THE FEATHER AND THE STONE

Also by Patricia Shaw

Valley of Lagoons
River of the Sun

THE FEATHER AND THE STONE

Patricia Shaw

St. Martin's Press
New York

THE FEATHER AND THE STONE. Copyright © 1992 by Patricia Shaw.
All rights reserved. Printed in the United States of
America. No part of this book may be used or reproduced
in any manner whatsoever without written permission
except in the case of brief quotations embodied in critical
articles or reviews. For information, address St. Martin's
Press, 175 Fifth Avenue, New York, N.Y. 10010.

Library of Congress Cataloging-in-Publication Data

Shaw, Patricia.
The feather and the stone / Patricia Shaw.
p.   cm.
ISBN 0-312-10462-6
1. Frontier and pioneer life—Australia—Fiction.   2. Women
pioneers—Australia—Fiction.   3. Young women—Australia—Fiction.
I. Title.
PR9619.3.S4815F43   1994
823—dc20   93-33501   CIP

First published in Great Britain by HEADLINE BOOK PUBLISHING PLC.

First U.S. Edition: January 1994
10   9   8   7   6   5   4   3   2   1

For
Desirée and Garry Shaw,
Dea, Pauline and Bron

Ode

We are the music-makers,
   And we are the dreamers of dreams,
Wandering by lone sea-breakers,
   And sitting by desolate streams;
World-losers and world forsakers,
   On whom the pale moon gleams:
Yet we are the movers and shakers
   Of the world forever, it seems.

Arthur O'Shaughnessy, 1874

1

At first it was rain. Blessed, cooling rain that washed the salt from the decks and sent passengers and crew alike rushing to collect it in all manner of vessels, from tubs to pans, and even hats.

After the limpid haze of the long summer crossing from the Cape of Good Hope, their ship, the sturdy *Cambridge Star,* stirred and shook like a dog from a bath. Sails lost their stiffness and billowed forth because with the rain came new winds, bracing winds that would send them speeding towards the coast of Western Australia.

Captain Bellamy's grin split his trim dark beard as he grasped the wheel. This was his first voyage to the Antipodes and he had advanced into the Great Southern Ocean with trepidation, heeding the warnings about the savage winds, the Roaring Forties, that would speed his ship but could hurtle into wind-strengths of ninety knots and drive the waves into massive craters. Instead, though, the ocean had been kind to him, almost too kind, for there was no heavy weather during all those long weeks, not even a squall to speak of, just the relentless drift eastwards that had placed him behind schedule and, worse, had caused a severe shortage of fresh water.

But now the worst was over. The passengers could stop grumbling and drench themselves in the rain if they wished, while this fine wind would push the ship on to Perth. He calculated that they should reach Fremantle at the mouth of the Swan River within four days.

Twenty-four hours later his optimism turned to apprehension as a storm developed. Rain lashed the ship in torrents, winds were building and the barometer falling, and he began the struggle for mastery of his vessel. For two days the *Cambridge Star* battled the storm while the crew fought, high in the masts, furling and unfurling the sails to keep her on an even keel. By night the ship thrashed on through the raging darkness.

Below decks, the officers assured cringing passengers that they would be through this bad patch in no time, so the women prayed as timbers smashed above them, and the men rushed to assist with the pumps. And then, mercifully, all was calm. On the third day a hush fell on the seas, the sky cleared to a yellowy tinge, as if the sun were striving to offer relief from the steamy air. Cabin-class passengers, the elite few, strolled forward, eyeing the damage with interest, looking for the captain to congratulate him, but he was unavailable.

He was resting, they were told, and so he would be, they agreed. The ship was hardly moving now. In a doldrum perhaps. They had heard of doldrums.

But in his cabin, Bellamy and his First Mate, Gruber, were studying charts.

1

'We're way off course, sir,' Gruber told him. 'Too far north.'

'And not a bloody thing we can do about it,' Bellamy worried. 'Not a breath of air out there. And we're so close,' he lamented. 'How much time do you think we've got?'

'Hard to say with these things. Could be a couple of hours. Maybe a full day.'

'Then get all hands working to repair what they can while they can,' the Captain groaned. 'We may have escaped.'

Gruber looked at the barometer and shook his head.

The three members of the Delahunty family were among the passengers on deck, but the stifling heat was too much for Mrs Delahunty. 'James, I must go back to the cabin. I am broiling up here.'

'Yes,' he admitted, 'the sun may be hidden but there's power in it.' He pulled his white panama hat down to shade his face and peered out at the milky sea. 'Settled in this great millpond one feels like the Ancient Mariner. You are right, my dear. The heat is appalling. A retreat is in order.'

'It's worse down there,' Sibell said, but her mother disagreed. 'Nonsense. There's no shade here. I already have a pounding headache.' She lifted her heavy skirts to negotiate the steep steps, relying on her husband for balance and Sibell as train-bearer.

'I must lie down,' Mrs Delahunty said. 'Now don't you go back on deck, Sibell, you'll ruin your skin with the reflection from the water.'

Her daughter sighed, wishing she had a penny for every time her mother had warned her about the ruination of her skin on this dreary interminable voyage with all these boring people. She was seventeen and there was no one else in her age-group among the cabin passengers, only older people and six atrocious grizzling children. Her parents' new friends, companions of the voyage, had often commented on Sibell's fair skin and good looks which, to her mind, was rather a waste since there was no one on board who really mattered to appreciate those good looks. Below decks, in intermediate and steerage, she had observed quite a few young people, but one could hardly associate with them; and, secretly, she had experienced some small satisfaction when members of the crew, rough fellows though they were, had nudged and grinned in her direction. Sibell had pretended not to notice these little flatteries but they did serve as tiny pinpoints of brightness to break the monotony of the dull days. She adjusted her bonnet and skirt and made for the saloon. At least the voyage would soon be over and the Delahuntys could begin their new life in the sunny land ahead.

James Delahunty was a gentleman farmer from Sussex who had become increasingly worried by a succession of severe winters and the economic malaise in rural areas. Just when he had reached a state of depression as to their future, though, a letter had arrived from his friend Percy Gilbert, inviting them to join him in the new British colony of Perth.

'In this country,' Percy advised, 'we can run, not hundreds, but thousands of sheep. The climate is excellent, with temperate winters, snow being unknown. There are fortunes to be made, beginning with the purchase of great tracts of land at only 2/6 per acre. To date I have

2

taken up several blocks and am faring exceeding well, with a house in the township to boot, but if the two families combine resources we could obtain large estates that would set us up for generations.'

To James, the letter was a godsend and he wasted no time in selling the farm and arranging to emigrate with all their goods and chattels.

'Be sure to bring your own people,' Percy had warned, 'for decent labour is hard to come by down here. Freed convicts are lazy and insolent and the blackfellows refuse to co-operate.'

So, also on board the *Cambridge Star* were two servants and two shepherds who had loyally volunteered to accompany Farmer Delahunty to the new world.

There were only four people in the saloon when Sibell entered, since most of the others were still recovering from the ravages of seasickness brought on by the storm. A fortunate few, including the Delahuntys, had suffered only the discomfort of queasiness which had passed quickly as the seas subsided.

Mr and Mrs Quigley were seated at a table, playing cards, and they invited Sibell to join them.

'Don't look over there now,' Mrs Quigley, eyes down, said to Sibell. 'But those two women in the corner don't belong here.'

Sibell, blinkered by her bonnet, hadn't taken any notice of the other two ladies in the room, but now she was curious. 'Who are they?'

'They're from steerage, Miss Delahunty,' Mrs Quigley hissed. 'I saw them down there when the steward accompanied me to the baggage room. I've just been telling Mr Quigley he should ask them to leave. Don't you agree?'

Sibell was bursting to look around but did not dare. 'They're not allowed in here,' she whispered. 'What would the Captain say?'

Mr Quigley, a mild-mannered gentleman, blinked behind his spectacles 'One would not wish to bother the Captain now. The poor fellow must be very tired.'

'That's true,' his wife said. 'And so it is up to you, sir, to request them to depart.'

'I'm sure that if you remind them this is the first-class section they'll understand,' Sibell offered primly.

'There!' Mrs Quigley said, pleased to have Sibell's support. 'I insist you speak to them, Mr Quigley.'

'Oh, very well,' he replied, straightening his black silk cravat before lifting himself from his chair. He stepped quietly over to them and Sibell took the opportunity to turn.

'Excuse me, ladies,' Mr Quigley began, 'but perhaps you are not aware that this area is reserved for first-class passengers.'

'So what?' one of the women replied sullenly, and Sibell gaped. They were young women, dressed neatly, but nothing could disguise their commonness.

Taken aback, Quigley could only stutter his reply. 'I'm afraid I shall have to ask you to leave.'

'Why should we?' the same woman asked, and her friend joined in angrily. 'It's slopping wet downstairs and like an oven, and we're fed up

3

with it. We're staying right here.' She reached over to a shelf that contained books and packs of cards, selected a pack and calmly began to set out a game of patience. Her companion watched her, laughing defiantly.

Quigley retreated, but his wife gained courage. 'If you wished to travel cabin class, you should have paid for it,' she called. 'You do not belong here. If you stay we shall have to report you to the Captain.'

The women ignored her. They didn't even look up from their game, which seemed to Sibell to be a worse insult than any bold reply. She was astonished.

Back in his chair Quigley whispered to the ladies, 'I fear this is shades of things to come. I have been told we might have to face similar incivilities in the colony.'

But just then two gentlemen came in, old Mr Freeman and his pompous son Ezra who had been appointed a magistrate with jurisdiction in the colony.

'Ah! Quigley!' Mr Freeman said. 'Just the man I want. I'm having a difference of opinion with young Ezra here . . .'

Despite the recent row with the female intruders, Sibell giggled and Mrs Quigley's mouth twitched. Ezra was all of forty years.

'It is my considered opinion,' the old man continued, 'that this storm is by no means over. I believe we have seen only the half of it.'

Ezra frowned. 'Nonsense, Father, you worry too much. And you must not upset the ladies.'

Obviously the argument had raged for a while, because Mr Freeman thumped his cane on the boards in frustration. 'I don't wish to upset the ladies,' he told his son angrily, 'and if you please, I am addressing Mr Quigley here. I ask you, sir, have you ever heard of a cyclone?'

'Yes, I have heard of such things, but surely, Mr Freeman, you can't believe that storm was a cyclone?'

'Not was, sir. Is!' the old man exclaimed vehemently. 'And we are in its centre. We should be making preparations for a worse storm . . .'

Never short of a word, Mrs Quigley intervened, taking Ezra's side, and dismissing the very idea of the storm turning back on them. Sibell was fascinated. She pictured their ship in a cyclone, spinning around in a tight circle like a doomed minnow in a storm drain. The first storm hadn't spun them around, so it seemed hardly likely that, if it came back, it could suck them into a huge whirlpool.

Ezra was putting up much the same view, but the old man shouted at him. 'Don't you understand? It isn't a case of the storm turning about. We are in the eye of the storm, dead centre where it is calm. We should be ready for the lifeboats if need be, such as they are. There are only two aboard.'

'He's right,' one of the strange women called to them. 'That's what they're saying down below. Some of the men, they say there's more to come.'

'Too right!' her friend added. 'That's why we're not shifting from here until we see what happens.'

It was Mrs Quigley's turn to ignore them. 'I'm sure the Captain understands the weather quite well,' she said to Mr Freeman, to reassure him. 'He got us through the last tempest; if it returns, we are in good hands.'

4

'Bah!' the old gentleman spluttered. 'You're a pack of fools! The foremast is split and half the sails are in shreds . . .' He stamped over to the two women. 'Would you ladies care to join me in a bottle of claret? I have some excellent stuff to hand. We might as well go down smiling.'

They were delighted to accept, which put Mrs Quigley in a huff. 'Come, Miss Delahunty,' she said. 'This is no place for a young lady now,' and Sibell dutifully followed.

The storm struck again that night with a roar, bearing down on them with torrential rain and deafening winds of terrifying ferocity. Whether it was the same storm or not seemed beside the point to Sibell, but people were still arguing about it as they huddled in the saloon, taking refuge from swamped cabins. Deep into the night she clung to her father as the ship bucked and crashed and the passengers screamed in fear. The saloon was in pitch darkness and foul from the stink of vomit, and as she tried to control her nausea, Sibell could hear the furious rush of the waves. She wondered if they really were spinning in circles.

They heard a mast crash down and were hurled together in a scrambled heap of shouts and screams as the ship plunged on to its side and water surged about them; then the vessel righted itself. In the panic she lost touch with her father. She could hear him calling her, but slithering among the throng, she couldn't reach him. Everyone seemed to be making for the door, so she went with them, fighting her way up to the deck which heaved and fell beneath her feet. She clung on to anyone and anything in the blinding rain, reacting to the shouts of 'To the boats!'

Out of curiosity she had gone to look at the two lifeboats Mr Freeman had referred to, and knowing the ship well after all this time, she was able to feel her way to the nearest one. Hands grabbed her, a crewman shouted, 'In you go, lady,' and she was pushed, stumbling, into the arms of men and handed on like a sack of soaking potatoes. She wondered, incongruously, how they could see in this darkness. But then she began screaming for her parents. Where were they? Who were these people clutching her, falling on top of her? She was in the bottom of the boat as it crashed, swamped, in to the sea, and the impact jarred every bone in her body, but she was in the safest place. She heard the screams around her as others were tossed into the churning ocean and tried to close her ears to the frightful, piteous cries for help, cries which were futile because it was impossible to see anyone in the dreadful dark sea.

Sibell could make out some people in the boat; men were shouting, cursing, pulling on oars. 'No,' she screamed. 'My parents! Mr and Mrs Delahunty! You must know them!' She was babbling, dragging at one of the men. 'We can't leave them. We have to go back for them.'

'Get off me, you stupid bitch!' an ugly voice shrieked at her. 'Let go of me or I'll chuck you overboard!'

Firm hands grasped her now, pulling her away, holding her down.

'Be still,' a woman warned her. 'Don't cause any more trouble, they haven't got time for you.'

'But the ship! We have to get back to the ship, it's dangerous out here!' It was madness, she felt, to be out in this tiny boat with the waves slamming over them, when they should be back on that big ship with all those people.

The woman shrieked, 'She's going down! Oh, God help us, she's sinking!'

'Where? Where?' Sibell cried frantically.

'Back there,' the woman sobbed, and as the first shreds of dawn cast a pale grey tinge on the terrible morning, Sibell saw the shuddering silhouette of the *Cambridge Star* as she dipped behind the shifting horizon, never to reappear.

A great wail went up from all around her, from ghostly voices that Sibell was sure she would hear for the rest of her life, and then the woman beside her began to pray . . . 'Our Father, who art in heaven . . .' and Sibell joined in, praying that her mother and her father were in that other lifeboat.

The cyclone, they said it was a cyclone, had passed on by, and Sibell sat silent and numb among these strangers as they struck for the coast, congratulating themselves that they were not stranded at sea without food or water, for the landmass of Western Australia was clearly visible. There were only fourteen people in the boat and room for many more, so Sibell resented them all. In her grief she blamed them for not rescuing her parents. As she looked out now across the gloomy sea, she saw a man clinging to a spar and imagined it was her father.

'Over there,' she screamed suddenly. 'It's my father. Row that way!'

And they did. They turned the boat towards him, straining at the oars, but as they closed on the man in the sea she saw it was a young man, not her father. He waved to them, urging them on to him, and suddenly the four oarsmen were working frantically, as if against time itself. Sibell saw their muscles bulging and the sweat on their faces before she realised that they were racing after a sharp black fin that was cutting through the water ahead of them. And then the man screamed, a terrible, agonised scream which was suddenly shut off as he threw up his hands and disappeared. A circle of churning blood coloured the sea.

Shocked by what had happened and conjuring up images of her dear parents at the mercy of sharks, Sibell began to scream hysterically until someone slapped her. 'Shut up,' he snarled. 'You're more trouble then you're worth.'

'But my mother and father,' she wept. 'They might be in the sea too. We have to look for them.'

A woman, soaked and distraught suddenly grabbed Sibell's hair and pulled her back. 'You've got my children!' she shouted, her eyes wild. 'Give me back my children!'

Men prised her away and shoved her to the back of the boat where she sat muttering to two elderly couples who must have stumbled into the lifeboat by a sheer miracle. At their feet a man groaned, clutching at a bloodied gash across his chest, but he was ignored as the men turned their attention to a woman with a broken arm, binding the limb with a torn cloth. Sibell stared in horror at her companions, still unable to grasp what she was doing in this boat.

Sunrise lifted a curtain on the desolate scene, and she rubbed her eyes, sure that this was some awful conjuring trick and that when she looked again the *Cambridge Star* would be there. It had to be! But the horizon was clear and the evidence lay on the surface around them, drifting wreckage of the doomed ship. And there was no sign of the other longboat.

As they drew towards the coast the four oarsmen became wary. 'Do you hear it?' one asked, and there was fear in his voice.

Sibell couldn't understand why. All she could hear was the welcome sound of sea breaking on shore; she recalled it from family holidays in Devon. She had thought it was romantic then, but now it was just respite from this nightmare of sodden heat and confinement before the real fears surfaced. Had her parents survived? And what about their servants, Maisie and Tom, and the two shepherds, father and son? Where were they?

While the oarsmen talked, the other passengers lay listlessly under the gruelling sun. Sibell knew something was wrong, although she couldn't imagine what else could happen to them. She leaned forward and tapped an arm. 'Is it sharks?' she asked.

'Not if you stay in the boat,' the man replied with a mad grin which frightened her.

The coastline became clearer. Sibell saw a long white beach, miles and miles of it spread out like a welcome mat before red-ochre land slightly tinged with tufts of green. The noise of the sea was louder.

'I can't swim,' one of the men said.

'It won't matter here,' another replied glumly. 'We'll have to ride the beast in.'

They were resting on their oars behind the breakers, rocking with the swell. A man with curly black hair and a dark beard squinted under the shade of his hand. 'God Almighty,' he muttered, peering along the coast, north to south, 'those breakers are dangerous. We've got to get out of here.'

'And where do we go?' another asked. ' 'Tis the longest beach I ever saw in me born days. There's no end to it. We can't row on forever, we ain't got no water. I say we give it a go.'

The bearded man looked nervously at their passengers. 'We can't afford to spill them, they'd never survive.'

The surf ahead of them sounded like a constant roll of thunder, and a sailor sneered at him. 'Since when did you care? He's only worrying about his own skin.'

'What are we waiting for?' Sibell asked, and the men turned to stare at her. 'We can't stay out here all day,' she said. 'Why don't you just row to that beach?'

Suddenly they were laughing. Even the ugly one who had threatened to throw her overboard. 'The princess has spoke,' he chortled. 'She's made the decision. We go.'

'Just a minute.' The bearded man turned back to Sibell. 'Will you shut your mouth. You don't know what you're talking about!'

'Of course I do. You're worried about waves when we've come through worse ones in this very boat.'

'It's not the same thing,' he snapped impatiently. 'That's surf ahead, not just waves, and it's my guess they're riding at about twenty feet, as high as a two-storey house. We could all get smashed up. Best you back out of this argument.'

'Why should I?' she declared. 'You people don't seem to be able to make up your minds. All the others are probably on shore by now.'

'Oh, Christ! She's away with the pixies,' the bearded man said. 'Let's row south for a while.'

'Why south?' a man they called Taffy wanted to know. 'Perth is to the north.'

'No, it's not,' a sailor argued. 'Gruber said we'd been blown off course and were to the north of Perth.'

Sibell listened to their arguments while the dazed old people held hands and the befuddled woman began shrieking again. The decision was sudden. She heard the shout: 'To the oars, mates!' and the bearded man shrugged, spat on his hands and grabbed an oar.

Quickly, Sibell moved about, rousing their companions. 'Wake up!' she yelled at them. 'Wake up and hang on.' She took hands and clasped them to the sides of the boat. 'Hang on tight,' she told them. 'The men are taking us in to shore and I think it might be difficult.'

They turned the boat shorewards with purpose, skimming merrily towards that shimmering sand, and at the first big swell, with everyone clinging on, they rode high, glimpsing the lilac-hazed mountains in the distance. Then they were down in a trough, but it wasn't too bad, except that the rowers made no leeway against the outward rip, their oars almost dragged from their hands.

Again they mounted a swell, riding high again, oars wasted in space, fielding only salt spray, and Sibell experienced the thrill of speed as they were borne safely homewards on the muscles of a huge wave, racing to the shore at an incredible pace, warm seas brushing, foam flecking. But like a spent horse, the foam told its tale. They plunged into yet another deep trough, losing sight of the shore.

Sibell wasn't afraid. This was the most exciting ride of her life, a journey that belonged in the void between life and death, in no man's land, cut off from everything she had ever known, beyond civilisation. Beneath her the crystal green sea was so clean and tempting that in her euphoria, she had to fight off the impulse to leap over into its inviting depths.

A family of dolphins joined in the fun, matching their skills against the power of the four oarsmen who were now dipping deep, jamming their oars into the fast-moving sea to climb the heights of the next breaker, desperate to reach the peak before it disintegrated into just another wave, for each one, closer now to shore, could be their salvation.

The dolphins leapt, dipped, dived and flew ahead of them, encouraging them to stay just behind the crest of the huge wave, balancing high above the dunes and enjoying a dolphin's-eye view of the land.

Sibell looked down at these joyous creatures with their knowing eyes; she could have reached out and touched them, stroked them, had they not all been travelling so fast. Then she saw them pull back: she saw them balk, squeaking their warnings as the oarsmen took on the summit. She watched them dive deep just as the boat shot skywards over the top of a massive breaking wave. No slide to a trough here, this wave carried them fast, foaming, belligerent, rushing forward with such awful power that oars were snatched away and the rowers clung on with their terrified companions. On and on they went, roaring at the shore like an invading horde, their flimsy boat held aloft as they flew, a winner's trophy high above the rest.

It was their last triumph. That wave, normal on the West Australian coast, did its duty, flung itself at the sands as waves had done from infinity, and having performed its task drew back in sucking rips to re-form and become just another roller, gathering green depths for a renewed assault on an anonymous shore.

Sibell knew it was too fast. She hung on as they swept up that wave. Before her the deceptive sea looked as dangerous as green jelly; they seemed to be enticed to slide up there, right to the foaming tip, and once again to join the hayride ever onwards. But something went wrong . . . the crest of that towering wave fell apart and their boat dropped headfirst into an abyss. The real strength of the wave loomed lower, catapulting forward, capturing the boat and tossing it like a matchstick into the sea-laden air.

Sibell was thrown, before she had time to gasp for air, into a long tunnel of green. Death rolled above her, a massive froth-laced curl of ocean that hung suspended for a few seconds before it thundered down on her, and she was pounded into the depths.

She fought for the surface, not knowing where it might be found and then the charge began. She was caught in a current that swept her to precious air but would not let her go, and her frail body was bundled, bouncing, crashing, twisting, turning, into the sand-logged shallows, and dumped unceremoniously, unconscious, on the shiny beach.

The bearded man waded through the surf, still unable to believe that moment when his feet touched firm ground and he could propel himself away from the churning green cauldron. As the last wave crashed about his shoulders he stumbled and allowed himself to collapse on to the smooth sand to watch the sea withdraw. Then, gasping with relief, he staggered up the hot, dry beach.

Taffy was standing there grinning at him. 'See! Weren't so bad after all.'

'I thought I was drowned for sure,' the exhausted man replied.

'You'd have plenty of company, mate. The boat's all splintered to hell and the passengers went to the deep. Can't find Leonard, he was on the oars with us, but Jimmy's down there throwin' up gallons of sea.'

'No one else?'

'Nope. There's a couple of dead 'uns dumped down there at the water's edge and another one further up. You was right, it were too rough to tackle.' He looked up in wonder. 'By Jesus, look at them breakers! Can't see past them, so I reckon if there are any more right out there, the sharks'll have them.'

The bearded man shook his head trying to establish reality. Taffy seemed unconcerned that so many had drowned, and he himself couldn't muster distress for them either in his relief at having survived. The others didn't seem relevant any more.

'On your feet, then,' Taffy said. 'We'll burn up in this heat. We're heading for Perth.'

Soon they were arguing again, the three of them. North or south? Taffy and Jimmy were set for north, and in the end he let them go, stubbornly certain that Perth lay to the south. For some strange reason he was pleased to be rid of them, to be left alone. Feeling light-headed, he slumped down on the beach not ready yet to make a move. It was as if the ocean had set him free, given him the chance to begin his life again, and he wanted to savour his luck.

There'd been Belfast. And a fool of a job for a lanky lad, all bones and joints, wedged into the office of that factory, being ogled by girls at their machines and never game to ogle back. He'd seen himself, that adolescent dope, as a great lover, but had had neither the wit nor the beauty to succeed. He laughed, listening to the whistle of the wind above the creamy waves. Nature took its own sweet time but he'd made up for the slack when his body filled out, his skin cleared and his jaw firmed, and the ogling was no longer a tease and a bluff.

But he'd moved on by then, working at all sorts of jobs, even as a bank clerk. He blamed women for his problems; they cost money to romance, and a bank full of cash had been too much for a poor man. He'd quit fast when the rumbles began, quit Belfast, too, and not sorry.

Liverpool was a raw place. Worse than Belfast. Hard on strangers, he mused, thinking back on those years. Never any work, but a man had to live: so, with the help of the bog-Irish girl, he'd found cash in the purses of fancy women, who were easy enough to charm. Then there were other matters, which he didn't care to recall and which had brought him to the decision that it was time to quit Liverpool.

Just his luck to choose that damned ship, the *Cambridge Star*, but he always kept his ears open. He'd heard the warnings of the men with him in steerage that this was no ordinary storm, and it had put the fear of God in him. To hell with shipboard rules – he was up and out of there, to stay hid by the lifeboat. This fellow, he said to himself, has one talent. He knows when it's time to quit. Now, he decided, it was time to get going: he would march south as far as his legs would carry him and he'd be bound to find someone.

As he rinsed his face with salt water he noticed a movement out of the corner of his eye. The woman up the beach had moved her head, startling him. He hadn't bothered to inspect those bodies, prepared to take Taffy's word for it that they had expired, rather than examine them. The very idea turned his stomach. But she was still alive and it was that damned girl from the boat, the one they'd called The Princess. Without enthusiasm, he moved over to take a look at her.

Someone was swabbing her face and it hurt. 'Don't,' she said, pushing him away, spitting sand from her dry lips. Exhausted, she dropped her face into the sand again and he let her be.

'Where am I?' she asked at length.

'Exactly where on a map I couldn't tell you, but right at this minute you're high in the sand dunes, safe in the shade of a fine pandanus tree.'

Somehow it didn't seem to matter anyway. She spat sand again. Her mouth was full of it, irritating her tongue, scratching her throat. She groaned as he pushed her, rolling her over on to her back. 'Go away,' she told him.

'Now, don't argue with me,' he said. 'It was hard enough getting you up here, what with me feeling battered too. I'm just trying to wash your face.'

'Leave me alone. My face is sore.'

'Of course it's sore, you must have come up that beach nose first. I just want to wash the sand away.'

'Ow!' she complained. 'That stings!'

He went on with the task, then sat back. 'You'll probably have a few bruises, but apart from that you seem to be in good order.' He pressed on her ribs. 'That hurt?'

'Everything hurts.'

'But not too bad?' He pressed again and when she didn't react he stood up. 'You stay there and rest, I'll have another look around.'

She opened her eyes and saw it was the man with the dark beard, and she was glad he had gone away.

In the morning she awoke with the light, confused and frightened, trying to shake off the terrifying nightmares that lingered ominously within her. She walked unsteadily across the wide beach, watching with horror the great breakers that blotted out the horizon. Had her waist-length hair not been so uncomfortable, matted with salt and sand, she would never have gone near the sea, but it was necessary, so she lay down at the water's edge, where a depression in the sand had formed a small pond, washed her face gingerly and soaked her hair. At least she was able to remove some of the sand. Then the impact of what had happened overwhelmed her and she sat shaking with fright, her hair drying in lank, clammy ropes.

She tried to take stock of herself. Her serge jacket and skirt were stiff and whitened with salt, and her blouse was torn at the neck. She had lost her shoes, so she slipped off her stockings and quickly buried them in the sand for modesty, and then that man came down, standing tall in shirt and breeches. He took her arm and helped her up. 'Come now, I'll take you back to the tree. I found a keg with some water, for which we can be grateful.'

Only then did Sibell notice that the beach was littered with wreckage. 'My parents,' she sobbed. 'They were on board. Have you seen them?'

'Were they in the boat with us?'

'No.'

'Maybe they were in the other one. We'll find out in time.'

'What about the rest of the people in our boat.'

'I fear most were lost when the boat overturned. Two old souls were washed up on the beach, drowned, so I buried them.'

Sibell retched into the sand, choking on bile.

Back in the shade he poured some water into a pan and gave it to her. 'I've been scavenging along the beach but there's not much of use to us, I'm sorry to say.'

'Isn't there anyone else?' His lack of concern upset her.

'Only two sailors, but they didn't want to stay. They've gone north, we're heading south.'

'I'm not going anywhere,' she told him. 'I'm staying right here to wait for the other boat.'

'It'll be a long wait, miss, there's not a boat in sight. That sea's as empty as my stomach.'

'Someone will come for us,' she insisted.

'That's possible, but we don't know when, so we have to look out for ourselves. Now you sit quiet there, I'm going fishing.'

'With what?'

'There's a great school of mullet running close to the shore. I might be able to trap some.'

Sibell was too disoriented to care what he did. She wondered vaguely what was behind the big sand dunes but was in no mood to investigate. 'Oh God,' she whispered. 'Help me. What is to become of me?'

He did bring back some fish, and filleted them with his penknife. 'I'm too hungry to waste time trying to light a fire with sticks – I never learned the art – but I've solved the problem. Look what I found . . . some jolly bottles of wine.'

'I don't drink wine.'

'You're not getting any, they're for the fish.'

She watched as he soaked the raw fish in red wine and handed the pan to her. 'There you are. Take a piece. It should soak longer but beggars can't be choosers.'

Sibell stared. 'I can't eat raw fish.'

'Please yourself.' He picked up a dripping piece of fish and ate it.

'That's disgusting!' she said, and turned away.

When he had eaten he placed the pan beside her. 'There's your share and you'd better get into it before those ants find it. There are whole armies of the big fat creatures marching about us.'

'I don't care.'

'Well, that's your decision. I'll have a look around and see what else I can find, and if you haven't swallowed that fish by the time I get back, I'll eat it myself.'

She was starving. She broke off a few flakes of the fish and tasted it. It was warm and horrible, but she knew she had to eat it, so nibble by nibble, so that she couldn't taste anything but the tang of the wine, she managed to get it down.

This time he brought back a sheet of canvas which he tore into wide strips. 'Wrap this over your head for shade,' he told her. 'I don't want you getting sunstroke. And by the way, my name's Logan, Logan Conal. What's yours?'

'Miss Delahunty,' she replied primly.

'Very well, Miss Delahunty. Take that pan down and wash it while I pack up our treasures. We've got more wine than water, so that should be interesting . . . hurry along, girl.'

She ran across the hot sand in her bare feet, vainly scanning the broad beach for signs of life, sluiced the pan and ran back, hating him, hating his rude manner and his complete lack of sympathy for her terrible situation.

The pan was shoved into a makeshift bag and he knotted the canvas at the corners. 'Now we go,' he told her.

'I don't want to go with you,' she muttered. 'We should follow the other sailors.'

He stared at her. 'I'm not a sailor.'

'What are you, then?'

'I don't know. I haven't decided.'

Sibell shrugged impatiently. She didn't know what to make of him. He was a stockily built fellow with the muscles of a farm hand under those rolled-up sleeves. Piercing green eyes gleamed from the heavily bearded face, eyes that offered more mockery than care. He had definitely not been travelling cabin class, so God alone knew what sort of a person she was stuck with, living with, in fact. If only someone else would come along. Anyone!

'Have you been to this coast before?' she asked.

'No.'

'Then why are you giving orders? The sailors must know where they are going. You should have insisted they wait for me.'

'Listen to me, miss. You thank your stars they ran off without us. You wouldn't want to be in the company of men like that for too long.'

'What do you mean?'

'You work it out,' he replied. 'Now get up. We'll travel at the water's edge to keep our feet cooled.'

Sibell stumbled after him, resenting his attitude but afraid to argue with him any more. She ran, trotted, walked and limped along the great empty beach, well behind the determined figure who kept moving on relentlessly, his outline distorted in the shimmering haze because of the stupid bonnet of canvas that he too had wrapped around his head. On principle she wanted to throw her head-covering away but her face was already burning from the glare. She sobbed: her mother had worried so much about her skin, she'd have a perfect fit if she could see her daughter now, her face slowly turning beetroot red.

And her father, Sibell told herself, he'd have something to say about this fellow's treatment of her. James Delahunty, she was sure, would be in Perth by now, with her mother. They wouldn't have climbed into a boat with a bunch of madmen as she had – her father had more sense. She would have to explain to him that she'd had no choice. He would understand. And dear God! What would her mother say about her being out here alone with a strange man? It was so embarrassing, she hoped no one would ever find out. In her befuddled, weakened condition, the girl saw Logan Conal as her ruination. He had forced her to spend a night with him, alone, sleeping only yards apart, and by the looks of things they would be together again tonight, maybe even for days or weeks. For however long it took them to walk to Perth, if they were going in the right direction. She had seen those magazines with stories about couples alone on desert islands, not that she would ever stoop to reading them, they were too sordid. Sibell blushed and tears stung her face. She would never live this down: this man had compromised her.

Logan Conal was worried. It was mid-afternoon yet they'd travelled only a few miles: the girl was constantly stopping to rest. This time she had a stitch in her side. That was unavoidable so he gave her a drink of water and waited. She was so upset and confused that it was difficult to push her any harder, but they had to keep moving or they'd die out here.

'Are you feeling better?' he asked.

'Yes, I think it has gone.' She struggled to her feet and walked a few paces, the hem of her long skirt heavy with sand.

'Let me cut some inches off that skirt,' he offered, 'to keep it above ground. It will make walking easier for you.'

'You'll do no such thing! I am not arriving looking like a ragbag. Have you still got my jacket?'

He nodded. It had taken quite an argument to make her hand over the serge jacket, even though she was wearing a blouse underneath, but the heat had forced her to relinquish it, on the promise that he would keep it intact in his canvas bag.

'Come on, then, we must hurry.'

'I have decided,' she told him, 'to stay here. I shall find shade up under those shrubs and when you reach the town you can send people back for me.'

'That's out of the question. You're coming with me.'

'I refuse to walk any further along this stupid beach. It's far too hot out here in the open. Why don't we go inland and find a farm-house?'

'Because there seems to be nothing out there but empty plains.'

'I have looked out over the land, too, and at least there are trees, we'd have some shade as we walked. Did you think of that?'

He sighed. 'Miss Delahunty, I am in charge of this expedition and you will go where you are told.'

She plodded away, taking slow, deliberate steps, and he strode after her, tempted to give her a good whack on the behind as he would a stubborn donkey. He chose, instead, a tongue-lashing.

'I don't want to die of thirst out here, but if I do, it will be your fault. I've had enough of your shenanigans. You're not an old woman, you're young and, so far, healthy, so you get a move on or I'll take a stick to you.'

Her big grey eyes looked at him in shock and her mouth dropped open. Logan almost laughed: she was as pretty as a picture even with the sunburn and that honey-coloured mane of hair a tangled mess.

'How dare you!' she exploded, but she did pick up her skirts and run, presumably to get away from him. At least, though, they were on their way again. He smiled as he jogged along behind her, admiring her neat ankles and realising that it was easier to drive than lead her.

For four days they kept travelling south, living on fish and sips of water, and his companion had now fallen into a good loping stride. He blessed the Lord that fish were so numerous in these seas: migrating shoals of mullet made the catch easy.

The girl was quieter and by the end of each day was too tired to complain, sinking quickly into a heavy sleep among the warm dunes, her precious jacket for a pillow. He heard her call and cry out at night, sometimes even weeping in her sleep, but bad dreams or not he wouldn't wake her, she needed the rest, such as it was.

By the time they did find company she had stopped worrying about her appearance. They both looked like derelicts, their clothes beginning to

14

rot from constant dips in the sea as they tried to combat the heat and the subsequent baking along the shore.

Miss Delahunty saw them first. 'There are people ahead,' she screamed, and took off, racing away from him.

As they neared, he made out two naked black women doing what appeared to him to be some ritual dance in the sand, their hips swaying rhythmically, their heads down, intent on their movements. Then they stopped, watching the strangers approach.

'Steady now,' Logan called to the girl. 'Go quietly. We don't want to frighten them off.'

She stopped suddenly, as he caught up.

'Don't worry,' he told her. 'Put your hands out to show we are friendly, that we have no weapons.' He dropped his canvas bundle on the sand and approached, hands free.

'Come back here,' the girl said angrily. 'You can't go up to them.'

'Why not?' he asked, without turning his head.

'They are not clothed, Mr Conal.'

'Oh, Jesus!' he snapped. 'Don't be so bloody stupid!' He smiled at the two women. They were both young, their firm black bodies glistening in the sun. 'Good morning,' he said slowly and bowed to them, and they burst into paroxysms of giggles, large white teeth in sharp contrast to their dark skin.

'Speak English?' he asked, only to be met by more giggles as they studied this strange pair of white people.

Logan thought some attempt at conversation might help. 'What's in there?' he asked, pointing at their plaited dilly bags.

They understood and took out some small, closed shells to show him.

'What are they?' he asked, shrugging helplessly. The two black women enthusiastically recommenced what seemed to be their dance. Hips swinging from side to side, they drove their feet into the wet sand, dislodging more shells that were pounced on and placed in the bags. He realised that they were a food source and prised one open with difficulty. It was like a small white mussel shell, and, sure enough, inside was flesh which he dug out and put into his mouth, only to find it was thick with grit.

The native girls stared in astonishment, and he nodded. 'You're right,' he said. 'I think they have to be washed first.'

They were laughing again, probably at his foolishness, so he took the opportunity to begin drawing in the sand, his companion's silent presence behind him making him uncomfortably aware of their nakedness. He drew houses, pointed at them and in a charade tried to enquire where these houses might be.

They studied the picture he had drawn, looked at one another, mystified, and then the taller of the two clapped her hands and pointed inland.

'There you are,' Miss Delahunty said. 'I told you so. Inland!'

'Oh shut up!' he said. 'Where inland?'

But as he spoke, he realised that they were pointing at a fearful-looking Aborigine, standing high on the nearest dune and holding a huge spear. He jerked his head and the two girls grabbed their dilly bags and ran up into the dunes. Then he beckoned to the strangers to come forward.

15

The blue sky behind the stark black figure looked so dense that Logan felt he could poke a finger into it, and for a few minutes he was distracted by this impressive scene. An impatient gesture from above brought him back to reality.

'You stay here,' he told the girl, but as usual he might just as well have told the wind to stay put. He heard her scrambling up behind him.

'Good morning,' he called cheerfully, concealing a shiver of fear. The native was a large, muscular fellow, dressed, Logan thought ruefully, aware of his own unfortunate choice of expression, to kill. The Aborigine's hair was bound into a thick top-knot, secured with a bone, and his face and body were daubed with yellow and white paint. He wore no real clothing but around his neck was a brace of coloured cords, and his bulging biceps displayed similar tight cords. Slung low from his waist hung a narrow cord belt which seemed to serve no purpose at present since his substantial genitalia were well displayed. Logan grinned as he held out his hand in friendship. Serve her right, he told himself, thinking gleefully of the snooty Miss Delahunty who didn't want him to approach the naked women. This sight will give her a heart attack. Surreptitiously he glanced back at her and, sure enough, she had stopped dead in her tracks and was staring fixedly in another direction.

The black man did not accept his hand, but made some remark and tapped Logan with his spear, forcing him to keep his distance.

'Logan,' he told the black, pointing to himself. He indicated the sea to try to explain where he had come from, and having identified himself, pointed to the native with what he hoped was an expression of enquiry.

The dark eyes watched him closely, and then the Aborigine spoke, tapping his chest: 'Nah-keenah.'

Logan nodded and produced his precious penknife from his pocket. He might as well hand it over, he decided. It wouldn't be much use to him if the natives proved nasty, and right now he needed their help. 'A gift for you, sir,' he smiled.

Nah-keenah looked warily at the closed knife and then gave a piercing whistle. Three more blacks came up from behind the dunes and strode forward, all of them eyeing the newcomers curiously. They lined up behind Nah-keenah and watched as Logan undid the knife, demonstrating two blades, followed by a pipe cleaner and a corkscrew. He doubted the latter two would be of any use to them but they created interest simply by emerging from this small item.

At last Nah-Keenah took the knife. He studied the blades, tested them on his large hand and grinned. The gift was accepted. He spoke to his companions and then beckoned to Logan. Obviously it was time to move off.

Logan felt faint with relief. At least if they could travel with these people they'd find food and water. He remembered the bundle he'd dropped on the beach and pointed to it, so the two women, who had been standing well back in the dunes, were sent to collect it.

'We'll go with them,' he told the girl, 'so look pleased about it. His name is Nah-keenah.'

'Nah-keenah,' she repeated, smiling uncertainly at the native. 'My name is Sibell.' Gathering her courage, she pointed to herself: 'Sibell.'

Nah-keenah didn't seem impressed, which should have been a warning to Logan, but he was intrigued to hear her Christian name for the first time. Sibell. It was a very pleasant name . . .

The three other men turned to leave, and Nah-keenah motioned to Logan to walk in front of him, which he did, with Sibell moving forward to stay with him.

Affronted, Nah-keenah lashed out, slapping her across the face with such force that she went sprawling backwards into the sand, screaming in fright. Logan's first reaction was anger, but instantly the spears were levelled at him, so he backed away and tried to calm Sibell. She winced as he touched her face, and he realised that blow must have hurt like hell. 'Shush now,' he said, 'for Christ's sake, be quiet and I'll see what this is about.' She was still sobbing as he helped her up, and he noticed that the black women, who had returned, were unconcerned by her plight. 'I think you've breached protocol here,' he told Sibell. 'You mustn't be frightened. I think you must not walk in front of the boss there. Maybe you should walk with the women.'

He stood up and called to the black girls to bring Sibell along, and then, his voice firm, he turned, beckoning to Nah-keenah. 'Come on, boss, let's go.'

The order of march now seemed to please the blacks, who grinned at one another and set off with Logan, the women following.

As they began their trek across the hot, dry land, Logan looked back at Sibell, relieved to see that the native women were helping her. They were both taller than Sibell and their strong arms were lodged under hers, practically lifting her from the ground, as if this were a game to hurry a little child along. But several hours later, by the time they reached the blacks' camp by a large water hole in the dried-up bend of a river, Logan also needed assistance. His bare feet were torn and bleeding from the sparse, sharp grasses that lined the tree-dotted plain over which they had travelled.

Apart from the brutish attack on Sibell, the blacks seemed an amiable lot, talking cheerfully among themselves in a deep-throated guttural language. Over the last few yards two of the men picked Logan up and dumped him bodily into the wonderfully cool, clear water, while other blacks in the camp came to stare.

He looked about for Sibell, who arrived shortly afterwards, piggy-backed with ease by one of her minders. She was allowed to join him, and wallowed miserably in the sandy shallows.

'Are you all right?' he asked her, deliberately making no comment on the purple bruise around her right eye, so as not to upset her.

'No,' she replied. 'I hate these filthy people. We should never have come with them. My feet are red-raw, and I'm starving.'

'Don't worry yourself, now: they're lighting fires, so I think it's suppertime. If you're feeling faint, lie on the banks and rest while I investigate.'

His advice was based on self-knowledge: he was so weak with hunger he could hardly drag himself up to the camp, his dripping clothes a temporary insulation against the stifling heat.

No one bothered him as he skirted around groups of rowdy natives, all busy with their own affairs, and sank dizzily against a tree to watch

17

proceedings. He must have dozed off, because he became gradually aware that someone was staring at him. He opened his eyes to find an elderly, gnarled woman kneeling beside him, waiting. She had set out some food for him in two wooden gourds, one containing nuts and berries, and the other charred meat, unmistakably a bird of some sort. Logan gave a sigh of relief. 'Thank you,' he said to her, and pounced on the meat. Even though it had been scrappily plucked it seemed to him to be the best meal of his life – duckling, he was sure, marvellous, succulent duckling – and he had devoured almost a whole bird before he remembered Sibell. He looked anxiously around and saw her sitting nearby in the shade of a bark lean-to. 'Have you been fed?' he called to her.

'Yes,' she replied, sounding far from enthusiastic. He returned to his own meal.

Another woman, watching him curiously, brought him a large parcel of scorched leaves which she opened reverently and offered to him. It contained a fish, well steamed, and Logan wasted no time trying to work out what type of fish it was: he only knew that it was as fat as a salmon and tasted even better. 'Magnificent!' he said to his two native waitresses, and they grinned in acknowledgement. Since it was such a big fish he felt he should offer them some, not expecting them to accept, but they did, digging in with their fingers. That was a mistake, he told himself, grabbing at the last of the fish.

The nuts and berries, too, were delicious. Some other time, he told himself lazily, I'll enquire into the nature of these plants, but not now. Not now . . .

The women took their bowls and left, and Logan studied the company. Supper over, the sexes mixed easily now, reclining or sitting cross-legged in groups, talking quietly, while pot-bellied children scampered around them and dogs scavenged for left-over bones.

The setting sun was a fiery ball of orange, heralding, Logan guessed, another hot day on the morrow, and the dark skins of the blacks had taken on a coppery glow. They all seemed content, and he was, too, until, as the sun slipped from sight, hordes of mosquitoes descended in a fury. Logan slapped and thumped at them, noticing that they didn't seem to bother the blacks, which he considered grossly unfair. Wearily he lifted himself up and went over to see how Sibell was coping. 'Did you enjoy your meal?' he asked.

'Fish again,' she complained. 'When I get home I'm never going to eat another fish.'

'Is that all you had?' he asked, interested.

'These nuts,' she told him, showing him the bowl she'd been picking at. 'And some strange berries.'

A man's world, he thought, and made no mention of his feast of duckling.

Her minders must have decided it was time to leave them. Giggling again, the women pointed to the lean-to. 'Mia-mia,' one said, and Logan repeated the word.

'Mia-mia?'

She nodded, one hand on the bark shelter, waving the other one to include Logan and Sibell.

18

'I think she means this is our house,' he said, 'so we must accept. We mustn't break any of the rules by wandering around.'

Sibell was appalled. 'I believe they think you're my husband!'

'Quite possible,' he grinned. 'There's nothing we can do about it.'

'There is so. You can go away.'

'Not on your life,' he said, ducking under the shelter. 'As long as we're here I intend to do exactly as I'm told. They've got some nasty-looking weapons.'

'Where will we go tomorrow?'

'Not too far, I hope. Neither of us is fit to travel, with our suffering feet and not a boot in sight.'

A mild breeze rustled among the high eucalypts, and the people seemed to be settling down for the night. Some drew closer to the central fire, lying huddled together like puppies, others withdrew to shelters. Logan saw two men with those big spears disappear into the bush, and wondered if they were off hunting or taking up positions as guards. In the distance he heard animals that sounded like wolves howling, and he shuddered. Even though they'd been fed and treated fairly, these primitive men with their streaked faces made him nervous. He had noticed they were being watched all the time as if they might attempt to run away, in which case they could be prisoners. But what did they do with prisoners?

'I can't sleep,' Sibell complained. 'The mosquitoes here are terrible.'

'Then stay awake,' he said, too tired to worry about her any more.

His stomach satisfied for a change, he slept well, and when he awoke Sibell was outside, eating her breakfast.

'What's that?' he asked.

'Something like bread. The women have just cooked it.' She handed him a warm, doughy lump. 'It tastes perfectly frightful and you have to spit out the charcoal. Most of the blacks have gone out, thank God.'

'Blast!' Logan said, scrambling up. 'Has Nah-keenah gone, too?'

'Yes.'

'Damn it all! Now what are we supposed to do?'

'That's what I wanted to talk to you about.' She looked up at him, the grey of her eyes emphasised by a fine dark rim and then again by thick dark lashes. 'I suppose we shall have to be married now.'

He was watching a woman at her fire, wondering if he might ask her for more bread, and he turned back absently, thinking he may have misheard her. 'What did you say?'

'I said,' she told him seriously, 'I suppose we shall have to marry now.'

Logan blinked. 'What on earth brought this on?'

'Last night you slept with me. When people sleep together they should be married, otherwise they are breaking the commandments. And since you have now compromised me, then you'll have to marry me.'

'I hope you're joking.'

'I am not joking, Mr Conal.' A flush passed over her face. 'Oh, my God!' she exclaimed. 'Don't tell me you're already married?'

'I am not married, Miss Delahunty, and I have no intentions of marrying you.'

'We don't have any choice in the matter.'

19

Logan started to laugh. 'I don't know where your parents have been keeping you, young lady, but sharing a shelter does not necessitate a rush to the altar. I haven't touched you . . .' He stopped, seeing tears welling up in her eyes, and scowled. The silly girl really did think that her reputation was ruined, or at least as battered as the wretched clothes she was still forced to wear. He tapped her on the shoulder. 'You should be thankful that we're safe,' he told her. 'People will be so glad to see you return from a shipwreck, that they won't be worrying about details. Why, lass, you might even be famous.'

'What?' She was so shocked that he groaned, realising he'd put his foot in it again. 'I don't want to be famous! I don't want people to know I've been living with a man for days and . . . and . . . staying out here with undressed savages! Don't you dare tell anyone! Who will marry me then?'

'Oh, for Christ's sake, I never heard the likes of you. I never knew a lady so obsessed with marriage.'

'Then you don't know much about ladies, Mr Conal,' she retorted, 'for all your clever talk.'

Logan gave up. He went down to the lagoon to bathe. Even though it was still early morning the sun blazed from the huge blue sky with the force of a battering ram.

Some children came dashing in to leap and splash around him, and he played with them for a while, pulling them along in the water and cupping his hands to catapult them into wriggling dives. They were thoroughly enjoying themselves and were disappointed when he called a halt to the games and marched up the bank. They stood crestfallen in the shimmering water like live shadows and to cheer them up he stopped, pointed to himself and called: 'Logan.' Immediately they understood and came flying towards him, shouting joyously: 'Logarn! Logarn!' In a body they tramped up to the camp, to the amusement of the women and the glint-eyed appreciation of three old men who were sitting cross-legged in the shade of their mia-mia.

'Nah-keenah?' he asked them. 'Where is Nah-keenah?'

Heads jerked over their shoulders, and voices replied amicably.

Logan hadn't expected any more from them – it was obvious that Nah-keenah and the younger men had gone off, probably hunting – but he had achieved a rapport of sorts, so he sat down and began testing them for English. 'Perth?' he asked. 'Where is Perth? English? Do you know any English?' They laughed and exchanged rumbling remarks among themselves, and he was struck by the lightheartedness of these people. They laughed a lot, merriment came easily to them, and he was certain, by the casual way they had accepted him and Sibell, that they were not unacquainted with Europeans.

Once again he drew houses on the ground, outlines of simple sheds with doors and windows, and pointed at them. 'White man's houses,' he said. 'Where are they?'

The old men hunched broad, scarred shoulders over his drawings, and one took his stick while Logan watched hopefully, but he only added to the picture by drawing a fish. A fish! It was developing into an art class. Logan went one better by smoothing another space and drawing a ship

20

with high sails, which achieved nothing but applause, so he reverted to his original question. 'Perth?' he insisted. 'Where is Perth?' There was desperation in his voice. 'We have to go to Perth.'

The men discussed this as he pleaded with them, 'Can you show me the way to Perth?' Just as he was about to give up he heard three words which he was certain were English. 'By and by!' he cried. 'Did you say "by and by"?'

One of the men, with a flowing white beard, nudged the others and repeated triumphantly, 'By 'm by.'

'Oh! Good fellow,' Logan beamed. 'Well done! What happens by and by?'

'Pfeller comen,' the old man said carefully, then with an extra effort, 'blackpfeller comen.'

'What blackfeller? Who is coming?'

But he couldn't find out any more: apparently the old man had exhausted his knowledge of English. He tried to explain something to Logan in his own language, becoming a little irritated that Logan could not understand him, and finally pointed a determined finger at Logan's picture of the houses. He dug his finger hard among them, tapping the ground to make sure there was no mistake. 'Pfeller comen!' he explained testily.

Logan hurried back to tell Sibell, who was sitting sulkily, picking burrs from her skirt, but she was not impressed. 'How far is it to Perth?'

'I don't know.'

'Then I hope this person brings horses.'

'In which case, Miss Delahunty, I hope you can ride,' he snapped. She was most the most annoying brat of a girl. In all his twenty-four years he had never come across such a wretch.

'I ride extremely well for my age, my father says.'

'And what age would that be?'

'I shall be eighteen in a few weeks,' she announced loftily. 'My father will probably arrange a ball for me in Perth.'

Logan was astonished. She was living in a dream world. There was every possibility that both of her parents had gone down with the *Cambridge Star*, but she couldn't seem to understand this. Or maybe her attitude was just bravado. He hadn't told her that the old man had said a blackfellow was coming for them, which could mean anything – another cross-country barefoot trek seemed on the cards. He had been definite about the European houses, though. They must have sent a message to someone that they had two white people in their camp, and a reply was expected. What that reply would be he couldn't guess. For that matter, the old man could have been talking nonsense.

'What do your parents plan to do in Perth?' he asked Sibell.

'They intend to take up a large pasture and farm sheep. My father has a partner, a gentleman of consequence in Perth, Mr Percy Gilbert. Do you know of him?'

'I do not. I have never been to Perth.'

'Sheep farmers do very well in the colony,' she said. 'And are very highly thought of. I've been thinking, Mr Logan . . . What we must say is that I met you here among these people, and that will head off any gossip.'

21

'And rescue your chances of making a good marriage?' he grinned.

'There's nothing wrong with wanting to protect one's reputation,' she sniffed.

'Do you think of anything but marriage?' he asked her. 'Is that all you want? To find a husband as soon as possible and be relegated to his household.'

'What a question!' she pouted. 'It's a perfectly natural arrangement. What else would you expect of me?'

He studied her carefully. 'You're a good-looking girl, you're educated, you've got brains and, as I've noticed, a will of your own. Why this headlong rush to tie yourself down to some feller and jump to his tune for the rest of your life?' He leaned forward and gazed at her. 'A girl like you, shouldn't you want to be captain of your own soul?'

Embarrassed, she pulled away from him. 'I don't know what you're talking about! You seem to have no sense of propriety.'

Logan shrugged. 'Oh, well, if I'm still in Perth I hope you will invite me to your wedding.'

The look she gave him as she stood up and stalked away made it clear that this would be highly unlikely.

After the first day in the camp, their situation deteriorated. Sibell was expected to help, to crush bulbs into flour using a rock and the wooden gourds, to crack hard nuts between stones without smashing the kernels, to soak those shells the women had collected on the beach, stirring them endlessly in water from the lagoon to rid them of sand. The chores were not difficult, but several women were obviously pushing jobs on to her in quick succession all eager to use this new pair of hands.

Logan had taken himself down along the banks, examining the vegetation, finding pretty little wild flowers scattered among the thinning gums, and delighting in the wildlife that shared this oasis. Hundreds of magpie geese rose screeching at his approach, and white cockatoos added to the clamour as they too removed themselves from nearby trees. Across on the far bank, several grey kangaroos, all of them at least six feet tall, stopped grazing to observe the commotion, and then bounded effortlessly away. He was disappointed: this was his first sighting of kangaroos, and they intrigued him. What a time he would have in this wild country. There was so much to see. But since he had lost his travelling stake of ten pounds to the deep, he'd have to find work quickly, and stay on the west coast until he had saved enough to head east. Logan was ambitious to find fame and fortune in this land, but he had to acknowledge he'd made a poor start.

When he returned to the camp he found Sibell involved in a screaming row with the women. He was amused to find she was holding her own, too: despite the language barrier, she was getting her message across by hurling bowls away and shooing off a press of would-be employers. Then, suddenly, the scene erupted into violence, the native women whacking viciously at each other with heavy sticks. Logan dashed over to pull Sibell out of the mêlée, and they took refuge further back in the trees.

Two days later Sibell fumed: 'I can't stand this stinking place any more. I shall die of the heat and the dirt! You have to get me out of here,' she demanded. 'Right now!'

'I can't,' he replied. 'Nah-keenah made it plain to me last night, we stay.'

'We were better off on the beach,' she grumbled. 'The food they're giving me is vile.'

He nodded. The previous night he'd been handed the haunch of a small animal which had obviously been thrown on to the fire with the fur intact. He'd heard that natives in other countries ate monkeys cooked in the same manner but had never imagined that one day he'd be so hungry by sunset that he would devour every morsel he could separate from bone and fur. 'Just close your eyes and eat,' he advised. 'You must eat.'

'Their food stinks!'

'Then eat the nuts and berries, they're good for you.'

On the fifth day, he was surprised to see that Nah-keenah and several of the men remained in the camp, working on their implements. Hoping for some information, he sat with Nah-keenah, who sharpened the penknife on a stone and whittled happily at a long sapling, proudly showing off his treasure. The old man with the white beard came trundling over on his skinny legs to speak to Logan. 'Pfeller comen,' he said, pointing to the sun.

'Today? Pfeller comen today?' Logan asked excitedly.

The old man translated to Nah-keenah, who nodded to Logan. Something was happening. Logan prayed now that they would find a way to civilisation and at the same time wondered how they knew someone was coming. If they knew.

But at last it happened. A man rode into the camp, a blackfellow wearing a check shirt and torn, flapping trousers.

Logan leapt up, but Nah-keenah ordered him to stand back. Protocol again, Logan assumed.

The rider dismounted, and Nah-keenah went to greet him, surrounded at a respectful distance by his excited people. The two men greeted each other merrily with much back-slapping and chest-punching. The newcomer glanced towards Logan and Sibell, who were now standing in the crowd, and Logan picked up the warning to stay back. He held Sibell's arm as the strange blackfellow began unpacking a saddlebag, placing its contents on the ground.

There was meat, wrapped in muslin, a large cheese, tins of tobacco. He pointed to Logan and dug deeper into the pack for a tin of tea and a small bag of flour, then, indicating Sibell, unpacked some sugar and a jar of sweets, which were immediately handed around, accompanied by whoops of joy from the children.

'I think he's buying us,' Sibell whispered.

'I'd say you're right,' Logan replied. 'Let's hope the offerings are accepted.'

Nah-keenah studied the gifts and then pointed at the tomahawk stuck in the stranger's saddle pouch. They seemed to argue over this, but eventually the newcomer handed it over, and Nah-keenah threw his arms wide. He beckoned to Logan to come forward.

'You fellers come quick,' the stranger said. 'We go now.'

'I'll get my jacket,' Sibell said, but he grabbed her arm.

23

'No bloody fear. Go now. These fellers changem mind too bloody quick.' He turned and began to lead the horse away. Logan shoved Sibell after him, then bowed to Nah-keenah with a smile, not daring to attempt to shake his hand. 'Thank you, sir,' he said. 'We are very grateful for your help.'

Nah-keenah stood tall and dignified, inclined his head a little as if acknowledging Logan's gratitude, then grinned, not looking at Logan but at the haul which constituted their purchase price.

Logan laughed, waved to the rest of the tribe and ran after Sibell who had already disappeared into the bush. No one followed them.

Logan was full of questions. 'Who are you?' he asked the stranger. 'Where did you come from?'

'Me Jimmy Moon,' the man explained. 'Comen quick from whitefeller farm. Get you out.'

'How did you know where we were?'

'Nah-keenah send message. White people pay or his people killem you. Bash head in.' He seemed to find the ultimatum quite normal.

'I don't believe you,' Logan said. 'They were very good to us.'

'Not to me,' Sibell said. 'That man struck me.' Her face was still bruised.

The black man hoisted her up on to the horse. 'That mob bad fellers, you plenty lucky fellers, I'll say.' He chortled, nodding to himself. 'You got no boots,' he said to Logan, amazed that a white man should be out here barefoot.

'Neither have you.'

Jimmy shrugged. 'Whitefeller feet burn up.' He led them across a dried-up section of the river and then on through the bush that bordered the watercourse. Once out on the plains he gave Sibell the reins and set off at a run, calling back to Logan in a voice that was unmistakably a challenge, 'You puff up pretty soon I reckon!'

He was only a young man, clean-shaven, with a large fuzz of crimped hair, and his body was long and lean. Logan knew Jimmy could outrun him but he was determined to make a go of it.

'How far do we have to go?' Sibell called, riding astride without protest, but Jimmy had sped away.

'Why didn't he bring three horses?' she called to Logan.

I've no idea, he thought, refusing to waste his breath by replying. They were on their way to Perth, that was all that mattered.

24

2

A whitewashed stone farmhouse sat low in the foothills overlooking the Moore River, which ran swiftly westward, dropped south and then meandered to the coast where it met the great Indian Ocean. The sheep farm harbouring the house was just a dot in the huge state of Western Australia that could swallow Europe at a gulp. So far, settlements were huddled in the southern corner of the state or at tiny coastal outposts like Geraldton and Shark Bay. Exploration inland and in the northern regions had amounted only to thin trails marked by brave men who had battled into the Kimberleys or across the deserts to reach the interior and connect with that wonder, the International Electric Telegraph Line.

'No longer,' newspapers crowed, 'do we have to wait months for news of the Mother Country: we are at last linked to the rest of the world.'

Few knew how the thing worked, but work it did, and messages came tapping from Singapore to Java to the first continental landfall at Palmerston on Port Darwin, and went zinging on across the savage dry interior, right down to Adelaide. It was a massive project, with British and Chinese labourers toiling side by side across the dead heart of the country, and when the connection was completed, men who called themselves Australians were giddy with delight, despite the fact that at ten shillings per word only the rich could indulge.

Jack Cambray had no interest in the new-fangled communication line. Back home in Gloucester he'd had no use for such inventions, so there was no reason why he should waste time thinking about it now. Besides, it didn't come anywhere near Perth. He was too busy concentrating on his farm, which he had acquired through a series of fortunes and misfortunes.

By the time he had arrived in Perth, most of the viable land near the town had been taken up, so he looked to the northern coastal country between Perth and Geraldton. As an emigrant he was entitled to a grant of land equal to the value of the property he had imported. Property, as such, included livestock, goods and chattels. Armed with his share of furnishings and farming implements, kitchenware and linen, and his tiny, weary herd of sheep, Jack was well placed to claim his entitlements. But the lives of farmers are ever controlled by 'swells' at the top, and by the time the Cambray family arrived, the rules had changed.

A system of free selection had been introduced, the word 'free' a misnomer, since prospective landholders had to pay 2/6 per acre. Nevertheless there was no shortage of applicants: settlers, ex-convicts, experienced farmers and hopefuls, agents and dummy buyers all raced into the coastal plains, selecting their land, limited to 640 acres per man, to make their fortunes as sheep or wheat farmers.

This was a terrible blow to the Cambrays.

'We'll just have to buy,' Josie Cambray told her husband.

'And then what? We've precious little cash, we'll run out of ready before the farm begins to pay. I counted on buying horses and a wagon and more sheep, and I set aside a shepherd's pay.'

They sat sweltering in a rented cottage on the outskirts of the sun-bleached town, worrying at the problem, feeling let down. They had disembarked at Fremantle and sailed up-river to Perth in a small cutter, impressed by the tranquil beauty of the Swan River and its surrounds, relieved that the long and dangerous sea-voyage was behind them, and delighting in the prospects ahead. Now, though, depression had set in. Country folk, they were intimidated by the rush and bustle of the burgeoning town built on a peninsula of land jutting out into the wide reaches of the river.

It was a strange place, Perth. Horsemen raced through the streets with no care for life and limb. All manner of rattletrap vehicles clattered among sleek landaus and carriages, and even bullock teams were permitted in the main streets, struggling past with huge loads attended by whip-cracking teamsters. No one seemed to notice the lack of decorum. Ladies strolled the streets with their parasols, ignoring the men and youths who blundered around and the sad-eyed natives who congregated under shady trees. To Josie, Perth was a confusion of glaring white buildings stuck among scraggy trees and dusty roads, and it lacked the neatness of English villages. She was an orderly person, and everything about the place bothered her. The people looked rough and ready on the whole, more like frontiersmen than villagers, and while her husband searched for work, she stayed in the cottage, insisting that their eight-year-old son, Ned, learn his lessons.

Josie had grown up on the small farm next door to the Cambrays, and it had been taken for granted that she would marry Jack, her childhood sweetheart. Their second son had died of pneumonia when he was only two, and it was about that time that they began thinking of moving away to a more temperate climate, so it was no surprise to her when Jack announced his decision to emigrate. They all knew that the farm could not support Jack and his three brothers, so, as the eldest, he volunteered to leave. If he made good, he told them, Andy, the youngest son, ought to be sent out to Western Australia to join him. Miserably, Josie doubted that anyone else, family or friends, would be following them, because Jack would tell them the truth about this place. She felt lost, and homesick for the green of England, but for his sake she kept the boy quiet and put on a brave face.

At thirty years of age, strong of limb and a hard worker, Jack had plenty of confidence. He strode off into the town to enquire about employment, but made an unwelcome discovery there: the well-to-do employed cheap labour, convicts. Even though transportation had ceased years back, men still under sentence had to finish their time. The ticket-of-leave felons, people who were on parole, got the better jobs, while the rest of the convicts were employed by the government on roads and public buildings. Jack was shocked to see fellow-Englishmen clanking around in chains, and to witness the brutal treatment they received from the

26

foremen, who kept them slaving in the heat, using the whips with a ferocity that would have shamed the bullockies, who took better care of the animals. Watching the teamsters, he'd been interested to hear that each one of the bullocks had a pet name and that the animals were held in high regard. Not so these poor convicts. Feeling humiliated for them, he'd turned away and kept on with his search for the elusive job.

He approached customers in the hotels, asking for work as a farm hand, but none would give him the time of day.

'A free settler, eh?' one man said, his voice loud with arrogance and spite. 'Well, let me tell you, mister . . . I came out here a convict. Most of us here was convicts, and your lot flogged us bloody blind. Now it's our turn. We're free now, see, and we got our own families and mates to look after. You don't get no work on our farms or in our stables, no bloody place. We only employ our own mates and their sons, so hoppit!'

Other men in the bar jeered as he backed away, rage in his heart. 'If that's how it is,' he muttered to himself, 'when I get my farm none of your sons will get work with me, either.'

In desperation he sought advice in the office of the Government Surveyor, where he met a young man called Stuart Giles.

'That's the way it is,' Stuart told him. 'It's them and us over here. Right about now they estimate there are near as many convicts and their descendants in the colony as free settlers. The jailbirds have had twenty years to breed and brood, and they do plenty of both. I tell you, sir, they're a vicious lot . . .'

'By the way they're treated, I'm not surprised,' Jack retorted, but Stuart grinned.

'Don't get soft for the bastards, they won't lift a bloody finger less you flog 'em. And as for the freed ones, you say one word out of place to any of them, and the whole bunch quits. Bloody hopeless lot! It's better in the eastern states: a chap like you, a decent chap, you ought to get back on a boat and keep going. Go on to Adelaide or Melbourne.'

'Not me,' Jack replied. 'I don't quit that easily. I'll make my way here. But if you hear of a job I'd be much obliged.'

He saw the clerk's eyes narrow expectantly, and added, 'I'll make it worth your while.'

During the next few months Jack could find only poorly paid odd jobs, and as their money dwindled Jack and Josie did consider moving on to Adelaide. 'The land is bound to be dearer, though,' Jack told his wife, 'and even further out from the town than this. We'll have to hang on.'

And then Stuart Giles came looking for him. 'I've found you a farm. Going begging.'

'What sort of a farm?'

'They run sheep. But the bloke who owned it, he didn't know a sheep from a stag. Made a right mess of it. Then he went and got himself killed. Fell off his horse and broke his neck.'

'How terrible,' Josie said. 'The poor man.'

'That's the way it goes,' Stuart said. 'It's dangerous country out there.'

'What do you mean?' Josie cried.

Jack intervened. 'You might as well say it's dangerous here. Tell me about the farm.'

27

'Nothing much to tell. It's a fair spread of six-forty acres, in the foothills to the north – sheep country – half paid for, but the widow's had enough. She's walking off, asking fifty pounds including stock. The house isn't any better than this hut of yours, seeing her old man wasn't much with the carpentering either . . .'

'Why is it so cheap?' Jack asked.

Stuart shrugged. 'Mrs Crittenden – that's her name, the widow – will take fifty pounds for a quick sale. Plus a few pounds for my services in helping her.'

'And how much are your services?' Jack asked.

'Five pounds.' He saw Jack frown. 'If you don't take it, I could sell it down the street for her in ten minutes.'

He was right, of course. The widow was foolish selling at that price, but Jack knew that if he didn't snap it up, someone else would. 'Very well,' he said. 'I'll take it.'

A few days later, Jack stormed into the surveyor's office and found Stuart. 'You bloody little wretch,' he yelled. 'You lied to me. Crittenden didn't die from a fall from his horse, he was speared by blacks. Everyone in town knows about it.'

Stuart was unconcerned. 'I could hardly say that in front of your wife. I started to tell her about the dangers out there, but you cut me short. Anyway, there are hostiles everywhere once you leave the town, you just have to be careful.'

It was too late to turn back: he'd paid for the farm and ordered their goods in storage to be brought to Perth. In his heart of hearts Jack was terrified of the savages. No one at the shipping or emigration offices had mentioned hostiles: they were too concerned with their lists of required provisions for the steerage-class voyage and advice on clothing needed in the colony – flannel shirts and night-shirts, even night-caps, stiff shirts and collars, and intimate attire for ladies. Not a word about the blacks, though. Jack Cambray considered himself a fair-to-middling brave man in normal circumstances – when push came to shove he wasn't afraid to step out front – but wild blacks! He hadn't given them a thought. He recalled that, as a child, if he didn't go to sleep, his mother would threaten him that a black savage would come in the dark and cut his head off! The fear had stayed with him.

Josie was so excited about the farm that he kept his worries to himself and put on a cheerful front as they prepared for the eighty-mile journey in the wake of the bullock wagon carrying all their worldly goods. Determined not to take on anyone from the convict class, Jack had hired a young emigrant lad, Selwyn Stokes, as a shepherd and handyman. It was Josie who introduced the fifth member of his household. Laughing, she brought home an Aborigine youth about the same age as Selwyn. 'You've hired and I've acquired,' she said. 'He wants to come with us.'

'What are you doing, woman?' he yelped. Even the presence of the grinning, shiny black face made him nervy. 'We can't afford to feed him.'

'But Jack, he's so good with the boy. He can look after Ned in the wilds when I'm busy. And he'll be able to help you, too.'

The bullocky, Tom Pratt, gave a shout of laughter. 'Help? He'll be gone in a week or so. The blacks won't work, stubborn lot they are, missus! They don't like us much, you see,' he continued, tempering his comments as Jack had noticed local men were apt to do in the presence of women.

Jack shuddered. From what he had heard lately, that was a serious understatement! Attacks, murders, grisly slaughters by blacks, were the talk of the town, and it was hard to separate fact from fiction.

'His name is Jimmy Moon,' Josie announced firmly. 'I don't know his Aborigine name but he says he comes from the Whadjuck tribe and they live out our way.'

Tom considered this. 'That's true,' he said at last. 'If he's telling the truth. Your farm on the Moore River is in their territory and you might as well know there are still plenty of wild blacks camped out there.' He turned on Jimmy. 'You speak Whadjuck feller talk?'

'Speak plenty good English, too,' the lad replied.

'You're a full-blood black,' Tom said. 'How come you talk English, wear English clobber?'

'My mother Mary-Mary Moon,' Jimmy said proudly. 'She show me whitefeller place.'

'Oh, cripes,' Tom said, glancing at Jack. 'She's the town bike.' Instantly, he stammered his apologies. 'Beg your pardon, ma'am.'

'That's quite all right,' Josie said, surprising her husband. 'I spoke to the poor woman and she wants me to take him away from here. She said this town is no good for him and I can quite well believe it. She also told me Jimmy is a good tracker. I'm not too sure what she meant by that . . .'

'Bloody good tracker,' Jimmy echoed, and Josie sighed.

'I'll also have to do something about his language.'

'Trackers?' Tom said. 'If they're really good at it, they're magic! Someone gets lost in the bush, we wouldn't see a mark. I reckon those fellers could track a man through the centre of London. Might be a good idea to keep him, after all,' he told Jack. 'You want to send a message through to Perth or someplace, you got a ready-made runner.' He jerked his head at Selwyn. 'That kid'd be lost in the scrub within the first mile.'

'Very well,' Jack said. 'He comes too. Now let's get on with it.'

Before Jack could change his mind, Josie ordered Ned, Selwyn and Jimmy to jump aboard the wagon, and she climbed up front.

'That's if he stays,' Tom said to Jack.

'Who?'

'The black kid. They're still tribal. Every so often they go walkabout. There's no stopping them. Half of it's holiday, and the other half I figure is like them Arab fellers who go off to Mecca. The Abos do the same thing: they go on the same old routes way out into the hills for hundreds of miles, visiting the sacred spots, that sort of thing. As far as I can make out, they're very religious, everything hangs on their Dreaming, a sort of other-life.'

'You travel the country a lot?' Jack asked.

'Oh, yeah,' Tom said, sucking on his pipe. 'I go to the limits, right up to Geraldton if needs be.'

29

'And the blacks don't worry you?'

'Ah, well now . . . I've had a few close shaves but I try to buy them off.Once you get to know them, they seem friendly enough, but there are always a few show-offs that'll shove a spear at you given half a chance. Another time they'll feed you: they've helped me get the teams across rivers, nursed me when I got crook with the fever.' He shook his head. 'I've been a teamster since I got my ticket-of-leave nigh on ten years ago, and I still can't tell you much about the Abos. They're a mysterious lot, you just never know which way they'll jump. Me, I take my chances. A new chum like you, I'd say keep the rifle handy. Don't give 'em an inch and never turn your back.'

Jack glanced nervously at Jimmy Moon, who was listening to their conversation with childish delight, as if Tom's remarks were studded with compliments.

'Come along, you fellows,' Josie called. 'We haven't got all day!'

Even though it was only five-thirty, the sun was already sharp yellow, glaring a warning of the heat to come, and for the first time in this land, Jack realised that the light was different from home. On the sunniest days in England he had never experienced such strong light, especially at this hour: the shadows were already like cut-outs and the huge wattle tree near their hut was showered with tiny balls of yellow fluff as clearly defined against the slim green leaves as if each one were a lamp in itself. He sighed as the contrast gave him a pang of homesickness.

Their new neighbors had gathered to see them off, wishing them good luck and 'Godspeed'. Men stood by, smoking their pipes, as women rushed forward to hand up small gifts to Josie – a bag of apples, cake wrapped in muslin, a bunch of carrots, all tokens of goodwill from people they hardly knew. She was touched by their kindness.

'Ho! Nellie up front there!' Tom called to the lead bullock with a crack of his whip, and the team lurched forward. Jack swung up on to the wagon beside Josie, taking the reins quickly since his two horses were eager to be on their way. Behind him, young Ned and Selwyn were tucked in among the provisions, with Jimmy Moon perched loftily on a bag of potatoes. Josie took her husband's arm as they set off down the track to the main road. 'I hope we haven't forgotten anything,' she laughed. 'There'll be no running into the village for extras.'

'No,' he said grimly. Their farm was eighty miles away 'as the crow flies', he'd been told, but on the far side of the Moore River, which they'd have to cross by barge ferry.

At the crossroads they had to wait as the Governor, resplendent in uniform, rode back into town at the head of a platoon of mounted marines. Behind them, other men on horseback trotted past.

'What's going on?' he asked Jimmy, who shook his head, mystified.

'Catch up with Tom and ask him,' he told Jimmy.

The black youth leapt down and raced ahead to confer with Tom, but came back shaking his head. 'He doan say. He jus' say: "Bad business".'

Further along, groups of pedestrians were also straggling back to the township. 'It must have been some sort of dawn service,' Josie said.

'Would have been pretty important to bring the Governor out,' Jack replied, and reined in the horses to ask one of the men at the roadside, 'Where have you been?'

'To the hangin',' the fellow replied. 'The Guv'nor hanged them two niggers as killed the shepherds. They killed two shepherds . . . he shoulda hanged ten of them!'

'Oh, dear God,' Josie breathed.

'Don't feel sorry for them, lady. Them two blokes have made history. We've never hanged blackfellers before. Shootings never seem to worry them, so the Guv'nor's teaching them a lesson. He reckons hangings will frighten the lights out of them, make them think twice.'

They continued in silence. Hangings were not new to the Cambrays, but this event had cast gloom on their day, and, even worse now, they could hear a terrible wailing ahead of them.

Rounding the bend, they saw hundreds of Aborigines gathered, weeping and wailing around a tall tree, and, high above them, two men hanging limply from taut ropes. Four armed marines guarded the bodies to prevent the blacks from cutting them down, as distraught spectators threw themselves to the ground, screaming in anguish.

Josie covered her face. It was too late to do anything about Ned, who was watching in awe. Jimmy Moon yelled angrily and ran across the road into the crowd.

When they were well away from the terrible place, Tom halted his bullocks and came back. 'Your black boy didn't last long,' he commented. 'We won't see him again, and that's a nuisance. He would have come in handy as a guide. I'll just have to give you directions. You can travel faster than me, Jack, so you go on ahead and make camp at Budgie Creek tonight, and I'll catch up. Give the horses a rest at midday, they get pretty knocked up in the heat, worse than us.'

Jack listened carefully to his instructions, and set out again with the wild country ahead of him. A huge flock of cockatoos screamed overhead, shrieking like banshees as if in protest at the events of the morning, and then the Cambray family were alone on the empty road.

Hanging above him, his neck broken, was his uncle – his mother's brother, Tarwonga – and a friend, Gabyelli. It was the most terrible sight Jimmy had ever seen. He moaned and swayed and wrung his hands in shock before he could muster the courage to find his mother.

She was hysterical, clinging to her friends, tearing at her floral shift as if to rid herself of the white man's taint. Angry voices were raised and drowned again in the helpless wailing as his mother threw her arms around him, her good son who was at her side when he was needed. 'You speak for us,' she urged him. ' We must bury our brothers. Jaljurra will speak for us.' Jaljurra was Jimmy's real name.

'No use,' some friends said, miserably. 'We can't take them down until sunset, that is whitefeller law.'

There were murmurs of mutiny among them, but the soldiers stood fast, rifles with bayonets fixed pointed at the mourners. They settled again, chanting death songs, for if sunset it had to be, then they would stay all day.

His mother took him aside, tears streaming down her plump cheeks.

31

'You go fast to Nah-keenah. His warriors killed the shepherds, not our brothers here, so he must make the payback. You tell him what the whitefeller has done.' She lowered her voice. 'Then you get away quick so the whites can't chase you for blame.' Despite her misery she managed a grim smile. 'We all stay here and tonight we will bury our brothers, make a corroboree for the spirits. The whites will be watching us, so no blame on us either.' She stood up and shook her fist at the redcoats. 'Make them pay!' she ordered Jimmy through gritted teeth.

He slipped quietly into the bush and began to run with long, measured strides across country. He cut across farmlands, keeping to scrub as much as possible, forded creeks, sped into wooded hills, until in the late afternoon he picked up a trail that took him to a place where a family of blacks were camped. He ate with them, enquired after the whereabouts of Nah-keenah without informing them of his mission, and went on into the night, following a low ridge in sight of the sea.

For a few hours he rested and at dawn he began to track Nah-keenah's mob, picking up the signs – a leaf here, broken twigs, the secret marks designating hidden water holes unknown to the whites, stones still damp, the discarded head of a snake, an empty lizard's nest . . .

Nah-keenah was amused at his whitefeller trousers. 'Do they itch?' he asked.

'Only when fleas get in,' Jaljurra told him, and then they sat down to business.

He delivered his message to a ring of sombre faces, explaining to them what was meant by hanging, which they seemed to find very interesting, and then, with their permission, he left. These people, he knew, would never give in to the whites, and although they were friendly enough, they despised blacks who had succumbed to living on farms or in the town for the sake of the white tucker. There were at least five hundred wild blacks, as the Englishmen called them, still living in the bush around here, and sometimes Jimmy had become so depressed he was tempted to go back and join them. Something always happened, though, to make him change his mind. This time it was the job with Missus Cambray, his first real job. He thought it might be good fun for a while.

But now he had to find them again. He took a different route south, making for the ferry on the Moore River, and by the time the Cambray family and the bullock team arrived, on the second afternoon of their journey, their black boy was innocently waiting for them, a big smile on his face.

'How the hell did you get here?' Jack asked, amazed.

'Run fast, catchem up,' he grinned. 'All pfellers crossem river here.'

From the ferry they turned east, passing large farms with sheep grazing contentedly. With a loan from the bank, Jack had added to his flock and had paid a drover to follow them with a hundred sheep and his small herd of dairy cattle. He was anxious to get settled before they arrived.

The wagon bumped along a narrow track with the horses heaving and sweating. 'Tom says the next farm is our neighbour,' he told his wife. 'Mr and Mrs Randolph James. We can't stop, we have to keep moving, but we'll make their acquaintance as soon as possible.'

'It's very dry country,' she said anxiously.

'Ah, yes, but Tom says that when the rain comes, everything springs into life and the wild flowers out here are a wonder.'

The last few miles seemed to take an eternity. Ahead of them through the bush Jack could see the flash of white paint that Tom had said to watch for. They would be the boards mounted over the track to the James' farm. Although none of these properties were completely fenced, settlers seemed to like to dress up the entrances – some had archways, and one they'd seen even had a moon-gate for luck.

He wondered if the horses knew they were coming to the end of their journey, for they were becoming fidgety and nervous, whinnying and snorting as Jack tightened his hands on the reins. Then he saw the bodies. 'Christ Almighty!'

Josie screamed and climbed clumsily into the back of the wagon to clasp Ned to her so that he couldn't see yet another terrible sight.

'Whoa! Whoa!' Jack tried to hold the horses but they had taken fright and were dragging away. Jimmy raced forward to hold them to a slow trot until they were well past.

'Stay here,' Jack told his wife. 'You stay with them, Selwyn.' He himself ran back to stare at the naked bodies hanging obscenely from the board that proclaimed: 'Randolph James, Esq.' He was almost certain that the two bodies hanging here were Mr and Mrs James! As he stared into the vacant faces, his stomach rebelled and he reeled away, vomiting. He didn't know what to do. Should they go on? Surely they couldn't just leave them? And who had done this? Were they in danger? What should he do to protect his family?

He took out his gun, loaded it and put his wife and son under the wagon to wait until Tom caught up with them.

'Can you get up there and cut them down?' he asked Jimmy.

'No fear!' Jimmy replied, rolling his eyes, feigning fear. If the white people wouldn't cut down his people, then he wouldn't cut down theirs. He noticed too, without commenting, that the man and the woman were not hanged with ropes, white men's ropes, but with plaited vines. Nah-keenah had caught on quick! Blacks didn't hang people: they might spear them, or bring them down with boomerangs, or even chop them up, but never hang them. Until now. Nah-keenah was making certain the whites knew what this was about, a special revenge. The message was clear.

Hours later, the bullock team crunched up the road.

Tom stared. 'That's them all right. Randolph and Annie, God rest their souls. Let's get them down.'

They had to climb up on Jack's furniture to get enough height to cut the bodies loose. Then they wrapped them in canvas.

'We'll take them up and bury them near their house,' Tom said. 'A bloody shame this. They'd just finished their new house too.'

'Who could have done this?' Jack asked, still feeling sick.

'Blacks, I'd say.'

'Oh, my God!' Another fear clutched at Jack. 'Did they have any children?'

'Fortunately, no.'

The little convoy travelled at a funereal pace around the undulating

33

countryside to the Jameses' homestead. As they reached the row of young pines that led directly to the house, they stopped again. Only the chimney stood among the smouldering ruins.

'That does it!' Jack said. 'We're going back to Perth.'

And there, in the middle of all this horror, beside the dead bodies of their neighbours, in the presence of the bullocky, the emigrant youth, their son Ned, and a blackfellow, Jack and Josie had their first serious row.

'We stay,' she said. Demanded. 'We can't turn back now, we'd be ruined.'

'A damn sight better than being murdered.'

'We just have to be on our guard.'

'What about the child, woman? You're risking his life, too.'

'It was your idea to come to the colony, Jack Cambray, remember that.'

In the end they kept going, but their fond relationship was over. Their hut was still standing but was in such a foul condition that they had to camp out again. Jack elected to stand watch over them, but he had a bottle of rum with him, and by the time they were all asleep, he was dead drunk, slumped by the slab walls of his new home.

Jimmy Moon patrolled all night. He liked the missus they called Josie: she had plenty of fire in her, and she had been just as pained at the sight of the hanged black men as at the deaths of the white pair. Jimmy appreciated that. He moved quietly among the trees, watching in case any of Nah-keenah's warriors were hanging about, so that he could warn them off: for Jaljurra held rank in the Whadjuck tribe. Never mind about his mother – she had her own reasons for drifting into the town – his father had been an important man and he had been killed, not by the whites, but in a fight with a blackfeller. Nah-keenah! So now Nah-keenah, a bloodthirsty bastard, owed him. Nah-keenah could never touch him. Besides, Jimmy smiled to himself, Jaljurra was known to be fleet of foot and strong in the arm, a well-trained warrior. In the morning, he decided, he would make himself a cache of weapons in case he ever needed them.

Jack never told his wife of his dread of stealthy black savages, and, forced to live in his own nightmare, he built a cottage that was more like a fort. There were no windows, only auger holes, dark slits to accommodate his choice of deadly weapons, and to allow him a view of the land he was constantly clearing. He worked hard, long hours through the heat of summer and the kinder chill of the southern winter, with a revolver nearby and a rifle shoved into a leather pouch on his saddle, always looking over his shoulder, always afraid that a spear would plunge into his back.

At night he ate his meal in silence, then sat outside in a bough shelter with his comforters, his rifle and his rum. Sometimes, thinking the blacks were creeping up on him, he would race wildly down the hill, firing in all directions, the dogs yapping ecstatically behind him. Most times, though, he would just slump into a heap and Josie would have to lift and drag him inside to bed.

He became known in the district as Mad Jack, but: 'Give him his due,'

34

they all said, 'he's making a real go of that farm.' They knew from bitter experience that the recipe for prosperity in this frontier land was hard work . . . blood, blisters and backache.

No one felt sorry for Josie, not even the woman herself. There were plenty worse off. Jack didn't beat his wife or his son, and even if he were fanatical about protecting them, as Josie understood the situation, then that was no crime. Out here, so far from the town, pioneer women had enough worries without sighing over their husbands. Accidents were commonplace: an axe could slip, a horse rear, children were lost in the bush or drowned in seemingly shallow water holes, anything could happen. They coped with snake-bites and spider-bites, illnesses and childbirth, and they worked in their houses and in the fields. Some women even envied Josie: 'At least her husband passes out every night,' they whispered.

Selwyn didn't last long and neither did any of the succession of shepherds who came after him. They soon discovered that shepherding on the Cambray farm also meant chopping down trees and digging post holes, building fences and grappling with crowbars to oust old tree stumps with roots of iron. Mad Jack never ran out of jobs, so one by one they ran away.

Jimmy Moon, as they had been warned, came and went. He seemed to regard the farm as his home and was willing enough to give a hand at jobs that suited him, but he preferred the company of Ned, and the boy loved him. Jack shouted at him, called him a lazy good-for-nothing, gave him the occasional clout on the ear, all to no avail, Jimmy remained more of a companion to the family than a labourer, and, thanks to his unfailing good humour, they put up with him.

This particular day, Josie took Jack's lunch down to him because she knew he was angry with her. He was building a new dip-run for the sheep and as he straightened up she saw the sweat pouring down his face, which was burned dark these days from the sun. 'You should wear a hat,' she told him. 'You'll get sunstroke again.'

'They're a bloody nuisance,' he growled, reaching for the billy of hot black tea which she had brought him. 'No sign of that bloody Jimmy,' he complained. 'You've done it this time. We'll be lucky if we ever see that horse again, or him.'

'We had to give it to him,' she said. 'What else could we do?'

'He'll make a bloody laughing-stock of me. Giving a black a horse!' He took the lid from the billy and drank a great gulp of tea, turning his back to stand staring down the track. Jack had never felt so guilty: he should have gone out there himself, but he just didn't have the guts to volunteer. He couldn't bring himself to ride into blackfeller country that was so fiercely defended by mobs of savages, even on a mercy mission.

Jimmy had provided him with an excuse, and he'd grabbed at it to save face. Now, though, he was beginning to think that the whole affair was just a yarn, and that Jimmy had pulled a fast one on them.

Three days ago he'd come racing across the fields, brimming with news. 'The people say a white lady and her husband bin catchem out there by blackfellers,' he yelled at Jack.

Gradually Jack had prised the story out of him. He claimed that a white man and woman were being held prisoner by wild blacks who were willing to trade them for tucker.

'What white people? Where did they come from?'

'They got no horses,' Jimmy said, wide-eyed. He expected all whites to have horses. 'Blackfellers say them allasame fell off big ship, washem up on sand like dead fish.'

They fetched Josie, who was more patient with Jimmy.

'A shipwreck?' she said to Jack. 'We haven't heard of any shipwreck.'

'Could be . . . that big rainstorm we had a few days back, they say that was the tail end of a hurricane that fizzled out once it crossed the coast.'

'Someone will have to go and find out,' she said. 'We can't just leave them there.'

'If they exist. All a lot of bloody rot. You know he gets things all mixed up.'

'No fear, boss,' Jimmy cried. 'Gotta pickemup or blackfeller mebbe killem. Mebbe hangem,' he added, for extra drama. Jimmy was eager to do this himself, he wanted the glory of rescuing the white people, he would be famous. 'Them there all ri'',' he told them. 'All bloody true!'

'What blackfeller?' Jack asked suspiciously. 'Who wants to trade?'

Jimmy's toe scratched in the dust to avert attention from his face. No one ever mentioned Nah-keenah's name to the whites. They were always sending out troopers to bring in what they called ringleaders, so a wall of silence had been built around the tribal bosses. Contrary to the European opinion, they had no chiefs as such, only tribal elders and men who by prowess in war and hunting had placed themselves in positions of authority. He looked around him, searching for a name, saw where Jack had been burning off, and then looked up with a grin.

'Marradong,' he announced. 'Jimmy Moon make trade with big blackfeller boss Marradong.' The word meant 'burnt log' in his language, but they wouldn't know.

'You ought to get some of the neighbours together, Jack,' Josie suggested, 'and go to meet this fellow Marradong.'

Laughter bubbled up inside Jimmy Moon, but he controlled it.

'No fear,' he advised. 'You send plenty men, blackfellers get frighten. Run off. You send this feller with plenty good tucker.'

They talked it over and finally agreed, not without misgivings, to pack a supply of food for the trade.

'How far away are they?' Josie asked.

'Two-feller day march,' Jimmy said.

Josie turned to her husband. 'We'll have to let him take a horse.'

'What? Are you daft, woman?'

'He travels fast, you know that. A white lady couldn't keep up with him, and if she has suffered a shipwreck she won't be in any condition to walk all the way back here. You men either go yourselves or you give Jimmy a horse!'

Jimmy Moon couldn't believe his luck. He was an excellent rider, and he loved horses, and to be allowed to ride free, alone, filled him with pride. He travelled north, detouring occasionally to visit camps so that he could show off his animal, riding high just like the white bosses, nodding magnanimously to his friends squatting in the shade, giving cheek to the old blokes, who cackled in delight. For a while there, giddy with his own importance, Jimmy did contemplate taking off, far away, with the beautiful horse, but common sense prevailed. The whitefellers shot or hanged their own people if they stole horses: if they caught him their revenge would be awesome. And then, of course, there was Nah-keenah, waiting for his presents. He would not dare cross that black bastard: Nah-keenah's men would track him to the end of the rainbow.

Half-way to Nah-keenah's latest sitting-down place, Jimmy took some of the stores and hid them, so that he would have food to share with the two strangers on the return journey. This precaution was necessary in case Nah-keenah decided to take the lot.

Which he did. There was no holding back, he had to hand over all of the provisions in exchange for the two white people. Jimmy was beside himself with glee. He couldn't get over the expression on Nah-keenah's face when he saw this blackfeller arrive on horseback. He was so impressed that he greeted Jimmy with unusual warmth, thereby signalling to his mob that this important man, Jaljurra, was his friend. He seemed to believe it could be possible to get Jaljurra to hand over the horse as well, which was why Jimmy hurried the white pair out of the camp. If he allowed time to discuss and debate the question, he would lose, and the whites would blame him.

The man and his wife were a curious pair, their clothes in rags like any old town blacks, but the lady had a lovely smile and did exactly as she was told, which was another first for Jimmy. Telling white people what to do! The man, whose name, he learned, was Lo-Gan, was a big feller, but thin, and, as he told Jimmy, hungry, since they'd spent days with only a little fish to eat.

Jimmy was perplexed at this – there was plenty of food in the bush, especially along the coast – but he made no comment. Lo-Gan was a bit of a pest, slowing him up, needing rests all the time, but both of these people were immensely grateful that he had rescued them and thanked him over and over, so Jimmy was happy. Counting old Mad Jack, he now had four whitefeller friends, and that was important. They were powerful people.

Mad Jack galloped down the track to meet them. 'By Jesus, Jimmy!' he called in astonishment. 'You did it!'

Sibell was embarrassed. She was dressed in an ugly brown paisley dress that Josie had given her, and it was miles too big, even though the farmer's wife had sewn lumpy darts all over the place for a better fit. She was also wearing a straw hat, and shoes several sizes too large that slopped off her feet when she walked.

Mr Cambray had brought them into town in his wagon, and all along the way people had come to meet them, insisting they rest up, anxious to hear all about their appalling news. The *Cambridge Star* had gone down! They had no news of any other survivors, but Jack assured her they'd hear more in Perth.

They were taken to the home of a Mr Anderson, the Surveyor-General, she was told, but it meant nothing to her. The surroundings, all these people, were just a blur. She kept asking for her parents and could not understand why they didn't fetch them. Women fussed over her. In a daze she was bathed and assisted into a large, clean white bed, and the room was darkened. It was so cool, so luxurious, that she felt herself drifting among puffy white clouds, out of touch with the confusion around her.

'She's slept for days, poor thing,' a woman said, and another one, moving about, clucked and sighed.

'Mrs Gilbert is waiting to see her, but I told her she'd just have to wait. The girl is exhausted, she must not be disturbed.'

Sibell snapped awake! That name, Gilbert. Who was that? It sounded so familiar. She would have to ask her mother. 'Where is my mother?' she demanded.

'Shush now, dear, everything is going to be all right, you'll see.'

'My mother is Alice Delahunty. Will you get her, please?'

Instead of doing as they were asked, the women brought her a cup of coffee that had a strange taste.

'Just a little brandy, dear, to perk you up,' a plump old woman said. She pulled up a chair and sat by the bed with the other woman hovering behind. 'Drink your coffee first, Miss Delahunty, then you'll feel better. You've had a very nasty experience.'

When they took the cup and saucer away, Sibell eyed them suspiciously. 'My parents will be worried . . .'

'Now, Sibell,' the woman began, taking her hand. 'You must be brave. You know the ship went down and you were a very fortunate girl to survive. We must give thanks to God for that. There were other survivors, twelve other people were saved, but I'm afraid . . .'

'No!' Sibell screamed. 'No!'

The quiet voice droned on. 'But I'm afraid your parents were not among them. God in his wisdom has chosen to take them . . .'

'I don't believe you!' she shouted. 'You don't know what you're talking about. They were in the other boat!'

'They were lost at sea, dear. I'm terribly sorry to have to tell you this, it's a dreadful tragedy . . .'

'They drowned?' Sibell whispered, clutching her hand.

'Yes, dear.' The woman put her arms around Sibell and rocked her like a child. 'There, there, now, that's a good girl, keep your chin up. You are fortunate, you have friends here. Mr and Mrs Gilbert have come to see you, and when you're feeling better they'll take you home with them.'

Sibell went down to her room, ground floor at the back, and sank helplessly into the lumpy armchair. For three months she had been living with the Gilberts, no longer a guest, more a servant granted the distinction of taking her meals with the master and mistress, and with the added discrimination of no pay.

'She's like our own daughter,' Margot Gilbert told her friends, with the smarmy smile that Sibell had come to hate, because the woman was such a hypocrite. The Gilberts resented having to support her, but public sympathy for the poor lass hindered any plans they may have had to be rid of her after their initial show of support.

'A charity case, that's what I am,' Sibell muttered. 'Just like her daughter, indeed!' Miss Elizabeth Gilbert had been sent to boarding school in Adelaide, and her large, airy room upstairs, filled with her dolls and trinkets, was dusted every day, cared for like a shrine. Sibell envied the girl's good fortune at being cut loose from this nagging, niggling woman, and fought off reminders of her own mother far too painful to contemplate.

At first she had appreciated the Gilberts' obvious distress at the loss of her parents, their friends, but gradually she came to realise that there was more to their mourning: the shipwreck had embarrassed them financially. Percy Gilbert was a sheep-farmer. He maintained his house in Perth, and an overseer managed his property somewhere to the south. After some years Percy had come to the conclusion that bigger properties were necessary in this country to make real money, and that he should expand, following the example of the squatters in the eastern states. Those men had huge estates, called stations, where they ran thousands of sheep – hundreds of thousands of them – and wool sales were skyrocketing.

Sibell gave a grim smile of satisfaction. They argued over this situation at the dinner table, not caring that Sibell was forced to listen, or possibly making certain she heard of their woes so that she understood that her very presence now was an imposition. Occasionally, though, Margot, fortified by claret, shifted the blame from James Delahunty to Percy himself.

'If you had bought all that land in the first place when it was going cheap, Percy, we'd be rich now. Your lack of foresight will cost us dearly.'

'I'll have you know, madam, that my first acquisition of land was more than sufficient in English terms. I was never advised that these fields suffer so severely from droughts such as we had last year. You will give me credit for discovering the solution, which is to acquire property with more permanent water supplies. I have done that.'

Percy's solution was to buy more land, and since that required extra capital, he had invited James Delahunty to become a partner in this enterprise and to manage the new properties. Now, since Delahunty had been so foolish as to embark with his family and finance on a ship captained by an inexperienced fool – for that was the finding of the enquiry into the disaster – he was left high and dry. The necessary finance was at the bottom of the ocean with his proposed partner, and, his hopes dashed, Percy seemed to have only two alternatives: sell the new land, or sell his house and move to the country. He considered moving to the new sheep-run and working it himself with the aid of a foreman, but Margot stubbornly refused to give up her house and her position in Perth society.

Tears stung Sibell's eyes, but she sat stony-faced, listening to them casting blame on her father, and her chagrin equalled theirs, because there was also the matter of her reputation.

Whispering women looked at her slyly, they talked in huddles with Margot, and when Sibell entered the room there was pursed-lip silence until finally Margot confronted her behind closed doors.

'I want to know exactly what went on between you and that fellow Conal.'

Red-faced, squirming in humiliation at having to discuss that time, Sibell could only reply: 'Nothing.'

'You will give me the courtesy of the truth,' Margot demanded. 'The whole town is talking about it. You lived with that fellow for days!'

'Yes.'

'Did he touch you?'

'No.'

'Are you still a virgin?'

'What?' That side of things had not occurred to her. This was too much. 'How dare you ask me such a question. Who do you think you are? Get out of my room!'

'Your room? This is my house, you are wearing my clothes and eating my food. I am entitled to know what you've been up to. And what about those natives? You come back into decent society admitting you were in their camp for days . . .'

'I didn't say anything. Everyone knows that's where they found us!'

'And you take it all so calmly. Were they dressed, these natives? Were they properly clothed?'

Sibell stared at her. Margot was titillated by her experience, she had a hot gleam of curiosity in her eyes as if she were reading one of those sordid books. Sibell had had enough of the Gilberts: she decided to give Margot something to go on with.

'No,' she replied defiantly, 'they weren't clothed. They were naked, the whole lot of them. Completely stark naked. Men as well as women. What a shame you missed it.'

Margot lashed out at her, but missed as Sibell ducked. 'And don't you ever try to hit me again,' she shouted, 'or I'll hit back.' She recalled her shock and fear when Nah-keenah had whacked her with that steel-like hand. 'No one will ever strike me again and get away with it.'

'Captain of your own soul', she remembered Logan saying to her, in a different context, but it gave her courage.

'You foul-mouthed little brat,' Margot stormed. 'I'll have you out of this place as soon as possible. Certainly before my Elizabeth comes home.'

'Good idea. Give me the fare back to England.' She knew that was just bravado, she'd need more than her fare. And what would she do when she did get home? Land back on her uncles, still a charity case? And she also knew that the Gilberts, being pressed for cash, would not pay her fare, they'd already discussed that option.

Sibell moved the armchair, shoving it across the floor with her feet, not caring that it scratched the lino, and stared at herself in the mirror. Margot's clothes! She had only two dresses, awful black crepe, and her long, wavy hair was in two ugly plaits that Margot had insisted upon, hoping that they would make her look plain and virtuous. Well, she wasn't plain, she was no longer the skinny scarecrow who had come in from the bush. Her looks had improved in this fresh climate, and her skin was flawless again. She undid her plaits, frowning at the prissy crimp. Her mother had always done her hair for her, pinning it into lovely soft rolls around her face, but Sibell couldn't manage it: even with the handful of combs and hairpins she'd scrounged from around the house, it just kept falling down! The process of hairdressing was a complete mystery to her, so she took the scissors and cut her hair off to

40

shoulder length, and a very good job of it she made, too. Her fair hair now bounced and fluffed in thick, natural, loose curls, and Sibell nodded at the mirror. 'Well, goodness me, Miss Delahunty,' she laughed. 'Even if I do say so myself, you look quite beautiful!'

She thought her new hairstyle would startle them, but they ignored it when she came in to supper.

'Mr Gilbert and I have been discussing your circumstances,' Margot announced, and Percy intervened.

'Leave this to me, madam. We have decided that the best thing for you to do is to marry as soon as possible,' he said to Sibell. 'You need someone to look after you.'

'If anyone will have her,' Margot sniffed, still sulking from their row.

'I have a gentleman in mind,' Percy said. 'I shall broach the subject with him.'

Sibell didn't care. Marrying would get her out of this house, away from them. And then she thought of Logan. He wouldn't approve, of course, but he wasn't caught in a trap as she was. Her thoughts must have been conveyed to Percy.

'That fellow Conal came to see you this morning,' he said, 'but I chased him off. You must not associate with him, it will only start all the talk again.' He sighed, and slurped his soup through his moustache. 'It will take years for her to live all that down,' he told his wife.

For an instant Sibell entertained the marvellous idea of tipping the hot, greasy soup into his lap. What right did he have to turn her visitor away? Even if that visitor were Logan Conal.

She had dreaded seeing him again, and yet in an odd way she was pleased that he had called. Her irritation with him seemed to have been dampened down by these long, lonely months, and he didn't seem so bad after all. It would have been a change to see his familiar face, although she had no idea what they would talk about. Surprising really that he had bothered to call. Did he consider himself a friend? She supposed so, now that all that other business was behind them, and admitted that it was a gentlemanly act for him to come to the house to enquire after her. The last thing she'd expected of Logan Conal. At least now he might admit that she'd been right – she had been horribly compromised, according to Percy and Margot Gilbert and their friends – and probably she owed him an apology because he had behaved honourably.

They were watching her, so she sipped her soup slowly, coolly, as they waited for her reaction to this marriage idea. Marriage would give her respectability, and, despite what Logan had said, she would be mistress of her own home, to which the Gilberts would never be invited. Never! Knowing that her prolonged silences infuriated Margot, she said nothing, and affected a calm expression that revealed nothing.

She couldn't talk to these people. She couldn't tell them how much she missed her dear parents, or about the nightmares that remained with her. Awful dreams of them screaming to her for help, and of their servants, who had been so fond of her, lost forever in the vicious green depths, never understanding what had happened. As she tried to shut out the terrifying dreams, Sibell closed her mind to all waking thoughts of them, and by utilising that defence, she unwittingly bottled up her grief, refusing to face it, so becoming colder, more remote.

Josie Cambray, the woman at that farm who had been so kind to her, had kept in touch. She had written every so often, long cheery letters, not terribly interesting to Sibell, but ever so welcome in giving her some contact with the world out there. Sibell decided she would reply with her first piece of news: that she was considering marriage.

Once they were established at Cambray Farm, Josie found the months passed as vacantly as that long stretch of empty road that came to a dead end in the hills above them. No travellers came by, no strangers rode down from those rocky, straggle-treed inclines to share their table . . . that was blackfeller country and they were welcome to it. Josie didn't even know what was on the other side of the ranges. Some said it was good grazing land, others warned that it deteriorated into desert.

When the first thrill of owning such a large property, big enough to carry a dozen farms back home, dwindled to a deadly round of chores, she missed people. She missed the interchange of farm owners and workers, the gossip of villagers, the raised hats and nods of passers-by in narrow lanes, the sounds of voices. This land was quiet, unless you counted the squeals and trills of the birds, but at least the blacks had never bothered them. Not that she could convince Jack: he still sat out there every night drinking himself senseless. If a native did leap out from the dark, he probably wouldn't notice. It was Josie's considered opinion that the shock of coming upon the bodies of their former neighbours had addled his brain. And yet it was strange that she had managed to shut out the tragedy and that Ned was not scared. He probably didn't associate the murders with the blacks, since Jimmy Moon, when he was around, was his much-loved playmate.

The nights were the worst. With Ned asleep, and Jack outside, Josie was lonely. She tried her hand at embroideries, and then knitting, but she felt that she had something within her that was bursting to emerge, something better than just more work, something to occupy her mind. She began filling scrap-books with important world events cut from the few newspapers that came their way. Her hero, General 'Chinese' Gordon, was sweeping across the Sudan, giving 'what-ho' to rebels and dervishes and slave traders. The Queen was having trouble with those sons of hers, but it must be some consolation for her to be bearing the proud title of Empress of India.

Out here, a local hero, Alexander Forrest, whose brother had crossed the terrible Nullabor plains from Perth to Adelaide, was planning to explore the northern regions of the state. Josie was intrigued to note that Nullabor was not a native word but Latin for 'no trees'. And over in Victoria, a fellow called Ned Kelly was leading the police on a merry chase, robbing banks right under their noses. Some said he was a modern-day Robin Hood, others insisted he was just another cold-blooded bush-ranger. Josie couldn't decide, but she followed his career with interest.

'Why are you doing all that snipping and pasting?' Jack asked her.

'For posterity,' she told him, reckoning inwardly that it fair beat sinking rum every night.

'What's the point? Newspapers theirselves keep copies of every one they print. If posterity wants to look, posterity just goes in and turns the pages.'

Josie hadn't known that. The information was a blow to her dignity, but it opened another outlet. They were, after all, pioneers in this valley, even if no one had the time to care, so she would record her experiences, for posterity, in letters.

She made a list of family friends back home, and chose three people whom she considered would make reliable correspondents, and who would appreciate her reports. Within two years, two fell by the wayside, but her Aunt Flora remained faithful. However, there was such a long time between sending and receiving that Josie needed new contacts. Failing any volunteers, she began to write a series of letters that were never posted. She could hardly write to herself, so she addressed them to 'Dear Victoria', considering that the Queen, if she were to receive such letters, might be quite interested in the life and times of Josie Cambray in this far- flung outpost of the Empire.

The day they took Ned into town to deliver him to the headmaster at Bishop's College, Josie was fluffed up with pride. Jack was, too, not admitting it, of course – he wore the same dour expression that had contributed to the isolation of the Cambray family – but she sensed a swagger in his step.

'Who'd have thought,' she asked, as they walked out through the gates, 'that we'd be putting our lad in a college? That'll be something to tell them back home.'

'And they won't thank you,' he grunted. 'They'll say we're putting on airs. You go on back to the lodging house. I've got business to do.'

Josie had no intention of spending the rest of the afternoon in their room. She had made herself a new hat and a smart navy ensemble for this important occasion, and she wanted to step out in the town for a change. She strolled down King Street, looking in shop windows and taking the opportunity to admire the neat cut of her jacket, which accentuated her small waist and still firm figure. Then, when she came to the front steps of the Royal Perth Hotel, on impulse she marched up into the cool, carpeted lobby.

Her next impulse was to turn and run out again – she had never been inside a place as grand as this before – but a porter sprang forward to open glass doors for her. 'Will you be taking tea, madam?'

Josie nodded, and was swept forward by a waitress through a sea of sparkling cutlery and starched napery.

'Will anyone be joining you?' the girl asked briskly, and Josie felt such a fool. 'No,' she admitted.

'Good-oh then, this will be a nice table for you. You're a bit early but it don't matter.' She chatted cheerfully as she deposited Josie at a table for two. 'We're just setting out the cake dishes but I can bring your tea.'

'Thank you,' Josie whispered, and sat stiff as a poker in the proffered chair, hardly daring to breathe she was so nervous. If Jack knew she was in here, he'd have a pink fit! Then she smiled to herself . . . But he wouldn't know, would he?

She watched as a meagre scattering of customers was distributed throughout the large dining room, and sipped her tea with as much aplomb as she could muster, given that she was the only one so obviously devoid of friends that she was forced to take tea alone. The experience brought home to her the true loneliness of her life now, but she brushed aside her miseries as the waitress, still chatting, set out the most delicious afternoon tea Josie had ever seen. For an instant she panicked at the possible cost, but she had money in her handbag, money for provisions for the next few months. Jack wouldn't notice any discrepancy. It was her job to see the bills were paid.

'There's only me,' she admonished as the waitress served ham sand-wiches, scones with blackberry jam and clotted cream, and two large wedges of sponge cake bulging with whipped cream and topped with a thick layer of passion-fruit icing. Passion fruit was one of the many new fruits Josie had discovered in Perth, ugly purple-black crusts that revealed the sweetest pulp when you cut the top off to eat it with a teaspoon, like an egg. She had never thought to put it in icing, though.

'Bet you don't leave a crumb,' the waitress laughed. 'Cook prides herself on her teas.'

As Josie tackled the sandwiches, she saw an older woman, also alone, come through the doors, Her dress, Josie thought, was rather old-fashioned, a billowing, plum-coloured taffeta, and her hat was a no-nonsense black felt, but she also wore a rope of fat pearls, which, if they were real, must have been worth a fortune.

She proceeded grandly, unescorted, to take the table next to Josie, and sat down, her skirts subsiding with a ballooning puff. The waitress rushed over with a welcoming smile. Obviously the woman was known to the staff, as others came by to chat with her.

Josie felt better then, since she wasn't the only lonely soul in the room, and turned her attention to the scones before moving on to the cake. The girl was right: even though it didn't seem ladylike to polish off the lot, she couldn't resist that second slice of sponge.

Two waitresses hovered around her neighbour, offering to pour her tea, enquiring if she might require anything else.

'No, no,' she said. 'You girls go about your business. I'll survive, thank you.' Her voice was strong, clipped, authoritative. It seemed to match that hat. She adjusted her spectacles and gazed about her until her eyes rested on Josie. 'Are you staying in the hotel?' she asked, startling Josie, who was afraid that her staring had forced this reaction.

'No,' she mumbled. 'I'm sorry. I just came in for afternoon tea.'

'Nothing to be sorry about,' the woman replied peremptorily. 'Do you live in Perth?'

'No, out on the Moore River. We have a farm there.'

'I see. Sheep, I suppose?'

'Yes.'

'And is the farm successful?'

That took Josie by surprise. Men talked of the ups and downs, mainly downs, of country life, but this hardly seemed a polite question for a woman to be asking. 'Biding fair,' she replied, hearing herself echoing her husband's words.

'Good to hear it. You're English, are you?'

'Yes.' Josie nodded again, sipping on the last of her tea.

'I've never been to England,' her persistent neighbour continued. 'It must be a marvellous place, all those castles and the white cliffs of Dover. I was born in New South Wales.' She laughed. 'Up north they call us Sydney cockneys.'

'Up north?' Josie echoed, intrigued.

'Yes. I live in the Northern Territory, this is my first visit to Perth. Came down to see an eye specialist. My eyes have been giving me hell.'

Before Josie could commiserate, the woman took over. 'You've finished eating. Why don't you join me in a fresh pot of tea?' Without waiting for Josie's reply, the woman summoned a waitress to transfer Josie to her table. 'I'm Charlotte Hamilton,' she said, as Josie was being settled.

'How do you do, Mrs Hamilton? My name is Josie Cambray.'

'Call me Charlotte,' the woman said, to Josie's astonishment. 'Where I come from, no one stands on ceremony. This is a very pretty town, isn't it?'

'Yes,' Josie said uncertainly, and, feeling compelled to contribute now, asked where in the north the woman came from, this strange character whose presence seemed to dominate the room.

'I live in Palmerston, that's the township for Port Darwin.'

'Darwin?' Josie said, interested now. 'We hear all sorts of strange stories about Port Darwin. Not that one believes them,' she hastened to add, but Charlotte smiled.

'You can believe them, my girl. We've got the lot up there, from the bluest blood of England to tramps and outlaws. They call it "Darwin the Damned".'

'Good heavens! And you live there!'

'Of course. I've been in The Territory for years. Wouldn't live anywhere else. It's a grand place once you know what you're doing. I started off mining with my husband. He'd been prospecting back east for years and never did any good, so we decided to take on Pine Creek.'

'Where's that?'

'About a hundred and fifty miles south of the port. We really roughed it there, I can tell you, but we struck it rich and opened a pub as well. But you get nothing for nothing in this life. The heat and the booze got to my husband and he died.'

'I'm so sorry.'

Charlotte shrugged. 'These things happen. I leased the mines and the pub, took my two sons in to Palmerston, and bought a proper hotel, the Prince of Wales. It's the best in town.'

'And do your sons run it for you?'

'Good God, no! I didn't want them taking after their father. I run it myself. I invested in a horse and cattle station, and shunted them out on to the land. They're doing a fine job, too, my boys. You wouldn't think it, on a cattle station, but education helps. I saw to it that my kids got a proper schooling as soon as I could afford it. I sent them off to a boarding school in Adelaide.' She laughed. 'And oh, my! Didn't they yell! But I told them, three years at school, two years working as stockmen, and then I'd buy them their own station. And I kept my promise. Black Wattle's a good station, five thousand square miles, so that keeps them busy.'

'Five thousand square miles, did you say?' Josie was stunned.

'There are bigger stations,' Charlotte commented amiably, sipping her tea. 'Victoria River Downs, Wave Hill, quite a few. But you need the land, you can only run so many cattle per acre. We go in for shorthorns but the horse-breeding is important, too.'

'And do you go out there? To the station?'

'I've only been out a couple of times. I'm getting too old to enjoy camping, but we're building a homestead on the property, and when that's finished I'll retire from the hotel business. I'm past sixty, you know, and a person gets sick of keeping the men in order around pubs. I don't mind a drink myself, but I've got no time for drunks.'

Josie felt her face redden, thinking of Jack, so she changed the subject. 'What did the specialist say about your eyes?'

'Nothing much they can do. It's the dust up there, even the blacks have eye trouble. He used some high-falutin' words, said I should have come to him sooner, but how are you supposed to know? You think your eyes are just weepy from the dust and grit, and by the time you wake up it's worse than that, it's too late.'

'Too late?' Josie was startled. 'You don't mean to say . . .' She hesitated, but Charlotte was a very forthright woman.

'Going blind, my dear, if that isn't just the limit!'

'I'm so sorry,' Josie said.

'Don't be. I'll manage. It won't be for a while yet.'

When they parted, Charlotte gave Josie her card. 'Now, you must keep in touch. You can come to visit, perhaps – we do have a social life, it's never dull in The Territory.'

'I don't know if I'd ever get up there,' Josie said. 'But could I write to you?'

'Would you? I'd like that. We're isolated in the Top End, so everyone loves getting letters. And reading! They'd read anything. I'm taking a crate of books back with me to start a library at the station. I'm even thinking that when my eyes give out I ought to employ a secretary to look after my accounts and read to me. I've heard older ladies do have companions like that.'

'Oh, dear,' Josie said sadly. 'I hope that time is a long way off yet.'

Mrs Hamilton smiled. Despite the cloudy eyes, she was a handsome woman. 'Oh, yes,' she agreed. 'Time will tell, but I won't allow blindness to beat me.'

All the way back to the boarding house, Josie rehearsed her story for Jack: 'I went to afternoon tea and met . . .'

No, that wouldn't do, he might ask where. Begin again. 'I met a lady today, a Mrs Hamilton, a very interesting woman, and amusing, too, when one becomes accustomed to her rather brusque way of talking. But what was really astonishing, Jack, was that her sons run a horse and cattle station in the Northern Territory and it's enormous. Five thousand square miles . . .'

Josie began to doubt her ears. That seemed impossible. Maybe it was acres, not square miles, but even an acreage that size was huge. Best not to mention that bit to Jack, he'd say she was all wrong. A bloody fool. His favourite name for her these days.

It would be lonely at Cambray Farm now, without Ned. She would miss him terribly. The excitement of seeing him enter the College had worn off, and Josie was dreading returning home. Unlike his father, Ned was such a cheerful boy that he'd always been good company for her. Suddenly, in her mind's eye, she saw Ned's face as he walked away from them with his teacher. It had been a picture of delight, as if he had found freedom, not the confines of a boarding school. Most of the other boys had looked miserable and depressed, but not Ned. He hadn't even glanced back at them. He had been glad to go.

Feeling sad and let down, her meeting with Charlotte forgotten, she opened the fly-wire door and stepped into the gloom of the boarding-house lobby to find a visitor waiting for her.

'I was just about to give up on you,' he said. 'I saw you down the street a while back and then I lost you.'

'Why, Mr Conal! What a surprise! I'm sorry I wasn't here to meet you.' She glanced about her to make certain Jack wasn't lurking in the background. 'I went to tea at the Royal Perth Hotel,' she whispered. 'It was just wonderful. But what brings you here?'

He ushered her into the sitting room where several guests looked suspiciously at them. 'I haven't had a chance to come out to see you, and I've been feeling bad about that, because I owe you a debt for buying us loose from the villain Nah-keenah.'

'Oh, mercy, that was nothing. You can't believe how relieved we were to see you.'

'And astonished too, I'll bet,' he laughed. 'What a pair of ragamuffins we must have looked.' He touched his chin, which was now clean-shaven. 'After that episode, I got rid of the whiskers: by that time it was like wearing a rat's nest.'

'You look much better without a beard,' Josie said, and then she blushed. He was very handsome indeed, with a smooth, polished face, strong features and thick black hair that curled at the nape of his neck like a child's. But she shouldn't have made a remark like that.

'I'm glad you think so,' he replied. 'And might I say you're looking very smart, too. You must have turned heads at that hotel.'

'Heavens, no. But I met this lady from up Port Darwin way. She was quite attractive for her age, and plain-spoken, but easy to talk to. She's going to write to me.'

He nodded, intrigued. 'Port Darwin? I can't imagine anyone attractive coming out of there. They say it's the pits of the world.'

'To tell you the truth,' Josie confided, 'I'm not at all sure where Port Darwin is. This country confuses me.'

'Would you like some maps? I could get you some.'

'That would be very helpful. It would be strange to send letters off not knowing where they might land. Mrs Hamilton said this was her first visit to Perth; her sons live on a cattle station . . . Now don't laugh at me, but I think she said their property was five thousand square miles. Would that be right?'

'I don't know. It sounds an awful lot. It'd keep a surveyor busy for a year. I'll find out for you.'

'How?'

'I'm a surveyor, my colleagues would know.'

'Do you have work already?'

'Yes, that's why I couldn't come out to thank you for your kindness to us. I'd like to invite you and your husband to dine with me this evening at the Palace Hotel, if you haven't any other plans.'

Josie's heart rose and sank at the same time. She had never dined out in her life, she would adore to have dinner at the Palace, another fine hotel. But Jack would never agree. He didn't believe in putting on airs, that's what it would be to him.

'Thank you, Mr Conal, it's good of you to ask, but we couldn't.'

She was grateful that he didn't ask why, since she was still scrambling around in her head for a reasonable explanation.

'It is short notice,' he said. 'Maybe tomorrow.'

'I'll have to ask Jack,' she told him, and changed the subject. 'Have you seen Miss Delahunty?'

'No, I've tried to, but can't get past the front door. Her guardians, Mr and Mrs Gilbert, are in with the social set, but Sibell never appears.'

'Still in mourning, I suppose, the poor girl. A terrible thing to lose your parents like that. She's lucky to have the Gilberts to care for her.'

'I'm not so sure,' Logan said. 'They're a charmless pair. I've met them at a couple of functions and asked after her, and been cut dead for my troubles.'

'But that's dreadful! If it hadn't been for you, goodness knows what would have happened to Miss Delahunty.'

He laughed. 'I think that's the problem. There's been quite a bit of chat in the town about Sibell and me . . . You know the sort of things gossips enjoy.'

Josie was appalled. 'They ought to be ashamed of themselves!'

'My name didn't help,' he grinned. 'The English seem to think the Irish are over-sexed, and a young Irishman out there for days on a lonely beach with a helpless, pretty English maiden makes for juicy talk.'

His amusement was infectious. Josie found herself laughing too. 'The fact that your lives were at risk has been forgotten?'

'Of course. That part is all over, the rest will live on.'

'Oh dear! I should call on Miss Delahunty myself.'

'I was hoping you would. They can't very well turn you away.'

'What if they do?'

'Then you insist on seeing her. Can you do that?'

Emboldened by the success of her day, Josie nodded. 'My very word, I can.'

Jack didn't appear for supper, and Josie sat alone in the dining room, praying that he would turn up, aware that the landlady was not impressed. When she had finished her meal she tried to escape unnoticed, but the landlady stopped her at the door: 'When guests are not coming in to meals, I expect to be advised.'

'Yes, I'm sorry,' Josie mumbled.

'You'll have to pay for his meal just the same. I'll be charging two shillings on your bill, and I don't want no arguments.'

'I'll be happy to pay,' Josie replied, having been made to feel thoroughly guilty. No doubt Jack was in a pub somewhere.

Alone in their room, she put on her nightdress and climbed into bed, but she couldn't sleep, because, at every sound, she thought she heard Jack coming in, hoped it would be him. Eventually she must have dozed, because, late in the night, a loud banging wakened her and she knew from experience that Jack was out there, hammering on locked doors. A couple of times at home she'd tried locking him out when he became too drunk, but he'd raised Cain, and now he was at it again.

She heard a shouting match between Jack and the landlady as she let him in, and then she could hear him stumbling noisily around. Josie pretended to be asleep, too embarrassed to emerge.

It was the landlady who hammered on her door. 'Mrs Cambray, your drunken husband is laid out on my stairs. You get out here and shift him.'

Feeling sick with humiliation, Josie put on her wrapper and hurried out to shake and shove at Jack until she had him up the stairs to their room. Meanwhile, the landlady stood, brawny arms folded, muttering about the sort of people she had to contend with.

Furious with her husband, who was so drunk he had no idea what was going on, Josie shouldered him out of sight, flinching as he slumped to the floor, making enough noise to wake the whole place.

'This establishment caters for gentlemen . . .' the landlady began, determined to express the full measure of her disapproval.

'Mrs Bolton,' Josie snapped, 'you wouldn't know a gentleman if you fell over one!' She slammed the door in her face.

The next morning, she rounded on Jack. 'A fine performance you put on! We'll probably get thrown out of here now.'

'Ah, stop your bleating, woman! She'll not throw cash out the door. Get dressed, the breakfast gong will go soon and I've got a busy day.'

'Did you find shearers?' she asked him.

'Shearers? Bloody gods they think they are in the country!'

Josie didn't encourage him to enlarge on that. Every year he had to find new shearers, since there were always rows over their wages. They ranked high on his list of hates, along with blacks and crows.

He ate his breakfast quickly and left before Josie had finished her chops, but she didn't mind. It was such a pleasure to be served meals, especially breakfast, which she always ate on the run, and she wanted to enjoy herself. Mrs Bolton, she had to admit, did serve a good hearty breakfast of porridge and the usual mixed grill of mutton chops, lamb's fry and bacon, with toast and Worcester sauce. After such a meal, the walk out to the Gilbert house in Wellington Street would do her good. She took out the slip of paper Logan had given her and studied the sketchy street map as she drank her tea. And then she came to thinking about Logan. He really was a charming man, and she was flattered that he saw her as a friend, a rare occurrence for her these days. Josie had not mentioned his invitation to Jack, it was too risky. Like as not, Jack wouldn't accept, or, worse, he'd be drunk, and she couldn't bear a scene in front of Logan. For that matter, she hadn't even told Jack he'd called. Why should she? Jack never told her anything, just went his own cranky way, getting into rows with everyone. He didn't know about Mrs Hamilton, either. Josie was wondering if she could visit the Royal Perth again this afternoon. Mrs Hamilton had said she was there every day. But maybe not, she might think Josie was imposing. Being too pushy.

The wind whipped at her skirts, and tawny dust whirled along the sandy street as, head down, clutching her hat, Josie made her way towards the Gilbert house. A dog ran out, snapping at her heels, and she kicked it away, hoping no one was watching. She was not so sure of herself now, and her mind raced with questions. What if Miss Delahunty didn't want to see her? She'd look a silly fool and they'd know she'd come all this way on foot. And as if to emphasise her inferior status, a carriage rolled by, horses trotting haughtily, the driver looking down at her without expression.

Josie had never ridden in a carriage. The upkeep, she suddenly realised, must be enormous, what with horses, and a driver to boot, because no one drove their own. How marvellous it would be to own one.

Spots of rain dotted her path, and she looked up to see clouds gathering, usually a welcome sight, though not now. She didn't even have an umbrella. Ahead of her, a man was clipping a hedge.

'Excuse me,' she said. 'Can you tell me which one is the Gilbert place?'

'Five houses along,' he replied, 'you can't miss it. Stone fence. And you better get a move on, lady,' he grinned. 'It'll be rainin' cats and dogs in a minute.'

'Thank you,' Josie said, tempted to run, knowing rain would ruin her hat, but preferring to protect her dignity in this neighbourhood.

Fortunately she made it up the drive and on to the veranda of the large sandstone house before the rain set in, and, after composing herself, tapped the brass knocker.

Miss Delahunty herself opened the door, tossing an apron aside. 'Mrs Cambray!' she said. 'What are you doing here?'

Josie was taken aback for a minute. Not only had she expected to be admitted by a maid, but this girl looked different from the waif who had stumbled into the farmhouse. Even in a simple blouse and skirt, she was so elegant! So beautiful! And she seemed taller now, with the unmistakable look of that class of people 'Oh!' Josie exclaimed, searching for something to say. 'You've cut your hair!'

The girl smiled. 'Yes, I did. Do you like it?'

'Why, yes. It's lovely . . .'

'It was too long, I couldn't handle it. My mother used to roll it up for me, like yours, and it looked so smart, but I couldn't do that, not with ninety pins.'

Josie touched her hair uncertainly. 'Once you get used to it . . .' she mumbled.

Miss Delahunty swung about, fluffing her hair. 'You don't think it is unfashionable?'

Josie studied the soft, fair waves that framed her face. She couldn't think of anyone else who had cut her hair into a mop of golden ringlets

50

like that, but it certainly was attractive. 'No,' she replied firmly. 'It's very becoming.'

'Oh! Good! No one here has even noticed. Or they pretend they haven't. Anyway, come on in. Did you want to see Mrs Gilbert?'

'No.' Josie followed her into a very large sitting room. 'I came to see you. I was wondering how you were getting on.'

'Me? Well, of course, I'm so sorry. It's very kind of you.'

They sat facing each other on two stiff, expensive chairs, and Josie despaired at the silence. She took off her gloves. 'Miss Delahunty, thank you for your letter. I was delighted to hear from you, and I'm sorry I didn't reply, but we've been quite busy lately.'

She saw the blue-grey eyes mist for an instant, and then the cool gaze returned. 'Call me Sibell,' she said. 'I'm the one at fault, I completely forgot to thank you for your kindness.'

'Oh, goodness, I'm just so pleased now to see you looking so well. There's no need for thanks.'

'Yes, there is,' Sibell said. She rose to close the door. 'The truth is, I owe you. Jimmy Moon told us you supplied the provisions to pay for our release.'

'That was precious little. We didn't miss a few supplies from the farm.'

'Nevertheless,' Sibell continued, 'I would have repaid you, but I am afraid I don't have any money.'

'Oh, well,' Josie smiled, and then she stared. 'Good God. I hope you don't think I have come here for payment? It didn't enter my head. I just wanted to see you, Sibell. You've had a bad time, but you seem to have come through it, so I won't take up any more of your time.'

She stood, convinced now that her visit had been misinterpreted, but Sibell remained seated, staring at the carpet as if engrossed in the pattern.

'Are you all right, Sibell?' Josie asked from the door, but there was no answer.

'Perhaps I should have a word with Mrs Gilbert?'

That brought Sibell to life. 'No! I don't want her in here. I hate her!'

Josie nodded, not surprised. Logan didn't like the Gilberts either, she recalled. 'You'd better tell me about it,' she said, returning to her chair to listen, as Sibell outlined her life with the so-called friends.

'What can I do?' she asked at length. 'I'm trapped here.'

'I don't know,' Josie said. 'I'll have to think about it. But I must say you're bearing up well.'

'What do you mean?'

'Considering your experiences, you do have your nerves well under control: to be able to tell me about this situation without shedding a pond of tears is most impressive.'

'Thanks, but I don't cry. And I'm not going to let them beat me.'

'That's the spirit. Did you know that Mr Conal called on you? Since he wasn't able to see you, he sends his regards.'

'Oh, yes. That's another matter. Margot Gilbert is so damned suspicious, she thinks something went on with him. Isn't that awful? Anyway, I'm glad I couldn't see him. He laughed at me.'

'Surely not? When was this?'

'Oh, back then . . . I don't want to talk about it. But the latest plan here is to marry me off to the first eligible gent who'll have me.'

'So you're not really "considering marriage", as you put it in your letter,' Josie said. 'You mustn't get pushed into anything. You just refuse.'

'I don't know.' Sibell was thoughtful. 'It would get me out of here.'

'Out of the fat into the fire, more like it.'

'Would you like tea?' Sibell asked.

'No, thank you, I won't stay. I'm not really anxious to meet Mrs Gilbert, and I'd rather go now while the rain has stopped. But you must write to me again. I'll keep in touch with you, and if there is anything I can do, just ask.'

Sibell walked with her to the gate. 'Thank you for coming, I feel a lot better now.'

'Yes, don't be worrying. And when you are in the township, call at the Survey Office. Mr Conal would be pleased to see you.'

'And start all the tongues wagging again?'

'You can't be worried about things like that. In years to come, you'll be telling your grandchildren all about that shipwreck, and about Logan Conal pushing you along a deserted beach.'

'I am bored,' Logan said, over a pint at the Esplanade Inn. 'Bored, displeased and dissatisfied. Also broke. Poor deluded soul that I am, I thought I was coming to the land of milk and honey, the land of free spirits.'

'Ah, they're far from free here,' Charlie Grant mourned. 'Whisky's double the price, and there's no such thing as a penn'orth of gin.'

'Nothing's changed at all,' Logan muttered. 'Only the sky. I might as well be back looking at the Mersey for all my grand plans, still keeping my head down to dodge the rent, still giving the nod to the locals. I swear half the bad lads of Liverpool have taken up residence here by the Swan.'

'Have a brandy,' Charlie said. 'It will cheer you up. My treat.'

'Make it a double, then, and I'll owe you. Might as well get properly drunk. What I mean to say is . . .' His words were tripping over themselves. 'What I mean, Charlie, is I thought a man could rake in the cash out here, but I'm not making much at all, and I spend half my life hanging around the court-house.'

'That's because you're a real live land surveyor, qualified, not a hit-and-pinch fellow like me. They asked me if I could do the job and it sounded cushier than the army so I switched. Give me a couple of chain-men and I'm up and away. Measure anything I can.'

'So I've noticed, boundaries like a mad woman's knitting, left to me to sort out.' He beckoned to the bosomy girl behind the bar. 'Two double brandies, if you will.'

'No tick,' she retorted. 'Cash up.'

'I'm paying,' Charlie told her, placing the coins on the sticky counter.

'Would you be from Liverpool?' Logan asked her.

'Not me,' she said, delivering the brandies. 'Me dad's from Liverpool, though.'

'A ringlock passenger,' Charlie whispered, but she overheard him.

52

'Transported and bloody proud of it, too,' she snapped. 'He owns this place, lock, stock and barrel. What do you own?'

'Nowt, lass,' Logan grinned. 'Not a thing. No offence.'

'You're the surveyor feller, aren't you?' she asked.

'Yes, Logan Conal at your service.'

'That's never an English name?'

'It is not. The world's a-shifting. My old grandpa came from Belfast but got no further than Liverpool,' Logan lied effortlessly.

'A ringlock man, too?' she challenged.

'Close enough,' he laughed. 'What's your name?'

'Iris. Here's my dad, he'll be wanting to meet you.'

'I bet he will,' Charlie commented amiably, sinking the brandy. 'Drink up, old chap, the next one'll be on the house.'

The burly innkeeper came down, hand outstretched, his pockmarked red face beaming. 'Ah, lads. I know Mr Grant here, and Iris tells me you're the famous Mr Conal. Pleased to meet you.' He clutched Logan's hand. 'I'm Tommy Blackburn. You're one of the blokes came off the *Cambridge Star*?'

Logan nodded.

'I remember now,' Blackburn said heartily. 'You saved that little girl, too, brought her in from the wilds.'

Logan warmed to him. In loftier circles he was still the butt of sly jokes about Sibell. 'I didn't actually save her,' he replied. 'Or myself. The Lord dumped us there. And I'll tell you what, being a woman, she wasn't too pleased about it at all.'

Blackburn's laugh boomed to the rafters. 'That'd be right!'

Until now, Logan had been on the defensive about that subject, but in this company, he found he could laugh too. 'She was a little tartar,' he said. '"I'm staying right here, Mr Conal," she told me. "You go for help!" Played the duchess. Now when I look at the maps and see where we must have been, my legs buckle. If the blacks hadn't found us, I'd still be there arguing the point with her.'

'By God, you were lucky. And this calls for a celebration. Iris, same again for these gents.'

She delivered the brandies, and Blackburn leaned on the counter, lowering his voice. 'I wanted to have a word with you my own self, so to speak, Mr Conal. I've got a problem with the bloody courts.'

'What sort of a problem?'

'My land, you see. I've got a sheep-run up the coast, had the title all cut and dried, legal-like, and next thing this bloke on the next block claims half me land.'

'I know your case,' Charlie said. 'It's cut and dried all right, or it was until you moved the boundary stones, you rascal.'

'Mr Grant, I never did no such thing.'

'Tommy, I surveyed it in the first place. You're poaching, and you know it.'

Blackburn poured himself a slug of gin and considered this. 'The way I see it, gents, there's plenty of land for everyone out there, millions of acres to go yet. What's a few square miles?'

'Everything, to the other chap.'

'So why doesn't he move a couple of miles further up? Live and let live.'

'Because it doesn't work that way,' Charlie told him.

'The hell it doesn't,' Tommy said. 'Don't try pulling the wool on me, mate.' He turned to Logan. 'Charlie here's real obliging when it comes to boundaries, only now that you've come along, the toffs don't need him in court any more, not amateurs like him. You're the specialist, see, they ring you in, and we're the losers.'

On the far wall, a bearded gnome decked in tartan was painted over a silvering mirror advertising whisky. He seemed to wink at Logan

'Put it this way, Mr Conal, blunt as you like,' Blackburn said quietly. 'The squatters are slipping quids to the courts and surveyors, to get every square inch their way.'

'I don't work anybody's way,' Logan said. 'I just go by the rules.' He didn't add that the rules were mostly his own.

'Well, out here, rules can be bent, doing no one any harm. And me, for one, I'd make it real worth your while to see things my way.'

Logan looked at Charlie, who shrugged, and Logan relaxed. Takes one to know one, he thought. He'd been aware for some time that Charlie was on the take, but had been unable to locate the sources. It wasn't something you could ask up front. As it was, he'd been treading on thin ice until they all began to take him for granted. Having chosen a new name, 'Conal' being his grandfather's Christian name, and 'Logan' pulled out of the blue for Sibell's benefit, he was quite pleased with it. To his ears, Logan Conal sounded honest, upright and true, if ever a name did.

Then, being fêted in Perth with some of the other survivors – in total there were only sixteen of them from a company of a hundred and thirty souls – gave him a sense of importance. He'd advised the authorities that Taffy and Jimmy had survived and marched off in the wrong direction, and a boat had been despatched to search the northern shores, but to date they seemed to have walked into oblivion, or, as some muttered, into spears.

Logan was disappointed that Sibell's parents had not survived, because she had said they were rich, and they surely would have rewarded him for saving their daughter. He'd made himself known to the Gilberts in the hope that they would do the right thing. No such luck: that pair of skinflints only gave him the cold shoulder.

As he'd guessed in his run for the lifeboat, only a couple of the steerage passengers had survived, and fortunately they were not known to him, leaving him free to do as he pleased without looking over his shoulder for the law.

Feeling magnanimous now that he was on the right track, Logan ordered another round of drinks, leaving Blackburn's question hanging in the air.

He'd heard that the Survey Office was looking for staff, and without giving it further thought announced that he was a qualified surveyor. A castaway could not be expected to produce papers and certificates. He had worked for a brief time as a chain-man in County Armagh, where they were building a new road, so that knowledge sufficed for a foot in the door. After that, it had been no trouble to nick a few books from the office and read what this surveying business was all about. He still marvelled that his opinions, which were mostly guesswork, were taken as gospel. These colonials, he smirked, were a pack of simpletons. He would go far in Australia.

Blackburn was becoming impatient. 'What do you say then, Mr Conal?'

'I don't know,' Logan replied, assuming an air of righteous caution.

'Well, just think about it,' Tommy Blackburn said, undeterred. 'You give it some thought, mate.'

When they left the tavern, Logan pretended indignation. 'You've been taking bribes!' he said to Charlie.

'That's not terribly polite. I'm simply being practical. There are only two classes in this wretched place, the winners, and the losers. When I go home, I'll be travelling first class: what you do is your own business. Now, cheer up, old chum. You look as if you've swallowed a bad oyster.'

In the next few weeks, Logan began paying more attention to the workings of commerce in Perth. He found that the average fellow in the pubs thought it was riotously funny to 'see off' the squatters, cheering on bushrangers who preyed on wealthy travellers or robbed banks. He unearthed evidence that rich settlers were taking up far more than their quota of land by nominating dummy buyers, known as harbourers. And he realised that as the boundaries were extended, a class contest was underway for ownership of the land.

He rode about the town attending to his duties on a tired old mare provided by the department, and listened, interested, to the boastings of former convicts as they sang the praises of their mounts, for good horses were prized above women. High and low, men talked horses day and night; Thoroughbreds, Arabs, brumbies were discussed in detail, and horse-stealing was the worst crime. Yearling sales were of paramount importance, and the races, besides being social events, were just another arena where Jack could take on his master.

When the Blackburn land wrangle came to his attention, Logan saw, with renewed interest, that the complainant was Percival Gilbert of Wellington Street. He smiled, and rubbed his hands.

Tommy Blackburn won his case, and Logan Conal's finances took a turn for the better. And Tommy had many friends who also sought Logan's advice. Logan had come down on the side of the winners.

The magistrate, Ezra Freeman, another survivor of the *Cambridge Star*, claimed Logan as a friend, bound together by the tragedy. He had no interest in the outcome of these cases, only a determination to rid himself of the huge backlog on his lists, and he appreciated Logan's efficiency.

'In and out, Logan,' he said. 'Shift these squabbles along. I have far more important matters to confront, real crimes.'

Ezra was a boy at heart, Logan decided: he loved the excitement of the courts, the swaggering cowboys who roamed the streets, pistols swung on their hips, and the ongoing war with the blacks. He had even bought himself a silver-handled Colt which he waved around in the court-house, occasionally firing to restore order.

And it was the rollicking disorder of the colony that appealed to Logan.

55

There were as many brothels as pubs in the town, to keep a man happy, and fishing trips on the Swan on Sundays. What more could a man want? he asked himself, as his bank balance improved. No more back streets for him: he was now a legitimate member of local society.

'The man's a scoundrel,' Percy Gilbert snorted. 'He ought to be tarred and feathered! I complained to his superiors, but I might as well talk to the wall. It's an outrage! They claim they don't have the staff to investigate: too damned slack, bone lazy more like it.'

'Excellent port,' Ezra Freeman commented, undoing three of his waist-coat buttons to allow his wide girth some comfort after a heavy meal. 'The civil service here is hard pressed: we're seriously undermanned. And heavens, don't I know it? I'm up to my ears in work, with no relief in sight. People clamouring at me from all sides. Even the warden at the jail hinted I should stop sending him so many customers. Have you ever been out to that Fremantle jail? A fascinating place, the solitary cells gave me the shudders! Black as pitch. One cell built inside another so that no light can enter . . .'

'Yes, so I hear,' Percy said impatiently. 'But as I was saying, since they won't lift a finger in the Survey Office, perhaps you could put a stop to Mr Conal.'

'On what grounds?' Ezra murmured. This was a delicate situation. He didn't want to offend Gilbert: his future happiness depended on staying on good terms with the fellow.

'Far be it from me to instruct you in your duties, sir. But if you were to locate illegalities in his methods, shall we say, you could bar him from your courts, and he would no longer be of use to them.'

'It wouldn't be easy,' Ezra remarked, furrowing his florid brow for effect. Such action would be a simple move, but he needed Percy to be obligated to him. 'I may be able to assist you.'

'Do not regard this as assisting me, sir, but as a service to the colony.'

Magistrate Freeman reached for the port bottle. 'Of course, of course.' For personal reasons, he had made his own enquiries about Percy Gilbert, and discovered that he had been hoping for Delahunty money to bail him out, since he had taken up more land than he could afford to maintain. But when that source dried up, or more aptly, sank, he had subdivided his properties in the south, selling them off to new chums at top prices. One of the new owners was now in bother, left with no access to the river. Apparently Gilbert had assured him that he only had to sink wells to obtain water, but the block was bone dry.

'The settler's as mad as a cockatoo in a cage,' Ezra's clerk had told him, 'and the surveyors are on his side.'

'You will look into this matter?' Percy insisted.

'Certainly. But it is getting late. Have you spoken to Miss Delahunty about me?'

'Not yet. There are a number of young gentlemen who have expressed interest in her. The girl hardly knows which way to turn.'

'Oh, I see,' Ezra said sadly. He certainly did. Percy had been trying to marry her off for months, but a girl with no dowry and with her repu-tation coloured by that miserable shipwreck would not attract ambitious gents out here. Fortunately Ezra knew Logan Conal and had made it his business, over a few drinks, to acquaint himself with the facts. He knew that the gossip was unfair and ill founded, and he felt sorry for the poor girl. But not so sorry that he would admit to this knowledge right now. The very fact that she was compromised gave him an edge, it kept other suitors away. When they were married, he would speak up.

After that conversation, Ezra made his own plans. He spoke to the Surveyor-General. 'It's really too bad, sir, my courts are jammed with disputed land claims. Mr Conal is doing an excellent job in sorting them out, excellent. But if I may say so, sir, we could avoid all this time-consuming litigation if you were to put a qualified man like him out in the field. He's the one who should be sent to survey new blocks, opening up the land. He'd get it right the first time, and then we'd all know where we are.'

It didn't take long for Percy to hear that Logan Conal had been banished, and he wasted no time in inviting his friend, the magistrate, to dine with them again.

Logan went in search of Charlie. 'I've been promoted at last. I'm to head an expedition to survey land over the Darling ranges and I want you to come with me.'

Charlie stared. 'You must be mad. There's nothing exciting in that country but some very large blackfellers with very large spears.'

'Oh, come on! We'll be well armed, and the blacks aren't as bad as you think. They saved my life, remember? Listen, Charlie, we get to take two chain-men, a general help – which means cook – and plenty of supplies. That means our keep all the time we're away, so we'll save a heap of money.'

'Surveying's bloody hard work in the bush.'

'They'll let me have the newest theodolites, all the most modern instruments. Don't turn down an opportunity like this.'

Charlie considered the proposition. 'Do you suppose we could claim a couple of prime blocks for ourselves?'

'Wake up, Charlie, why do you think I agreed to go?'

'Well, in that case it could be worth my while. We'll need a guide, a blackfeller.'

'I know the very man. A feller called Jimmy Moon. All I have to do is find him.'

Margot was entertaining two friends at morning tea: Mrs Judd, the vicar's wife, and Mrs Enderby, whose husband was a wool-buyer. Sibell had stayed long enough for a cup of tea and to collar a cake, and then escaped from the parlour to sit on the veranda in a long, low canvas chair. This was her favourite spot, at its best when Margot was busy with guests and therefore unable to pounce on her with some new chore. Margot, as she often said herself, couldn't bear to see people doing nothing.

But Sibell wasn't actually doing nothing. She was thinking hard, as usual, about the problem of how to get away from this house. She could hear their voices droning from within the tall open windows nearby, and they seemed to match the high-pitched buzz of cicadas emanating from the garden. There were thousands of cicadas all around, she mused, but you never saw them. Clever little things, keeping well out of sight.

A lone magpie warbled fruitily from a nearby tree, with none of the usual purpose in its song. The notes were vague, almost introspective, as if it were simply filling in time, making up its mind what to do next. 'You and me both,' Sibell said to it, and the bird turned an inquisitive eye on her.

The cicadas stopped simultaneously, for some unfathomable reason, and in the sudden silence, Sibell heard Margot's voice. 'Excuse me for just a minute, ladies.'

Oh no, Sibell thought. She's not coming out here, is she? She braced herself for the call, but obviously Margot had gone in the other direction.

'Poor Margot.' Sibell heard Mrs Enderby's whining tone. 'She's having a terrible time with that girl.'

Sibell stirred herself to listen, with no qualms about eavesdropping.

'Which girl? Miss Delahunty?'

'Yes. A real little hussy, she is, and after all Margot has done for her.'

'Oh, dear, she is a problem for them. Percy came to see my husband,' Mrs Judd replied. 'He wanted the vicar's advice on decent young men in our community, with a view to matrimony, you understand . . .'

Sibell's face flamed with embarrassment.

'. . . but it's an awkward situation. My Ted honestly didn't know who to suggest. Percy even mentioned a couple of lads in the Governor's set, but that wouldn't do at all.'

'Of course not. But they'll have to find someone soon. They can't keep her forever . . .'

Embarrassment turned to rage as Sibell forced herself not to barge in on them.

Mrs Enderby continued. 'I mean to say, Margot has to feed and clothe her, and it's costing a fortune. I believe she buys anything that pleases her.'

'Damn liars,' Sibell whispered.

'But how could she do that?' Mrs Judd, at least, had reservations here. 'All Margot has to do is stop giving her money.'

'Not necessarily,' Mrs Enderby said airily. 'Margot has accounts: the girl has only to walk into Garbutt's Drapery and order things. I wouldn't put it past her. Margot says she's as bold as brass.'

But then the conversation was curtailed as Margot returned.

Sibell sat fuming. Should she go in there and tell them off? What could she do? She thought wistfully of her own dear parents, and tears stung her eyes, but she brushed them aside. No crying, she couldn't allow herself to cry, she had to be brave.

The magpie took off, flying fast and sure for a far tree, and Sibell nodded. Yes, a move of some sort was needed. She'd give them something to talk about.

She hurried to her bedroom, stumbling at the back door, her head busy with tangled plots and angry threats. She'd show them! She'd . . . what? She ought to burn their rotten house down. Take all Margot's clothes and throw them out of the window. Sibell brushed her hair vigorously, deciding on a simple act of disobedience: she'd take Margot's horse and go into town.

The only bonnet she possessed was a faded black, so she threw it aside and left the house hatless. That would annoy Margot, for a start.

As he strapped the side-saddle on to the horse, the groom was nervous. 'Does Mrs Gilbert know you're taking Bonny?'

'Of course she does. I'm in a hurry, don't dawdle, Leonard.'

And then she was on her way. She'd been out before, only in the gig, with Margot and Percy, her keepers. Now she felt free of them, pleased with herself as she cantered down the tree-lined street.

With no real plans as to what to do next, she rode quietly along the Esplanade, down to the docks and past the Governor's house. She turned up into Hay Street, enjoying her tour but still far from calm. Her stomach churned at the thought of those women, and others, no doubt, at the cruel things they were saying about her. She wished she could strike them all down, like God did in the Bible. Dash them on rocks . . . She read a large sign outside a shop, and sat staring at it. Garbutt's Drapery. And she remembered that Margot had an account there.

It wasn't London, but they did have some pretty dresses. Sibell had a wonderful time. She bought a soft white Indian muslin dress with double flounces to the floor, a dressy blue faille two-piece suit that had a neat peplum to accentuate her slim waist, and a lacy blouse to go with it. And then she couldn't resist a blue printed cotton with full sleeves and a velvet sash.

'It looks lovely on you, dear,' Mrs Garbutt almost sang. 'See how the skirt is stiffened at the hem so that it doesn't catch on your shoes. Now put on this lawn petticoat – slip it under the skirt. It's only a half underslip, but it will make the skirt stand out.'

Sibell whirled around in front of the mirror, delighted with it.

'Blue does suit you, Miss Delahunty, a pretty girl like you should wear more blue.'

'Yes, you're right. I'll take it. In fact I'll wear it right now. You can throw out my black skirt and the blouse, they're worn out.'

Mrs Garbutt fussed around her. 'No need for them any more, dear. Your time of mourning is well over. I haven't had the pleasure of meeting you before, but do accept my condolences on the loss of your dear parents.'

'Thank you,' Sibell said. 'Margot has been so kind to me. You can put these things on her account.'

'Certainly, dear, but what about some shoes? If I may say so, those lace-ups are a little heavy for these garments. I do have some very neat black pumps.'

'Ideal,' Sibell purred. 'And I'll need some gloves and stockings, and that nice straw hat, the one with the blue ribbons. It will match this dress.'

Her shopping expedition completed by a light handbag and some handkerchiefs, Sibell signed Margot's account, not bothering to examine the prices. She stared at herself in the mirror, amazed at the transformation: the blue dress with its accessories made her look stunning. She was anxious to show off now. 'While you're wrapping the parcels, I think I'll take a stroll.'

'We can deliver them if you wish,' Mrs Garbutt suggested.

'No, don't bother. I'll come back for them.' She sailed out of the shop and into Hay Street, strolling along, looking in windows, wishing there was someone she could visit, now that she was dressed to advantage.

Logan Conal, she recalled. Why not? The new clothes had given her confidence. So she stopped and asked a shopkeeper, 'Could you please direct me to the Survey Office?'

'Yes, miss.' The old man beamed at her. 'Around the corner in King Street. A lovely day, isn't it?'

Sibell smiled. 'Yes, it is indeed. The blue dress was perfect for such a day.

The clerk, too, seemed to come under her spell. 'Mr Conal? Yes, miss, he's out the back, packing up. I'll take you there myself.' He led her through the building to a large yard where half a dozen men were busy sorting through a small maze of packing cases. Supplies, saddles, camping gear, blankets, were scattered everywhere in tidy heaps, and a man was checking them against a clipboard. All eyes turned as Sibell stepped out into the glare, but she wasn't concerned, she was pleased with the attention.

'Where's Conal?' the clerk called.

'In the shed,' someone replied.

'I'll get him for you,' he told Sibell, and dashed away.

While she waited, a young black man moved closer to her and whispered shyly, 'Good-day Missibel.'

Sibell looked at him blankly for an instant, and then Missibel realised who it was. 'Why, Jimmy Moon! It's Jimmy, isn't it?'

He nodded, face crinkling with pleasure.

'How are you?'

'Good.'

'I hadn't forgotten you,' she said. 'You were very brave to come and get us.'

'Good job,' he agreed, laughing. 'You ride the horse good, too. Mr Conal he never run more better in his life.'

Sibell giggled, remembering how Logan had pushed himself to keep up with Jimmy, refusing to take a break by climbing on the back of the horse with her. Which she had only offered half-heartedly anyway.

'What's going on here?' she asked him.

'Mr Conal, he take us allasame walkabout. I ride a horse again,' he said proudly.

'You've got a horse?' she asked. He had told them, when they camped overnight, that he would get a horse of his own, 'by 'm by'.

His face fell. 'No, these feller horses belong bosses.'

'Never mind,' she said brightly. Today she felt capable of anything. 'I'll buy you a horse one day.'

'For me own self?'

'Yes.'

Jimmy capered on the spot. 'That one fine time,' he laughed.

'Well, will you look at you!' It was Logan Conal, standing admiring her, and Sibell was thrilled, because now he seemed so different, so smart and manly in a check shirt and white buckskins and brown riding boots, his curly dark hair hanging languidly over his brow. She looked at those green eyes, which once she'd thought to be hard and mean. Now, they twinkled with merriment.

She pulled herself together. 'Good morning, Mr Conal.'

'It's afternoon,' he grinned. 'How are you keeping, Sibell?'

'Very well, thank you. I see you are packing. Where are you going?'

'Out into the bush. We're off on a survey trip.'

'How interesting? When are you leaving?'

'First thing in the morning, that's why this place looks like a general store right now. We have to take plenty of equipment.'

'How long will you be away?'

'A few months, I guess.'

'Oh.' She was disappointed. 'Well, I can see you're busy, so I won't keep you.'

He walked with her to the street. 'And what are you up to today?' he asked.

'I have a lot of things to do,' she told him. 'Shopping, and various other bits and pieces.'

He looked at her keenly. 'Is everything all right with you, Sibell?'

She had thought of asking him to loan her some money, to give her some independence from Margot, even just a little to buy some lunch, but she couldn't bring herself to ask.

Logan seemed to read her mind. 'Have you had lunch?'

'Yes, thank you,' she answered, too quickly, and she could have kicked herself. Her pride had prevented her from spending more time with him.

'Well, then,' he said, farewelling her. 'I'll look you up when I come back. Did Josie tell you I did call?'

'Yes. But you mustn't take any notice of them. The Gilberts, I mean. They don't own me.'

'Good for you. You look out for yourself, Sibell. I should be back around Easter. I'll look you up then.'

The shine seemed to have gone out of the day as Sibell collected her parcels and rode back to Wellington Street. She was glad she had visited him, but she was hurting now. All she could think of was Logan, his wide smile, his new kindness. She was certain he was fond of her, and to her, the meeting was bittersweet: she had found the real Logan Conal, only to have him leave Perth. She was more than fond of him – she thought he was the handsomest man she'd ever seen – and was thrilled by his concern. Logan understood her, he would take care of her as he had done before.

Sibell's thoughts of Logan Conal sustained her during the tirades that ensued when Margot found out what she had done.

'You vicious little wretch. It's stealing, that's what it is! You've booked up more than thirty pounds on my account, made a fool out of me!'

'No, I haven't. Mrs Garbutt thinks you're the most generous lady in the world. If you take them back you'll look a fool.'

'You wait until Percy hears about this.'

Sibell shrugged. 'What can he do? Beat me? If he dares, I'll have the law on him.'

Percy roared. He shouted at her. 'You take those clothes back yourself!'

'No.' She sat through his rage without another word. Thinking of Logan. Looking forward to Easter, enduring the murderous atmosphere in the house, refusing to hand over the new clothes. 'I'll tear them up first,' she warned Margot, who had decided she might keep them for herself. The cook and the maid, enthralled by Sibell's audacious behaviour, became her allies. They told her everything that went on in the house.

As she was dressing for dinner one evening, in the white muslin, Lena, the maid, came to her door. 'Miss Delahunty,' she whispered, 'Mr Freeman's downstairs.'

'How exciting,' Sibell replied sourly. Poor old Ezra was often at the house lately, still talking about the *Cambridge Star*, still lamenting that no one had listened to his father who had warned them they were riding a cyclone. Ezra called it a hurricane, for more dramatic effect, Sibell suspected. She had looked the words up in a dictionary and found they meant the same thing, a godawful storm.

'Could be for you,' Lena grinned. 'He wants to marry you.'

'Oh, very funny!'

'No, it's the truth, I swear. And, what's more, I heard Mr Gilbert give him the nod. You're for the altar, lovey.'

Sibell pulled Lena inside and slammed the door. 'How do you know?'

'I served the sherry. I heard them talking.' She bobbed around Sibell, doing up the tiny pearl buttons on her dress. 'Come on, now, look sharp. You don't want to keep your fiancé waiting.'

'He's not my fiancé,' Sibell fumed. 'I'm not going to marry Ezra Freeman. He's old enough to be my father, and he's fat and boring. I won't go down.'

'Steady on, miss, don't break the traces. He's a good catch as men go. Since old Mr Templeton's finally gone right off his head, Mr Freeman's the chief magistrate now. That makes him a powerful man in Perth . . . and besides, he's not short of a quid. You could do a lot worse.'

Sibell plomped down on to the bed. 'I won't marry him, and they can't make me.'

'Don't be so sure. Cook and me didn't want to upset you before this, but the missus has been carrying on about you, talking about you a lot to Mr Gilbert. We didn't know who they had in mind then, but they said if you didn't do as you were told, then you'd have to go. You be careful, miss, they're talking about chucking you out.'

'Good, I'll be pleased to leave here.'

'And go where?' Lena's work-weary face was strained as she bent down to whisper to Sibell. 'Now you listen to me. I'm past fifty years of age and I've done it hard, rearin' a family here. I come out, transported, so I learned the ropes bloody quick, There's only one way to get on: you shut your mouth and do what has to be done.'

'Not me,' Sibell said, straightening up. Logan would be back by Easter, and then things would be different. Every night now she lulled herself to sleep with lovely dreams of Logan, of how he would come back and take her in his arms, and they would be married and live happily . . .

Exasperated, Lena pulled her back to the present. 'Miss Delahunty, have a bit of sense. If you leave here, where will you go?'

'I don't know,' Sibell shrugged.

'And have you got any cash?'

'No.'

'For cryin' out loud! Don't you know the law, girl? You'd be a vagrant, no visible means of support. The sentence for that is three months' jail. You'd be up in front of the magistrate, your Mr Freeman. And let me tell you, a man scorned is worse than a woman . . .'

Sibell gritted her teeth. 'They're not going to do this to me.'

'Then stall,' Lena said. 'Don't go down mean, go along with them. Something else might turn up.'

Sibell looked up and smiled. 'That's right, something else might turn up.' She threw her arms around Lena. 'You're a genius! That's what I'll do, I'll pretend to agree.'

Lena sighed. 'You might get away with it for a while, but I still say you ought to get it over with. You'll be somebody in the town then.'

'I'm going to be somebody anyway,' Sibell laughed, sure of herself. Sure of Logan.

'I really value your friendship, Miss Delahunty,' Ezra murmured, sliding a finger around his starched collar to separate it from reddening flesh. He was uncomfortable and very nervous once the Gilberts had withdrawn and left him to his mission, and Sibell had no intention of offering sympathy.

'Thank you,' she said.

'We have come through a lot together,' he added. Hardly together, Sibell thought, staring at a touched-up portrait of Percy Gilbert that hung over the mantelpiece.

'I was wondering,' Ezra began, 'if . . .' He took out his handkerchief and mopped sweat from his lip. 'If you would . . .'

Oh no, Sibell thought, not already. So much for stalling.

'If you would care to accompany me to the races?' Ezra blurted in a rush. 'Next Saturday. I am a member of the Turf Club and I can assure you of a pleasant day.'

'Why, Ezra, I should love to go to the races. Mr and Mrs Gilbert haven't thought to invite me before this, so it should be quite a treat.'

'Good-oh, then,' he smiled, relieved and encouraged. 'That will be splendid.' He fished in a fob pocket. 'By the way, I have a little present for you – just a locket, but I thought it was so pretty it reminded me of you.'

'A present! I adore presents!' Sibell opened the red plush box and stared at the locket and chain. 'It's beautiful. Is it gold?'

'Oh, yes, and that's a ruby, the stone set in the front.'

'Ezra, it's superb,' Sibell enthused, wondering how much it was worth. 'But my birthday isn't until next week.'

'Your birthday? Oh, no, I had no idea.' He glowed. 'We shall have to think of something special for your birthday.'

'Goodness me, no, you mustn't,' she said.

'But I must, my dear, because I want us to be the best of friends.'

Sibell rushed to the mirror to fix the locket around her neck, wishing he would leave. But there he was, standing behind her.

'The truth is,' he said, looking into the mirror, 'I am greatly enamoured of you, dear girl. I want you to be my wife.'

Sibell tried to feign surprise. 'Oh! Ezra, I had no idea.'

'Didn't Percy mention me to you?' he asked, breathing hard on her neck.

'No, he did not.' She went to move away, but Ezra's hands were about her, clutching clumsily at her breasts, his fat, pudgy hands sickening her.

'Don't,' she cried, breaking loose. 'You forget yourself, sir.'

'Oh,' he said, hands twitching. 'Forgive me. But I did speak to Percy, and he has given his blessing. I have to know. Will you be my wife?'

'Well, I shall certainly think about it, Ezra. It's immensely kind of you.' She took refuge in a lone armchair.

'You will have the best,' he told her. 'I am building a fine house on the river. Apart from my salary, I am a man of means, having inherited my poor dear father's estate. The woman who marries me,' he said, speaking to her as if she were a child to be informed of important matters, 'will be most fortunate, and that's for certain. It is not as if I'm coming to you empty-handed.'

Sibell resisted the urge to kick him on the ankles. 'You're too generous,' she replied.

'I was wondering,' he ventured, seeming to take her response as normal, 'what compensation you were paid by Lloyds. Your late parents, as I recall, were travelling with servants, livestock and considerable goods and furnishings.'

'Not to mention money,' Sibell added.

'Well, then, did Lloyds assess the compensation fairly?'

She was surprised. 'I didn't know they'd pay anything. I haven't any idea.'

'Perhaps Percy knows,' he murmured slyly, and Sibell took the hint.

'Perhaps he does. Thank you, Ezra, I shall enquire.'

'It might be a good idea, Miss Delahunty. If Lloyds haven't paid you, then a person in my position can make sure they do.'

A new element had been introduced to this friendship situation. Sibell was sure Ezra was trying to tell her something. Had Percy claimed the compensation? Or was Ezra making sure that his intended did not come empty-handed?

'I don't really understand these things,' she murmured. 'Could I leave it to you? Obviously a claim must be made, but I wouldn't know where to start. I'd need your guidance.'

'And you shall have it, my dear.'

Ezra's courtroom was closed on Fridays to allow him to sift through cases, placing boring matters to the bottom of the pile, and to attend to his own business affairs with the assistance of his clerk. Normally he enjoyed Fridays, because they gave him the time to prepare his social arrangements for the weekend, but this day was being shattered by interruptions. First a gaggle of petitioners had to be sent on their way, but not without noisy arguments, as Ezra tried to explain to them that they had no right to be pestering a magistrate, that their presence was illegal.

'They have no concept of the law,' he told Pastor Whitney who was waiting patiently in his office. 'None at all. And what can I do for you, sir?'

'I wanted to speak to you, Mr Freeman, as regards the blacks.'

'Oh, yes?' Ezra lit his pipe. This one would get short shrift too. The blacks were not his concern, and he wouldn't be drawn into the conflicts.

'We are taking up a petition to have the blacks excluded from the boundaries of Perth, and intend to force the Governor to listen to us. Your support for this request is needed.' He took out a paper with a list of names. 'We are calling a meeting on Sunday night, and your name has been suggested . . . You are to have the honour of chairing the meeting.'

'Not on your life,' Ezra said calmly.

'I beg your pardon?'

'You heard me, Pastor. You haven't got a hope in hell of getting that past the Governor. We've got enough trouble with the blacks without stirring up more.'

'Trouble. That's exactly what we're talking about. They're a filthy lot, a pack of thieves . . .'

'Thieves are dealt with in the courts.'

'Mr Freeman, you must know what is going on out in the countryside. No one is safe from marauding blacks . . .'

'Troopers are out there, they can contain them.'

'Leaving us unprotected here. Pretty soon they'll outnumber us in Perth, we'll be overrun by them, we'll be at their mercy. And God knows what will happen to our women.' His pale eyes bulged and his sidewhiskers quivered.

'I think our women will be safe enough,' Ezra muttered impatiently, rearranging papers and hoping that Whitney would take the hint. He glanced over at the pastor. Of course! Ezra loved gossip, and he'd heard a juicy bit about this fellow. His neighbours reported that Whitney beat his wife, they often had to shelter her when she ran squawking from the house in her nightdress. He smiled: 'Seems to me,' he said, 'that certain women we know would be safer with blacks than with their own husbands, wouldn't you say?'

No sooner had he rid himself of the pastor than another caller loomed up in his doorway. Colonel Puckering, no less, commander of the local regiment, personal friend to the Governor.

Ezra sprang to his feet, regretting now that he'd replaced his boots with slippers to protect his feet against the cold flagstone floor. 'Come in, Colonel, he cried, staying behind his desk. 'Take a seat. Would you care for coffee? Or tea?'

'Thank you, no. No time to waste today. Quick call. What did that pimply priest want?'

'Nothing, really, he was just here to talk about the blacks.'

'Indeed! Well, he may have pre-empted me. A word of caution, sir. Not to tell you how to suck eggs. Sure you'll take this in good part. A request, that's all.' He strode across the room and straightened a portrait of the

65

Queen. 'About the blacks. Got to ask you to ease up on the floggings. Don't help, flogging the poor buggers, y'know. Only makes the rest belly-ache, gets 'em nasty!'

'My dear Colonel!' Ezra was confused. 'That fellow, that Pastor Whitney, I've just had to contend with him. He wanted me to lead his group in having all blacks expelled from Perth.'

'Lunatics! Lunatics! Hope you set him right.'

'That's what I'm trying to tell you. First he wants me to be harder on them and now you want me to ease up.'

'Just cut out the floggings . . .'

'But, Colonel, some of these blacks are arrogant. Why, one savage even turned on me in my own courtroom. Do you know what he said to me? Bold as brass! "This our country, not yours!" Well, I never heard the like. I couldn't let that pass. A few strokes of the whip soon showed him whose country it is.'

'You're missing the point, old chap. Can't say I blame the feller meself, but my men have to keep order, and these floggings incite trouble.'

'What am I supposed to do, then?' Ezra grumbled. 'The warden doesn't want them in his prison, we've got enough white criminals to fill ten jails.'

The Colonel laughed. 'We could start transporting our convicts to England! Fair exchange, what? Take my tip, Freeman. Governor would appreciate it, y'know.'

By the time he arrived at the Palace Hotel to lunch with Percy Gilbert, Ezra's confusion had put him in a sour mood. And he'd had enough of Percy's procrastination. He came straight to the point before the soup. 'A little bird told me that Miss Delahunty was paid a healthy sum by Lloyds insurance.'

'They did pay her a few pounds,' Percy admitted.

'I heard it was in the vicinity . . .' Ezra paused, enjoying his companion's unease, 'of eleven hundred and nine pounds, eight shillings and ninepence halfpenny.' He flicked his napkin open. 'So now my fiancée does have a dowry.'

'You don't seem to realise, Ezra, what it has cost to keep the girl. There's her room and board, and her clothes – she's mighty extravagant in that area. She'd have little left.'

'I was under the impression she has no money at all.'

'Good Lord. Who gives a girl that age money? I've been minding it for her.'

'Then you should have said so,' Ezra told him amiably. 'Miss Delahunty has asked me to take care of her affairs now, so all you have to do is draw up a list of her expenses, we'll subtract them from the insurance money, and the balance belongs to the lady.'

Percy stalled. 'It might be difficult to work out . . .'

'You'll manage. My clerk will be pleased to assist, if necessary. Room and board shouldn't run at more than two and sixpence per week since she's only using a spare room in your house, not purchasing it.' He was enjoying Percy's predicament, it made up for his morning. Ezra was just beginning to realise that he had been rapped over the knuckles by Colonel Puckering. His face reddened at the thought. 'You can pay the balance into my bank account where it will be safe,' he instructed Percy, who bridled.

66

'I was just about to open an account for Miss Delahunty myself, since she is under age.'

'Oh, that won't be necessary. You might as well give her the cash, Percy. She will need the money now for her wedding dress and her trousseau. Poor girl hasn't even got a glory box. She will need plenty of linen for our new home – I can advise her what to buy.'

Colonel Puckering strolled through the grounds of Government House in the company of his friend, Governor Ord. The afternoon breeze, so welcome in high summer, wafted in from the ocean, adding briskness to their steps.

'Best time of the year here,' Governor Ord said, 'coming into autumn. Perfect weather! Perfect weather!'

Puckering made no comment. Discussions on weather bored him, especially here in Perth where he considered that the balmy climate contributed to the lackadaisical attitude of the citizens, and his men. He felt they all needed a good strong blizzard to shake them up. And next to the weather, the populace was entranced with the park that overlooked the township. A fine park, he was ready to admit, a thousand acres set aside to preserve forever the beautiful wild flowers that bloomed in profusion in the colony. But having done that, in a land that wouldn't miss *ten* thousand acres, Puckering felt they should get on with more important matters.

'There's talk,' Ord said, 'of changing the name of Kings Park to Forrest Park, since John Forrest had the land set aside. What do you think?'

The Colonel sighed. He didn't care what they called the place. Abruptly he changed the subject. 'I spoke to the Chief Magistrate about the floggings. Flogging blacks. Told him to cut it out. Only aggravates the situation. Might need a word from you as well, though, sir.'

'Quite so.' The Governor stopped and pointed with his cane. 'I thought of putting a gazebo here. Lovely view, what?'

'Yes,' Puckering replied. 'Had a visit from one of the blacks. Strange feller. First voluntary contact. Name of Jimmy Moon. You know him?'

'Never heard of him.'

'Feller made an appointment, too. That in itself drew my attention. Wanted to speak to me about his people.'

'About the floggings?'

'No. He wanted to talk about the wild blacks. A nice feller he was, talks fair-to-middling English. Told me that out in the bush the whites are still going out on blackfeller hunts. Shooting whole families. Would this be right?' Puckering had only been in the colony six months and was finding it difficult to ascertain the truth of these matters.

'Deplorable though it may sound, I believe it could be true. There's a tight lid on these doings. The squatters keep mum on what they get up to, but on the other hand they bombard me about atrocities committed by the blacks.'

'I did mention that side of it to the Moon feller, and he said the tribal people don't understand how strangers can walk on their land. Says white people are leaving them no place to tread.'

The Governor shrugged. 'That's true enough. I don't know why they can't be like the Indians and accept the British.'

67

'India?' Puckering snorted. 'I've a few battle scars to prove *they* didn't come quietly.'

'Of course. Of course.' The Governor put his hand on Puckering's shoulder. 'You lost your dear wife in India. Those infernal fevers. How are you settling down now? It must have been a great blow to you, Beth was so young.'

'Keeping on,' Puckering replied sternly. 'I had in mind we might be able to use this fellow as a go-between, help to keep the peace. Choose a decent officer and a couple of troopers to go out with him. Investigate. Talk to both sides. Pour the oil, so to speak.'

'Did he mention a blackfeller called Marradong? Every time there's been trouble with the blacks lately that name has come up.'

'Ha! Now I've heard of Marradong myself. Asked him straight up. Told him this Chief Marradong has a bad reputation. But all the fellow did was laugh. Said there's no such person.'

'He's lying. They all lie when it comes to that chap. I'm afraid Moon won't be much help to you. Could be a trap.'

'But he says Marradong is a joke. A standing joke among the Aborigines.'

'He's no bloody joke to me,' Ord said. 'Pull Moon in again and question him.'

'I can't,' Puckering said, much relieved. He had liked Jimmy Moon, a sturdy chap, he'd felt. Clear gaze. And looked you straight in the eye. He'd have been willing to bet Moon was telling the truth. 'He's gone off with Logan Conal's party surveying in the north. I was hoping to set up a reconnaisance party with him when he returned.'

'Then have a talk with Conal when he gets back. He'll know more about your man by then.'

The subject was closed as far as the Governor was concerned, but Puckering made a promise to himself that none of his men would be sent out to find this elusive and probably nonexistent Marradong.

Puckering did miss his wife, and since this post required quite an amount of socialising, he felt her absence keenly. He'd become an office-wallah, which didn't sit well with him after years of activity. Decidedly unhappy, he'd told himself, in this strange little place, his men no more than policemen. The Colonel was giving serious thought to resigning his commission.

Sibell Delahunty saw her life as before and after – A.M. and P.M. Back there in England, in the morning of her times, there were days of delight, days when good fortune flowed in abundance. Not monumental gifts, but small things to make her heart sing. On one of these days, she recalled, she'd found a field studded with luscious mushrooms, then she'd been surprised, amazed, to hear that she had topped her class at school, and when she'd arrived home, there'd been a new pair of shoes for her. Pleasant days, they were, in sharp contrast with the churlishness of the Gilbert household. She couldn't put her finger on any occasion since she'd been in this place when even tiny stabs of joy had brightened her day. Until now.

First there was a letter from Josie Cambray, who mentioned that Logan had called in at their farm with his companions. She wrote that the group had been held up there by storms which caused flooding in the district, but Sibell skipped that part. She read and reread that Logan sent his regards, and hoped she was keeping well.

Logan. In the privacy of her room, she allowed herself the luxury of relishing his words. He could hardly say he sent his love, but she knew that was what he meant. Logan, with his big bright eyes and teasing smile. She sighed. It would be ages before he could get home, that storm would add precious days to his absence.

And then there was Josie's other news. Sibell smiled. In different circumstances she would have jumped at the chance to get away from Perth. Apparently Josie had a friend, a Mrs Charlotte Hamilton, who owned a hotel in Palmerston, in the Northern Territory. Josie had taken the liberty, she apologised, of acquainting Mrs Hamilton with Sibell's present unhappy situation, and the woman had responded quickly. Because her eyes were failing, she needed an educated young lady as a companion, and she was offering employment to Sibell.

Josie urged Sibell to give this offer her attention. 'Mrs Hamilton,' she continued, 'is a kindly, humorous person. They have a huge property, too, and seem quite well off. Mrs Hamilton also insists that you will be paid for your services and will have your own quarters. She will also pay your fare to Port Darwin which will necessitate a sea voyage . . .'

That made Sibell jump. Another ship! She doubted if she would have the courage to venture to sea again. Not that it mattered. It was kind of Mrs Hamilton to invite her, but she couldn't take up the offer, for she was waiting for Logan to come back. Logan, whom she loved more and more each day, certain that the old adage, 'absence makes the heart grow fonder', was absolutely true. And she was sure that he would be feeling the same. She refused to take Ezra's courting seriously, but gave the impression she would accept him as a husband to keep the Gilberts at bay. To her mind, they were all stupid to think she would consider Ezra, so she treated the whole affair as a joke. At least she was going out these days. Ezra took her to functions and, at every opportunity, to inspect his house, which was nearing completion. It was an ugly, garish, Tudor-style mansion which seemed, to her anyway, to be quite out of place looking out over the wide sweep of the Swan. But she viewed it politely, smiling to herself, telling him it was quite delightful. Who cared?

And that same morning, Percy called her into his study to present her with a hundred pounds. In cash! Sibell was flabbergasted. And thrilled. She had never owned so much money in her life!

'I'm allowing you this money to buy your trousseau and other pieces ladies need,' Percy told her. 'And here is a list. Margot compiled it.'

Sibell glanced at the list which included tablecloths, napery, towels, nets, bed-linen, then looked suspiciously at Percy. 'Why would you want to give me the money to furnish his house? Because that's what this is, necessities Ezra has been hinting I should bring with me.'

'He's quite correct,' Percy replied. 'You can't marry without a glory box, so Margot and I are willing to help you.'

'Rot!' Sibell exclaimed. 'This is my own money. I bet you got it from the insurance people.'

'I am your guardian,' Percy explained calmly. 'It is wicked of you to question my generosity. I didn't have to give you anything.'

'Except that Ezra insisted,' Sibell grinned.

Percy ignored her. 'Margot will take you into town and help you to choose the linen.'

'I prefer to do my own shopping.'

With the precious money safe in her handbag, Sibell took the gig into town, instructing the driver to stop at the drapery store. She sailed into the shop, and, to the surprise of all inside, went right through and out the back door, making for the Commercial Bank.

At the bank, she filled in the necessary form stating her age as twenty-one, and deposited the hundred pounds. All of it.

Now, she told herself as she emerged, when I marry Logan, I will have a dowry. He'll be very pleased with me.

3

The river was angry, churned up by moon storms that lashed the earth in their final assault before retreating into the north, leaving the southland to bake in its long, hot summer. Jimmy knew, as all the people knew, that storm spirits did not disappear, they simply took their wares – their thunder, their bolts of lightning and fireballs – and went on to that other land, which, it was said, was closer to the great sun. Up there, Jimmy had heard, the powerful rainmen drew together with the storm spirit and surged over the land with massive rains that turned deserts into lakes and rivers into seas. Such stories had instilled in Jimmy Moon a yearning to see these wonders for himself, to travel until he ran out of land, meeting different tribes and hearing their words, their legends.

It was this curiosity that had brought him to follow his mother in among the white fellers. People said other tribes in the strange lands spoke different languages, but he was more confident now, since he was managing the English words so well. He would learn to make himself understood in the same way. Besides, all tribes used sign language, so there must be common ground. One day he would go.

Right now, though, he squatted on high ground and watched as Logan and his men dried out their supplies. The ferry had overturned on its second trip across the turbulent river, throwing men and horses into the rushing water. Fortunately they'd all made it ashore, but a day had been wasted as they toiled to right the ferry, using winches and the muscles of men and animals. He marvelled at the resourcefulness of these white men, at their determination to rescue the ferry which he had thought was doomed. And, with a temporary break in the rain, they were still working by their fires, drying out blankets and clothes and sorting through equipment caked with mud.

He wasn't sure why he'd agreed to guide this expedition, except possibly that he had a soft spot for Logan. Having brought him and Missibel in from the wilds, Jimmy had a proprietorial interest in their welfare, and he'd tried to explain to Logan that his mission into the back country was far from wise. But none of the white men seemed concerned, except for Charlie, the second boss, and he made a joke of everything.

Nah-keenah, Jimmy knew, was no joke. Forced to the outskirts of his territory, he had to fight, or go, head bowed, into Juat country, asking permission to stay. Why couldn't the whites understand this? Juat people wouldn't be pleased about sharing their hunting grounds.

And as Jimmy pondered, he realised that the Juat people would be next, followed by all the rest, as soon as the whites reached them, spreading like weeds across the good earth. Maybe his mother was right. She didn't care any more. 'Family finished,' she'd told him. 'Dark people die now. The white man stole our Dreaming.'

In despair, he'd found the name and gone to see the boss-soldier to discuss this awful problem. He'd been kindly received, but he'd come away dispirited. It had been a shock to discover that even a big white boss like that couldn't control the invaders, and, worse, had no solution to offer.

When he told them that he'd been to see Colonel Puckering, his mother and her friends had laughed, had fallen about in fits of giggles. 'Colonel Bugger-im? Damn fool name that! You're the silly bugger. White men won't help us.'

Another voice joined in. 'They rather kill us.'

A woman sneered. 'So our warriors kill them.'

Jimmy's mother took a swig of a powerful clearwater drink that a white man had given her. 'Only kill or be killed in the bush now. Depends on who gets up first. Safer here.'

Safer? Jimmy shook his head and walked away. These were busted people, the precious land that fed them taken away. Nothing to do, nowhere to go, they hung about on the river banks in desolate groups, waiting for death to come, and yet fearing death because their spirit places were lost. Come the Dreaming, they would never be able to find their spirit selves and would wander in darkness forever. Jimmy knew that their desolation went far deeper than the miserable existence they displayed to the white men, and that their laughter was fraught with tears.

He had visited his spirit place, which once had been an emu stamping-ground, far upriver, but was now a big farm. Even the emus had been chased away. He was of the emu clan, so he had found a feather to cherish and taken a stone from there to protect himself and keep his spirit with him. Both the feather and the stone were in a small bag that hung about his neck, sacred, secret things that together made for strong magic.

'We'll push on to the Cambray farm in the morning,' Logan told him, 'and go north from there.'

'More storm comen,' Jimmy said. 'Missus lucky, high house, plenty water comen down them hills.'

'Floods?'

'Yes. More better we stay outa there.'

'I'll have to risk it,' Logan told him. 'I want to repay Farmer Cambray for those provisions you had to give Nah-keenah.'

'Only tucker,' Jimmy replied. 'What matter?' But Logan wasn't listening.

That night, Logan wished he had listened to Jimmy. By noon, they were battling heavy rains, slowed down by trails that had become quagmires. High winds sent trees crashing around them, the packhorses whinnied and moaned as they struggled for solid ground, and it was well after dark before the six men, with their two spare mounts and two packhorses, rode up the track towards the house.

Shots rang out, blasting the air like lightning cracks, and Charlie's horse reared. 'What the hell?' he shouted. 'I thought these people were friends of yours, Logan!'

'Who goes there?' a voice boomed, and Jack Cambray loomed up, dead ahead.

'It's Logan Conal,' he called. 'All's well, Jack.'

Cambray, shrouded in a heavy oilskin, strode forward. 'What do you want?'

'Don't you remember me?' Conal asked.

Jack was unimpressed. 'Aye, that I do. Who are these other blokes?'

Jimmy Moon swung down from his horse, laughing. 'Them fellers not bushrangers, boss.'

'Christ! It's you, Moon. About time you bloody showed up.'

Drenched to the skin, Charlie was in no mood for conversation. 'Can you give us shelter, sir? We're travelling upcountry.'

Cambray considered this. Finally he turned to Jimmy. 'Show 'em the barn.' He turned and disappeared among the dripping trees.

Jimmy grinned. 'Boss doan like visitors.'

'That's obvious,' Logan said, and followed Jimmy around the house to the welcome of a warm, dry barn.

With Jimmy's help, the two chain-men, Len and Alex, took care of the shivering horses, while Charlie lit another lantern and explored the barn. 'There's feed here,' Charlie said to Logan. 'Do you think your good mate would mind if we fed the horses?'

'I'll pay him,' Logan growled. 'You get them fed and I'll go up to the house and find out what's happening.'

As he was about to knock on the door, it opened, and Josie appeared in a heavy topcoat and scarf. 'Why! It's you, Logan! I was just coming down to see who our visitors were. Come in quickly, you'll drown out there.'

He walked into the familiar kitchen. 'Didn't Jack tell you we were here?'

'Oh . . . well,' she replied, stammering a little, 'Jack, he likes to be outside at night . . .'

'In this weather?'

She pushed the big black kettle to the centre of the stove, her back to him. 'He has to keep an eye on the place. You never know who's about.' Then she turned back to him. 'What are you doing out this way?'

Logan remembered then that Cambray hit the bottle at night, and hung about near the water tank. His host's peculiarities had slipped his mind, and now he was sorry he'd embarrassed her, so he went on to explain his expedition.

'I'll make your friends some supper,' she said. 'I've got a fine stew here, that'll warm them up. What a night to be out.'

'By the way,' Logan said. 'We've got Jimmy Moon with us. He's our guide.'

'He'll be an excellent guide,' she smiled. 'He's a good lad, but Jack will be disappointed. Even though he won't admit it, he's always pleased to see Jimmy. Gets him to give a hand with the heavy work.'

Logan liked her. She had clear, sharp features, softened by rolls of chestnut hair fastened expertly into a thick coil on her crown. She worked as she spoke, quietly, efficiently, setting a large wooden tray for the men, and he wondered what sort of a life this was for her, stuck with an eccentric like Jack Cambray. Her figure, too, he noticed, would do her proud in any company, a true hour-glass shape.

As they were eating their supper, Jack Cambray marched into the crowded barn. Nervously, Josie explained to him that she'd been able to find the men some 'leftovers'.

'We'll pay for the meal and the feed for the horses,' Logan said cheerfully. 'And I want to fix you up, Jack, for the supplies you gave the natives for Miss Delahunty and me.'

Jack looked around him, heavy eyebrows beetling. 'Three quid will cover it.'

'I was thinking more than that,' Logan offered, but the farmer declined.

'Three quid, sir. Pay the woman.' He inspected his barn, shifting a lantern to hang it on a hook away from the hay stall, standing a rake in place, and disappeared out of the rear door.

Logan escorted Josie back to the house, and sat talking to her in the kitchen – on the pretext of waiting for her husband to come in, but more because he liked being with her. She laughed easily, which surprised him, since he didn't consider she had much to laugh about in this lonely place: it was a wonder she hadn't forgotten. He drank two glasses of port, but eventually had to go, leaving the rest of his bottle for Jack.

'If this rain doesn't let up,' she said, as she saw him out, 'you mightn't get away in the morning. The river has been rising for days. Jack has shifted the stock to high ground, we could have a flood.'

That night, sleeping on his blanket on the floor of the barn, Logan dreamed of Josie, and awoke, pleased to hear the rain drumming on the iron roof.

Dawn saw them stranded on the Cambray farm, surrounded by a small sea that stretched to the foothills. Jack was squelching angrily around his island property.

With nothing else to do, Logan and his men pitched in, carting fodder to the livestock standing miserably in muddy paddocks, and pulling out bogged sheep that had wandered away in the night. Jimmy Moon took over the milking for Josie, and Logan put a box of supplies in her kitchen, since the visitors were forced to remain and he didn't want her to feel obliged to provide for them.

In the afternoon he walked around the farm with her, watching the water lapping at the borders of their large vegetable garden. Josie stared at it disconsolately. 'After all my work! The lettuces and cabbages are ruined. Do you think it will come any higher?'

'No,' Logan told her.

'How do you know?'

Caught out, he laughed. 'I don't. I just wanted to make you feel better.' He took her arm as they made their way along the slippery track through the soggy orchard, feeling the warmth of her, wanting her, and nursing a delight that she remained so close to him. A misty rain was still falling, and her old felt hat drooped around her face.

'What a sight I must look,' she said, pushing aside wet strands of hair.

Logan stopped. 'You look lovely,' he said, and kissed her on the cheek, a kiss so moist and cool that he felt a rush of desire for this woman. Looking down at her now, he seemed to see a reflection of his own needs. As he put his arms around her, her face tilted up to him without a trace of shyness. It was as if she'd known this would happen. Standing there in the shelter of the trees, Logan kissed her again, and held her to him, experiencing a rush of excitement at this clandestine encounter. He wanted her desperately, this strong, firm woman, whose body was arching into him, and he knew he could have taken her there and then had it not been for the rain and all this mud and slush.

As they trudged back, he took her hand. 'Josie, we can't leave things like this. Meet me tonight.'

'Come over to the kitchen,' she whispered. 'After supper.'

Again, though, he was frustrated. As soon as he slipped into the house they were in each other's arms, kissing passionately. She allowed his hands to roam urgently over her body, but when he tried to move her towards the bedroom, she held back. 'No, we can't. He's out there, Logan, too close. It's so wet tonight.'

'Josie, I need you. Where can we go? What about one of the sheds?

'He'd see us. Darling, I want you too, so much. I've been praying I might see you again one day, but I never dared hope you'd care for me.'

The expedition was held up for three days, waiting for the waters to recede, and in all that time, with Jack Cambray stalking about like a warder, they were only able to snatch fervent minutes together, short embraces that became more and more rapturous but left them feeling cheated.

On the last night, he walked past Cambray to take the stew pot and utensils back to her kitchen, and stood apart from Josie, both of them aching to be together. 'I wish I could take you with me,' he said.

'So do I.'

Logan studied her intensely. 'Do you mean that?'

'Yes,' she said, moving as close to him as she dared, and Logan felt that the passion between them was almost visible. He had to have this woman – no one else had excited him as Josie could.

'Do you *really* mean that?' he breathed.

'You know I do.' Her eyes were full of trust.

'Then, by God, I'll come back for you. We can return this way: will you come with me then, and be with me?'

'Leave with you?' she asked, uncertainly.

'Yes,' he said, and took her in his arms again. Damn Cambray.

Josie edged reluctantly away. 'You'll have time to change your mind,' she told him, 'but if you don't, darling, I'll be ready. I'll be waiting for you.'

Had any Easter ever been so long in coming? As a little girl, standing at the cold windows looking out over frosty fields, Sibell had counted the months and then the dragging days, first for the joys and surprises of Christmas, and then for Easter, when she would receive the rare treat of iced marzipan eggs. The days had seemed like years, the months like decades. But that waiting had been trivial compared to the awful strain of these days. Her moods fluctuated between excitement that April, at long last, had struggled into view, and fear that something had happened to Logan out there in the wilds.

Her days in the Gilbert house were even worse now. Long, empty hours spent mooning from room to room, day-dreaming about Logan, wafting about in what she considered the useless occupations of engaged young ladies. Sibell had no trouble accepting the role of being 'spoken-for', as they called it. She had convinced herself that she was – only not to old Ezra. Her new status kept Margot from nagging her too much, though to Margot's irritation, Sibell would not discuss what she had ordered on that shopping expedition.

Fortunately, Ezra was a busy man and didn't bother her too much. He took her out on Saturdays, to luncheons or to race meetings, after first taking her on the mandatory visit to his dreadful house to supervise work on the interior of the building. He also escorted her to church on Sunday mornings, in company with Margot and Percy. Her fiancé puffed and wheezed all the time, still complaining about the heat, although the weather had cooled down considerably. Sibell agreed that he was wise to keep out of the midday sun, while she looked elegant and cool to emphasise his discomfort.

His men friends were old and dull, and their fawning wives told Sibell that she was lucky to have caught the eye of Ezra Freeman. Resenting them, she remained aloof, appearing to be quiet and dignified. Underneath, though, her fears mounted. Trying to keep up this façade, she seemed to be becoming two different people. During the day she managed to keep control, but at night she suffered. Fearing sleep, she had induced insomnia, and sat waiting for the dawn, her imagination running wild, mulling over the unfairness of her lot and preparing reckless plans of escape. Only thoughts of Logan – constant reflections on his dark good looks, his smile, his smooth, even features – could calm her nerves and give her the strength to face the day again.

'Come, my dear,' Ezra said, interrupting her meditations. Sibell groaned. She had been content to sit in her deck chair under a canvas awning, pretending to watch boat races on the Swan River, which she found excessively dull, while Ezra beetled around with his friends in a betting circle. 'That was the last race. Dear God, it is hot! I have your aunt's permission to take you to dine this evening at the Palace Hotel.'

'I'm not dressed to go dining,' she countered, standing to smooth her dress and plonk her leghorn hat back in place.

'Not to worry. I shall take you home and call back for you later in my carriage. This is a very special occasion.'

'What is?'

'Tonight, my dear.'

'Why?' Sibell had a premonition of trouble, as the crowds on the green lawns drifted away.

'I'll tell you tonight.'

'No, tell me now.'

Ezra's laugh was more of a snort. 'You're a little rascal, you can get anything out of me. I'm hugely fond of you, Sibell.'

Two ladies, in Boat Race Day uniform of summery white dresses and imposing hats, strolled by, nodding to Ezra, who responded enthusiastically. 'Do you know who they are?' he asked Sibell.

'No.'

'I didn't think you did,' he said. 'What am I going to do with you?

You never seem to be interested in meeting anyone. The first lady, in the hat with the yellow roses, is the Governor's cousin, the other lady is her travelling companion.'

'Really,' she said, unimpressed. 'What is tonight's occasion?'

'Oh, goodness me.' He took her hand. 'Come up here with me. I have to sit down: the glare of the sun is too frightful, and I hate those deck chairs. I can't get out of the things.'

Sibell smiled. That was why she had chosen one.

They walked up to the pavilion, where Ezra found sturdier chairs. 'We've got time. Would you care for a glass of iced champagne?'

'Yes, please.' Sibell wondered what her parents would have thought. None of the Delahuntys drank. These people drank like fishes – and especially champagne, which she had thought from her reading was reserved for dukes and duchesses, and actresses, who drank it from their slippers, a mysterious accomplishment she was determined to try one day. Preferably from new, unworn slippers, she hoped, although that might spoil the bouquet.

She coolly sipped at her champagne. Absolutely delicious! Her favourite drink. When she and Logan were rich, they would have a cellar full. It made her feel so grown-up and worldly.

But Ezra brought her down to earth with a thump. 'I want you to wear your finest tonight, my dear. I mean to say, you always look beautiful, but tonight we'll announce the date.'

'What date?'

He patted her on the cheek. 'Time to order the wedding dress, my love.'

'What?'

'The courts close down at Easter for two weeks. I have arranged my schedule so that we can be married on Easter Saturday.'

Stunned, Sibell drank her champagne and allowed the waiter to refill her glass. She wasn't feeling so worldly any more: just a very young girl caught in a trap set by this fat old man.

'We'll have the wedding breakfast at the Palace Hotel,' Ezra was saying. 'That's why I thought we should go there this evening – to discuss the arrangements with Mrs Page. Her husband owns the hotel, she'll do us proud.'

The wedding! Only weeks away. What was he talking about?

'No need for us to go away for our honeymoon,' Ezra continued. 'My house will be completed in time. Gracious,' he said, mopping drops of sweat from his jowls, 'what a relief it will be to move into my own house after those dreadful rooms I've been occupying.'

Sibell had almost forgotten their stupid engagement. It was unreal. Unwanted. It had been around for months, a bother, that was all. Wasn't it her right to set the date for her wedding? Who did they think they all were?

'I don't believe that date will be suitable,' she announced.

Ezra flushed a beetroot red. 'Forgive me, my dear. Which week would be suitable?'

Sibell stared into her champagne glass, sure her face was as red as his. The implications of the conversation disgusted her, and she lashed out at him. 'No date. I don't wish to be married.'

Ezra gaped. He stared around him. He fumbled in his pockets. His spectacles came out and landed on his nose with a jolt. 'I beg your pardon?'

'I told you, I don't wish to marry you.'

'But, Sibell,' he stammered, 'you are my fiancée. You have to marry me. You must.'

'Why must I?'

'Because . . . Good Lord! Sibell, you *will* marry me. You don't seem to realise who I am. I shall not permit you to jilt me. Now, don't be foolish.' He glanced around to make sure no one was listening. 'I have arranged to meet Mrs Page this evening.'

'Then cancel it. I have changed my mind.' She looked down at her engagement ring, and, with regret, removed it. The only expensive piece of jewellery she had ever owned. 'Here's your ring back.'

'This is an insult,' he cried, almost weeping, grabbing the ring. 'What shall I tell people?'

'Simply that I have changed my mind,' she said. 'That's reasonable, Ezra. I don't know why you're making such a fuss.'

'You'll find out,' he hissed, 'when I speak to your uncle.'

'He's not my uncle.'

'He's still responsible for your appalling behaviour.'

'Good,' she smiled, spurred on by the wine. 'Blame him.'

Ezra charged into the house, demanding to see Percy and Margot, and Sibell was paraded before them like a criminal. She now had a headache as well as a new fear at this confrontation. They were hounding her, all three of them: she was terrified that she would be turned out immediately, into the hands of the police, and charged with vagrancy. She began to sidestep their questions, their demands.

'I'm just not ready to get married,' she said defensively, feeling cornered.

'Nonsense,' Margot said. 'I was married at your age.' She turned to Ezra and Percy. 'And I wasn't a bold brat like this one.'

'She's too knowing for a girl of her age,' Percy stated ominously

'About what?' Sibell challenged.

'Everything,' Percy said. 'It just goes to show what education can do to women. It damages their mentality.' He turned on his wife. 'I want my daughter home from that school right away. Do you hear me? All this high-falutin' talk, look at the result.'

'Yes, dear,' Margot said, and Sibell intervened.

'You two are so stupid. This has nothing to do with education.'

'She's right,' Ezra said. 'I have nothing against a woman who is literate.'

'Thank you.' Sibell was grateful for that much, but Ezra continued.

'If this girl is determined to jilt me, then she must have a reason, and I believe there is another man involved. I see enough of this sort of thing in my courts.'

'That's not true,' Margot cried. 'She will marry you. She's just got the jitters, lots of girls do that. There isn't another man, I can assure you. Tell him, Sibell.'

78

Tell him? Tell them? Sibell was tired of their arguments, fed up with them handing her around as if she were a jar of jam, with no feelings at all. The Gilberts only cared about getting rid of her, so why not tell them? That would shut them all up . . .

'Ezra is right. There is another man, and I intend to marry him as soon as he returns to Perth.'

Uproar! All three of her elders, these people who thought they owned her, were shouting at once.

'I told you so!' Ezra yelped, staggering to a chair, which collapsed under his weight.

As they rushed to assist him, he rose in a rage. 'How dare she jilt me! You'd better do something about this, Gilbert! I've grounds here for breach of promise.'

'My dear fellow,' Percy assisted him to a solid couch, 'don't be hasty. I'm sure this is only a misunderstanding.' He rushed to the brandy decanter and poured a drink for Ezra, while Margot hushed and fussed around their guest.

Sibell sat calmly, defiantly, taking in the scene as if she were simply an observer, until Margot turned on her. 'You wretched girl. I've always said you're quite peculiar. Your dear mother would turn in her grave if she knew of your disgusting behaviour. Who is this person? This person you intend to marry? I don't think there's anyone at all. You're lying!'

'I'm not lying, Margot. The gentleman is very well thought of in the community. His name is Mr Conal.'

'Him? I might have known! I knew there was more to that business between you two. And all this time you've been under our roof, playing the innocent!'

Percy was shaking with rage. 'You are engaged to Mr Freeman and you will marry Mr Freeman. I will not give my permission for you to marry anyone else.'

'You forget, Percy,' Sibell said, 'I am not related to you. I don't need your permission to do anything.'

'We'll see about that!' Percy shouted, but Ezra had cooled down. He looked at Sibell, and for the first time she saw him as the magistrate, his hard eyes demanding that she reply correctly. 'You say you are engaged to Logan Conal?'

'Yes.'

'I know Mr Conal. He did not mention this engagement. When did he ask you to marry him?'

When? A wave of panic swept over her. When had Logan proposed to her? Had she allowed her day-dreams to get out of hand? She fought back tears, determined not to let them get the better of her. Logan would be back and he would marry her. She was certain of that, fate had thrown them together . . . 'Mr Conal is away at present,' she replied firmly.

'I am aware of that. You haven't answered my question.'

Sibell frowned. She was a match for Ezra too. She wouldn't allow them to bully her. Logan had said something about being captain of her own soul: that conversation was fading now, but she clung to it. 'I don't believe it is any of your business, but since you know Mr Conal, you may ask him yourself.'

'That I will,' Ezra growled. He stood up and made for the door. 'I'll see myself out,' he said. 'You haven't heard the end of this, Percy, not by a long shot.'

As the front door slammed, Margot wept, Percy ranted. 'Ezra Freeman is a powerful man,' he yelled at Sibell. 'Is this how you repay our kindness to you? Go to your room, miss. Get out of my sight! You will apologise to Ezra, and the wedding will proceed. That is my last word on the subject.'

Sibell did write a letter of apology to Ezra, but not the words dictated by Margot. She simply apologised for any inconvenience she may have caused him. She was still stalling for time. Where was Logan? Easter was now only a week away and there was no word from him.

Then she received a letter from Josie, which she opened eagerly, hoping for news. And there was news, devastating news! Sibell was shocked! She stumbled once again to the lonely stillness of her room and read the letter through a blinding rage, realising that it had been posted in Perth.

'. . . By the time you receive this letter, Logan and I will have left for Geraldton. We will be in Perth just long enough for Logan to complete his report: under the circumstances, we thought it better to begin a new life elsewhere . . .'

Sibell crumpled the letter and hurled it from her, then picked it up again to reread it, hardly believing what had happened. Josie and Logan! It couldn't be. She was a married woman!! How could he respect a woman who had deserted her husband?

'I was able to call on my son, Ned, at his boarding school . . .' Josie wrote, and Sibell almost exploded. She had deserted her son too? What sort of a woman was this? Obviously, being a married woman, she had seduced Logan. Turned his head. A Delilah! 'A positive snake in the grass,' Sibell hissed. Pretending to be a friend when all the time she was after Logan. Her Logan!

'I hope you will understand, Sibell,' Josie wrote. 'This wasn't something we planned. It just happened, and our feelings for each other are so deep that we couldn't bear to be separated.'

'I feel sick,' Sibell spat, disgusted, but she read on.

'. . . Be happy for us. Even though this has been a big upheaval in my life, I have never been happier, because we are so much in love.'

Sibell hated her. Hated them both. Now she had no one. Deserted by the only people she trusted. She sat on the floor, despairing, distraught, and then she remembered the Gilberts. Why had she told them she was engaged to Logan? She had made an awful fool of herself. What an idiot she would look when they heard the news. As they would. Oh God! Oh God! She held her head and rocked in pain. She had to get away somewhere to avoid the awful humiliation that was about to crash on her. What a fool! If only she hadn't mentioned Logan, it wouldn't be so bad.

Yes, it would. She had lost him!

She scrabbled in her bottom drawer. Who was that woman who needed a companion? Where was that letter from Josie? Hands shaking, she dug out the letter, searching frantically for the address: Prince of Wales Hotel,

Palmerston. That was it. She would go there, right away. As soon as possible. Still shocked and trembling, she decided to go straight into town and find out how to get to this place.

The clerk in the shipping office was keen to help. 'You're in luck, miss, there's a ship leaving on Wednesday for Port Darwin. You come here bright and early, by six on Wednesday morning, and I'll take you down to the cutter. I've gotta go to Fremantle myself, so I'll be pleased to see you on board ship. It's the *Bengal*, she's as good as any coastal vessel operating between Adelaide and Port Darwin.'

'Thank you,' Sibell replied, wondering how to avoid Margot and Percy for two days. She wished she could stay right here in this office until it was time to leave, hidden from all of them.

'Miss Delahunty,' the clerk enquired, 'aren't you the young lady who survived the *Cambridge Star?*'

'Yes,' Sibell said absently, having made a new decision. She would go home, pack her things and leave the Gilbert house. They weren't likely to object. But this time she'd tell them nothing. She wouldn't tell them what she was doing, or where she was going. Never again would she allow anyone to dominate her life.

'I must say you're brave,' the clerk commented. 'Taking on another sea voyage.'

'What?' Terror clutched at her. What was he saying? A sea voyage. She had thought Port Darwin was a short journey up the coast. 'It isn't very far, is it?' she asked him nervously.

'I'm afraid so,' he told her. 'Look here at the map. It'd have to be a couple of thousand miles landwise: by sea it takes about ten days. Not that you could go by land anyway. But don't you be worrying. The *Bengal*'s as safe as a house.'

Sibell nodded, as if it didn't matter. In actual fact, she was so frightened she couldn't even attempt a reply.

She paid for her ticket and left. What did it matter if she drowned? Who would care? Perhaps drowning was to be her fate after all, and she had only achieved a postponement. She booked herself into the nearest hotel, which the clerk assured her was suitable for ladies, and returned to the house for her belongings.

Lena informed her that Percy and Margot were attending a church 'sociable', so there was no need for a confrontation. Sibell didn't even bother to leave a note.

That night she sat alone in her room, listening to the community singing coming from the parlour below, the sounds of a happy world from which she was excluded.

The barque *Bengal* sailed serenely up the coast of Western Australia. Colonel Puckering was enjoying the voyage, and the occasional glimpses of the majestic landfall. He had resigned his commission with the regiment and accepted the post of Chief Inspector of Police in Palmerston. His bailiwick extended for hundreds of miles into what was called the 'wayback', and from all accounts the job should keep him hopping. He had decided that since his duties in Perth encompassed more police work than military, he might as well take on the former officially. His new post carried a much higher salary, and no interference from resident bureaucrats, since the Northern Territory was governed from South Australia.

Puckering had travelled to Adelaide to receive his instructions from a grateful Minister of Police, who was anxious to please. The fellow had been truthful, though, in explaining that it had been difficult to find someone suitable to take on this responsibility. The Territory had a lawless reputation, the climate could be trying, especially in the wet season, and several policemen had either quit in disgust or suffered untimely ends.

'Accidents?' Puckering had asked.

'Not all,' the Minister admitted. 'But take heart, sir, we pay ample compensation for injuries . . .'

'Kind of you,' the Colonel grunted.

'Also,' the Minister hurried to add, 'we do permit remunerations after a few years, for length of stay. Sort of payment for hanging on there, so to speak, far from the amenities that a gentleman of your calibre would be accustomed to.'

Better than India, the Colonel thought, but accepted the news without comment.

'Plenty of Chinese there,' his Minister continued. 'More than Europeans, but if you get sweet with their bosses you won't have any trouble with them. The blacks, I have to tell you, are numerous and dangerous, but most of the murders can be traced back to white men stealing their women. Your main problem is our own people: you're dealing with belligerent miners or men on the run, and the female population is minimal, a ratio of about four hundred to one. That exacerbates the situation.'

Puckering felt the man was exaggerating. Other Englishmen in faraway posts suffered the same deprivation, but discipline was maintained. He was becoming bored with the interview.

'Don't stick to the letter of the law up there, Colonel,' the Minister warned, nervousness in his voice. 'They don't like it. And Territorians bear arms. Nothing you can do about that, either.'

'Sounds as if I should sit in my office and let the world go by,' Puckering said eventually, and was unprepared for the Minister's reply.

'More or less! More or less, I'd say.'

The Colonel had the impression that the government of South Australia believed it had made a serious mistake in annexing the huge expanse of no man's land which they now called the Northern Territory of South Australia, and that they felt the less heard from it the better. That suited Puckering, he was looking forward to taking on this badland. A real challenge. He had checked on the background of Port Darwin-cum-Palmerston, and discovered that this was the fourth attempt to establish a British settlement in the north; all the others had been defeated by isolation, fever and a horrific wet season. He approved of the courage of these people, however appalling their reputations, to try again to defy the elements. Britain needed a strong port in the north, and Palmerston, so far, was the only outpost on that impossible stretch of coastline closer to Singapore than to Sydney. For the first time in many years, Puckering experienced a sense of purpose, a determination to make his mark. He could, and would, contribute his expertise to Palmerston in the hope that the settlement, this time, would stay on its feet.

The ship was crowded, over-crowded, he complained to the Captain, but fortunately the worst of the wet season had passed, so they survived a potentially dangerous voyage. Most of the passengers were eager gold prospectors, the rest were cattlemen returning to their properties, or a collection of young Englishmen employed by the British Australian Telegraph Office, known as BAT, in Palmerston. Some even had Indian servants with them. 'White sahibs,' Puckering growled to himself, but concealed a certain amusement that these gentlemen could be in for a shock at their new base.

There were only two women aboard, so they shared a cabin. One – a strange addition to the company – was Miss Delahunty, whom he recognised as being the fiancée of Ezra Freeman. The other was a Miss Lorelei Rourke, several years older than Miss Delahunty and greatly more experienced. She informed the Colonel that she was going to Port Darwin to open a 'little business'. A euphemism, he knew, often used in the colonies to describe a brothel, but he took no offence. Judging by the ratio of women to men on the ship, bordellos, accepted in Palmerston, were needed. He doubted that Miss Delahunty had any idea of the occupation of her cabin companion, and for her part, Lorelei informed him that she had gleaned the truth from Miss Delahunty. Sibell had run away from Ezra! Had bolted! And was to take up employment as a lady's companion in the north. Puckering couldn't blame the girl – he appreciated her pluck – and Lorelei, if that were truly her name, was a bright little sort. He took them under his wing for the voyage, and, by dint of his authority, kept them clear of ardent suitors, and even the impulsive offers of marriage which came thick and fast.

Five days' ride took Logan and his team on to sheep-runs that had been marked out by their owners, who had jumped the gun and simply squatted on the land. Because of the drier conditions, these holdings were far more extensive than their southern counterparts, and instead of leading, the authorities were now following pastoralists who were spreading out across the land. It was left to surveyors to identify the boundaries of these properties so that a scale of leasehold fees and land-use inspections could be established. And, of equal importance, provision had to be made for roads through these properties, official carriage-ways to connect with other areas and eventually bring order into the maze of tracks and trails forged through the bush by the pioneers.

Logan had anticipated problems over the boundaries, but operating on a larger scale, these squatters had made fairly amicable arrangements. It was the roads that caused the trouble. The squatters were loath to surrender ribbons of land, especially across cleared blocks. Logan knew that clearing virgin scrub was tough, back-breaking work, and he did his best to accommodate the pastoralists, but when he made his final decision, he was firm. He pushed steadily on, with the squatters breathing down his neck, informing them that they did have the right of appeal.

Charlie wasn't much help in the field, so Logan preferred to work with the chain-men, leaving his friend to suffer being entertained by their hosts with kangaroo shoots and a spot of fishing. It suited Logan to keep Charlie out of the way so that his friend would not spot his unorthodox methods

83

and his short cuts to speed the work up. His mind was on Josie, so he had no passion to spare for this 'noble' occupation, for the good of the state. He worked the men hard, ignoring their complaints, until they became accustomed to the pace, and he took great care with his maps, making certain that, if not quite correct, they looked neat and matched his notes. Drawing on the civil service fondness for the pleasing page rather than the accurate contents, Logan knew his maps would make his employers happy, at least for a few years.

Jimmy Moon searched out local Aborigines, enjoying their company, occasionally introducing the white men as curiosities. Charlie was so nervous of the tribal blacks that he stood over the cook and the two labourers like a warder, afraid they would upset their visitors. Since Charlie was trigger-happy at the best of times, the men were willing to oblige.

When he encountered other mobs of blackfellows who were not so friendly, Jimmy kept the peace by explaining that they were only passing through. He didn't bother to mention that Logan and his mates were measuring the land, because he couldn't see the point of what they were doing. Any blackfellow could tell them where they were, and the bastard squatters were everywhere, gobbling up the best hunting lands near rivers and springs. But they were all having a good time, they had plenty of tucker, and, best of all, Logan had promised to pay him ten pounds when they returned to Perth. Ten whole pounds! He would be rich. Other white men only paid him in tucker or clothes and a blanket or two.

Logan was pleased that Jimmy had volunteered to take his turn on watch at night. Jimmy wanted to help all he could, though, for he knew that if they were attacked, he wouldn't be spared. They sat by their campfire each evening, swapping yarns, and listening to Len's alarming tales of his convict days and Alex's songs of old England which they all enjoyed. The informality left Logan open to ragging about Mrs Cambray.

'What's going on there?' Charlie teased. 'Come on, Logan, you can tell us.'

'She had that lovin' look, Mr Conal,' Len laughed. 'You've won a heart there!'

'Better watch out, mate,' the cook chimed in. 'Old Mad Jack'll plug you full of holes.'

Logan had hoped that his meetings with Josie might have passed unobserved, but he should have known that these men wouldn't miss much. He hoped, for Josie's sake, that Jack Cambray had stayed true to form, obsessed with his own concerns.

'I'd appreciate it if we could leave the lady out of our conversations,' he said stiffly.

'Spoken like a true gentleman,' Charlie intoned soberly. 'We must have respect for Logan's true love.'

Before Logan could react, Charlie burst into a heartfelt rendition of 'Rose of Tralee', and, grinning broadly, the others joined in.

Logan decided to let the matter rest. To demand an apology would upset the harmony in the camp, and with months of work ahead, he couldn't afford disruptions. Instead, he turned his attention to Jimmy Moon.

'What about him? Where have you been the last two nights, Jimmy? Who's the girl?'

Their guide's eyes lit up, delighted to be included in the whitefellow jokes. He had met a beautiful girl. He was entranced by a comely young gin with velvety skin and lovely dewy, dark eyes. 'Her name is Lawina,' he told them. 'Bloody pretty gin, eh?'

'You can say that again,' Len, who had seen and admired the girl, agreed. 'Has she got any sisters?'

Jimmy's face clouded. 'You doan touch them people. Good people.'

'No offence, Jimmy. He was only joking,' Charlie hurried to explain. 'Tell us about her.'

'She make a good wife. Right skin. I make a proper deal with her brothers.'

'Are you going to marry her?' Logan was interested. They had all thought Jimmy had just gone back to have his fun with the girl. He thought of Josie. His desire for her was still overwhelming, and he worried now that his absence would cause her to change her mind. She'd have had time to reconsider and she might decide to stay with that stupid bloody husband. Listening to Jimmy outlining the intricacies of arranging his marriage with the gin, Logan felt sorry for himself. He poured another mug of rum.

'Have you slept with her?' Len asked Jimmy with a leer, and Jimmy was shocked.

'No bloody fear. Family punish badfellers. Not moral,' he smiled, pleased with his English word. 'You know moral?'

'Sure,' Alex said, 'but you should have brought her along.' He winked at the cook. 'Ernie there could do with a helper, couldn't you, mate?'

'That I could.' Ernie grinned enthusiastically, but Jimmy missed the implications.

'That bad form,' he replied with quiet dignity. 'Lawina stays with her family until proper time. I show them respect. Marriage laws sacred.'

The men were suddenly quiet. Embarrassed, Logan took his drink and made for his tent, but as he walked away he heard Jimmy expand on the subject. 'When we go back that ways, I ask for Lawina proper and we have big whoopee feast. Stealem gins bad magic.'

Logan sat on his bunk, assailed by doubts. Soon, though, he threw them aside. A man shouldn't let the superstitions of a native spook him. In his world, things were different, there were extenuating circumstances with Josie. He took out his maps and notebooks to concentrate on the work in hand; these simple surveys would earn him another promotion. The work was going so well, this time they couldn't refuse him. He had to think of the future now, his future with Josie. And that was a comforting thought.

Months later, as the weary group returned to the familiar trails over the ranges, the surveys completed on schedule, Logan gave Jimmy permission to ride on ahead and claim his wife. The bantering over the women had long since ceased and they were all anxious to avoid any more delays as they headed for Perth. Charlie had secured some fine pasture land for himself, but Logan had declined, not ready to commit himself at this stage, needing Josie's opinion. Needing Josie.

Jimmy rode down the long valley to find Lawina's people. His heart was singing as he passed by large stands of sandalwood along the banks of the idling river. He had proved that he could live in the white man's world, and be accepted by them as a good person, and with this power he would be able to protect his wife as their Dreaming world crumbled around them. Many people believed that the white tribes would go away one day and leave them in peace, or that the spirits would send huge magic to destroy the intruders who had defiled their chosen land, and while Jimmy hoped that would happen, he understood that to survive, he would have to be practical. He now knew he could ask for payment in money for his work: it was possible for a black man to earn money. He would learn more of their ways and he would teach Lawina too. And with the teaching and the loving and the blessings of this marriage, they would sing their happiness like mother and father kookaburras and make strong babies.

Right now, the birds of the forest weren't singing much. There seemed to be a quiet in the bush, and the further he travelled the more concerned he became. There was a hush in the valley broken only by the mournful caw of a crow who fluttered, agitated, to the treetops.

He searched all day but was unable to find a trace of Lawina's family, nor could he find anyone to direct him. The valley seemed deserted. But surely not. They knew he was coming, they would never break the spiritual bond that already existed between him and his promised wife. That would give him the right to track them down, demand his wife and punish those responsible for such an outrage. It was unthinkable, there was no reason for them to invite trouble. But he worried. Maybe Lawina had run off with someone else and her people couldn't face him.

On the far side of the river, the hills shaded into purples, bereft of sunlight, while above him, the last golden rays clung to stubby cliffs and crags. He dropped down to a sandy bank, examining the relics of a campsite, and stared morosely at the deep, darkening waters, moving softly and stealthily now, creeping past as if not wishing to attract his attention.

Patches of mist descended like grey spirits, floating in the woods, and Jimmy's horse whinnied uneasily. He stroked her silken neck, slid down to tether her to a tree, and climbed to a ridge to call his presence.

'Coo-eeh! Coo-eeh!'

His strong voice shattered the stillness, echoing about him until it faded into the distance, but there was no reply. He waited until the first stars appeared before he made camp. They would see his fire. Someone would investigate.

Later that night, as he sat waiting, he felt movement in the bush and grasped his knife, but that seemed foolish. There was nothing to fear here, he'd been with white men too long, men who jumped at every shadow. His keen eyes searched the white shafts of the stringy-bark trees that edged the clearing, and rested on a dark figure standing motionless only a few yards from him.

'Come out,' he laughed, aware that he was dressed as a white man. 'Can't you tell a blackfeller fire?'

As the man emerged, Jimmy was startled to see that the stranger was daubed in skeleton markings and the white-face paint of mourning.

'Who are you?' he asked.

'Guldurrim,' the man replied, remaining erect, his spear firmly planted in the sand. 'Brother of the woman who is mother of Lawina.'

'You have had grief in your family?' Jimmy asked, his formal politeness covering a sense of foreboding.

'Much grief,' Guldurrim said angrily. 'One woman dead, two women gone, taken by white men.' He whipped his spear into both hands, holding it before him like a barrier. 'You go from here or we will kill you. Men say you are one of them.'

'One of who? I have been away for months.'

'You wear white men things, you ride the big beast, you have joined them. You go!'

Jimmy stood up slowly. 'No. Lawina is promised to me. You give me Lawina for my wife, and then I'll go.'

He saw pain in the stranger's eyes, this man who was Lawina's uncle, and grasped the meaning. 'Who did they take?'

'They took her,' Guldurrim said, his voice breaking with emotion. 'They killed my little girl and took away Lawina and her sister.'

'Who did?' Jimmy shrieked. 'Who took her? What sort of men are you to let this happen to your women?'

'You go!' Guldurrim insisted, but Jimmy moved swiftly, wrenching the spear from him and slamming the heavy body against a boulder, the spear at his throat.

'You tell me what happened, or you will receive the punishment you deserve right now.'

'It is not becoming that you treat me like this,' Guldurrim complained.

'Nor should you threaten a kinsman.' Jimmy released him. 'Sit there and speak to me of this matter. When did this happen?'

Guldurrim squatted cross-legged in the sand. He looked up at the sharp outline of the crescent moon. 'One full month past,' he began, his face grim, 'the women were building fish-traps past the falls, when three white men came.'

'How do you know?' Jimmy groaned to himself. A month gone.

'With them was Lawina's young brother. He hid. The white men grabbed our women, tied them to trees with rope. Like this . . .' He indicated that they were roped by the neck. Like cattle, Jimmy thought, a fury building.

'They ravaged my little one, whose name I cannot say,' Guldurrim continued, head bowed, 'but she fought them. They bashed her. Ah, may the spirits cleave open their hard hearts.'

'It won't be the spirits. Go on.'

There wasn't much more to tell. When they were missed, the families searched for them and found the terrified boy hiding, shocked, in a cave. Guldurrim found his daughter's body in the river, but the other two girls were missing.

'Shame on you,' Jimmy charged, 'that you did not go after these murderers.'

'We did. But they were horsemen with a day before us to get clear. We searched until we reached the white man's road, right to their fences, but our people were chased back by gunshots, no one would listen to us.' He wept. 'Our shame is truly great.'

87

Jimmy yanked him to his feet. 'I want to talk to that boy.'

They forded the river and travelled through the darkness, back into the hills, until they came to the silent, sorrowing people. All eyes were on Jimmy as he sat down with Lawina's brother, a slim, frightened seven-year-old.

'Don't be afraid,' Jimmy said. 'Tell me the story that you will ever remember, and I will reward you for your great powers of memory.' He unstrapped his hunting knife and placed it on the ground. 'This will be yours.'

The questioning was tedious, but the boy maintained a stoical respect. He answered carefully, Jimmy's questions leading him into areas that his own people would not have known to explore.

'Horses? How many horses?'

'Four horses.'

'And only three men?'

'Only three men.' Good, Jimmy thought, they've got a packhorse, so they're not local stockmen.

'Clothes?' Although the boy did not understand white men's clothes, Jimmy was able to establish that the men were not troopers or squatters. The boy described rough clothes – no uniforms or polished boots – drooping hats, not the smart, straight squatter style.

The boy had seen a great deal. 'How had they taken the girls? Were they put on the spare horse?'

'No.' He showed Jimmy that they had roped the girls by the neck and tied them to the saddles, and as they rode away, the girls had to run. Hating to hear this, Jimmy understood. His mother had told him that white men lassoed young gins and carted them off like this to the stations. Some were for the men, some were taken in by the women, locked into cupboards to break them in for housework. His mother knew all these things – she made it her business to know all these things – and she talked about them all the time so that the people would remember, but the knowledge had destroyed her. She too had been captured, but she had escaped, changed her name and chosen the freedom of town life, since her husband was dead and no tribal man would take on a woman defiled by her captors. Her freedom, though, was just another prison.

Jimmy kept on with his interrogation. He was no longer tribal, he carried his ancestors with him. He would have Lawina back, he would make this up to her.

'The spare horse? Was it loaded up with goods?'

The boy nodded. 'Food-serving implements. Fat bags. Earth-chopping implements.' Jimmy smiled on him.

'Good boy.' They had to be gold prospectors with pots and pans and lanterns, picks and shovels. The white men were always searching for this elusive stuff called gold, which, they said, was to be found in the earth. As far as he knew, their searches were in vain. He had heard the surveyors talking about it.

'A waste of bloody time,' Charlie had said.

'Not so.' Logan had disagreed. 'I'm dead certain there's gold out here somewhere. All the signs are there. They've found millions of pounds of gold in the eastern states, so there has to be plenty in West Australia too.'

'Why aren't you looking for it, then?' Charlie had challenged.

'I might do just that one day,' Logan said.

Jimmy had given himself a little message to find out, when he could, exactly what this gold stuff looked like. He wondered why these whitefellows didn't ask the blacks where this gold was hidden, for they all knew every speck of their land.

With full packs, the villains had to be travelling away from Perth. And in more discussions with the boy he learned their descriptions. One older man with a scrappy grey beard, and two younger with bushy black beards, fearful fellows to the lad. Demons.

'I want a name,' he demanded, but the boy shook his head.

'Search deep inside,' Jimmy insisted. 'There is a name you did hear, and you will recall it.'

The boy tried, and with a surprised yelp he came out with one English word: 'mate'.

'Well done,' Jimmy said. 'Now we will have another. They call me Jimmy. Did you hear a name like that.'

The boy concentrated. He tried the word 'Jimmy', and it seemed to help. And Jimmy Moon waited without a sound. Finally it came, a name. 'Jacko,' the boy said. 'A man called Jacko.'

'Which one?'

The boy did not know.

The interview completed, Jimmy thanked him and handed him the knife, but it was refused. 'My sisters are lost to us,' the lad told him. 'You must punish the bad men. You will need the knife since you do not have a spear.'

As he rode back to catch up with Logan at the ferry, Jimmy's plans were in place. The boy was right, he didn't have a spear these days, but he could do better than that. He would have a weapon, a real bloody weapon, one that he could hide in his shirt. And he knew just where to get it.

Josie had said Jimmy would be at the ferry, and she was right. He was there, eyes dancing, broad teeth like a band of white across his dark face, and once again he'd returned the horse, as promised. Now they could all go on into Perth and celebrate, and who had better reason than Logan himself, with Josie at his side?

He had gone to the farm alone, heart pounding, and knees knocking against his saddle. How would she receive him? And when it came to the point, what sort of an itinerary would the day present? He couldn't plot this stage with his usual efficiency, it was fraught with problems. Ever helpful, Charlie had suggested that his main requirement was a fast horse in case Mad Jack reared up with his shotgun! Thanks, Charlie! It was hard not to admit, even to himself, that he was scared stiff. Too late to turn back.

But Jack was nowhere to be seen. Josie said he was working with a neighbour, fencing their boundary, down in the back block. So they embraced, urgently, and Josie packed quickly. The letter to her husband was already written. She took it from its hiding place and laid the sealed envelope on the kitchen table. Then she added some stock to the stew that was simmering softly on the stove. 'His dinner,' she explained, and Logan nodded, as if he appreciated her thoughtfulness. In truth, though, he found it irritating. He saddled her horse for her and they rode away. As simple as that, after all his worrying.

The men acknowledged her awkwardly, excessive in their politeness, and it was a relief to reach the ferry for a change of mood.

'Where's your bride?' Len asked Jimmy, and he nodded.

'She comen by 'm by.'

No one pursued the subject. With the other 'bride' in the company, it seemed more appropriate to avoid further discussion, like keeping well clear of a tall cactus.

'What's the matter with Jimmy? Why does he look so strange?' Josie asked.

'He's excited about his wife, I suppose,' Logan said. 'And he probably thinks this is quite an adventure, with you along.'

'No. He's all wound up. Brittle. Something's wrong.'

'Don't worry about him, darling, he'll be fine.' It was the first time he'd called her that, and she took his hand as they crossed the river together.

On this, the last night on the trail, they camped by the river and the ferryman's wife put Josie up in her cabin, as she had done many times before, unaware of the changed circumstances.

Dawn saw them all up and eager to go. Logan and his lady forgotten, the men were in high spirits, presenting the ferryman with the last of their provisions, and promising to sink a few for him when they hit the Perth hotels. But as he packed, Logan realised that his German revolver was missing. He checked his pack again, worried that a box of cartridges had disappeared too. He wandered about, hoping someone would mention them – there could be a reason – but they were mounting up, shouting at him to get a move on.

Len had Jimmy's horse. 'He's gone walkabout again,' he laughed. 'Come on, boss. Let's go.'

Charlie assisted Josie on to her horse: she was becoming impatient, too, worrying perhaps that her husband might catch up with them. This was definitely not the time to be holding an enquiry, and, besides, he was fairly certain now that Jimmy had stolen the weapon. Who else could have entered his tent unnoticed? He could have stolen it last night while they were eating, or even during the night, given the way he glided around as quietly as a nocturnal animal. But why?

He shrugged and swung up on to his horse. 'Right!' he called. 'Perth it is!' What the hell was Jimmy up to? Whatever it was, Logan had no intention of reporting the theft. It was an offence to sell or to give Aborigines firearms, there would have to be an official enquiry, and Logan wasn't about to spoil his good record with a lapse like that. Better not to mention the revolver. Jimmy would have to forgo his pay, but he was a smart fellow: he could hunt more easily with a gun, it was worth far more to him than the ten pounds he'd been promised. And he liked to show off to his mates. With a new wife and a gun he'd be kingpin with the mob. Let him have it.

The setting sun gave Perth a welcoming apricot glow as the small group rode in, relieved to be back in town at last. They made straight for the Esplanade Inn, but Josie was unwilling to meet people until she'd had a chance to brush up, so Logan took her on to his rooms. There, at last, in his warm bed, they made love through the night, deep, passionate love, fired by the frustrations of the last few months, and Logan wondered ecstatically how he could have waited so long for her. He lit the lantern to look at her, to stroke her full breasts and her long, firm body, to kiss her and bury his face in the smooth skin, beside himself with joy that he had found a woman who would not hold back. Her sensuality astonished and delighted him, and he felt a stab of jealousy that Jack Cambray had known her, maybe had taught her to give, to enjoy like this. He lifted her under him and plunged down on her, seeking to eradicate the vision of that other body, and she seemed to understand. 'Logan,' she whispered. 'My Logan. I do love you.'

In the morning, Logan was in no hurry to report to work. Taking his time, he bathed, shaved, put on his neat town clothes, combed his hair down with water and a touch of pomade, and presented himself at the office with his leather pouch of maps and accompanying notes.

His immediate boss, Ralph Purvis, took them into Surveyor-General Anderson's inner sanctum while Logan relaxed with the rest of the staff, listening to their gossip, interested to hear that in their absence, gold had become the main topic of conversation. The government was offering bounties for any men who could locate gold-bearing reefs. 'Who would want the bounty?' he laughed. 'If you found gold, why bother?'

They were instantly suspicious. 'You didn't find any, did you?'

'No, worse luck.'

At last he was summoned into the Surveyor-General's office. 'I must say, Mr Conal, you've done excellent work here,' Anderson said. 'You are to be commended. I think a few weeks of leave would be in order now. You're looking a bit thin on it.'

'I have lost some weight,' Logan agreed. 'We all did, spared the enticements of cake shops and bakeries and home-baked pies. I'm looking forward to a slap-up meal.'

'Well then. Two weeks, shall we say?' Anderson asked Purvis.

'Yes, that is acceptable. Half-pay, I think.'

'Half-pay?' Logan echoed.

'You won't be working,' Purvis explained.

'In that case, I think I'd just as soon stay at work, if you don't mind. And while I'm here, sir,' he turned to Anderson. 'You have proof now, fair proof of my qualifications. I was hoping for a promotion to senior pay.'

'Not right now,' Anderson said. 'You go on leave and we'll discuss this when you return.' He began to turn the pages of Logan's notebooks, precise descriptions of hundreds of blocks ready for entry into the records, reading them with exaggerated interest, as though they were the pages of a saucy novel.

'I would prefer . . .' Logan began, but Purvis pushed him out into the narrow corridor. 'Say no more, Conal, for God's sake. You're lucky you still have a job, coming home from official duties with another man's wife. The whole town's talking.'

'Already? That didn't take long,' Logan said. 'But that is my personal business, nothing to do with my work.'

'Then keep it your business. I've done my best for you. The old man has agreed to give you leave until this blows over. You must have known you'd be causing a scandal.'

Logan stared along the sickly-green calcimined walls towards the open back door. 'Am I being given the sack?' he asked.

'Not at all. Just take a breather, old chap. But if I were you, I wouldn't be lording it around town with Mrs Cambray. Not looking for trouble, so to speak.'

'If you'd given me a chance, I wanted to ask for a transfer to Geraldton for that very reason. No one can complain if I'm five hundred miles away, and you need someone to take charge of that office.'

Purvis considered this. He lit his pipe and moved away from Anderson's door. 'I'd be sorry to lose you, but I think that's possibly the best solution. I'll put it to the old man for you. Now pick up your pay and run along.'

The new arrangements delighted Josie. 'Time off? I'm so glad. I was wondering what to do with myself all day. We'll have to find a place with a kitchen, you must have proper meals.'

'No need to bother. I've asked for a transfer to Geraldton, we'll have a house there.'

'Geraldton? Why that's wonderful. I've heard it is such a pretty place, and right on the sea-front.'

His enforced leave gave Logan the opportunity to enjoy her company. They slept late, bought cooked fish and pork pies from street vendors, rode up to explore Kings Park, took long walks along the river bank, and dined each evening at the Esplanade Inn, where Josie was accepted without question. They had seven days of contentedness, delicious days of love-making and long talks about their future as they drank wine together in the little sitting room.

On the Sunday afternoon, Josie went alone to visit Ned, to explain that she had left the farm, left his father, but not deeming it necessary, just yet, to mention Logan. The boy was angry with her. She had thought he would understand. He knew better than anyone else how difficult Jack had become, to put it mildly, but he would not accept her pleas.

'You go back! Go home!' he shouted at her, wrenching himself from her arms, running wildly away from her.

'He'll get over it,' Logan said, trying to comfort her. 'Kids don't like change, but they adapt. Give him a week and see how he is next Sunday.' He grinned. 'Take him a big tin of toffees, that'll put a smile on his face.'

But on the Monday morning, the blow fell. A police constable appeared at their door, enquiring for a Mrs Jack Cambray.

'What is it?' she breathed anxiously, afraid that something had happened to the boy, that he might have run away from school.

Logan put an arm around her. 'What's the trouble, Constable?'

He huffed into his large moustache, jerking at his uniform jacket, preparing his speech. 'It is my sad duty to inform Mrs Cambray that her husband has passed away.' Having made that effort, he dropped into less formal language. 'Dead,' he told Logan. 'Shot himself.'

'Oh, my God!' The two men caught Josie as she reeled away. They gave her a glass of brandy.

Logan took one himself and offered a glass to the constable, who declined, then, in an afterthought, ventured, 'Well, just a sip, sir. But about Mr Cambray. He sent a letter to a lawyer, here in town, Mr Spencer. Had his will and all in it,' the policeman explained. 'So Spencer had some troopers sent out to investigate, and there he was, dead, round the back of the stables. A neighbour identified him.'

'What should we do now?' Logan asked. 'A funeral? We shall have to arrange his funeral.'

'All done. In his letter he said he wanted to be buried on his farm, and no fuss. They buried him on Saturday.'

Logan took her to the police station, where she was required to sign papers, and then on to the office of the lawyer.

Josie, still in shock, sat mutely as Logan spoke with Spencer, an old gent with a whiskery face and hard, accusing eyes.

'I won't keep you long,' he said sternly. 'Mr Cambray's instructions are quite clear, as you can see from his letter.' He handed the two sheets of paper to Josie, who turned away.

'Please, Mr Spencer, I can't . . .'

Logan read the letter for her.

'As you can see,' Spencer continued, 'there's no suggestion of foul play. It was a planned suicide. And,' he peered over his spectacles, 'the poor fellow has given his reasons.'

'I can see that,' Logan said angrily. Cambray had blamed his wife for this calamity, in a rambling tirade. 'Is there anything else?'

'The will. I have that also. It is not witnessed, but it is in the deceased's own hand and so acceptable under the law. And under the circumstances, I should warn you, an appeal by Mrs Cambray would fail.'

'What?' Josie asked, bewildered by the suggestion.

'Nothing to worry about,' Logan told her.

Spencer cleared his throat. 'Mr Cambray requests that his proper livestock, goods and chattels be sold, and all proceeds be placed in trust – in this case I am appointed trustee – to pay for the education and support of his son, Edward John Cambray. He expressly wishes that not one penny of his estate should go to Josephine Cambray, who left the property to enter into an adulterous –'

'Cut out the sermon,' Logan snapped. 'Mrs Cambray is his widow, she's entitled to that farm. Her farm, dammit!'

'I don't want it,' Josie said, understanding the situation now.

'But it's yours,' Logan argued. 'The will isn't legal.'

'I'd rather Ned had it,' she said firmly, and Spencer gave a grunt of satisfaction.

Against Logan's advice, Josie also insisted on visiting Ned the same day.

They were kept waiting in the polished lobby of the college, until the headmaster came to receive them. 'I'm sorry,' he said, looking more severe than sorry, 'but I have instructions from Mr Spencer, acting on the last wishes of the deceased, that you should not be permitted to see young Edward. He is in good hands, the masters have informed him of his father's death, and he is holding up quite well.'

'His mother has a right to see him, regardless of that will,' Logan argued, but the headmaster was adamant. 'Mr Spencer is paying the bills: I have to comply. I did speak to the lad myself, and I have to inform you that he does not wish to see his mother. He is quite determined on that score, so I think it would be best if you left the premises.'

He took her back to his rooms, nursing a presentiment of more trouble, a logical progression, since the scandal had now been compounded. It was no great surprise for him, therefore, to find a gloomy clerk marking time outside the premises. 'A letter for you, Mr Conal. They said I was to hand it to you personal.' He peered cheekily at Josie, adolescent eyes bulging at this first-hand glimpse of lust, so Logan took the letter and gave him a clout on the ear to help him on his way.

'Who is that from?' she asked, climbing the stairs ahead of him, each step a burden, as if she were carrying a cross up with her. She didn't even notice that he made no reply.

'I think I'll lie down for a while,' she said as he ushered her into the bedroom.

'Can I get you anything?'

'No.' She looked up at him, her eyes red and puffy from tears. 'Oh, Logan, I feel so guilty.'

'That's how you're meant to feel. Don't let him get away with it. He didn't have to kill himself, remember that. He was just trying to take revenge on you. Now get some rest.'

'But he's dead, Logan. He's dead!' She was asking for pity, but he chose not to encourage her.

'Good. So now we're rid of him.'

Josie was taking off her hat. She stopped, the hat-pin suspended in mid-air. 'That's a terrible thing to say! How can you be so callous?'

'Easily. You didn't care a jot about the man or you wouldn't have left him. I can understand you're upset about Ned, but spare me the crocodile tears over Mad Jack.' He left the room, and she slammed the door behind him.

Logan squatted on a lumpy ottoman in the sitting room. 'Well,' he sighed, 'you won that round, Jack, you bloody bastard, and I wouldn't mind betting you've just won another.' He turned over the sealed envelope with the government stamp on the back, and opened it slowly and deliberately, as if it really mattered.

Anderson's laborious copperplate signature decorated the half-empty page – the message above it was short and to the point.

'In the light of further unfortunate events,' he intoned, mimicking the old man's voice. Then he jumped to the last line. '. . . dispense with your services forthwith.'

'I see,' he told the room. 'I've got a grieving widow and bereft mother on my hands, no job, and I hate this bloody ugly room.' He stared at the clutter around him, the cheap sofa, the rickety table with its mismatched chairs, the old oak dresser, and the two foolish paintings of 'scenes' on the walls. Once upon a time, he had found these rooms quite fun, somewhere he could put his feet up and not give a damn. But that seemed so long ago now.

There was a knock at the door: it was Charlie, laden with gifts. He handed Logan a posy of violets. 'These are for your lady, I thought she might be feeling a bit off. And this is from Iris – women are so much more

94

practical, aren't they?' Iris had sent them a box of sandwiches garnished with slices of boiled eggs.

Logan was amazed. 'That's kind of you, Charlie. And Iris . . .'

'Think nothing of it. Your mates at the Esplanade, they hope you're bearing up. And Iris says that's rare beef and her own pickles in the sandwiches, so you have to eat them. And this is from me.' He held up a quart bottle of claret. 'A jolly good brew, this one. Where's Josie?'

'She's resting.'

'Of course, voices down, eh?'

'Yes.' Logan produced two glasses and they settled themselves in their familiar places at his table.

As Logan poured, Charlie looked at him keenly. 'So Mad Jack shot himself, eh?'

'A successful suicide,' Logan said. 'She's blaming herself.'

'She'll get over it.'

'I hope so. I'm not going to wear it.'

'Why should you? He was probably pissed anyway.'

Logan nodded, he'd thought of that, too, but hadn't voiced it.

'That's a nice-sized farm,' Charlie commented. 'Josie will own it now.'

'No, she won't. He left it to their son.'

Charlie was disappointed. 'I didn't know they had a son.'

'He's at boarding school. But we didn't only lose the farm. I got the sack today.'

'What? I didn't hear about this.'

'You will tomorrow, it'll be hot news. But what gripes me is that they were going to give me Geraldton. If that lunatic hadn't shot himself, I'd have been on Easy Street, boss-man up there.'

'Oh, Christ, and you didn't get the farm either. You're having a bad run, Logan, old pal.' Charlie refilled their glasses. 'What now?'

'I haven't the faintest bloody idea.'

'Drink up then, and let's think. What about Adelaide? It might be an idea for you to move on to South Australia. They'll blackball you here for government jobs, which are the only ones worth having in these shaky times. Perth is on its knees, you know.'

'Since when?'

'Since the wool prices dropped and the State is close to or actually broke. We're too far from anywhere to find markets. Why do you think they're offering bounties to anyone who can locate gold? They're desperate.'

'Jesus, yes,' Logan muttered. 'I'd swear there's gold out there somewhere, but it might as well be on the moon.'

They worried Logan's future past the pint mark on the bottle, by which time ideas came more easily to mind. 'You were accepted as a surveyor without papers,' Charlie said, 'so why don't you set yourself up as a geologist, a metallurgist, or whatever they're called? A man who knows all about gold-bearing quartz and so forth.'

Logan looked at him quizzically, wondering if Charlie had guessed that he was no more qualified than Charlie himself was. 'Why would I want to be a geologist?'

'Because syndicates here are investing heavily in gold exploration and gold mines. You could talk yourself into a good job: mining experts are sparse on the ground in Perth, my lad. You stay put for a while and I'll make some enquiries.'

When Charlie left, Logan went quietly into the bedroom. Josie was sitting on the edge of the bed, staring down at the frayed carpet as though she were looking over a cliff, preparing to jump. Her posture irritated him. 'Did you have a sleep?'

'Yes.'

'Are you feeling better?'

'I don't know.'

He gave her the flowers, and that brought on more tears. 'Iris sent us some sandwiches, too. They look tasty, come and have something to eat.'

'I'm not hungry.'

'Well, I am.' He went back to the table and attacked the sandwiches. They were tasty – moreish, as his father used to say. He ate the lot. 'I'll go out and buy some more,' he told her, but she was curled up in the middle of the bed again, and gave no indication that she'd heard him. The white cotton coverlet was neatly folded over the tall iron railings at the foot of the bed, like a small screen, separating them. Angrily, he stepped out and made for the pub.

Josie had listened to the murmur of their voices until they had lulled her to sleep, but when she awoke, they were noisier, and the clink of glass told her that Logan and Charlie were drinking out there. Even laughing. She sat on the edge of the bed, chilled by the night and by Logan's lack of compassion. Worry enticed new fears: why had she slammed the door on him? She should have called him back, but instead she'd shut him out. It was such a foolish thing to do. Her misery was upsetting him. While she was deciding that the best thing to do would be to tidy up, and try to be decent company with a guest in the house, another voice inside her rang warning bells: 'Don't let this one bully you too. You never stood up to Jack. You have to stand up to this one.' And another worry intervened: 'Is this one also a boozer? Women do that, you know. They marry the same sort of man the next time, and end up in the same mess. Everyone knows that.'

Then he was back again, with flowers, a bunch of violets, and Charlie's kindness ruined both arguments as she dissolved into tears, annoying Logan again. She climbed back on to the bed and hid her face in a pillow.

She was alone now. And he was off drinking somewhere. Just like Jack. Exhausted, she tried to sleep again, but she was shocked by Jack's death and worried about Ned. Poor boy, how confused he must be. She wondered if they had told him that his father had taken his own life, and if Ned would always blame her, and she wept again.

'It's no use, Charlie, you know Percy Gilbert wouldn't give me a job.' Weeks had passed and Logan was still unemployed. It was obvious in this close-knit community that he was being blackballed.

'Gilbert might not have any choice: he hasn't found a replacement yet.'

Logan scowled. 'You mean I'm the last resort.'

96

'Put it round the other way – this could be your last resort unless you want to take pot luck in Adelaide. You'd be the manager,' he coaxed. 'Logan Conal, Manager, Gilbert Gold-Mining Company! Nothing wrong with that.'

'Did you hear what happened to the last manager?' Logan asked Josie.

'No.' She looked to Charlie for an explanation.

'They hanged him,' he laughed. 'Apparently he got into a fight with one of his men over a woman, and he shot the fellow, so the victim's mates strung him up. Rather wild and woolly, that country.'

'Good heavens!'

'The town is called Katherine,' Logan grumbled, 'and it's in the Northern Territory, right out in the middle of nowhere.'

'I should imagine,' Josie said, 'that all goldfields would be in the middle of nowhere. You couldn't expect them to be underfoot.'

'It's good money,' Charlie reminded Logan, 'and there'd be nothing to stop you doing a bit of prospecting on your own. You could come back a millionaire.'

Outside the open window, a breeze rustled the leaves, as if urging Logan to pay attention, and a shiver of excitement ran through him. Gold! The word made his palms itch with anticipation! He had been so busy trying to think how to earn an honest, or dishonest, quid here in Perth that the word hadn't registered. This town was too small and he was too well known to resort to petty theft, and there were no other jobs on offer. The talk of gold hadn't seemed real to him until now, but in this land they were actually picking it up out of the ground! The concept astounded him, and he was staggered by the possibilities. 'I'll think about it,' he told them, containing this new enthusiasm. 'In the mean time, Charlie, you might as well line me up to see the gentleman.'

And Charlie was right. Percy's investment in the mines was more important than their previous differences.

'I understand you have knowledge of metallurgy,' Gilbert said to Logan.

'Understanding the properties of metal was part of my studies as a surveyor,' Logan replied loftily. 'A required course at the Belfast Academy,' he added, and then changed the subject to cut short that line of questioning. 'I regret I was unable to assist you on that boundary appeal, Mr Gilbert, but I was only following orders.'

'Whose orders?'

'I'd rather not mention names,' Logan said darkly, 'but I was in no position to take on my superiors. However, my work speaks for itself. I was in line for another promotion.'

'Until you created a scandal.'

'Mr Gilbert,' Logan sighed, 'the lady's husband was well known as Mad Jack. She had no alternative but to leave him, she feared for her life.'

'That may be so,' Gilbert snapped, 'but you're no Lochinvar, Conal. I didn't come down in the last shower. It turned out damned convenient for you. However, I'll give your application my consideration. In the mean time, you might acquaint yourself with that section of the Northern Territory by calling on my junior partner, Mr Collins, at the Mines Department.'

Joachim Collins was eager to oblige. He produced maps of what Logan could only describe as a vast emptiness, with the telegraph line snaking across the centre, and not more than a half-dozen dots representing townships, leading south from Palmerston on the north coast. Being more interested in the remuneration he might expect, it didn't occur to Logan to enquire the size of these townships. Collins was able to inform him that the Mines Manager was entitled to a company house and a salary of 500 pounds per annum plus bonuses.

The high salary pleased Logan, but was no surprise, since Charlie had already pointed out that managerial staff prepared to go into the outback could expect recompense.

'I presume my fares and expenses will also be paid,' he said to Collins.

'Oh, quite,' Collins replied. He was a neat and nervy little man with a whine in his voice. 'I'd go up there myself but my health won't permit such exertions. It's all very well for Mr Gilbert to procrastinate, but I'm eager to see the mines reopened as soon as possible. I invested my life savings in the syndicate, and at present I'm not getting any return.'

'That's unfortunate,' Logan commiserated. 'But it's always the way. People with money don't understand these things, and, if you notice, they always seem to be the last to pay their bills.'

Collins nodded glumly. 'True. True.'

'I'm sure I could get the mines paying again in no time, but I don't know if Mr Gilbert will approve my application.'

'I'll put in a good word for you, Mr Conal,' Joachim said, and Logan shook his hand firmly.

'Yes, time's a-wasting, it would be terrible if someone jumped the claims.'

'Oh, I don't think they could do that,' Collins replied.

'From what I hear,' Logan laughed, 'they can do what they like up there north of the law.'

Having thoroughly shattered Joachim's day, Logan went whistling on his way.

'It looks as if I might have the job,' he told Josie. She, though, was having second thoughts. Her enthusiasm had seeped away with the realisation that Katherine was half a continent away from Perth.

'What about Ned?' she asked. 'I don't think they'll let him come with me.'

That annoyed Logan. He hadn't given Ned a thought. 'Be sensible, woman. You were pleased as punch to get him into a college. You can't take him out now.'

'But I mustn't go right up there and just leave him. What if he gets sick?'

'You don't have to go. You can stay here in my rooms until I come back.'

'And when will that be?'

'How do I know? People in those sort of jobs get annual leave.'

Now Josie was torn between the two of them. 'Logan,' she pleaded, 'I don't want to stay here on my own, not with all the gossip about us. I don't know anyone.'

'What are you talking about?' he asked crossly. 'You know Charlie and Iris and a few of them at Tommy's pub.'

She stared at him. Did he really intend to go off and leave her behind? She didn't wish to offend him by criticising his friends, but she found them rather a wild lot – kind enough, but not the sort of company she would choose. She envisaged herself, a lone woman, having to frequent the tavern for the sake of company, and the picture appalled her. She listened as he outlined his plans, talking about the information he'd gleaned from Collins. 'I should really go with you,' she remarked uncertainly.

'It's no place for a woman,' Logan told her.

'But you just said there is a house for the manager. We'd have our own home.'

'And then you'd be pining for Ned. I'll be earning well. I can leave you enough to live on, and I'll send you your keep.'

For how long? she wondered. Out of sight, out of mind, and Logan was reckless with money. Then what would become of her? What had happened to her life? What had she done? Her fears increased as she watched Logan dozing on the sofa. She loved everything about him – his handsome face, his physique – and she treasured their lovemaking. In fact everything she did with him and for him, was an act of love.

'Darling,' she called softly to him, 'please don't go. It's all too complicated. You'll find something else down here, a man like you. It's only a matter of time. We're so happy together, we mustn't let anyone separate us now.'

He opened his eyes, scowling. 'Oh, for Christ's sake, Josie! Stop moping. I've got to get past Percy Gilbert yet. Nothing's definite.'

In the following days, while she prayed that Mr Gilbert would find someone else, Josie took time off from her shopping to search for work. She thought that if she had a job, Logan wouldn't need to look so far afield. As long as someone was bringing money into the home, he needn't feel so pushed to find employment, he could afford to wait. She had no idea that Logan had the gold fever now and nothing would keep him from those treasure fields.

Her efforts, anyhow, were in vain. She applied at hotels as a housemaid or a scullery-maid, but was rejected, and she gave up when a portly woman told her: 'Go home, love. We can't use a lady like you. Be too strange, it would.'

She called at drapers and dress shops only to be brushed aside by busy proprietors. She even applied at a boot factory, to be met with laughter, since it was also a saddlery and all the workers were male.

Day after day she walked out past Ned's school, hoping to catch a glimpse of him, but obviously the boys were confined to the rear of the college precincts, and the well-kept front gardens became a colourful no man's land that she did not dare cross. She took cakes and sweets and sandwiches to the back gate and handed them to the gardener, requesting that her small offerings be given to Master Ned Cambray. Sometimes she even hid a shilling or two in the boxes, but she never received any acknowledgement.

Her dilemma seemed monstrous. Whichever way she turned, heartbreak was hovering.

She was sure that, in time, Ned's attitude would soften; he was only a lad. Eventually the masters would lose interest in the Cambrays' problems and she would be able to see her son. She would never give up, and persistence had to win out in the end. But to do this she would have to remain in Perth.

But if she lost Logan, her own world would collapse.

It was almost a relief when he made the decision for her.

'You must waste no time in reopening the mines,' Percy told the new appointee. 'It is imperative you follow exactly the routine set in place by the previous fellow. You are authorised to employ twelve workmen and two lubras.'

'Lubras?' Logan asked. 'What do they do?'

'God knows. Cook for the workmen I suppose. They are paid a few shillings a week, according to the books, but keep in mind that the company does not provide food. The Mines Inspector reports that our mines are still viable, but I expect you to keep expenses down.'

'How much gold do they yield per ton?' Logan asked, sounding knowledgeable.

'You'll be privy to that information when you get there. I don't need it bandied around here, attracting more prospectors. The postmaster in Katherine, Simon Pinwell, is holding the books and records and acting as temporary caretaker. A very reliable fellow, he will fill you in on local details. Now, are you sure you can manage this post? It's a very responsible position.'

'I'll do my best.' And that's true enough, Logan said to himself. He'd read up on gold mines, and there was nothing hard about them. Few diggers had any experience at all: they either found gold or they didn't. But Logan had already decided to run old Gilbert's mines like clockwork, to make a good impression in the town. The smaller the town, the longer the tongues, he mused. Once he'd been accepted as a leading light of upright character, he could start to look around for himself. He had still not understood that 'town' was a misnomer for these settlements in the northern wilderness, and that even 'village' was too grand a name for the stark environment. But his wily employer knew.

'I want a full monthly report,' Percy said. 'The gold is to be sent under escort to Palmerston each month, and my agent, Mr Albert Strange, will take charge of it from then on.' Unconcerned that his remarks could be construed as offensive, he continued: 'I believe in shared responsibility, Mr Conal.' He went on with a smirk, 'You deliver the goods to Strange and you send me your reports separately. That way, to protect my interests, I have a check on both of you. Mr Strange, by the way, is my wife's cousin, so don't get any funny ideas about collaborating with him.'

'Certainly not,' Logan said, Gilbert wasn't so smart after all: that was a vital piece of information, possibly the most important of his endless lecture. Logan would make sure to keep clear of the cousin.

'One more thing,' Percy said, hesitating, his pen poised over the papers certifying Logan's future authority. 'I don't want any more trouble with women up there. Disgusting as it may sound, the last fellow took up with a lubra, and I am advised that quite a few degenerate white men in the north are guilty on that score. I have been discussing this problem with Mrs Gilbert, and in her wisdom she insists that the only solution is for us to appoint a married man since quarters are available.'

'Married?' Logan only just managed to make that sound like an interested question instead of a yelp of surprise. 'I was under the impression my application was approved.'

'It is, on that condition. Surely not an impediment for you. After all, you are living with the widow Cambray. You do intend to marry her?' Gilbert's eyes were black pinpoints that left Logan in no doubt that his job was on the line. His mind raced. Marry Josie? God Almighty, she hadn't needed a shotgun to come to live with him, and she'd never asked for a wedding ring. He didn't want another wife around his neck. He had been congratulating himself that in the new life that had been handed to him, he was now free of the Irish woman he'd left behind in Liverpool. Now this prig and his ugly wife were trying to fix him again.

'We were hoping to leave a decent interval between her husband's death and our betrothal,' he said mildly, stalling for time, but Gilbert sneered at him.

'And you consider that sleeping with the woman in an extra-marital arrangement is decent? You have strange values, Mr Conal. The manager of our mines must be a married man,' he said, holding the pen aloft like a miniature guillotine. 'Is that a problem, or not?'

'No,' Logan said. 'It will make us both very happy. If you think it is the right thing to do, Mr Gilbert, we'll be married before we board the ship.'

He watched as Percy signed the papers with a flourish, blotting them with exaggerated care.

'I've been thinking,' he said to Josie, 'about having to leave you. I'd miss you, it'd be hard not having you around.'

'Oh, darling, I'd miss you too,' Josie said. 'Hold me close. I love you so much, I still can't believe how lucky I am.'

He enveloped her, rubbing his whiskery face along her chin, kissing her cheek and then her eager mouth. 'Let's get married.'

Her eyes shone and she hugged him. 'Darling, thank you. I've never brought the subject up, because I wanted it to be your decision, I didn't want you to feel you had to marry me. But now! I'm so happy. We'll have a wonderful life, you'll see.' But then she remembered the job in Katherine. 'You won't go to the north, will you? Not now?'

'I have to, Josie. It's too good an opportunity to miss. And you're coming with me. The voyage up the coast will be our honeymoon, and then we'll go on to our own home.' He saw her frown, her face creased with worry, and led her into the bedroom, where he knew she'd never refuse him. 'Come and make love to me to seal the bargain. You do love me enough to marry me, don't you?'

'You know I do,' she smiled, thrilling as this man before her began to undress. Her husband.

She slid into bed beside him, secure in his arms, that lovely future before her, abandoning herself to his love as he pushed up her voluminous nightdress, engulfing her. 'I'm not leaving you,' he muttered as he buried himself within her. 'You can't desert your husband. You're coming with me, I insist.' And joyfully, wildly happy, she agreed.

Later she whispered to him, 'That lady I met, Mrs Hamilton. She has a hotel in Palmerston. I'll have one friend up there.' But he was asleep. And later still, she consoled herself, 'Ned's in good hands. Logan's right. I shouldn't take him out of that college, he deserves a good education. But I'll write to him. I can still send him presents. I'll be able to afford better ones now. It's for the best after all.' And Josie slept peacefully at last, curled into the man she loved.

Two days before the ship sailed, Josie and Logan were married. Josie wrote Ned a long, loving letter, enclosing a pound note, promising to keep in touch with him.

Jimmy rolled his swag like the whitefellow travellers and took to the road, his revolver hidden under the old blanket, his eyes glowering like a snake in the shade.

Because of the swag, his English, and his ready-to-please smile, they took him for a half-caste, which amused Jimmy. Whitey seemed to think a half-caste was only half as dirty, half as dangerous and could be allowed half into doorways. Proud of his race, Jimmy patronised the settlers, chopping wood, digging holes to empty their poop cans, helping to slaughter and skin their sheep, accepting food with due deference. And all the while he listened, prompting talk of prospectors by mentioning gold, asking what was this 'feller'. They were all experts, it seemed, ready to enlighten him, reasoning that a blackfellow was not likely to compete for the riches.

One lady even showed Jimmy a tiny spoon with a smidgen of the magic metal on the handle. It didn't look much to him, about as useless as the silly little spoon itself, but he showed proper reverence, wondering aloud which way these gold-seekers might go to begin their digging.

And then, up by the dry lakes, he was on their trail.

Everywhere he went, he dropped the name 'Jacko', sadly, a common name among their mobs, and one day, he made a contact.

'That bastard!' a drover's wife snapped. 'If he's the one you call your mate, you could find better company than him. Got a couple of poor little gins in tow, him and his two bloody sons, a nasty pair of blockheads.'

Jimmy shied off, in case she refused to tell him any more, doubled back on the truth, claiming *his* mate Jacko was only a half-caste, and she was mollified.

Before he bade her farewell, he learned that his quarry had headed west towards a place the whites called Mount Magnet. Jimmy was, by this time, far outside his own tribal lands, but he didn't care: he would follow white men's trails, and once he was in the area he'd have the devils within reach. White men were easy to track, especially in mountain country: coming or going, they stuck to the same paths.

He loped into the morning sun, bare feet padding steadily through the flattened bush, until he came across a mob of dark people who were confused and unsettled by the incursion of so many whites. To them, he was able to speak the truth. They bunched around him in sorrowful communion, offering to show him easier routes into the ranges, but he declined, needing to stay on the clearly defined trails.

He did not want their help to find Lawina – he knew what he had to do, and they must not be involved – but since he would not be returning this way, he sought their advice on other peoples. They were Juat tribe of the Nyungar nation, as were Whadjuck, and over the ranges Jimmy would find Balardong tribes, who were also Nyungar. A gentle elder gave him a message stick to carry, not with messages such as the whites send on paper, but with clan signs and good magic.

No one had found the elusive gold. Prospectors were pulling out of the hills, and Jimmy greeted them cheerily, trotting back with them in his seemingly aimless travels, listening, listening, until he thought he had located Jacko. The men who gave him the information, though, spoke of a trio with one black gin, only one. Jimmy decided to investigate anyway, and he found them heading back across a high rocky plain – three horsemen, no packhorse, and a black girl dressed in men's clothes, her face hidden by an old brown hat. He smiled meanly: that was their way, they dressed the gins deliberately to look like boys, to escape criticism and hide the girls from other predatory males.

Jimmy moved around behind them and stayed with them until they had made camp among a clump of trees littered with garbage and cast-off equipment left by other retreating prospectors. They watered their horses in the stony shallows of a drying creek, and handed them over to the girl. Jimmy knew the procedure. The gin would hobble the horses, then come back and light a fire for them to cook their meal, so he slipped in among the trees to get a better look at her.

His heart sank. This was not Lawina, it was her sister. Where was Lawina, then? Had they sold her off to other men? He shook his head: never mind, he would find her. But for now, he would get this girl away from them, and, naturally, he would have to punish them. As he watched, they passed around a bottle and lit their pipes, but their rifles were handy. He could not attack them during the night: their guns were always close, and, besides, he wanted them to know *why* they were being punished. He raced away down the gully to a water hole that he knew had plenty of fish, and stayed there for the night.

In the morning, Jacko and his two brawny sons stumbled out of their tent. They stretched and spat, scratched at their long flannel underpants, and ambled awkwardly, barefoot, into the creek to drink and slosh the chilly water on to their faces.

'G'day boss!' Jimmy called, marching down to the water's edge. He held up two large fish. 'You feller want plenty good fish?'

Surprised, pleased, they reacted well. 'Yeah! We'll take them.'

'Good, you catch!' Jimmy laughed, and threw the fish into deeper water.

The girl, recognising him, stood by the tent, gaping, while the men laughed and jostled playfully in the water, each one intent on retrieving a fish.

When they stood up, the blackfellow was facing them, the wide grin replaced by a mask of rage. They weren't looking at his face though, but staring aghast at the revolver trained on them, and stumbling backwards in fear.

'What do you want?' the grey-haired man yelled.

'You took my wife!' Jimmy shouted. 'You dirty bastards, and you kill Whadjuck woman!'

They floundered in front of him, but the revolver was steady.

'Where's Lawina?' Jimmy demanded. With Lawina's sister behind him, they couldn't deny their involvement.

'Come on now, son,' Jacko wheedled. 'She's all right. She took up with another feller, back in the hills.'

'He lies!' the girl screamed. 'My sister dead. Hurtem too much.'

'Dead!' The word exploded in his brain. He had been ready to believe they had sold her off. He pulled the trigger, and Jacko fell back. His sons, screaming, lurched towards Jimmy, and he let them come, shooting the first one in the chest, and the second one in the face. The stream was running blood as he strode in and looked down at Jacko, who was threshing wildly in the water. 'You never touch another black woman,' he said, and shot him in the head.

He set the horses free, grabbed the terrified girl, and pulled her in among the trees. 'I must go now a long way, I can't take you with me.'

The bewildered girl stared at him. 'What can I do? I can't go back, they won't have me now.'

Jimmy understood. He gave her the message stick. 'Get rid of those clothes, white men won't look for a tribal girl. Go back to the Juat people, they will take care of you.' Her eyes were sharp now, no longer a shy native girl. She was a survivor, this one. He gave her careful directions to find the Juats, warning her to stay within their ranks, and she listened attentively.

'I'm sorry,' he said, as she undressed, noticing whip marks on her body, but she shrugged.

'Good you kill them.'

'You run now,' he told her. 'Keep to the bush until you find the people.'

As she slipped away he looked back at the camp, ignoring the bodies lying awkwardly in the water. Two rifles were propped by the tent. It pained him to have to leave them, but they would be too conspicuous. He rolled his own gun back into the swag, and set off inland.

Balardong men received him cautiously, and against their better judgement escorted him far to the east, to the lands of the desert people, another nation, where different languages were spoken. 'Terrible country,' they warned. 'A cruel sun, very little water and no shade but for rocks.'

Jimmy looked out into the dusty red horizon. 'But these tribes? Are they friendly?'

'They are good people, very shy, they don't see many strangers.'

'Where will I find them?'

'They will find you.'

He had come a long way already, and it was weeks since he'd taken his revenge, but he was determined that the white police would never catch him. He would cross this desert and find a new land, leaving behind the bad memories. He was Jaljurra once again. He wouldn't allow himself to think of Lawina, nor did he want to know how she had died: the hurt was too great. The trek ahead of him was the challenge he needed to burn out the pain and make Jaljurra a truly strong man.

4

Their progress up the steep hill from the jetty into the town of Palmerston was like a grand parade, and Sibell was delighted. They'd had so much fun on the ship it had been like a holiday. Since she and Lorelei were the only two ladies on board, they'd been swamped by suitors, and Colonel Puckering had acted as their chaperon, a very lenient one who'd been happy to see them enjoying themselves.

Several of the young men from the British-Australian Telegraph Office had already declared their undying love for Sibell, and she'd flirted outrageously with two of them, Michael de Lange and John Trafford.

Lorelei Rourke was her cabin companion – better than no one, Sibell, supposed, so she made an extra effort to be polite. In truth, though, she considered Lorelei rather common. She had a low-class London accent and wore cheap, gaudy clothes. On the other hand, she was amazingly self-assured, and quite hilarious company. She made everyone laugh, with her quick wit and sharp manner, and Sibell noticed that she told awful fibs, tossing them around with careless abandon like an incompetent juggler. She was on her way to Palmerston, she told Sibell, to open a little business, but her various tales of how she'd come to be in Perth defied logic. Surprisingly, no one seemed to mind: her stories were so entertaining, so ridiculous, she had everyone laughing. Even the Colonel.

Sometimes, though, Sibell thought that Lorelei wasn't as scatter-brained as she pretended. Not that it mattered now. They would be going their separate ways shortly.

'Is this China?' Lorelei asked, bewildered, and Sibell was wondering the same thing. There were Chinamen bustling everywhere, hundreds of them, in blue or black pyjama-like outfits, all wearing yard-wide conical hats, their pigtails flapping down their backs.

'It could easily be,' Puckering said, taking Sibell's arm and pushing away persistent Chinese who were eager to sell their wares to the new-comers, clamouring around them with trays of pearls and other exotic pieces, proffering hats and parasols and lengths of silk, even parcels of strongly spiced food. The noise was incredible, with everyone shouting at once. The Colonel was wearing his new high-collared black serge uniform with its silver buttons, and the peaked cap displaying his badge of office, yet instead of deterring the pedlars, the uniform seemed to attract them.

There were a few prettily dressed women in the crowd, wives of gentlemen from the BAT, Michael explained, walking backwards in front of Sibell so as not to lose her in the welcoming crush. Several men were rigged out in white suits and pith helmets, but the rest were a shabby, rough lot who shouted cheerily to the girls, doffing battered hats.

By the time they reached the top of the hill, coolies were already rushing past with luggage balanced on bamboo poles, and Sibell stopped to view the town. The land seemed flat as far as the eye could see, and a long, straight street lay before them, bordered by straggles of single-storey buildings. Some were neat sandstone, some timber, but scattered among them were shanties and tents, a motley collection as strange as the population. But it was the trees that had the most moisture in the sultry air. The intense greenery splashed with scarlet blooms seemed to hold the place together, and the fragrance of tropical flowers wafted over them, so welcome after the sour weeks aboard ship.

The sky was a dense cover of grey, the humidity warning of the true heat of the sun from which they were presently shielded, and Sibell felt a thrill of anticipation! This was the tropics, the real tropics, the land of adventure, and she already had friends of her own. She wouldn't be lonely here.

Michael and John and the ever-present Colonel escorted them to the Prince of Wales Hotel where Lorelei had decided she would stay until she found a permanent residence. They strolled along the street under rickety awnings, accepting the greetings of curious men who squatted in the shade, and drinkers lounging outside the hotel.

At the main entrance they read a sign which proclaimed baldly: 'Best Food. Best Beds, Best Ales and Spirits. Stables. Horse Feed.'

'Did you say a Mrs Hamilton owns this hotel?' the Colonel asked, studying the name of the licensee over the door.

'Yes,' Sibell said. 'I did write to tell her I was coming, but Michael said my letter would be in the mail on our ship.'

'You'll look silly if the job's gone,' Lorelei said, but Sibell wouldn't be deterred. She was never going back to Perth.

'It doesn't matter. I'll do something else.'

'Sibell could teach,' Michael suggested. 'Teachers and governesses are in short supply here.'

'If you marry me,' John Trafford smiled, 'you wouldn't have to work, dear girl.'

They trooped into the dim, carpeted lobby to be met by a short, plump man who introduced himself as Digger Jones, Proprietor. He untied his white apron. 'Off the ship, are we?'

'That's right,' the Colonel said. 'A lady here to see Mrs Hamilton.'

'Ah, yes. Mrs Hamilton,' he replied. 'Fine lady, Charlotte, but you've missed her. I bought the Prince from her a whiles back. Will you all be staying with us? Best rooms, best tucker in town, I can guarantee that.'

'Where can I find Mrs Hamilton?' Sibell asked, her newly acquired confidence slipping away.

'She's gone bush, miss. Out to the station.'

'Oh, well, not to worry,' Lorelei said. 'You and I can share a room, Sibell, it'll be cheaper.'

'Just the two ladies then?' Jones asked, but the Colonel intervened.

'You might as well stay here for the present,' he told Sibell in his usual brisk tone, 'but take single rooms. You've been cramped up in that cabin long enough.'

Sibell thought she saw Michael glance approval to John, and wondered, momentarily, what that meant. Meanwhile, the publican found their keys, and Michael suggested that they have a bottle of champagne to celebrate their safe arrival.

'A marvellous idea,' Lorelei cried. 'I'm dying of thirst. Hasn't anyone else noticed how hot it is here? I shall expire if I don't have a cool drink.'

'It is hot,' John agreed, 'but this is the end of the monsoons. The humidity won't be so bad in a few weeks.'

Michael laughed. 'That's true, the air clears and the real heat starts.'

'Spare me.' Lorelei sighed, making for the hotel lounge.

Sibell turned to the publican. 'Excuse me, Mr Jones. Where is Mrs Hamilton's station?'

'A long way out, miss. Black Wattle Station would be a couple of hundred miles. I'd reckon. Hard to say.'

'How would I get there?'

He stared. 'To a station? In The Territory? I wouldn't recommend it. Not for a lady like you.'

'Mrs Hamilton seems not to think so,' the Colonel said, but Jones shook his head.

'Ah, yes, but Charlotte's different. She's a real Territorian. She over-landed from Queensland in a buggy with her husband and a couple of kids in tow, a thousand miles of shockin' country . . .'

'Good God!' Puckering exclaimed, 'I'll be looking forward to meeting her myself.' He extended his hand. 'Introduce myself, sir. Puckering. Colonel. Taking up duties here. Chief Inspector of Police.'

Jones grasped his hand warmly. 'Pleased to meet you, mate. You'll find us all real law-abiding citizens, you mark my words.' A Chinese servant pattered out with a tray of glasses and the champagne that Lorelei had wasted no time in ordering, and Jones called to him, 'On the house, those drinks! And bring out the decent glasses.' He smiled nervously at the Colonel. 'No charge for you, sir. Proud to make your acquaintance.'

'Appreciate it,' Puckering said. 'Now tell me this. Is there any transport available to Black Wattle Station? Miss Delahunty expects to be employed by Mrs Hamilton, and until she can speak with her, she will be unable to make any plans.'

'Ah, right,' Jones said. 'But transport? Not a chance. Those cattle stations in the wayback, they only get supplies twice a year. I tell you what, though, I'll ask around. Someone from the station could be in town. But the best bet is to write to her.'

Sibell thought he was exaggerating about the supplies. 'If they only get their supplies twice a year, what's the point in writing?'

'A letter'd get there fast enough,' he explained. 'Maybe only a week or so. Riders pick up mail and newspapers and the like from depots, or they get handed on from one station to the next.'

'See what you can find out,' Puckering instructed, and took Sibell aside. 'I can't stay, I have to report in. They'll be wondering where I've got to. But don't worry, I'll arrange contact with Mrs Hamilton for you somehow.'

Sibell had lost interest in Mrs Hamilton. 'I don't think I'll bother,

Colonel. I might as well stay here in Palmerston, everyone is so pleasant and I can easily find employment.'

'You'll do no such thing. This is no place for a girl your age on your own, half a glance should have told you that. Didn't you see how few women there are here? It's too dangerous.'

'Lorelei isn't worried, why should I be?'

He gave a click of impatience. 'Lorelei is different. You have a reputation to protect.'

'I have?' she retorted. 'That's a change.'

'Don't talk nonsense. You can't stay here, a single girl, associating with Lorelei.'

It was only then that she realised, shocked, what he was trying to tell her. She couldn't go back, though, so she defied him, 'You can't make me leave!'

'I am the law here, I could deport you right now if I so wished.'

She tried to cajole him. 'I thought you were my friend.'

'I am your friend. I won't desert you. I can give you letters of introduction to decent people in Perth.'

'Like Ezra Freeman!' Sibell snapped. 'I don't need your help, Colonel. I'll find Mrs Hamilton myself, thank you.'

She turned on her heel and hurried into the lounge to join the others, but despite their gaiety she felt hot and uncomfortable sitting with Lorelei. She wondered if Michael and John knew what she was, and then it dawned on her that of course they did! And what did they think of her? Was she regarded in the same way? On the ship, Lorelei, too, had received proposals of marriage. Were these men so hard up they'd marry anyone? All the flattering attention she had received now tasted of ash, and to make matters worse, the proprietor came in to introduce his wife, a tiny Chinese girl who spoke no English.

Unable to decide what else to do, Sibell stayed with them, trying to be pleasant as more champagne appeared and the party grew. They moved on to the dining room where she ate strange Chinese concoctions. They were tasty, she had to admit, but served with rice, which to her mind belonged only as dessert, and she wondered if Palmerston were not an English colony after all, but an Oriental port.

Then, once again, alone in a strange room, disturbing thoughts began to fester in Sibell's mind. The shipboard happiness had been short-lived, ruined by the Colonel's awful remarks. Was Lorelei a prostitute? Surely not. And if so, the Colonel must have known all along. Why hadn't he told her? Reason argued that she would still have had to continue sharing that cabin, but she was in no mood to spare anyone. She resented all of them, believing they'd made a fool of her. Had they laughed at her ignorance? She felt so miserable she was nearing the point when she didn't have the heart to go on.

After all the setbacks, it seemed that life was hell-bent on betraying her, and a fear came upon her that the betrayals would go on until she succumbed . . .

She was in a highly nervous state, and although she was physically well, despair had begun to rap at the windows of her soul. 'No one cares about me,' she said to the flickering lamp. 'No one in the whole world.

I might as well be dead.' She walked over to the mirror and stared at her dim reflection. 'You hardly exist,' she said. 'You're the ghost of Sibell Delahunty who went down on that ship, still tramping the land looking for your grave.'

Common sense told her she was being melodramatic, but reality was no consolation. She didn't understand the need to let go, to find a shoulder to cry on. Her natural reserve forbade such a display.

By morning she saw herself at odds with the world, and so, in a spirit of defiance, she took herself alone into the dining room, head high, refusing to retreat when she saw she was the only woman present. White-suited gentlemen watched her as she walked past them.

The Chinese waiter placed her breakfast in front of her, and she stared. It wasn't Chinese food, nor was it the English fare that the Gilberts clung to. She looked down at a huge steak, dripping with juice. It was so big it hung over the edge of a dinner plate. On top were two fried eggs, and loaded over and around them mounds of bubble-and-squeak – fried, cooked vegetables. Anxious to assist, the waiter returned with a bottle of Worcester sauce.

Overhead, a punkah moved languidly, and her eyes followed the brassy cord to a far wall, where a bored Aborigine lad encouraged its endeavours with the cord tied to his toe.

Sibell smothered a wild urge to laugh at this ridiculous scene and the equally ridiculous meal, especially since no one else seemed to find anything amusing, and she felt better. So much so that she decided she might as well attack this breakfast if she could find a way to carve through it without losing half on to the tablecloth.

To her surprise she found that the eggs were perfectly cooked, the bubble-and-squeak crisp, and the steak so tender it cut like butter. Aided by chunks of fresh bread, Sibell cleaned up the plate and washed her breakfast down with strong tea. She had thought of taking herself for a walk, but recalled the Colonel's words about the town being dangerous, so now she sat, uncertain what to do next.

Digger Jones' booming voice made her jump. 'Hey, Miss Delahunty, someone said the Hamilton boys are in town.'

'Where?'

'I don't rightly know, but if they're still around we'll find them.'

'They brought in a mob of horses,' one of the guests called from the rear of the room. 'I reckon they'll be gone by now. Send Ling Lee around to Carmody's stables. He'd know.'

Sibell waited in the foyer, staring out at the grey day where misty rain steamed in the street like a low-lying fog. The muggy weather had caused large patches of condensation to seep down the plaster walls, so that it felt as though she were sitting in a cave, with attendant heat discomfort.

The Chinese servant came racing in the door. 'Missy see! Missy see!' He dragged her to the door.

'See what?'

'Hamiltons!' His Chinese pronunciation of the name was close enough for Sibell to interpret, and she looked anxiously down the street. Three men, shrouded in mackintoshes that hung in long, heavy folds, were riding towards her, faces hidden by wide, dripping hats. They looked huge from where she stood, ghostly figures on their tall horses, trotting almost soundlessly down the wet road.

'Who wants us?' one of them called, and, intimidated by them, Sibell was tempted to run back inside.

The servant answered for her. 'This missy,' he pointed at her, giggling. 'Her!'

'I am looking for Mrs Hamilton,' Sibell called, from the shelter of the veranda.

'Which Mrs Hamilton?'

Taken aback, Sibell hesitated. 'Mrs Charlotte Hamilton.'

'Oh! Charlotte. She's not here.'

'I know that. Perhaps you could tell me how to get out to Black Wattle Station?'

There was a silence. Their spokesman swung down from his horse. He was a big, rangy man, certainly not a boy (hadn't people referred to them as the 'Hamilton boys'?). He dragged his hat off, revealing a thatch of sun-bleached hair, blue eyes under heavy eyebrows, the stubble of a beard shadowing the lower part of his face. 'I'm Zachary Hamilton,' he said. 'Now, what's the problem?'

'Well,' she began, unimpressed by this uncouth fellow who, she guessed, was probably only in his late twenties even if he did speak with the authority of the Colonel. 'Mrs Charlotte Hamilton, I was informed, is looking for someone to work for her, to act as her companion or her secretary . . . actually I'm not sure about this at all,' she continued. 'But, anyway, I want to apply for the job. I have been recommended to Mrs Hamilton by – ' she balked at mentioning Josie's name, but then decided it was necessary. 'By Mrs Cambray.'

'That's the lady Charlotte writes to,' he said. 'But I don't know about a companion. Why would she want a companion? My mother's a very independent woman. It doesn't make sense. I think you might have the wrong person, Miss . . .'

'Delahunty. Sibell Delahunty. And I'm sure I have not. I gather Mrs Hamilton is looking for someone to assist her because of her eyes.'

'What about her eyes?'

Now Sibell was beginning to believe she had made a mistake. 'Oh, Lord, I was under the impression that Mrs Hamilton was going blind.'

'Did you say my mother is going blind? Where did you hear this?'

'From Mrs Cambray. Your mother visited an eye specialist in Perth, I know that much.'

He was worried. 'She went for a holiday to Perth, she didn't mention eye doctors to us. Oh, God, hang on a minute.'

Sibell knew she had upset him with this news, and she was sorry. She shouldn't have had so much to say. It was possible now that Mrs Hamilton would be angry with her. She watched as Zachary Hamilton discussed the situation with the two other riders, standing out there in the rain. It was all Josie's fault, she should have warned her that this was a secret. Damn her! Her anger with Josie was suddenly pushed aside when she realised that Mrs Hamilton's son knew nothing about this job, therefore, at least, the post was still open. Whether or not she would make it out to their station was another matter.

Zachary came back and took her into the foyer. 'We'd better talk.' His companions followed. 'This is my brother, Cliff,' he said. This man, just as tall, but obviously younger, clutched his hat and extended his hand.

'How do you do, miss.'

'And this is Cliff's wife, Maudie.'

Sibell watched amazed as a young woman dumped her dripping mackintosh on a chair. She was wearing a man's shirt and dungarees, and short riding boots, men's boots. Her fair hair was pulled back into a rough plait and tied with string. She shook Sibell's hand with a grip of iron. 'You coming out with us?' she asked.

'I don't know. Am I?'

'It looks like it,' Zachary said. 'When did you arrive here?'

'Yesterday.'

'Are you on your own?'

'Yes.'

He turned to Cliff. 'We'll have to take her, then, we can't leave her here.'

Cliff was dubious. 'I don't know. We haven't got the buggy. Can you ride, miss?'

'Yes.'

'Have you done any bush riding, though?' Maudie asked, her voice as rough as her clothes.

'As a matter of fact, I have.' Sibell thought of that terrible time when she'd been shipwrecked, but she'd never tell any of these people. That scandal was behind her.

Maudie was still suspicious. 'Takes us the best part of five days to get home. It's no picnic.'

'I'll manage,' Sibell said, not sure that she would, but determined not to be left behind.

'She ought to wait here until Charlotte comes to town,' Maudie said.

'That won't be for months,' her husband argued. 'Charlotte's busy with all her furnishings; wild horses couldn't drag her loose.' He explained to Sibell, 'We built a new homestead, fit for women, and we've only just been able to get the furniture out, after the wet.'

Zachary had an idea. 'Maudie, you can take Miss Delahunty downriver by boat and we'll go on home. We'll bring the buggy across and meet you at the depot.'

'I don't want to go by bloody boat,' Maudie argued. 'It takes twice as long. And it's boring.'

'You'll have to this time,' he said. 'It's too hard a ride for a new chum. If she doesn't break her neck, we'll probably drown her.'

Sibell listened to their discussion. 'I'll take the boat on my own,' she said, offended at the way they spoke about her, as if she were extra luggage.

Maudie burst out laughing. 'On her own, she says! You got a gun, miss?'

'No. And please call me Sibell.'

'Righto, Sibell. This'll be your first lesson: you never travel anywhere out here without a gun, and ladies don't board that boat with all those hoboes without protection.' She sighed. 'I'd better take her.'

111

Sibell wasn't sure this was such a good idea after all. What sort of protection would Maudie be?

She soon found the answer. Maudie took charge. Within the hour, her bag was packed and slung on to Cliff's horse, and Sibell emerged, feeling ridiculous, dressed in Maudie's bush clothes.

'Don't worry about the pants,' Maudie had told her. 'They might look like men's gear but they're not. I made them myself. See! No fly.' Sibell was mortified at the conversation, but resolutely donned the trousers, not daring to look at herself in a mirror as she tucked in the shirt.

Another horse was brought up for her, and as Cliff legged her up, Sibell noticed that Maudie had a rifle buckled on to her saddle. She seemed impatient to be off, and yelled to her brother-in-law, 'Come on, Zack, let's get going!'

As they wheeled the horses about, Lorelei appeared outside the hotel. 'Good God, Sibell!' she called. 'You look like a cowboy!' But Sibell, trying to settle on her large bay horse, could only wave to her.

Cliff and Zachary smiled encouragement as they trotted along the main street. 'Oh, Lord!' she said to Zack, 'I forgot to pay.'

'Not a problem,' he replied easily. 'We'll pay next time. Digger knows we're good for the cash.'

Sibell had imagined that the river they spoke of was just out of town, but it was, for her, a long difficult ride. They forged on through endless tropical bushlands, steaming in the heat, and crossed swollen creeks, clattering over narrow causeways. The countryside was teeming with wildlife: wallabies and kangaroos spied on them, birds by the thousands shrilled overhead, and bush turkeys scrambled across the track. Each time they stopped, Sibell prayed they had arrived, but the breaks were only to rest the horses and take some refreshment for themselves. That night they were allotted bunks in a farmhouse, obviously owned by friends of the family, but Sibell was too tired to take much notice, and the next morning they were off again.

Finally, they rode into a small shanty town set on the high banks of a river. 'This is Pearly Springs,' Zack told her. 'You can rest up here until the riverboat comes back. The Red Lion isn't much of a pub but it's clean, and they'll look after you girls.'

The men rode off, leading two horses, and leaving Sibell in Maudie's capable hands, one of which held the rifle.

As the little steamboat chugged upriver, Sibell was apprehensive: she was travelling into country that looked like darkest Africa, after having removed herself from one end of the continent to the other, and she was now beginning to have second thoughts about this adventure. She shared a murky little cabin with Maudie, with a rowdy family next door who were *en route* to the goldfields. All the other passengers, mostly men, bedded down in the saloon or on the decks. They were a rough lot, prospectors mainly, Maudie told her, and Sibell was nervous, but Maudie moved easily among them.

The beautiful dark reaches of the river impressed Sibell, and the magnificent greenery crowding the banks seemed massive, mirrored in the velvet waters. 'It's lovely scenery,' she said to Maudie. 'The river looks so cool and inviting in this heat.'

'Do you reckon?' Maudie said. She spoke to one of the men, who disappeared for a few minutes and came back with a lump of meat.

'Watch this,' he said to Sibell, hurling the meat towards the bank of the river.

Instantly, crocodiles came racing out of the muddy undergrowth to slide noiselessly into the river, snapping for the meat, huge horrible bodies churning the waters as they rolled, fighting for the prize.

Sibell was stunned. She had heard of crocodiles but had never seen any before, and their size shocked her. Now she stood at the rails, fascinated as they drifted on the surface, some of them at least twenty feet long with girths bigger than horses.

'You wouldn't want to fall overboard,' Maudie laughed.

Maudie was cool to her, accommodating, Sibell mused, but no frills. Definitely no frills. She showed her where to wash, stood with her in the food queue at the galley, warning her not to touch the soup which she claimed was fermenting, sat with her on the deck discouraging the advances of bolder men, but had very little to say until her curiosity got the better of her. 'What are you doing wandering around on your own, anyway?'

'I came out to Australia with my parents, but they . . . died, so I have to find employment.'

She had expected some sympathy from Maudie, but it was not forthcoming. 'Both of your parents dead, eh?' Maudie said. 'So are mine. But why didn't you get a job in Perth?'

'There wasn't anything available,' Sibell replied, rather than admit that her situation in Perth had become impossible. 'I was recommended to apply for the position with Mrs Hamilton, so here I am.'

'You sure are,' Maudie laughed.

Sibell found her reply unnerving, but since Maudie was a little more talkative than usual, she had some questions of her own.

'You live at the Black Wattle Station?'

'Yes. Moved there when I married Cliff.'

'Who else lives there?'

'At the homestead? Only Charlotte and Zack and us. Then there's the station hands, a couple of cooks and a tribe of blacks.'

'Blacks?'

'Yeah. Well, they were there first.'

'Oh. And where was your home before you were married?'

'Nowhere in particular. My mum and dad were drovers, and us kids trailed along. They used to drive cattle in Queensland, and then they brought a big herd across the top end, over here to The Territory, and here they stayed, working these stock routes. I've been all over,' she said proudly, 'even down as far as Stuart in the Centre. But when I met Cliff, that was it! I work the station with them now, and it'll be real nice living in a proper house.' She laughed. 'They got that finished just in time. The first hut Cliff and Zack built was eaten to the ground by termites. They learned their lesson: the new house is mainly cedar, termites don't seem to like the taste.'

'Did they build it themselves?' Sibell asked.

'Not this house. Charlotte drew up the plans and sent builders out from Palmerston. It's one of the first real homesteads out here.'

'When we leave the boat, how long does it take to get to the station?'

'Only about a day from Idle Creek Junction. They built the house near the boundary, and the station property extends west from there.'

'I believe it's a very big property.'

'Big enough to make a go of it. I wonder what you'll have to do, working for Charlotte?'

'I'm not too sure myself. I just hope I'm suitable.'

Sibell was uncomfortably aware that Maudie seemed doubtful too. 'Maybe she's lining you up to marry Zack,' she suggested brightly, and Sibell was stunned.

'Good Lord, no! Why, Mrs Hamilton has never met me!'

'I know, but the lady who writes to her must have told her you're a pretty good sort, and educated too.'

'That's ridiculous. Where on earth did you get that idea?'

'Well . . . Charlotte didn't mind Cliff marrying me,' Maudie said, and then she added moodily, 'but I think she'd like to see her number one son do better.'

'You mustn't say things like that,' Sibell said. 'I think Cliff's lucky to have met someone like you: you know the country and you know what you're doing. I'm like a fish out of water out here.'

'Yes, that's what I said to Cliff,' Maudie replied. 'I told him you'd be no good on a station, you couldn't drown a worm, but he thinks Charlotte's plotting, and Zack's suspicious.'

'He needn't be, then,' Sibell told her. 'I'm not in the market. I think they've got a cheek!'

'Don't take it to heart. If you were us, you'd be wondering too. She'd like to see him married and women are scarce. By the way, who was that female who came out to wave you goodbye back at the Prince?'

Still smarting from Maudie's comments, Sibell answered abruptly, 'Her name is Lorelei Rourke. She's a lady I met on the ship.'

'Lady? She looked more like a tart to me.' Maudie shrugged, and Sibell, anxious again, went forward to watch the ship cutting through the velvety water, heading for yet another turn in its meandering path. Why couldn't they leave her alone? She was simply looking for employment, nothing else, and certainly not marriage to one of these country bumpkins. She wondered if she should turn back, rather than go on and be humiliated. No, if she stayed at Black Wattle Station, she'd make it plain to Mrs Hamilton and to Zachary – especially to Zachary – that she was not interested, not in the slightest. She thought of Logan, and was angry with him too. Damn them all! Somehow she'd have to make her own way and stop relying on people, but with only twenty pounds left it wouldn't be easy. And then she remembered the source of her money. Had Lloyds paid that compensation to Percy? And how much? She would write to the shipping company herself and find out.

The girls were ready to disembark as the boat neared Idle Creek, and the diggers ranged around them on the deck. 'You can stay with me blondie,' one fellow called to Sibell, and Maudie grinned at him.

'Fat chance, mate.'

They were assisted by willing hands on to a small pontoon and up the bank to a clearing strewn with litter. Bottles and tins and rotting packing cases lay abandoned, and the air was thick with flies. Sibell stared. 'There's nothing here. No town, nothing.'

Maudie wasn't concerned. 'No, it's only a junction. A river stop. In the dry season it's busier because sometimes the boats can't go much further. But no one hangs about here, they walk the rest of the way to the diggings: the nearest is about eighty miles as the crow flies.'

When the boat sailed, they were alone on the desolate banks and Sibell felt the silence descend on them like an ominous presence. 'What do we do now?' she asked.

'We wait for the buggy, and put your hat on or you'll get sunstroke.' The hat, a large felt, was also part of her bush uniform.

'Should we start walking?' Sibell asked, but Maudie laughed. 'That's a good way to get dead. We haven't got any waterbags. You don't go no place out here without water, this heat'd kill you in no time. We'll just wait here by the river. I wouldn't mind a swim but there are too many crocs around this time of the year.'

Sibell shuddered. She wondered what would happen if no one came for them, she wondered about a thousand things, but since she always seemed to be asking questions, she let it be.

'Look at this mess,' Maudie complained. 'Those damned diggers! A blackfeller wouldn't leave a mess like this.' She broke a heavy branch from a tree, and, using it as a broom, began to sweep and rake the litter into a heap. Feeling she should help, Sibell bent over to pick up some tins, but Maudie stopped her. 'Don't do that, don't touch any of the garbage, you might cut your hand. Cuts get infected easily.'

Sibell backed away, feeling useless, out of place. What am I doing here? she asked herself. I must be mad.

When at last Cliff arrived in the buggy, with a spare horse, he decided they might as well camp by the river for the night and get an early start in the morning. 'Thought we'd do a spot of fishing,' he said, and Maudie agreed enthusiastically. Neither of them noticed Sibell's despair. She was beginning to think they'd never reach the Hamilton house, and wondered to herself how she would ever get away again.

Black Wattle Station was quiet in the afternoons, except for the occasional buzz of ever-searching flies and the mournful caw of crows who disdained the bush siesta.

The new homestead, an amazing sight for local Aborigines, who came for miles to stand and stare, was located at the end of a long, sandy track that wound through the scrub, past grazing cattle and on by the horse paddocks to a clump of large, spreading black wattle trees, from which, of course, the station took its name. The blossoms were as yellow as ever, more golden perhaps than the balls of fluff of the better-known wattles, and they reached out in short strings, like glittering beads, against the thick-fronded foliage which was, in fact, not black but a deep, dark green, unmistakable against the other busy greens of the north.

The track filed past a long three-railed fence which declared the home precincts, and around the corner to the stables and an enclave of out-buildings necessary for the maintenance of this great property, Visitors, however, would alight at the front gate.

Charlotte Hamilton had decreed that an expanse thirty feet wide should surround the house inside the fence, for her garden, which she would attend to in time. So far it contained only some tall gums and native bushes that had been spared to soften the clearing. To European eyes the rambling country homestead, painted white with a green trim, had a stately charm, and Charlotte was thrilled with it. Not one to experiment with such a difficult project as this house-building had been, so far from civilisation, Charlotte had copied the tried-and-tested designs of Queensland country homesteads, which, in their turn, were reminiscent of the sprawling, high-ceilinged bungalows built by the British to combat the heat of India.

A swing for her five-year-old grandson hung from the roof of the timber-deck veranda which surrounded the house, and she had placed tables and comfortable chairs on the deck to make the most of outdoor living. French windows at exact intervals around the house opened on to the veranda for light and air, giving the sturdy building, with its single-gabled roof, a delicate air.

In the battle against heat and damp, snakes and other ground-dwelling wildlife, the house was built six feet above the ground, so, on each side, white-painted timber steps led up from the garden for easy access. The heavy brass knocker on the front door seemed superfluous since the door was always open. It led to a central living room, and on to the dining room. There were four bedrooms, and on the rear corner was the station office, the focal point of management of the property. On the other side was Charlotte's pride and joy, the bathroom: a large indoor bathroom with an adjacent indoor water closet, a luxury almost unknown in the north.

When visitors came, impressed by the wood panelling in the house and the cooling effect of the twelve-foot-high ceilings, Charlotte would hurry them through to view the bathroom, taking the rest of the place for granted.

But now, as she rose from her afternoon nap, she realised she still had a long way to go to complete the furnishing, and sometimes she wondered if she'd ever be finished. There were gaps everywhere. The floors of the house were polished cedar but she needed carpet squares, and lino for the kitchen. More curtain material was also needed, since several of the windows were still bare. The mahogany dining-room table had arrived, but without the chairs, so she had to make do with long benches.

Her sons couldn't understand her impatience. 'What's the hurry, Ma? The stuff will turn up eventually.' They were amused by her single-minded concentration on the house but that was how she'd always been. 'If a thing's worth doing,' she told them repeatedly,' it's worth doing properly.' She hoped that while they were in Palmerston selling a mob of horses they would remember her instructions and re-order necessities for her. She knew they were proud of the house but it was hard to make them think past cattle and horses.

Outside, the dogs started barking and her pet cockatoo on the veranda tramped up and down squawking: 'Get the buggers! Get the buggers!'

116

Knowing that most of the men were out on the range she called to Netta, her black housemaid. 'Who is it?'

'Bosses comen, missus!'

'Good! Get Wesley! Tell him his daddy's home.'

There was no response so she guessed Netta had rushed away to do just that. She fumbled for her glasses and buttoned up her brown holland dress, hurrying to the dressing table to tidy her hair. As she brushed it, pinning it in place, she grimaced into the mirror at the faded greying strands. In younger days her hair had been silky-blonde, legacy of her Swedish daddy who had jumped ship in Sydney, and then she thought fondly of her sons. Daddy, God rest his soul, would have been proud of his big strong grandsons. As she was. Her Viking lads! They hated her to say that to people, it embarrassed them, but it was true: their father, a red-headed Scot, had hardly got a look-in. Although Wesley was a throw-back with his red hair and freckles.

But good heavens! What was she doing? Sitting here reminiscing!

She rushed to the front of the house just as the 'boys', who had been joined by the foreman, Casey, and other riders, arrived at the gate but she stopped abruptly at the top of the steps. 'Where's Maudie?' she cried, gathering her skirts to go down to them.

'Don't worry Ma,' Cliff replied. 'She's on her way.' He leaned down and swept his son onto the saddle in front of him, while the two Aborigine nursemaids, twins Pet and Polly, clapped encouragement to their charge.

'How's my boy?' Cliff laughed, handing the child the reins.

'He's as fit as a fiddle,' Charlotte said. 'For God's sake, Cliff, where's Maudie?' She knew the dangers of the outback, she'd spent years on the lonely trails.

'Don't worry about Maudie,' Zack said, dismounting and handing his horse over to Casey. 'She's coming by boat.'

'Why would she do that?'

'It's a long story, Ma,' he said, putting an arm around her, 'but everything's under control. Cliff will go over to collect her at Idle Creek.'

They walked through to the kitchen where Sam Lim, the cook, alternated between welcoming Zack home and shushing them out of his domain in his high-pitched broken English. Sam Lim had been Charlotte's cook at the hotel, and she'd brought him with her to the station where his excited bossiness was a constant source of amusement to the household. 'Living with Sam is like living with a brass band,' Zack laughed, but he retreated obediently to the dining room so that Sam could serve them drinks 'ploper'.

Charlotte relaxed. 'Did you remember to order the lino?' she asked. 'And did you bring me back the samples of curtain materials?'

'Yes, we ticked off the list one by one, marched around the town half the day, in and out of the shops like worker ants, we were.'

Sam Lim brought in a bottle of beer and two glasses on a tray, and Zack downed his first drink almost as soon as it was poured. 'That's better,' he said.

'What about the horses?' Charlotte asked. 'Did you sell them all?'

'No problem. Topped the sales. I banked the cash and I remembered to bring back the receipt this time.' He leaned across the table. 'Now, how have you been keeping?'

'Me? I've never been better.'

'Glad to hear it. And how are your eyes?'

'Oh, they're just fine so long as I use the drops the doctor gave me.'

'You mean the eye specialist, the one in Perth.'

'Yes, him.' She admitted, 'I just have to take care on dusty days.'

'Mother,' Zack said, and the use of that title meant a serious conversation. 'For the next six months we'll have nothing but dusty days. Don't you think you should confide in us?'

'What about?'

'About your eyes. Are they getting better, or not?'

Charlotte hesitated, then admitted, 'No.'

'Well, now. That didn't hurt, did it? I'm bloody sorry about this – we got a shock when we heard, so it must have been worse for you – but try not to worry. We'll always be here, you'll cope, you always do.'

'I know, Zack. I'm getting used to the idea now, but how the hell did you find out?'

'Ah,' he said, 'now we come to the next interesting bit of news. We met your secretary.'

'Who?'

'Miss Delahunty.'

'Who's she?'

It was Zack's turn to be caught off guard. 'Don't you know?'

'No, I don't,' Charlotte told him.

'Jesus!' he said. 'She's on her way here, with Maudie. That's why Maudie, under protest, had to come by boat. Your secretary can sit on a horse but she's no bushie. She's very British!'

Charlotte was bewildered. 'I don't know anything about this.'

'Then turn your mind back a page or two. Remember that lady you write to, Mrs Cambray?'

'Yes.'

'Did you tell her you were thinking of hiring a secretary-cum-companion to help you if and when your eyes got worse?'

'Yes, I had an idea like that.'

'Not an idea any more. Mrs Cambray has sent the goods.'

'Good God! Why didn't she let me know?'

'Apparently the girl herself wrote to you. I don't think she's very bright. She travelled on the same ship as her letter.'

'And Maudie's bringing her out here?' Charlotte was dumbfounded.

'What else could we do? She was at the Prince of Wales Hotel, looking for you. And she insisted on seeing you. We couldn't leave her there.' He burst out laughing at his mother's astonishment. 'I reckon if we hadn't brought her along she'd have started walking. Anyway, you can have a talk to her, and if you want to take her on, it's up to you. If you don't, then she'll have to hang around here until I can find someone to take her back to Palmerston.'

Charlotte was curious. 'How old is she?'

'I don't know, nineteen, maybe. Are you sure you didn't line this up?'

'Of course not,' Charlotte said, 'but I have to start sometime, and if

118

she's suitable, then I could begin showing her my books and what I want her to do. Although I did have in mind someone older, and a country lady.'

'And you've got just the opposite,' he grinned, finishing the beer and climbing wearily to his feet. 'I'm going to have a bath.'

He walked out of the room and then stuck his head back in. 'By the way, Mother, I don't think your lady pal is Maudie's cup of tea,' and with another hoot of laughter, he disappeared.

'Nothing wrong with that,' Charlotte muttered. She found Cliff's wife rather a handful at times, a girl who was quick to take offence at imagined slights. Although Charlotte had welcomed her warmly to the family, and treated her with due deference and care, Maudie, she knew, was not all that comfortable in this house, feeling put down by Charlotte's insistence on manners and dress. She wanted to set a standard, and her sons acquiesced with their usual good nature when she asked them to tidy up for dinner at night. 'Bathe, shave and clean duds,' was all she asked of them, not insisting they wear white jackets in the heat, as some of the bush families did back east. In a lot of those houses, it could be fetching 110 degrees but the men would not enter the parlours or dining rooms without their coats.

She considered that was too formal for the climate, but then again, she supposed Maudie saw her other innovations in the same light. Not that Maudie ever said anything, not to her anyway, but those sharp brown eyes of hers carried an unmistakable sneer.

'Oh, dear,' Charlotte sighed quietly. Maudie was a good wife for a cattle-man: in many respects she was a tremendous back-up for her husband. Born to the saddle, Maudie could run rings around them all. Charlotte just wished she would take more interest in her son, Wesley. She seemed to think that as long as someone was minding him – hence the two Aborigine girls who had been by his side since he was a baby – the child was fine, and her only role as a mother was to scold.

As usual, Charlotte made no comment. The way the youngies brought up their kids was their own business. But this girl, this Miss Delahunty, intrigued her. She must have plenty of spunk, even if she were a city type, to come all this way on her own on the off-chance of finding a live-in job. Or else she was desperate. Mrs Hamilton, senior, decided she would have to vet this young lady very carefully.

The house, the woman herself, the staring people, black faces among them, were all a blur as, exhausted, Sibell climbed down from the buckboard in a dimly-lit courtyard and followed Maudie inside. There was excitement in the voices and a flurry as she was escorted to a bedroom.

'Call me Charlotte,' the woman said. 'The girls are drawing a bath for you. It will ease the buggy bruises.'

She was still in her dressing gown when Charlotte came back. 'Do you feel a bit better now?'

'Yes, thank you, the bath was wonderful.'

'I put some Epsom salts in the water,' Charlotte told her. 'That cheers up tired muscles. Do you feel up to joining us for dinner?'

'Would you mind if I just went to bed? I'm very tired.'

'Not at all, I'll send you in some tea and sandwiches.'

She could barely stay awake for the light meal delivered to her by a cheerful black girl, but she managed, and ate her sandwiches slowly, relieved to be on her own in a decent bed after that impossible journey. It wasn't just the buggy bumps: having to sleep out in the open last night, at Idle Creek, with only a rug and a mosquito net, had been the last straw! Sibell was drowsy and disoriented. She thought she could hear her father recounting his youthful adventures, tramping the Scottish countryside, and sleeping under the stars. It had sounded so romantic, such a splendid thing to do, but in this land, to date, it was only drudging, hard necessity.

As she lay in the cool, fresh sheets, a warm breeze drifted in through the open window, and his voice seemed to chide her: 'Fine hot nights and you're complaining! It was freezing those nights in Scotland.'

'You never told us that,' she muttered. And slept.

In the morning Charlotte herself brought her breakfast on a tray and placed it on a table by the open windows.

'You shouldn't have,' Sibell said.

'No trouble. I've got porridge for you, sausages and bacon and eggs, toast and tea and I even found you some marmalade.'

Once again Sibell was staggered by the size of the meal, but she didn't like to comment, so she pulled up a chair. It was already very hot, and outside a blue sky blazed above a row of dark trees. Nearby something, or someone, screamed, and Sibell jumped in fright, dropping cutlery.

'That's only Cocky,' Charlotte explained. 'Don't let him bother you. He lives on the veranda and thinks he owns the place. I'll leave you to have your breakfast in peace and then I might come back and have a cup of tea with you. If that's all right?'

'Yes, of course.' Sibell was impressed by the woman's kindness and easy manner. She had expected someone different, a stern, tough woman, an older version of Maudie.

She washed, brushed her hair vigorously, and looked for her bag, only to find that her clothes had been unpacked while she slept and her dresses pressed and hung in the cupboard. She blushed. Now they'd know how poor she was, with only a few dresses and the bare minimum of underwear. It was humiliating, but she couldn't allow herself to dwell on that. She hurried to pull on her blue suit, shoes and stockings, then sat down to eat as much of the food as she could, as fast as possible. It was important that when Mrs Hamilton returned her guest would be looking cool and calm, although she didn't feel it. But she had slept well, for a change, with no bad dreams. 'Obviously,' she told herself, 'you have to wear yourself to a frazzle to get a decent rest.'

They sat in the shade of the veranda with a view of flowering shrubs and an ocean of trees beyond the track, while Cocky pranced and screamed, showing off.

'Now, let's see,' Charlotte began. 'Do you really think you'd like to work out here?'

120

'If you'll have me.'

'My dear, it's not a case of having you, I'd like you to stay.'

'That's very kind of you.'

'No, it's not. At my age one gets to be a pretty shrewd judge of character. I believe in first impressions.'

Sibell thought of Logan. Her first impression of him hadn't been too complimentary. Had she been right?

'This station – ' Mrs Hamilton was saying, 'don't be misled by the house. Any station in the north can be a trial. The summer might be over, but it won't get any cooler. Heat, dust and flies are our lot for the next six months. You're out in the middle of nowhere. Our nearest neighbours are fifty miles away, and that's only Jim Pratt and his men camped on Corella Downs. The nearest town is Pine Creek, a hard day's ride from here, and it's just a rough mining town. There are no medical facilities outside of Palmerston, that's why there are so few women. If they're not bush-bred they won't put their kids at risk.'

'Not even any doctors?'

'Doctor Brody travels about the district, does a great job, but it takes time to locate him. Midwives deliver babies and look after the mothers, and they're worth their weight in gold. They're only ordinary women with birthing experience, but they'll leave their own families and ride for days to take care of the younger ones.'

'They're very brave.'

'My word they are. But for here . . . Zack tells me you ride well, dear, but you have to understand that you must never leave the immediate area without an escort.'

'Is it dangerous out there? I mean wild animals?'

'Not animals . . . I mean, you've enough sense not to go near bulls or water buffalo, and we really haven't got any wild animals. You'd be unlucky to get bitten by a snake or a spider, that could happen anywhere. But you could easily get lost or suffer from the heat, and there are still tribal blacks, and plenty of them, who live by the spear.'

'I saw quite a few black people walking around this morning,' Sibell said.

'Yes, poor things. They work on the theory that if you can't beat them, join them. On the whole the women are very loyal to white women, a big help. They're very caring people, and the men who live in blacks' camps on the station are rarely any trouble. Some of them have taken jobs as stockmen but the others keep their distance.'

'It's all very interesting,' Sibell said, and Charlotte heaved a sigh, realising she wasn't getting through.

'You might find the isolation trying,' she continued. 'A young girl like you, you'll miss the bright lights . . . you'll miss your friends.'

'I haven't got any friends.'

Charlotte smiled, looking at her appreciatively. 'I find that hard to believe.'

'Mrs Hamilton,' Sibell said. 'I survived the sinking of the *Cambridge Star*.' She could not bring herself to mention her parents, specifically in case she became too emotional and thereby ruined her chances of appearing sensible and efficient. 'I landed with nothing and have been living on charity ever since. The circumstances were singularly unpleasant, so now as long as I can earn my pay, I need this job.' She was pleased that she had managed to slip in the matter of wages.

The older woman was startled. 'Good God! Are you the one? I'm so sorry, Sibell . . . Josie Cambray did mention you, now I come to think of it, but I lost her letter in the move out here, so your name didn't ring a bell. The *Cambridge Star*, eh? I remember that! God, you were lucky!' She stood up and surprised Sibell by shaking hands. 'You've got yourself a job as long as you want to stay. With pay,' she added, not missing Sibell's reference. 'What do you say to five pounds a week and keep?'

Five pounds a week! Sibell was thrilled. Margot only paid her staff ten shillings a week, and then she docked them for everything she could think of. 'That will do very nicely,' she replied.

'Now,' Charlotte said, becoming businesslike. 'Duties. I want you to help me with my accounts and correspondence, and with station-office work, so that as my eyes peg out, you'll know what to do and I'll be able to dictate to you.'

'I hope that won't be for a very long time,' Sibell offered.

'So do I. But even now, with poor eyesight, a couple of other jobs are difficult for me. The ironing – I've given up trying to teach the gins, they're worse than me – and I'm worn out trying to make the damn curtains for the house. Can you sew?'

'Yes, and I'd be pleased to help.'

'Thank God for that! I think you and I will get along very well, but when you get fed up with the place, you say so. You're not a prisoner here. Come on now and I'll show you around.'

One thing, Sibell mused, as she followed Charlotte from room to room, admiring, agreeing, discussing what was yet needed: she'd never be short of conversation with Charlotte, who rattled on happily.

She was introduced to Netta, the young black housemaid who had brought her tea. 'Netta's a good girl,' Charlotte said. 'She makes a lot of mistakes, but she tries hard and she'll get the gist of things in time.'

Then they went into the kitchen to meet Sam Lim, the Chinese cook, who bowed politely. 'If you want anything,' Charlotte told Sibell, 'stand at the door and ask. He only lets me into his kitchen, and can be a real twerp if anyone else comes in. But he's a damn good cook.'

She was surprised to see a little red-headed white boy playing bat and ball with some black children, egged on by a circle of yelling Aborigine girls. 'That's my grandson, Wesley,' Charlotte told her. 'Maudie and Cliff's son and heir. He's a great little kid. Very independent.'

Sibell realised that Maudie had not volunteered any information that was not immediately relevant, and felt a crease of worry that perhaps Cliff's wife did not want her on the station.

'I must write to Josie Cambray and thank her for recommending you,' Charlotte enthused. 'I haven't written to her since I sold the hotel.'

'She doesn't live on the farm any more,' Sibell told her.

'Oh! They moved, did they? Where do they live now?'

'I don't know,' she replied bleakly. Obviously Charlotte hadn't heard that Josie had run off with another man, with Logan. Sibell was still mystified that Logan could prefer a mousy older woman like Josie to her, but she didn't want to think about them. Ever again.

That night Charlotte collared Zack, Cliff and Maudie when they came in from the day's work. 'Now, listen here, you lot. I've hired the girl, Sibell. I need her, so I want you to treat her like one of the family, or she'll bolt on me.'

'Whatever you say,' Cliff grinned. 'She sure brightens up the scenery!'

Charlotte saw Maudie scowl. 'Enough of that, you two boys give her the respect she deserves.'

'Why me?' Zack complained. 'If you're happy with her, that's fine with me.'

'If she stays,' Maudie laughed. 'She's a city-slicker. Ten to one she won't last a month.'

'Who is she, anyway?' Cliff asked. 'What the hell is she doing in The Territory? She's as out of place as a chook up a tree.'

'I saw her mate,' Maudie told them. 'A little blonde piece dressed up like Christmas. I'd bet my socks that one's a whore.'

'Sibell's a decent girl,' Charlotte snapped, and turned to Zack. 'You remember the ship that went down off Fremantle last year? The *Cambridge Star*.'

'Never heard of it,' Maudie put in, and Charlotte ignored her, thinking that if her daughter-in-law would learn to read, she would know. It had been in all the papers.

'Sibell is one of the survivors of that ship,' she continued. 'I believe only a few people survived. Josie Cambray wrote me about her. Sibell's mother and father were drowned. She lost everyone and everything.'

'Oh, no!' Zack groaned, genuinely upset. 'The poor girl.'

'She never said nothing to me about that,' Maudie sniffed.

'Sometimes people have a hurt they can't talk about,' Charlotte said softly. 'She didn't say much to me, either, so you people treat her with care. The girl's a bundle of nerves, and that's no wonder.'

'This country isn't going to do her nerves a lot of good,' Cliff snorted, and Maudie laughed.

'She's scared stiff of snakes, for a start.'

'Who isn't?' Zack said moodily. 'I saw you panic one day and shoot a young python that was just minding his own business.'

'Never mind about that,' Charlotte said. 'Sibell can help me in the house, and learn about the bush all in good time. She had the guts to get herself here, all the way from Perth. I reckon she just might surprise you.'

Zack hid a smile as Maudie came into dinner. With competition in the air, she had made an effort for a change. She hadn't taken kindly to Charlotte's request that they shine up of an evening, keeping to the letter of the law by changing from trousers into a skirt, but topping it off with a man's open-necked shirt. This time she'd found a blouse, and it was buttoned primly through to the collar.

When Sibell came in, he had to make a much stronger effort to disguise his reaction. She looked a dream in a graceful white dress, her cloud of soft, wavy hair the colour of wild honey in the lamplight, and her complexion reminding him of creamy camellias.

'Good evening,' she said shyly, and he stared at the long, dark lashes brushing liquid blue-grey eyes, as if seeing her for the first time.

Charlotte placed them, said grace, and turned to Sibell. 'Welcome to the Hamilton household.'

Zack tried to concentrate on the meal, feeling very second-rate in the company of this beauty, this person from another world. And he was angry with himself for allowing her to get to him like that, as if he were some adolescent kid with an instant crush. He would not permit this. He had no time to be thinking about girls, especially this one.

When those eyes rested on him, he looked away, and made no attempt to address her as the meal progressed. Charlotte kept the conversation going, talking about station matters, and the girl listened quietly, politely. Sitting across from her, he noticed she was startled by a gecko running across the ceiling, but meanly, as if to punish her, he didn't bother to tell her that geckos were everywhere and they were harmless.

5

In Palmerston, the Colonel had his problems, too. When he left the hotel he called at the tiny Commercial Bank to establish an account, but found the bank was closed.

A passer-by directed him to the Bank of Scotland. 'The blokes from the Commercial Bank are on holiday, or gone prospecting, more like it, so all their books are at the other bank.'

Puckering found this extraordinary, but the advice was correct. 'We take it in turns to shut down,' a teller told him cheerily. 'So you don't have to worry, we've got all their ledgers and we keep their cash in our safe.'

'So bank robbers may rob two banks at once,' the Colonel commented, unimpressed by this laxity.

'Cripes! Don't say that,' the teller responded. 'Don't put ideas in their heads.'

His next stop was the police station, which was wide open and unmanned. It was only a small wooden shack with a high counter, and he walked through to the rear where he discovered a cottage which displayed the sign: 'Residence'.

An old man was clearing high grass around the cottage with a scythe.

'Who lives here?' Puckering asked.

The old man studied his uniform with rheumy eyes. 'I reckon you do, he drawled. 'You'd be the new boss, wouldn't you?'

'Chief Inspector of Police,' Puckering announced.

'Yeah. I thought so. You can go in. It's not locked.'

'Where are the local police?'

The old man drew a pipe from his shirt pocket. 'Well, now, let me see. The sergeant, Jim Morris, he's away. Some Abos bumped off a half a dozen Jap pearlers across the bay, so he's gone to sort that out. The constable, Bobby Slater, he's laid up. In hospital. Got malaria.'

'Thank you. And the other two officers?'

'Oh, them! They quit.' He stuffed tobacco in the pipe and lit it. 'Quite a whiles back now, if I recall.'

'Where's the jail?'

'The lock-up? Follow that track down through the bush there. Long stone building, full as the family po, it is, so the warders let the white blokes out at night, makes it easier for everyone.' He saw the Colonel frown, and added, 'There's talk of building a bigger jail at Fannie Bay, but they haven't got around to it yet.'

'I see,' Puckering said, astounded by this information. 'My luggage was to be delivered to the police station. Has it appeared yet?'

'Sure it has. I shoved it in the house for you.' He ambled over and opened the front door. 'Place needs a bit of a clean-up, I'd say.'

Puckering stepped up on to the rickety veranda and strode into the house, where he was assailed by the overpowering powdery smell of mould. 'Good God!' he exclaimed, hurrying forward to throw open the windows.

The light exposed walls black with mould and floorboards with damp white blotches. Rats scuttled behind cabinets, and a huge cobweb barred the way to the bedroom. 'Bloody place is disgusting!' he snapped.

'Not the best,' the old man admitted. 'You can't close a place up in this climate. But the mould, it washes off.'

Puckering looked about him in despair. He couldn't move in to this sordid hole. And it seemed that his first duty would be that of a lowly constable. Someone had to man the station.

'Who can I get to clean up here?'

'I reckon your best bet is to get yourself a Chinee servant. He'll take care of this. And keep him on, they're good cooks and laundrymen.'

'Where would I find such a person?'

'I suppose I could dig one up for you.' He held out his hand. 'A shilling would do it.'

Puckering handed over the shilling and returned to the police station to examine their files and the daily diaries left open on the counter. 'Damned place should be locked up when they're away,' he muttered, but then he remembered the mould in that house, and shook his head. He was sweating now in the steamy atmosphere and decided he might as well go back to the Prince of Wales and take a room there until his residence, such as it was, had been thoroughly cleaned and aired.

By the time he was installed at the hotel, Puckering was in a thoroughly bad mood. What the hell had he let himself in for? And to think he left his last post because discipline was too slack! This place was worse. He would seek an appointment immediately with the Governor – or rather the Administrator, as he was known in The Territory, since it wasn't a state, just an adjunct of South Australia. He spent the afternoon writing a letter to the Administrator, requesting an audience and setting out an agenda for discussion, which included the immediate appointment of extra police.

The young gentlemen from the BAT had pointed out the Administrator's residence, a picturesque building known as the house of seven gables, set in a sheltered niche of greenery in the side of the hill overlooking the bay. Feeling it would not be correct for him to deliver the letter himself, the Colonel asked Digger Jones for a reliable servant to act as his courier.

'No point just now,' Digger told him. 'The Administrator's not home. He and a mate have gone prospecting. Down at Pine Creek, a hundred miles away.'

'Good God!' the Colonel said, defeated.

He supposed he might as well explore the town in a less conspicuous manner, and changed into mufti, but on the way out he dropped by the bar to fortify his flagging spirits.

Keeping faith with the placard outside the hotel, the whisky was surprisingly good, so, as the humid afternoon gloom of cloud resolved into night, he stood at a window, staring disconsolately out at his startling bailiwick. Unruly drinkers staggered in the streets, riders galloped past at breakneck pace, a fight broke out, shots were fired, and pianos jangled from saloons. Chinamen hurried by, heads down, arms folded in deep sleeves, some accompanied by their women, who, he noticed with horror, were tripping along on bound feet There were no police in sight, no one to control the roisterers except himself, this lone man in the long, raucous bar.

Heavily bearded men in flannel shirts and rough trousers tramped past to join the crush at the counter, sparing him no more than a glance. Their hard eyes noted the tall, barrel-chested man with clipped grey hair and the unmistakable erect stance of a military man, but it cut no ice with them. All sorts of characters turned up in Palmerston, chasing gold or being chased by the law. Strangers were studiously ignored. It didn't pay to be nosy.

Early the next morning, in a drizzle of warm rain, Puckering found an eager young Chinaman called Tom Phong waiting at the police station, so he put him to work in the cottage. There was still no sign of his officers, so the Colonel spent a fruitless morning hanging about the station, with no callers and no complainants. Obviously, he mused, the locals avoid this office like a plague house. When it came to crime or the reporting of such, his policemen would have to go out and fetch, like women at the well. And from his observations of the town last night, this well was flush. He'd seen opium dens, sly-grog shops, illegal fan-tan games and had heard talk of robberies and bashings. A saloon was wrecked and a butcher's shop burned to the ground. 'Because,' an old-timer explained patiently, 'the fool overcharged the wrong blokes.'

But no one had come forward to lodge complaints.

After the day's frustrations, he made for the saloon bar of the Prince of Wales, where Lorelei Rourke waylaid him to recount her woes. 'I've been trying to buy a house, but the only ones I can find are dirty little hovels. I am disgusted they even showed them to me. What do they think I am?'

Puckering didn't answer that. He preferred not to know. 'Where's Sibell?' he asked.

'Oh! Don't you know? She found the people she was looking for, and rode off with them. The Hamiltons, Digger said. And she was dressed up like a cowboy, in men's clothes, if you don't mind! I couldn't believe my eyes!' And then she nudged Puckering. 'But you should have seen the two fellers she went with! Big, handsome men, they were. Half her luck! Digger said they're wealthy cattlemen, big-time! So I guess that's the last we'll see of her.'

Puckering edged himself out of her company, loath to be seen consorting with a prostitute, and shouldered his way along the crowded street to a cafe where he enjoyed a meal of soup and chicken, prepared by Chinese cooks.

Later that night, Lorelei appeared at his door. 'The bar's closed, I thought you might like a nightcap.' She waved a bottle of port.

'I was asleep,' he said.

'Go on! At this hour? What do you think of my kimono? I bought it today. Isn't it pretty?' She turned about, showing off a brilliant pink silk wrapper that certainly did look attractive against her blonde curls and pale complexion.

'Indeed, yes,' he admitted, looking down at the revealing swell of her breasts, and she giggled at his hesitation, slipping past him into the room. She put the bottle on the dressing table as he closed the door, and twirled around again. 'This silk is so soft against my skin, I couldn't bear to spoil it by wearing anything underneath.' As she turned back to him the kimono was open, and he sighed. No man could be expected to refuse an offer like this! His hands slid into the soft folds of the kimono and over the firm round breasts, gliding down, drawing her to him, glad that the proprietor had alloted him a room with a large double bed.

In the morning, Lorelei was still with him, and although he was remorseful, calling himself all sorts of a fool, he took her supple young body in his arms and made love to her again.

'You wanted me all the time on the ship, didn't you?' she whispered her tongue caressing his ear. 'But Sibell was in the way.'

When he wouldn't reply, she nuzzled down under his neck. 'Of course you did. And I wanted you, I like older men. I positively fizzed when you were around.'

She sat up to straddle him, and looking at her in the daylight, able to see and hold that lovely body, he didn't want to let her go, to share her with anyone.

By the time Mr and Mrs Logan Conal arrived in Port Darwin harbour, the wet season in the north had been replaced by a hard, dry heat that would scorch the land to its core. Already the pungent aroma of burning eucalypts, so familiar to Australians, was drifting lazily over the bay, as yet not a concern to the residents. As the dry months progressed, however, and the heat intensified, a land revived by annual floods would steel itself against the onslaught of fearful bushfires.

The ship was like a hotplate, at anchor between the vivid twin blues of sea and sky, the sun blazing mercilessly on this trapped vessel, and Josie cringed under a light canvas awning. 'This is terrible,' she told Logan. 'How long do we have to stay out here?'

'We have to wait for the tides,' he explained. 'They say the sea-level in this bay can drop twenty-five feet at low tide. Cheer up, we'll be ashore soon and you'll feel better.'

The voyage had been misery from day one. Instead of cabins, this overcrowded ship provided a series of small dormitories, separating males from females, and Josie had been forced to share with four other women and three noisy children, all of whom were bound for the goldfields. Even though it was only a ten-day journey up the coast of Western Australia, to Josie it seemed endless. The children were seasick, their cabin stank, the food served to the passengers was appalling, and drunken men roistered on the decks day and night, ignored by the Captain. She could hardly wait to get ashore and away from these awful people.

When at last they were able to make their way into Palmerston, Logan bought her a sunshade right away, agreeing that the heat was incredible. It was the hottest day they'd ever encountered. 'Trust us,' he laughed, 'to arrive on a day like this.' They did not realise that the temperature was normal for Palmerston, that winter did not exist in The Territory: only two seasons, the Wet and the Dry, prevailed.

Josie insisted in going straight to the Prince of Wales Hotel, and was dismayed to hear that Charlotte Hamilton no longer owned the hotel, and, worse, that she had left Palmerston. Since that hotel was fully booked and the publican was too busy to be bothered with them, she sat on a bench outside, minding the luggage while Logan made enquiries about accommodation.

She studied the passers-by, finding them as rough and ready as the town itself. 'If this is the capital of the north,' she said to herself, half amused, 'I hate to think what the rest of the towns are like.' She had not yet grasped the ominous truth of her comment.

When Logan finally returned, she was wilting in the heat, but the set of his jaw warned her not to complain.

'The damn place is packed out,' he growled. 'Apparently their rainy season is over and the roads are opened up again, so the world is on the march.'

'What about the agent for Gilbert Mines, Mr Strange? Did you see him?'

'I found his office, wide open and empty. The barber told me he's around somewhere, but I couldn't find him. The least he could have done was meet us at the ship.'

'What do we do now?'

'There's a room at a pub a couple of streets away. It's not much, but it will do for a few days.'

The room was a sweltering corner of a ramshackle hotel, but the linen was clean and a large china jug on the washstand was brimming with water. 'Thank God,' Josie said, 'the perspiration is pouring off me.' She took off her serviceable bombazine suit and her long cotton petticoat to sluice her face and neck, but Logan put his arms around her waist.

'Keep going,' he murmured, untying her bodice. 'I think I'm going to like the tropics. What better excuse to take everything off?'

'Everything?' she asked. 'At this hour?'

'Why not?' he laughed, stripping quickly. 'It's cooler this way. That voyage nearly killed me, missing my conjugal rights. And on our honeymoon, too. Did you miss me?'

'You know I did.' She smiled a little shyly as he undressed her in broad daylight and sprawled her on the bed, but she felt a rush of excitement at his boldness, her own dark and handsome husband.

'You should be in the nuddy more often,' he told her gaily, standing looking at her, running his fingers over her tingling skin. 'You look your best this way.' And Josie giggled, her hunger for him heightened by this naughty game. She stretched luxuriously, showing off her full, taut breasts, and reached up for him.

'I love you, Logan.'

It wasn't so much love-making as a swift, sweaty exercise, and then he was on his feet again, satisfied. He slapped her on the bottom. 'Come on, Jose, get dressed. We'll have a look around the town.'

She obeyed, feeling let down, but consoled herself that they had all the time in the world for loving. There would be many other occasions.

They left Palmerston in a buckboard which Logan had bought, together with two horses and supplies for the trail, in the company of about twenty miners from the ship, and a few women, all travelling together for safety and for guidance on the route. Josie was reminded of her first inland journey to Cambray Farm. She missed Ned now, and prayed he was happy at his school. Regardless of their regulations, she intended to write to him every week, and hoped someone would be kind enough to hand on her letters.

But the trek to Cambray Farm had been a joyride in balmy weather compared to this nightmare journey in the blazing heat, plagued by insects and accidents. The road was bumpy, uneven, corrugated by heavy bullock wagons which had sloshed through at the end of the wet season, leaving the surface to set into hard ridges, baked by the sun. A buggy overturned, and a woman was thrown out, breaking her arm, and late on the first day a wheel came off the buckboard. Fortunately, several men came to their aid, and they were able to catch the main party up by nightfall.

They camped by a drying creek, near a series of water holes strung out like amber beads along the creek bed, and Josie didn't mind that. Their companions were hearty and helpful, and it was such a relief to get off that bobbing seat. The next day, though, as they moved on again in the gruelling heat of this endless country, the travellers on horseback rode off without them, and the man and woman in the buggy turned back to Palmerston.

'Just follow the track,' a miner advised them. 'But don't follow it too far,' he laughed. 'It goes all the way by the telegraph lines to Adelaide.'

As they struggled on, Josie told Logan about Charlotte Hamilton, who had overlanded to this place from the east coast, thousands of miles away, now realising what epic journeys those people had undertaken. But Logan would have none of it. 'You're so gullible, Josie. Only you would believe a tale like that.'

'But they did,' she argued. 'Charlotte told me they overlanded their cattle that way, too.'

'Bloody rot! They shipped the cattle in. How do you think they got cattle to this country in the first place? You English brought them all the way in the holds of ships.'

'Us English,' she laughed, but she wasn't really amused. It was just another of the cutting remarks he made when things weren't going his way. They had both been stunned to hear it would take another three awful days on this track to reach Katherine. Josie turned her mind to her son, since the subject of being English had come up. She wondered whether Ned, when he grew up, would regard himself as English or Australian.

Pine Creek was a dreadful place, just a shanty town, but fifty miles down the track they came to Katherine, and it was worse.

The buckboard shuffled down a road deep in fine dust, and they pulled over, fascinated, as six haughty, snorting camels plodded past with their Afghan keeper, who grinned cheerily, peg-teeth yellow against his swarthy skin. Around them the dusty land was pitted with man-made holes and hillocks; tree-stumps and rickety mine-cages littered the area for miles, and battered national flags hung dismally from poles and the last few desperate trees in the goldfields, as bizarre as bunting in a graveyard.

With the wretched journey behind them, Josie felt better, and she wanted to learn all she could about their new home. 'What are camels doing here?' she asked a miner who was riding alongside them.

'Ships of the desert, lady,' he told her. 'They can cross the dead centre to Adelaide ten times better than horses.'

'Amazing,' she replied, and Logan leaned over to ask where he might find Simon Pinwell, caretaker of the Gilbert Mines.

'He runs the Post Office store,' the stranger said. 'Next to the BAT office. You can't miss it, nothing much else in Katherine but the pub.'

He was right. Three rough timber shacks in a windswept street composed the town of Katherine, along with another single-fronted cabin which made claim to be the Commercial Bank.

'Katherine River City!' Logan commented bleakly, and Josie laughed, wiping the grime from her face. 'Quite a metropolis!'

The postmaster and storekeeper, Simon Pinwell, was a sharp-eyed, skinny little man with bow legs that were accented by the gun belt and heavy revolver slung around his narrow hips. He rode with them for a mile, on past the town, as he called it, to point out the Gilbert mines. That done, he indicated a building up among the trees. 'That's the manager's house,' he said. 'I've been expecting you, so I've had a couple of gins keeping it up to scratch.'

'Thank you,' Josie said. 'That's very good of you.' She was anxious to get home, to be in their own place at last. As they approached, though, she felt a twinge of anxiety.

Two black girls were waiting for them, eyes shining in anticipation, and Simon introduced them. 'That one's Spud, and she's Turnip.'

Josie was appalled. 'What dreadful names for such pretty girls. They deserve better than that!' Despite their tangled hair, the girls, in their teens, had lovely brown eyes, sleek anthracite skin and wide smiles that revealed strong, even teeth.

'They don't know any different,' Simon muttered.

'It doesn't matter,' Logan said impatiently, walking on to inspect the house. They stepped into a bough shelter which hid the main dwelling, grateful for the shade, and Josie noted absently the rough-hewn table and chairs, and two canvas deck chairs which would be quite pleasant for sitting out.

Logan pushed aside a strip of hessian covering the doorway and marched inside, only to stop dead. 'What's this?' he demanded angrily.

Their 'house' was a single room, with unsealed walls made of bark slabs. Overhead, the bare, corrugated-iron roof generated ferocious heat. An ornately carved four-poster bed stood by the window, over which was tacked cheesecloth in the absence of glass. The only other furniture able to fit into this small space was an old dressing table which had lost its mirror, and a lopsided wardrobe with the door hanging from one hinge.

'It's the manager's place,' Simon repeated defensively, not impressed by Logan's attitude.

'It's a bloody dump,' Logan fumed.

'Plenty worse around here,' Simon told them. 'Most of the miners live in tents and humpies.'

'Do you?' Logan demanded.

'That's different. I've got the store. I was a carpenter by trade, so

I built the store myself, with rooms on the back for the missus and me.'

Josie stared at the strange bed, as Simon marched over to it. 'This is a beauty. The only genuine four-poster in the district, the very thing for mosquito nets, best arrangement of the lot.'

Josie didn't feel up to commenting on that, there were so many other worries. 'They haven't put a floor in this room.'

Simon stamped on the hard surface. 'My word, they have. This floor is made of crushed ant-hills. Sets like concrete. I've got the same thing myself. You only need to water it down, give it a sweep, and you're all done.'

'Where's the kitchen?' she asked grimly.

'Out the back,' he told her. 'Too hot to cook inside. You got a good brick fireplace and a bush oven, all you need here, and there's a shower contraption out there, too. The outhouse is a bit further into the bush. You don't want it too close to the house – flies, you know.'

'The whole bloody place is disgusting!' Logan snapped, but Simon only shrugged.

'Nothing to do with me, mate, I'm just trying to help.'

'Yes, of course you are,' Josie said, steering him outside before Logan exploded.

Simon was obviously relieved to be on his way. 'Meet you at the mine in the morning, Mr Conal,' he said, 'and I'll give you the lowdown.'

'That bastard Gilbert!' Logan stormed. 'He said it was a house! And he expects us to pay rent! He won't get a penny out of me for this hovel.'

The Aborigine girls watched nervously as Logan and Josie prowled around outside their new abode. Tiny lizards scattered and dried leaves crackled underfoot as they took stock, wasps visited a mud nest on a wall, and all about them, the high, parched bush smelled of age, like an ancient tomb.

'Maybe Simon will build us a house,' Josie suggested.

'What the hell for? We'd have to pay for it,' Logan said. 'And then what? When the gold runs out, we'll be stuck with a house in a ghost town.'

There wasn't any actual decision taken to stay, they simply began to unpack the buckboard, and the girls lit the fire to boil the billy.

Once they were settled in Katherine, the days proceeded with awful monotony. Logan rode down to the mines early in the mornings and returned after dark. Determined to make the best of the primitive conditions, Josie tried to adapt, but time was her enemy. She had very little to do. As a farmer's wife she had skills, but now she lacked opportunity: no soil to till, as the press of trees prevented her from finding space for a garden. The scarcity of milk in the settlement meant that the churn she had brought with her lay idle, no butter- or cheesemaking to fill the hours. Pottering about the hut hardly ranked as housework, and the irony of the situation didn't escape her. Now she had two full-time maids and not enough work for one person, let alone three.

The girls, whose correct names she had discovered were Broula and Tirrabah, spoke some English and were eager to help, although they

132

regarded whitefellow chores as games. They washed clothes in the buckets with such rough enthusiasm that Josie predicted early disintegration, and they were happy to march back and forth from the well bringing water whenever Josie needed it. But there wasn't much else for them to do, so they wandered away, returning with fish, honey-ants, nuts, bush parsley and other native vegetables, for which Josie was grateful. With no farms to back up the settlement, only far-flung cattle stations, fresh produce was hard to come by.

In all it was a desperate, ugly place, except way over at the river which was bordered by deep tropical greenery. Josie saw it as a lovely oasis but was warned to keep clear for fear of snakes and crocodiles. She visited the store every day and bought something – an excuse to talk to Simon and Mrs Pinwell – and she searched vainly for some books or even something to sew, but this establishment didn't run to 'extras', as they told her. And, like everyone else except Josie, they were busy, so she couldn't loiter. The miners' wives worked the small claims with their men, and Josie seemed to be the only person in the town who had time on her hands. She put effort into her cooking, baking fresh damper every day, with plain cakes to compensate for the sameness of their diet, which centred on beef and bacon and more beef. Her days were long and dull.

On lethargic afternoons she sat in the bough shelter by their hut, listening to things. Just to things. The clang of metal, a chained dog howling like a tired child, thirsty trees rustling, leaves shifting uncomfortably, dust blowing, spattering on the iron roof like rain. Or was that wishful thinking? She wondered if the yearning for rain became so urgent that you could conjure up the sound. And eventually she slipped down in the canvas deck chair, to doze the time away.

Later, the dinner ready, she would brush up and wait for Logan to come home, although she never quite knew when to expect him. It soon became his habit to stay out drinking with the men on Friday and Saturday evenings. At first Josie understood. They all worked hard, they were entitled to the fellowship of a few rounds of drinks. Then she became impatient, hating the waiting time, watching while the dinner burned, or dried up, as she tried to keep it hot over the fire. At least Jack Cambray had come in for his dinner at dusk, regular as clockwork, and *then* gone out for his nightly drinking vigil. Logan was just the opposite. He stayed longer and longer at the pub, and when his homecomings became drunken staggers she finally forced herself to confront him. 'I'm not going to put up with this any longer! I'm entitled to some consideration! And don't you realise that with liquor such a price out here you're wasting an awful lot of money in the pub?'

'I can afford it,' he muttered, pushing past her. 'What's for dinner? Stew again?'

'No. I made a steak and kidney pudding. Logan, I do wish you'd come home on time. It gets very boring here on my own.'

'That's why I don't come home,' he snarled. 'You're boring.'

'Oh, no!' she said. 'I won't allow you to use me as an excuse to stay out boozing.'

'I'm not boozing, I'm talking business. You don't seem to understand my responsibilities. You sit here doing nothing all day and begrudge me a drink with my mates, when we've been climbing down those filthy mines, working our insides out.'

The arguments continued, achieving nothing except ill-will, so Josie stopped criticising, blaming the town and its male-dominated society. They wouldn't be here forever, she concluded, and she did love Logan. It was foolish to aggravate him. She knew he was doing his best, and managing three mines was a responsible job. Eventually they would leave Katherine, and then they could resume normal living.

6

Living on a station, Sibell soon found, was vastly different from the cosy Delahunty farm, mainly because of the scale of everything. She seemed to have entered a world of exaggeration. Gangs of men – station hands, stockmen and boundary riders – rode large raw-boned horses, herds of big wild-eyed cattle roamed the land, tall fences enclosed a maze of cattle yards and horse paddocks, and every so often, riders, whips cracking, would come racing across the back country with a mob of wild horses which they would then trap in camouflaged compounds.

Maudie was always out there, working with the men, often absent for days at a time traversing the huge property, but Sibell stayed close to home. Charlotte still loved to ride, so Sibell accompanied her on early-morning jaunts down the main track or out to the colourful lagoons lit by pink and purple lotus-lilies, home for myriads of beautiful birds, from pretty finches to graceful brolgas.

'One day I must show you,' Charlotte said, 'the bora ring near the homestead. I think it must have been a meeting place for blacks once. A corroboree ground of some importance. I find it interesting, but the station blacks won't go near it.'

'Why not?' Sibell asked.

'I can't find out. Something must have gone wrong there a long time back. A lot of these people are what they call emu totem, and they say it is a sacred emu stamping ground. But Zack says he's never seen emus within a day's march of the place.'

The two women worked in the office until noon, sorting out Charlotte's papers and accounts as well as the station books, and Sibell wrote letters dictated by Charlotte. Her letters were mainly to her solicitor and her stockbroker in Adelaide. 'My hobby,' Charlotte told Sibell. 'I'd like you to learn to keep an eye on them for me.'

'I don't know anything about stocks and shares,' Sibell said.

'Won't hurt you to learn, my girl. I have a lot of money invested in mining and shipping. And bank bonds.'

She did, indeed. Sibell gradually discovered that Charlotte was a very wealthy woman. She owned the station, and a house in Palmerston which she referred to as 'the beach house', and her investments, as far as Sibell could ascertain, were worth around two hundred thousand pounds. No wonder she could afford to spend so freely on this house. She was always studying catalogues and filling out orders which would take up to six months to be delivered. The transport charges alone were outrageous. But Charlotte wasn't concerned. 'I saw plenty of stations in Queensland, and it has been my life's ambition to be mistress of a station homestead. Now that I've finally made it, Black

Wattle will be as grand as any of them. Which reminds me, I must get a piano.'

'A piano?' Sibell gasped, wondering how on earth they'd get a piano out here.

'Yes, they say the Steinway is the best. Every family should have a piano.'

'Oh, yes, of course,' Sibell mumbled.

Every evening, when they were home, Zack and Cliff would report in to the office to give Charlotte information on the day's events – stock numbers and movements, blocks cleared, staff matters, all sorts of things, even daily temperatures and water-levels in the various creeks. Sibell was amazed at the detail that went into the station journal. 'They had to do this themselves until I came along,' Charlotte said, 'but they reckoned they never had time to do the job properly, so I took over. The journal is important, it's the history of the station, as well as a record of the stock – which is all they want to know.'

She rarely saw Zack, Cliff and Maudie during the day, since they were up and out at dawn, but they all gathered for dinner at night. Zack was cool, laconic, with a quiet wit, but Cliff was more flamboyant, always joking and teasing, very much like his mother, Sibell thought, who was an energetic person with a loud, infectious laugh. She had never met a woman of Charlotte's age who was so full of fun and yet could be so devastatingly direct.

At the table, Cliff teased her for 'talking with her hands': it wasn't unusual for Charlotte to knock over a wine glass. 'If your eyesight gets any worse, Ma,' he laughed, 'we'll have to tie your hands or we won't have any glasses left.'

Sibell thought that remark was rather callous, but his mother was amused. 'Blow the glasses,' she retorted. 'I'll be too busy trying to find the food on my plate!'

Maudie talked easily with the family, and she smiled at Sibell, but it seemed to Sibell that her smile held a mouthful of nails. Apart from an awareness that Maudie in some way resented her, Sibell quite liked being with the Hamiltons, but she envied their self-assurance, which seemed to emphasise her own lack of confidence. She was still shy when the men were around, and she knew they found her rather stiff-necked, because Charlotte went out of her way to include her in their conversations, a bit too obviously at times. Her upbringing hadn't prepared her for their irreverent talk, their utter lack of respect for everything she held dear. Clerical people were God-botherers. Politicians were crooks. Sheep-farmers were derided. The gentlemen of the BAT were pompous fools, and the Royal Family was a joke. Only Queen Victoria was spared – they loved her, and often drank her health. Sibell supposed that was something.

She wryly observed that, although she had hated the Gilberts, she had fitted in more easily to their formal lifestyle, which was light years away from this dusty frontier existence, despite Charlotte's attempts to soften their lives with home amenities. The informality of the station confused her, what with an excitable Chinese cook, bewildered black housemaids, and the noisy family. Zack and Cliff made enough noise for ten when they were home: they laughed, shouted, argued, tramping around the house or slumped out on the veranda with their long legs propped up on the rails. And worse, to Sibell's embarrassment, they didn't seem to own dressing gowns! They strode around to the bathroom with hardly a stitch on except for towels slung about their hips, and no one seemed to care, not even Charlotte. Sibell became expert at dodging them in the passageways to hide her blushes.

And so, weeks passed, and although there were always eruptions and incidents out and about on the station, Sibell was cocooned from problems, attending to her work and pottering around on her own when Charlotte took her afternoon nap. It worried her that her own sleep was still disturbed by nightmares, and she would wake trembling and afraid. She kept telling herself that there was nothing to be frightened of, that she was safe here, but every morning she would wake filled with an appalling sense of dread.

'Are you all right, Sibell?' Charlotte asked her one day. 'You look peaky.'

'I'm quite well, thank you.'

'That's good, but if anything is upsetting you, Sibell, you spit it out. It's bad to brood on things.'

'No, there's nothing. Really.' How could she let these vigorous people know that she suffered from bad dreams, like a baby?

'If you're worrying about the job, don't,' Charlotte said. 'You're a big help to me, and I enjoy your company. You should regard Black Wattle as your home as long as we can keep you.'

'Keep me?' Sibell echoed. 'Where else would I go?'

Charlotte laughed. 'My dear girl, once word gets out that there's a lovely single young lady living at Black Wattle, suitors will be beating a path to our door.'

'Oh, I don't think so . . .'

'They'll be here, mark my words. I wouldn't be surprised to see you married to one of our cattle kings one day if you stay in the north.'

In the massive silence of her room that night, trying to read, trying to stay awake, while the whole world seemed to be at a standstill, Sibell dismissed Charlotte's predictions as irrelevant, just a kindness: she didn't believe she belonged on a station in any capacity except as she was, an assistant, a companion to the lady of the house. On the other side of the compound was a long barracks and cookhouse, home for all those horsemen who tipped their hats to her as they passed by, but their exact roles out there in the wilds were a complete mystery to her and, she expected, would remain so.

Visitors did come to the station. Always men. Horse-breakers came for a couple of weeks at a time, causing a great deal of excitement. Whinnying, storming brumbies were brought in from the bush, and all other activities on the station seemed to be suspended as everyone gathered to watch the action. Sibell hadn't realised how many Aborigines lived on the station, but they all turned out for this occasion, as keen to watch the sport as were the 'whitefellers.'

Sibell secured an excellent vantage point, perched up on a high

137

fence, with Charlotte on one side of her and Netta, the housemaid, on the other. Those not fortunate enough to find a seat on a fence crowded at the rails, peering through at the dusty arena with excited anticipation.

The breakers went about their work steadily, methodically, day after day. The main interest fell on the high-flying fighters, the wild horses that valiantly resisted taming. This was the chance for local horsemen to prove their skill, and there was no lack of volunteers.

Men rode over from other stations to compete, joined by watchful horse-dealers. The violent spectacle fascinated Sibell, since the magnificent horses prowling and pawing the sturdy pens were an awesome challenge for bareback riders. She'd never seen horses like this before: to her, they had always been tame animals, sometimes flighty, but bred to the bridle. These mounts were downright dangerous, not above biting, shrieking and lashing out with all the power of their muscular legs.

Rider after rider was thrown in seconds, smashed against the fences, hurled under pounding hooves, or chased out of the ring to the cheers and derision of the crowd. And there were injuries – some of the riders limped out, and two had to be carried away.

Charlotte grew more nervous as the men began to call for 'the bosses': it was time for the Hamiltons to make their mark. She knew that Zack and Cliff, as bosses, were expected to do better, to give, here and now, a good, hard reason for their authority over the rest.

With only a hessian halter between him and the ignominious earth, Cliff mounted a black stallion which was wedged into a narrow pen, and flew atop it into the ring, while the audience counted the seconds. No show-riding here: Cliff hung on to the leaping, bucking horse across the centre, racing wildly, dangerously at the fences until, at last, with a sudden, jolting halt, the stallion dropped swiftly to its knees, and Cliff was thrown over its head.

And then it was Zack's turn. Blond hair flopping over his face, he was up there on the flailing black horse, hanging on to the halter but maintaining his seat by the strength of his legs, which were gripped around the horse's wide girth. The stallion reared and whirled in a dizzying circle, like a dog chasing its tail, yellow teeth snapping fiercely at the rider's leg. It arched its gleaming body and sprang high on all fours, hind legs lashing out repeatedly as it careered around the ring. Just when Sibell thought Zack was winning the struggle, the wily horse threw its great weight crashing to the ground beside a fence, hoping to trap and crush the rider. Zack leapt clear.

The audience whistled and yelled as Zack retreated and the snorting animal climbed up, unhurt, to take off in a triumphant bucking tour of the ring.

Zack had stayed on longer than Cliff, so he had won the contest on this horse, and Sibell watched the men laughing, jostling, congratulating him as bets were settled. Sibell thought it was all good-natured fun, but as they walked away, she heard a sour note. It was Maudie. 'You should have won,' she was saying to Cliff. 'You wore him down and made it easy for Zack.'

138

Sibell thought the remark was rather silly, since even now the horse looked far from tired. Those two short rides would hardly affect the strength of such a powerful animal, and she expected Cliff to laugh, but he did not. He was watching Zack with an expression of sullen resentment that disturbed and disappointed her.

Charlotte had not missed the incident. She touched Sibell's arm. 'Now you see why I still own the station,' she said. 'You can't keep two bulls in the one paddock. Cliff is starting to challenge Zack's authority. It's time to look around for another station.'

'Another one?' Sibell said, astonished. 'Surely this is big enough for two?'

'Not for two bosses. It confuses the men. This had to come, it's no surprise. I'll tell Zack to start making a few enquiries.'

'Which one will stay here at Black Wattle?'

'They can decide that for themselves.'

Other visitors arrived at Black Wattle. Rangy cattlemen, stock-buyers, government officials, and a friend of Charlotte's, Doctor Brody. The younger men hovered awkwardly around Sibell, who found excuses to retreat at the earliest possible opportunity, since the Hamiltons seemed to find their attentions a source of great amusement.

On Saturday nights, the foreman, known simply as Casey, came over from the men's quarters to have dinner with the family, obviously to establish his seniority in the station pecking order. He was a tow-headed Irishman, about fifty, and a real bushman, but by no means intimidated by the homestead rules.

After dinner they played cards, rowdy games with money on the table, and they insisted that Sibell join them.

'I can't play cards,' she had said at first, but they made her learn, and she began to enjoy herself, especially since she became quite good at the game of poker, and often won.

'It's that poker face of hers,' Cliff teased. 'You never know what she's thinking.'

'Not really,' she said. 'I have to concentrate. I'm not used to cards. My family didn't believe in gambling.'

'I wouldn't say that,' Zack drawled. 'They took a helluva gamble coming out here.'

Later he found Sibell to apologise. 'I'm sorry,' he said. 'That was a thoughtless remark of mine about your parents. I hope you'll forgive me. A bloody stupid thing to say. I just meant that any new venture is a gamble, or something like that . . .' His voice had dropped to an embarrassed mutter.

'It's quite all right,' she said, touched by his solicitude, seeing a new side to this aloof man. Later, though, she brooded over his remark. She supposed it had been a gamble, of a kind. And they had lost.

'But one of us survived,' she whispered grimly. 'One of us has to succeed or it will all have been for nothing.'

A dingo howled in the distance, and to stave off her depression, Sibell sat on her bed to count her winnings. Fifteen shillings and sixpence. Poker, she decided, was a very entertaining pastime.

*　　*　　*

139

One Sunday morning, she was sitting out under the trees, reading to Wesley and his two enthralled nursemaids, when Cliff called to her, 'Hey, Sibell! You're wanted out the front.'

Surprised, she stared at him. 'Who wants me?'

'I don't know,' he replied. 'Bring the nipper.'

She took Wesley's hand, the two girls following, and walked around to the front gate, where a small group, including Charlotte, Zack and several of the men, was gathered.

'What's happening?' Sibell asked, bewildered. 'Who wants me?'

Cliff picked up Wesley and put him on his shoulders. 'Take a look down there.'

Sibell turned, to see Casey coming towards them, leading a glossy chestnust horse with a blond mane. Around its neck was a gleaming green and gold garland of black wattle.

'What a lovely horse,' she said, thinking she'd been invited to view one of their prize mounts.

'It's yours,' Charlotte said.

'Mine?' Sibell was stunned.

'Yes. We decided you should have a horse of your own. Her name is Merry.'

Sibell rushed forward to pat the horse, and then back to throw her arms around Charlotte. 'Thank you! I can't get over this! It's so good of you! And what a beautiful horse, she's so pretty!'

With everyone watching, she had to ride the horse up and down, listening to instructions from the smiling audience. When she dismounted, Zack made a mock-formal speech. 'We don't give good horses to just anyone,' he announced, 'especially to strange English girls who wander on to our property, but I think this one has earned her spurs. What do you say?' They all clapped, and he added: 'Besides, Merry here was born on Black Wattle Station, so she knows her way home. When Sibell gets lost, we won't have to go looking for her.'

As they dispersed, Charlotte's horse was brought around from the stables. 'Do you want to take Merry out now?' she asked.

'I'd love to,' Sibell said.

'I'll show you the bora ring,' Charlotte told Sibell, after they'd travelled cross-country for a while, heading for some thicker bush.

On closer inspection, this was trackless open forest, and the horses trod easily between the trees, light filtering from above through a tracery of leaves. As they moved deeper into the stillness Sibell experienced a sense of unease. It seemed like a lost world, with weird green creepers dropping from the very tops of the trees, smothering branches and hanging across their paths. They pushed them aside and kept going, the horses skirting strange squat trees that jutted up from the scrappy grass.

'We call those trees black boys,' Charlotte said, 'for want of their proper name. They seem to be a cross between ferns and palms. Casey says they're ancient plants.'

Sibell looked around her anxiously. 'It's all so empty,' she said, but Charlotte laughed.

'Don't you believe it. The animals here are nocturnal, furry little rascals. Casey knows all about them, you should get him to bring you out here one night.'

'Oh, yes,' Sibell replied politely. She couldn't think of anything worse than being in this place at night.

When they came to a clearing Charlotte dismounted, hitched her horse to a tree and walked around, pointing at carved stones like small tombstones. 'See here,' she said, 'this is the bora ring.' She pulled matted grass away from a stone. 'They're almost buried now, but if you look hard enough you can find them. They form a circle. I'm probably standing in the middle right now.'

'Do they have any inscriptions?' Sibell asked, riding around the out-skirts.

'Oh, Lord, no. The Abos don't use writing. Only cave paintings and word of mouth to pass on their history.'

Sibell was disappointed: there wasn't much to see after all, only crumbling old stones. But since Charlotte had chosen this spot to rest, she decided she might as well dismount too, and made her way over to a fallen log that lay at the edge of the towering old trees.

'How's the horse?' Charlotte asked.

'She's a delight to ride – so even – and she seems to know what she's doing in the bush. She found her way through there very daintily.'

'That's good. By the way, we're not Indian givers. If you decide to leave at any time, you can take her with you.'

'That's very kind of you. Not that I'm going any place.'

'You like station life?'

Sibell laughed. 'From where I sit, I'm fine, but I'm no Maudie. I'm not cut out for the real jobs out here.'

'Don't be so sure. If the north wants to progress, we have to encourage women to settle, and stations needs both types.'

'Which are?'

'Well, Maudie's one for the hard grind. She mucks in, she's as good as any station hand, as solid as a rock.'

'And the other type is the useless one?'

'Lord, no. The other one brings the lighter touch. She has to turn a rough-house into a home, and set a standard, not only for the men, but for the children coming on. Someone has to educate them.'

'But if they haven't got Maudie's skills, they'll be as helpless as I am. I wouldn't be game to go any further than the gate on my own, and I've been warned often enough.'

'Yes, we'll have to remedy that,' Charlotte grinned. 'But as for the rest, life's a good teacher. What do they say? Necessity is the mother of something?'

'Invention.'

'Yes, that's it. Come on, we'd better get back.'

A few days later, Sibell noticed that an entry had been made in the station diary indicating that the chestnut mare, Merry, was the property of Sibell Delahunty. They also kept a stud book, and she looked up Merry to find that she was a two-year-old out of a mare called Ladybird, sired by Stonehenge. That reminded her of the bora ring. Such a lonely place. She wondered how many tribes of blacks had met there over the centuries, what they had discussed and why it had been abandoned.

She was pleased to see that, like everyone else who worked here, her wages were totalled each week so that she could draw on them if she wished, and it pleased her to watch the balance growing. She was suitably employed and was earning week by week, a satisfactory situation, if only she could rid herself of her terrible fits of depression.

Charlotte's certainty that she would eventually marry and settle in The Territory was disconcerting, reminding her of the speculation that she might be a prospective bride for Zack. That made her all the more determined to avoid him as much as possible.

Not that she saw much of Zack, and they were rarely alone. He treated her as he did Maudie, a big brother, usually pleasant in a remote sort of way, though occasionally grumbling at them.

'I can't find my socks,' he complained to Sibell one day. 'A house full of women and a man can't find any socks!'

Familiarity had caused her to lose her shyness, and the old Sibell was beginning to emerge. 'Then you'll have to go without, won't you?' she replied, making no effort to assist in the search.

'I suppose I will,' he said glumly, so she relented and found him a pair in the wash-house, only to return to find him laughing at her.

'That shifted you, didn't it?'

Mostly, though, he was a presence who stamped through the house intent on his own affairs. Sibell liked him – everyone liked Zack – but it was plain that he was boss of the walk. He had a voice like thunder when things didn't go his way, and from the house they could hear him roar at the men above the usual station clatter.

It wasn't Zack who bothered her, it was Cliff. He was far too familiar when no one else was around, and he always seemed to be looking at her. He often winked at her as if they had a secret between them, and of an evening, when they all sat outside in the cool darkness, without lanterns to attract insects, he would brush by her, surreptitiously managing to touch her on the shoulder or on the knee. Apart from resenting his attentions, Sibell was nervous that Maudie might notice. Maudie, whom she'd seen racing that big brute of a horse of hers, chasing cattle, the stockwhip cracking! God! The last person she would want to offend would be Maudie Hamilton! Sibell felt she ought to speak to Cliff, to ask him to desist, but she had nothing specific to complain about, and there was always the possibility that she was imagining his interest.

In all, though not madly happy, she did feel a lot calmer at Black Wattle, and she was regaining her confidence. The nightmares were still with her, but not as frequent, and she began to believe they would eventually disappear, since her luck had changed at last and she could stop worrying.

But, as she eventually told herself, she might have known this new-found calm couldn't last. She was a real jinx. Something always went wrong, and it happened so suddenly.

A rider came through with satchels of mail for the station, always an event at Black Wattle, and Sibell helped Charlotte to sort letters, magazines, newspapers and Charlotte's joy, the mail-order catalogues.

She bundled up papers and letters for the men and took them over to the cookhouse where she handed them to Harry, their cook, for distribution. Not needing to hurry, she stayed to chat with Harry, watching as he pounded huge lumps of dough for bread or damper, she wasn't sure which, then made her way back to the office.

Charlotte had opened her mail and was sitting studying several pages, so Sibell didn't disturb her. She checked a pile of newspapers, all weeks old, and was pleased to see they were in correct chronological order. No one minded, out here, that the papers were out of date, but they did like to read the news in order.

She heard Charlotte gasp, and as she turned, interested in what Charlotte may have read, the older woman moaned and began clutching at her chest.

'What's wrong?' Sibell almost screamed in fright, as right before her eyes, Charlotte's face turned an awful blotchy yellow and blue. She seemed to be gasping for breath.

Sibell snatched Charlotte's glasses from her face and undid the collar of her dress. 'What's the matter?' she cried. 'Charlotte! What's wrong?' But she was slipping from the chair now, groaning in pain, and all Sibell could do was hold on to her, to break her fall, as she dropped to the floor.

'Netta!' she screamed. 'Netta!' And Netta came running. She flung herself down by Charlotte, who was clutching Sibell's hand as if to ride out the pain, fighting for breath.

Netta was crying. 'What's up with Missus?'

'I don't know,' Sibell cried. 'She's having some sort of attack.' And then Sam Lim rushed in, having heard the commotion. He pushed Netta aside and unbuttoned the front of Charlotte's dress.

'She need big-air breathing,' he hissed, pumping on her chest.

'Go find boss,' he shouted at Netta, who dashed away.

Charlotte's eyes bulged with fear as Sibell put a cushion under her head. 'Don't panic,' she whispered. 'You can breathe, you can. Just go slow!' She hoped she could, she prayed she could, feeling so helpless as Charlotte lay stricken in front of her, saliva dripping from her mouth.

Casey was the first to arrive, charging into the office, stunned. He and Sam Lim lifted Charlotte on to a couch in the parlour. 'Get some scissors!' Casey yelled at Sibell, who was standing by, so frightened that she was slow to react.

'What for?' she asked.

'Get them!' he shouted, and she ran.

He cut away Charlotte's bodice, and Sibell stared, shocked that a man should take such liberties, until she saw he was cutting swiftly through her corsets as well. 'Bloody stays,' he was muttering. 'Beats me why women have to wear the damn things! That should give her some relief.'

Sibell brought a rug and Casey tucked it around Charlotte. 'There now, mate,' he was saying to her. 'Settle down. The worst is over, you're gonna be all right. You just stay still there, and Missy here will look after you.'

He went quietly out of the room, and Sibell, feeling jittery, sat by Charlotte, brushing strands of hair from her face and using the soft, damp cloth Sam Lim handed her to cool Charlotte's forehead. She was glad Sam Lim was with her, afraid the attack would begin again.

And then they were all home, hovering around, worried. Casey had sent two riders out to try to locate Doctor Brody, but in the mean time, all he could tell Zack was to keep her comfortable.

Not wanting to intrude too much in the sick room, with Zack and Cliff in a state of shock, Sibell went into the office to try to tidy Charlotte's desk. It occurred to her that something in the mail might have triggered the attack which Casey said seemed like a heart attack. She found a letter from Charlotte's solicitor in Adelaide, and as she read the carefully penned pages, she subsided slowly into Charlotte's chair.

The letter was a month old, and it carried bad news. Two banks, the Provincial and Suburban Bank in Melbourne, and the better-known Australian and European Bank, had both closed their doors after a run on their coin. Charlotte's stockbroker, Mr James J. Percival, had invested in the latter bank, and when anxious shareholders had insisted that he give a reckoning of their situations, a further problem had been uncovered. The solicitor felt it was his sad duty to advise Mrs Hamilton that, on inspection, Mr Percival's dealings were found to be dubious. Mr Percival had in fact forged share certificates and kept his clients' money for his own purposes. As these matters unfolded, Mr Percival had suddenly disappeared and no trace of him could be found to date.

The solicitor, signed, Your Obedient Servant, J. Leighton-Waters, had personally examined Mrs Hamilton's portfolio, and found it to be near to worthless, and her balance of seven thousand pounds in the A&E Bank to be lost.

'Oh, my God!' Sibell whispered, shoving the letter into a drawer, well out of sight.

When Doctor Brody came, confirming that Charlotte had indeed suffered a severe heart attack, Sibell took him aside and showed him the letter.

He put on his spectacles and read it slowly, and then looked at Sibell, his eyes weary. 'Yes . . .' he said, 'yes . . . scoundrels all of them, fiddling about with other people's money, never seeing the real damage they do. Ah, poor Charlotte, a letter like this, it's enough to give anyone a collapse. Don't be talking to her about this, let her bring it up in her own time. It'll take a while for her to get over the shock of being broke.'

'But she's not broke, not really,' Sibell said. 'She still has the station.'

'Sure she has, and the boys are doing just fine, but Black Wattle, like Rome, was never built in a day. She didn't buy the property with a pin and a bit of string, like a lot of them have. She had the capital behind her to keep the operation well funded.'

'She spent a lot of money on this house, shouldn't she have done that?'

'It's a great thing she did, or she'd have lost that cash, too.'

'I guess she would have. But she hasn't got anything to worry about. Zack and Cliff know what they're doing, they'll keep going. After all, it's only money that is lost, the family still has their home and livelihood.'

'Only money?' he snorted, cross with her. 'All very well when you're young, but Charlotte has just seen thirty years of hard work go down the drain. She hasn't got the time or the strength to do it again, that's the hurt.'

As Charlotte recovered, she was not the best patient, resenting her inactivity, demanding to know what was going on around her.

'All's well,' Zack said. 'Everything's under control, and Sibell is managing in the office. You have to stay in bed and rest.'

'Oh, stop fussing,' she said. 'I'm not ready for the marble angel yet.'

'I hope not,' he grinned.

She leaned back on the pillows and closed her eyes. 'I lost the lot, didn't I?' she whispered. 'What a damn fool I was to trust that bastard.'

'You weren't to know,' he sighed. 'He did well by you for years, and then he must have run off the track somewhere. These things happen.'

'Not to me they don't,' she said grimly.

'What are we going to do now, Zack?' she asked, tears welling in her eyes. 'Can we hang on?'

'Sure we can.'

'I wish I could believe that, but there are bills to be paid, and we haven't got any cash.'

'You know I wouldn't lie to you,' he said. 'We'll pull up. I'm going to start mustering a herd and take them south myself, down to the big markets. If I go, it saves the cost of drovers, and, besides, I can sell them myself at the best prices, with no middle man.'

'Cliff will stay here?'

'Yes. But in the mean time, if you're well enough, I want to take him to Pine Creek and down to Katherine.'

'I'm all right. I told you to stop fussing. What's in Katherine?'

'More and more gold miners, a good handy market. I'll have a talk with the butchers, and Cliff can deal with them direct while I'm away.'

She nodded, tiring, but as he went to leave, she called to him. 'You won't be away long?'

'No, only four or five days.'

'Good. Then you can take Sibell with you.'

'Sibell? What the hell for?'

'Because it's the only chance she'll have to get a break from here before next Christmas. I was going to take her into Palmerston for the annual race meeting, but that's out now.'

'But, Mother . . .'

'Don't "but" me. I want her to see a bit of the country.' She smiled. 'She hasn't the faintest idea where she is, you know, and she ought to see those towns.'

'Towns? I don't think they'll impress her.'

'A change is as good as a holiday. I need Sibell more than ever now, and it's not much to ask of you. Who else could take her? She'll be safe with you two, and Maudie can hold the fort in your absence.'

She saw that Zack was still preparing to argue, so she brushed a hand weakly across her face. 'I'm not feeling too well. Could you ask Netta to bring me a cup of tea.'

'Yes, of course,' he said, hurrying away.

145

As soon as Maudie heard the news, she confronted Zack. 'Why her? Why can't I go?'

'Because we can't leave Charlotte here with only Sibell in the house. And you have to keep the men working.'

'Casey can do that.'

'Casey can't stay in the house. And he's too soft on the men. We can't afford to let them slack off now.' He was annoyed with them all now, since Sibell hadn't welcomed the plan with much enthusiasm, either.

Sibell was in two minds about it. She would go, to please Charlotte, she supposed, and it would be interesting to see those towns and have a look at the goldfields. She was sure she could cope with the ride, especially since she was now so comfortable with her own horse, Merry. On the other hand, though, travelling alone with two men bothered her. She had even casually questioned the propriety of it with Charlotte.

'My dear,' Charlotte had said, 'this is a man's world. If you don't travel with men, you don't travel at all. I could send a black girl with you but that will only cause more complications when you get to the towns. There's a hotel in Pine Creek where you can stay, but they won't let gins in the door. Anyway, if you don't want to go, just say so.'

She was still debating with herself, when she heard Maudie arguing with Cliff. 'Casey should go, not you!' Maudie told him.

But Cliff objected. 'I man the bloody station, too,' he shouted. 'I'm not just a bloody stockman. Can't you get it through your head, Zack's going out looking for new contacts, Zack the boss-man! Well, I'm entitled to be there, too. I'm not just the also-ran.'

'I don't know why either of you have to go,' Maudie sulked.

'Because we're up against it, you bloody fool! Charlotte can't help us any more. We have to sell as many cattle as we can, and you better pray we have a bumper season of calves this year, because we're gonna need every bloody one of them.'

'All right, you go then, but I don't see why you have to take *her*.'

'Then you'd better argue with Charlotte about that.'

'Always Charlotte,' Maudie complained. 'If she told you to stand on your head in a bull-ring, you would. Zack's not the boss here, and neither are you. She is!'

Sibell moved quietly down the veranda and into her own room. She didn't want to hear any more. She resented Maudie's remarks about Charlotte, and she hated being called 'her'.

'Bad luck, Maudie,' she said to herself. 'If that's how you feel, I'm going!' She went to her cupboard and began taking out shirts and dungarees for the ride.

It occurred to her then that if anything happened to Charlotte, her position in the household would be shaky, given Maudie's attitude, and that reminded her of her own finances. She had received a reply from the insurer, advising her that compensation of more than a thousand pounds had been paid to Percy Gilbert, as her guardian. On Charlotte's advice, she had then written to Percy, demanding that the full amount be repaid

146

to her, since he had no authority to claim he was her guardian, and no legal entitlement to this money. Percy had not replied.

She decided to write to him again, and to post her letter in Pine Creek.

When the trio rode into the dusty gold-mining town, Sibell began to understand the status of the cattlemen. The two tall, bearded Hamiltons were instantly recognised, and men tipped their hats in good-natured salute. The manager of the BAT office came out to greet them, followed by his wife, who smiled dutifully as she was introduced. Sibell picked up the woman's sharp glance of disapproval at her male attire. Mrs Dowling was wearing a heavy black serge dress with a high, boned collar, long tight sleeves and a full skirt that trailed in the dirt. Sibell wondered how these women survived in this heat, the average temperature being well into the hundreds, and she was grateful for Maudie's common-sense approach.

They met the postmaster and his wife, and dozens of other people before they were installed in the Lucky Strike Hotel, a long, low, ramshackle building which Mrs Dowling assured them was the best in town.

Sibell stifled the laughter bubbling up inside her. Pine Creek a town? More like an open-house bedlam of rickety huts with a mad mix of residents: Chinamen hurried everywhere, their high-pitched chatter rising above the shouts of the diggers and the rumble of wagons, a blacksmith was hard at work, and drovers herded a mob of complaining cattle along the street, raising clouds of dust. Aborigines in tattered clothing were wandering aimlessly about, their dogs yapping at their heels.

'Are you all right?' Zack asked.

'Yes, thank you,' she gulped, trying not to offend anyone. 'I'm just tired.'

It seemed that the arrival of the Hamiltons was cause for celebration so they dined that night with the leading lights of Pine Creek at trestle tables set up under the trees, a stone's throw from the rowdy bar from which a procession of men emerged to pay their respects.

Zack laughed. 'You're the attraction, Sibell. There are plenty of beaux here. Which one do you want?'

But Cliff didn't take the intrusions so lightly, becoming more and more annoyed as eager men hovered around, hankering for introductions to Sibell. Finally, he told three young fellows to 'Piss off!'

'It's a free country!' one of them retorted, and turned back to Sibell. 'You're the prettiest girl who ever came to Pine Creek,' he told her. 'Are you staying long?'

'No,' she said. 'We're just passing through.'

Cliff jumped up and grabbed the man's arm. 'This is a private party, now get out of it!' But the digger shoved him away.

'You high and mighty squatters! Don't try to tell me what to do!'

In a swift reflex, Cliff punched him, and the digger shaped up: 'Right, mate, you asked for it!'

Shocked, Sibell looked to Zack. 'Stop them!'

But he went on eating. 'Why? Cliff started it, let him finish it.'

As the two men began to fight in earnest, it was the hotel-keeper's wife who intervened with a simple solution. She was a huge woman, almost as wide as she was tall.

Sibell jumped as a gunshot rent the air, and the two men stopped in their tracks. The woman ambled over, a rifle levelled at them. 'I don't allow no fighting here,' she roared, 'so you gents behave yourselves or both of you get out.'

Order was restored, but Cliff used the altercation as an excuse to stay by Sibell, monopolising her company until, irritated by his attentions, she went to bed.

The room was clean and plain, with just a bed and washstand, and one chair, but with no lock on the door. Sibell was nervous, with so many men around and the noise from the bar increasing. She climbed into bed, deliberately leaving the lamp on, certain she wouldn't sleep a wink. Of course, she did . . .

When she awoke, Cliff was standing beside her bed, bare chested, in just his trousers. For a few minutes, she thought it was morning, and struggled to clear her head, then she realised that the closed window was black, and the hotel quiet.

'What are you doing in here?' she demanded.

'Sssh!' he grinned. 'You'll wake the dead.' He moved on to the bed so fast, kissing her, his arms encircling her, that Sibell was taken by surprise. She pushed him away, trying to prise herself loose from his strong arms, but he was all over her, whispering, stripping aside the sheet which was her only covering in the heat, his hands slipping up under her nightdress.

Gritting her teeth, Sibell began to fight him, kicking and punching where she could, but she was no match for his strength. 'Come on, Sibell,' he whispered. 'You've been asking for this.'

'I have not,' she hissed angrily, afraid of waking the household 'Get away from me!' She knew now why Maudie carried a rifle, but she hadn't expected an attack from this quarter. A couple of times, Maudie had let Sibell try out the rifle, but she'd been hopeless, couldn't hit a thing. Maudie had said she ought to learn, but she hadn't bothered. A mistake.

His mouth was smothering her. 'You never minded when I touched you,' he was saying. 'You loved it. Be quiet, Sibell, let me love you now.'

And then she wondered why she had to be worried about anyone hearing them. Why did she have to care? Damn them!

'Cliff Hamilton,' she shouted. 'Get out of my room.'

Her shout had more impact than the gunshot. He leapt up, stunned. 'Shut up, you bloody fool,' he cried, attempting to cover her mouth with his hand. She twisted away.

'Cliff Hamilton!' she shouted again. 'Get away from me.'

He stumbled off the bed as Zack appeared in the doorway. 'What's going on here?'

Cliff was standing by the bed, fumbling with his pants. 'The bloody bitch!' he snarled. 'She invited me in here, and then changed her mind. Just trying to make a bloody fool of me.'

'Well, she's succeeded,' Zack said.

'He's a liar!' Sibell screamed as Cliff shot past Zack and disappeared.
'No need to tell the whole world,' he commented blandly.

Other people, roused by the commotion, must have come out into the passageway, for she heard Zack talking quietly. 'Just a family argument. No trouble. Go back to bed.' Then he looked in at her again. 'Are you all right?'

'He's a liar,' she insisted.' He came in here while I was asleep.'

'I asked you if you were all right.'

'Yes,' she said, calming down. 'I suppose so. How dare he attack me like that!' She clutched the sheet up to her neck. 'And you!' She turned her wrath on Zack. 'Standing there as if just nothing had happened!'

'What do you expect me to do? Start another fight? We'd all get chucked out.'

'Well, he is a liar!'

'I know,' Zack grinned. 'Now go back to sleep.'

'Are you going to leave me here alone again? With no protection?'

'That voice of yours is plenty of protection. You'd do an auctioneer proud.'

He closed the door, and left Sibell fuming.

The next morning, Sibell went shopping, unnerved now by the admiring stares of the predominantly male population. There had been no sign of Cliff at breakfast, and Zack only remarked to her that Cliff would apologise.

'I don't want his apologies!'

Zack had merely given that infuriating shrug of his. Nothing seemed to matter to him. 'You stay here,' he told her. 'I've got some people to see, some butchers and some cattle-buyers at the sales yards. And I might even get a shave and a haircut since we're socialising.'

'Can't I go to the stores?'

'Oh, yes. Sorry. Just don't wander away from the main street.' He took out his wallet and handed her two twenty-pound notes: 'Is this enough?'

'Yes. Thanks.' The day looked a lot brighter.

The Chinaman who owned the biggest store bustled about as Sibell wandered through the maze of goods, unable to find anything she wanted among the confusion. Hardware, clothing, tinned food, linen, firecrackers and jars of sweets were lumped together in no particular order, on and under tables and on wide shelves. She accepted the high chair he offered and called her requests to him as he scurried through the aisles, his little black hat popping up here and there. He knew about ladies' riding clothes, and produced calf-length divided skirts from a tea-chest. Never having come across them before, Sibell thought they were peculiar, but when she ducked behind the screen and tried on a beige skirt (they were all beige and all the same size), she found it to be rather swish. The Chinaman, who introduced himself as Mr Lee, was delighted to hear she was from Black Wattle Station, and insisted she buy boots to match, higher riding boots so no leg would show.

Sibell bought four skirts, two for Maudie, and another pair of the boots so that Maudie wouldn't be left out. And a silk kimono for Charlotte, and a long wooden toy train for Wesley. Then, wandering around this lucky dip of a store, she found some special items.

After quite a discussion with Mr Lee, she made her choice, then resumed her browsing, picking out a supply of combs and ribbons for the housegirls, and an assortment for herself. Mr Lee brought her tea in a tiny china cup, and her morning progressed happily.

Zack found Cliff at the sales yards. 'That was a bloody fool thing to do,' he said. 'You'll have to apologise to Sibell.'

'Like hell! It was her idea.'

'And I suppose that's why she yelled the place down.'

'Who knows, with stupid bloody women! Forget it, Zack, it's nothing to do with you.'

'What if she tells Maudie?'

'So? What's Maudie going to do? Be your age.'

'I'm trying to, you goat. We can't have these sort of ructions in the house.' Zack hadn't been surprised at Cliff making a move on Sibell, it had just been a matter of time. Wherever they went without Maudie, Cliff found women. He'd always been a womaniser, and marriage hadn't changed him.

'There won't be any ructions at home.' Cliff grinned. 'Sibell wouldn't say a word, she wouldn't dare.'

'You watch your step, mate,' Zack warned him. 'I don't think she's the type you should dare. That girl's got a wild streak in her, for all her genteel ways.'

Cliff burst out laughing. 'So you noticed, did you? You're not as dumb about women as you pretend! You've had plenty of time to stake a claim, Zack. I've given you a head start. I figured that, since you're not interested, it's my turn.'

'It's not your turn,' Zack growled, 'and it never will be. You keep away from her.'

'You can't have it both ways. If you're keen, why don't you marry her?'

Sooner or later he'd been expecting Charlotte to confront him with this question, but it was easier to explain to Cliff. 'She mightn't want me.'

'You've got nothing to lose by asking.'

'I've been thinking about it, but I don't think it would work. She doesn't belong out here. She's too citified. She just doesn't fit, and I don't think she'd last the distance.'

'Who cares? You'd have fun while it lasted.'

Zack's reaction was swift. He punched his brother, sending him flying against a water barrel. 'I should have done that last night,' he said, and because they were suddenly the centre of attention, watched by men hoping to see a fight, he pulled Cliff to his feet and marched him around behind a shed. 'Why do you have to be such a shit?'

'I was only fooling,' Cliff growled, rubbing his jaw, not anxious to push for a head-on fight with Zack, knowing he'd lose. 'You're too serious, that's your trouble. And if you're stuck on Sibell, why don't you marry her and get it over with?'

'Don't start that again! See if you can find Paddy Lynch, I heard he's talking about opening a butcher shop. He was one of the old man's mates, so he's our best shot.'

Zack tried to concentrate on the sales, tried to listen to the ringing voice of the auctioneer and the thump of his gavel, to see who was buying and at what price, but his thoughts were on his own problems. Barring any seasonal misfortune, which was just the luck of the draw, he could keep Black Wattle afloat. The present shortage of cash was only temporary: cattle sales this year would put them in front, and at long last the station would be able to stand on its own, without Charlotte's backing. He shuddered. Only just in time, though!

But he and Cliff had agreed that once Black Wattle was operating at full capacity, they would buy another station so that each would own a property and they could co-operate in practical ways. A double spread would also help them compete with the massive British-owned cattle stations in The Territory. This plan, approved by Charlotte, had depended on her financial support. Since that was no longer available, they were left with two choices: to postpone purchase of another property until they could afford to pay cash, by which time, Zack knew, land prices would have risen; or to borrow the stake with a mortgage on Black Wattle. They'd have to think this through very carefully. And so would he if he was thinking about taking a wife.

What would he have to offer Sibell? A woman needed her own home. Could he ask her to share with Maudie? And yet, on the other hand, if he had his own station, could he ask her to lead a life of isolation? He'd be away for weeks at a time: could she manage as the only white woman on a property, expected to be like Maudie and run the show in the absence of her husband? That was what he'd meant when he'd remarked that she wouldn't fit. His concern was for Sibell, he felt she deserved better. And he wished he could stop thinking about her. She was so sweet. She reminded him of sweetly perfumed frangipani. But then he smiled wryly. A strange comparison. The frangipani might have a delicate flower, but those stubby, stocky branches were tough. Break one off, plant it, and away it went, growing a foot a year! Why the hell did she have to come to Black Wattle and complicate his life? It was time to forget about her and concentrate on important matters.

They found Sibell, looking prettier than ever in a crisp new blouse and skirt, sitting serenely on the front porch of the hotel with the publican's wife, Kate Stirling. Through the open doorways, they could see that the bar was busy as usual, but not one of the customers even peeped at the ladies, not with big Kate in control.

She scowled at Cliff Hamilton and departed.

'You told her!' Cliff accused Sibell.

'I didn't have to,' Sibell said. 'She heard.'

As they pulled up chairs to join her at the table, she smiled sweetly at them. 'I've been shopping this morning.'

'That's good,' Zack said, obviously pleased to change the subject. 'What did you buy?'

'Oh, all sorts of things.' She put a battered leather pouch on the table.

151

'Mr Lee gave me this for nothing. A souvenir, he said: these are the bags they carry gold in.'

'You don't say.' Cliff's voice was heavy with sarcasm.

'I do say,' Sibell told him, 'but I have another use for it.' She drew out a gleaming Colt revolver and pointed it at Cliff. 'How do you like this?' she asked him, and Cliff froze.

'Put that bloody thing away!' He began easing out of his seat, but Sibell put her finger on the trigger.

'Sit down! And you stay back, Zack!'

'I have to tell you, Cliff,' she said quietly, the gun very still, 'I can't stand being bullied, and I won't be manhandled.'

'Is that gun loaded?' Zack cried urgently.

'Yes,' she said, still staring at Cliff. 'Apologies won't make up for your behaviour last night. I just thought I'd let you know that if you ever touch me again, you're going to hear a very loud bang.'

'Jesus wept!' Zack said, as, white-faced, Cliff pleaded:

'Take the bloody gun away from her.'

But there was nothing Zack could do.

'Have I made myself clear?' Sibell asked Cliff, who gulped, nodding.

'What's going on here?' Kate Stirling arrived with a tray of drinks. 'You shouldn't play with guns, Sibell.' She put down the tray and took the revolver. 'Christ Almighty, girl, it's loaded.'

'I know,' Sibell said, and Kate stared at them, then burst out laughing, guessing what had taken place. She emptied the chambers and passed the gun back to Sibell, together with the bullets.

'Drinks on the house,' she continued, handing them out. 'A nice cold gin squash for you, Sibell. Beer for Zack, and for you, Mr Hamilton,' she told Cliff, 'sarsaparilla.'

Sibell grinned: for the first time, she'd seen Zack shaken out of his cool composure, his indifference, and she realised that she enjoyed making him pay attention to her. Zack was, in fact, a very nice man. This mad episode that she'd dreamed up seemed to bring Zack into focus, and she looked at him as an awkward silence descended. Clean-shaven now, with his thatch of blond hair neatly trimmed, he was very handsome, and she felt a surge of affection for him.

But Cliff had the last word. He pushed aside the sarsaparilla and stood up. 'You were right, Zack,' he sneered. 'She doesn't belong with us!' And he stormed down the steps into the street.

His remark was a physical blow to Sibell, and it hurt so much she was shocked. Had Zack really said that? He made no attempt to deny it.

Kate tried to ease the situation. 'You young people,' she said, shaking her head. 'You get into all sorts of arguments. It's the heat and that bloody blue sky, never a change, that's the trouble.'

Zack drank his beer without a word, and Sibell was too upset to think of anything to say.

'Listen here, Zack,' Kate said. 'I was just telling Sibell, she shouldn't bother going on to Katherine. It's only diggings and the cable office so far, no accommodation worth the name, and the pub is only a sly-grog shop.' When Zack didn't reply, she kept talking. 'Mind you, the gorge is pretty, but it's too soon for young ladies to be going there. I'd sure like it if Sibell could stay on here with me for a few days. I'd appreciate the company. Why don't you lads ride down there, take a look around, and pick Sibell up on the way back?'

'It's up to Sibell,' Zack said, his face bleak.

Kate had invented that earlier conversation – they had not discussed the possibility of her staying on awhile at Pine Creek – but Sibell recognised the sense of it.

'Yes, I think I'll remain here for a few days.' And she couldn't resist adding: 'Then I won't be in your way.'

'If that's what you want,' Zack shrugged. He picked up his hat. 'I'll find Cliff. We might as well get going.'

They watched him leave.

'He's very fond of you,' Kate said.

'Zack? You're joking. You heard what Cliff said.'

'I did, but it's not the end of the world. Zack's like Charlotte, he thinks things through. The other one's always been a bit of a rake.'

Sibell was depressed. 'But Zack's probably right. Maybe I don't belong at Black Wattle.'

'Where do you belong?'

'I don't know.'

'Then give it time. It's my bet that Zack's thinking of you, not himself. He could be worried that a girl like you would end up a misery stuck out there. How many white women have you met since you've been there?'

'None.'

'Right! You're sheltered now, with Charlotte and Maudie, but don't set your sights on Zack Hamilton unless you're sure you can handle station life.'

'I haven't set my sights on Zack.'

'Of course not,' Kate laughed. 'By the way, do you know how to use that little pop-gun?'

'Not really,' Sibell said.

'I'll have to teach you, then, and in the mean time, never let me see you waving it around again. I nearly had a heart attack myself.'

Every morning as he trudged down to the mines, Logan cursed Charlie and his bright ideas. This particular morning he had a few more complaints. Miners took their turns at delivering their ore to the only battery in Katherine, and to protect their interests they stood guard over every inch of the process, watching carefully as the crushers and sieves did their jobs, so that the full measure of gold came through to them. It was a long, tedious process, often continuing overnight, and since Logan was tired, he allowed one of his men, Ted Taft, to stand in for him.

Ted Taft! If he could spare him, Logan would fire the fool, but with labour scarce, that option was not open to him. Taft had taken a bottle with him and ended up dead drunk, with the Gilbert gold shuttling by, unprotected from light-fingered battery staff.

It was fortunate that Simon Pinwell had walked into the battery and seen what was happening. He sent a runner to fetch Logan. 'You better take over yourself, mate. Your offsider here's in a sorry state.'

Taft wasn't just drunk, he was barely conscious. Logan picked up the bottle and sniffed it. 'Christ! What the hell has he been drinking?'

'Local brew,' Simon told him. 'They mix gin, kerosene, ginger and sugar and come up with a walloper!' He searched around and found another bottle, half full, and hurled it out into the bush. 'That stuff would make a rabbit bite a dingo,' he laughed.

Logan didn't think it was funny, nor did he appreciate the men's demands for Saturday afternoons off. 'Useless bloody lot,' he muttered to himself. But then again, by this time he knew that the real workers owned their own mines, and put their backs into them. His labourers were a shoddy lot.

There'd been trouble at the Gilbert mines right from the start. Several of the original staff had returned to work, but they'd brought lubras with them to push down into narrow shafts. Logan had banned that practice right away, then on payday had discovered that the former manager had claimed pay for the lubras, wages that the black women never received. The money was called 'Saturday shout', and was used to buy drinks for the miners at the end of the week. Logan refused to hand over money for nought, and his men missed out on the free drinks, which caused more grumbling.

The mines were producing well under his management, and neither Gilbert nor his agent had any complaints, so Logan was determined to stay on the job. Soon he would find the time to look about for pickings of his own.

But he could number a thousand things that made this place a hell on earth, not the least his constant worry about outlaws raiding the gold consignments as they were being taken by packhorse up to Palmerston. Then there was Josie! She had become a problem. In a different climate, this rough living wouldn't be so bad, but the heat was savage, food rotted, stinging flies filled the air, there were snakes everywhere . . . almost everything in nature conspired to make their lives a misery. Their lives, not just hers. And she begrudged him his few pleasures. Fortunately, she hadn't heard about the black gins they sneaked into the shed on card nights for a little extra entertainment.

As he approached the mine, he saw a familiar figure sitting on the single-rail fence. 'Good God!' he said. 'As I live and breathe, Jimmy Moon!'

'That old name now,' Jimmy replied quietly. 'Proper name here, Jaljurra.'

Logan stared at him: he looked older, road-weary, like many of the diggers. 'Where did you come from?'

'Been walkabout. Come all the way through the big desert, that mighty tough place. Comen on to whitefeller message shops.'

'The cable stations?'

'Sure. Follow that north to camp Stu-art.'

Logan nodded: that was another budding town on the Ross River.

'Got a job now, boss. Policeman at Stuart give me a job, send me on up here.' He seemed to find this hilarious. 'Working for police fellers now,' he laughed. 'Blacktracker number one.'

'Yes? Well, listen to me, number one blacktracker. You pinched my gun. Where is it?'

'Ah. Long time lost. Gone now.'

'You owe me then, you villain,' Logan said, not really concerned. 'Where's your wife?'

'No wife,' Jimmy said. 'No marrying, woman gone, run off.'

'That's bad luck,' Logan said. At that moment, Sergeant Bowles rode down the track.

'A word with you, Mr Conal.'

'Yes. What's doing?'

'I see you've met the lad here,' Bowles said, but before Logan could reply that he already knew Jimmy, the Sergeant continued. 'Did you tell Mr Conal the latest, Jaljurra?'

'What latest?' Logan asked.

'You know that kid who went missing? Young Snowy Dickensen? Well, it was Jaljurra who found him. We'd just about given up on the kid.'

Logan had heard of the six-year-old child lost in the bush for more than five days, and the great relief in Katherine when the child was brought in. 'You were the tracker?' he asked, and Jimmy nodded shyly.

'He's a bloody beauty, this one,' Bowles said. 'Tracked him in strange country, too – he comes from one of those desert tribes.'

Logan picked up a warning glance from Jimmy, and made no comment. So Jimmy was now Jaljurra, and a desert black. What the hell? Half the whites up here had false names, too.

'Is your consignment ready to go out today?' Bowles asked Logan.

'Yes, we've had a good run this month, and I'll be pleased to get it out of Katherine.' Logan kept the gold in a heavy safe in the makeshift local bank. It was far from secure, but he had no other choice.

'Well, it will have to stay put for a while longer,' Bowles said. 'My offsider, Constable Plummer, broke his leg showing off how he could ride Duffy's mad horse. He didn't last half a minute, so now I'm on my own. I can't leave here.'

'But it has to go,' Logan said. The Gilbert Company sent their gold to their agent in Palmerston, who immediately transferred it to a coastal ship that sailed for Perth from Port Darwin at the end of each month.

'The other miners are not worrying,' Bowles said. 'What's a few weeks?'

'They're not on a contract,' Logan argued. 'I have to get each consignment into Palmerston in time or I'll have Percy Gilbert on my back again.'

'Tell him this is the bush, not London Town.'

But Logan was an impatient man, and he knew what a 'few weeks' could mean out here. The gold would end up in the safe for at least another month, and everyone would know that two months' supply from the Katherine mines was on the road. Asking for trouble.

'You could still send it with the pack-mail,' Bowles suggested, 'but there's no escort. Unless you send a couple of your own blokes along.'

'Like hell I will! Those layabouts, we'd never see them or the gold again.'

'So you either leave it here with the rest, or you go yourself,' Bowles told him. 'Nothing else I can do. You'd only have to take it to Pine Creek: the police there will take it the rest of the way, as usual.'

That idea didn't appeal to Logan either. The two mail-men with their packhorses were no heroes, it was a two-day ride to Pine Creek, and he'd be riding shotgun on his own. A different proposition from the bush policemen, who knew the country, knew their duties, and were fearless crack shots.

'We go,' Jimmy offered. 'I go with Mr Conal.'

Bowles scratched his head. 'Yes, he could go with you. Take him and introduce him to the blokes at the Pine Creek station. They could use him, too.' He glared down at Jimmy. 'Don't you go walkabout on me – you come right back, you hear?'

'Yes, boss. Comen back with Mr Conal.'

Logan understood Bowles' reasoning. Good blacktrackers were in demand: the police would call for their services from hundreds of miles away, mainly to track criminals, and so they needed to know who was available to assist them.

That night he took Jimmy up to see Josie, explaining to him that they were now married, since Jack Cambray had died. He realised that neither he nor Jimmy was telling the whole truth, but in his usual way, he shrugged off the minor worry.

Josie was delighted to see Jimmy. She prepared a special fish dinner and asked him to join them. It was the first time he had ever sat down at a table with white people, and he was so impressed he insisted Josie show him how to use cutlery. Logan noted that it was quite a change to hear Josie laughing, as Jimmy, highly amused, struggled to master the knives and forks and spoons. It seemed he wanted to know everything in a hurry.

'Where's Ned?' he asked.

'In school,' she told him. 'In Perth.'

'Why you leave him back there?'

'He has to learn his lessons,' she said, an eternity of sadness in her voice. Jimmy nodded, silent now, not understanding.

To break the chill, Logan pointed to the worn skin pouch that Jimmy still had hanging around his neck by a thin hide cord. 'What's that?' he asked. 'You're still carting that bag around. What's in it?'

'Me,' Jimmy said simply.

'What do you mean, me?'

'Leave him alone,' Josie said. 'I think it's private. Tell us about your travels, Jimmy. Do you realise, Logan, that he has crossed the continent? From the west to the centre? I don't think many white men have done that.' She urged him to tell them about the country he'd passed through, about the tribal people he had met, and Logan wished she'd show a similar interest in the local people at Katherine. They had stories to tell, too, but she didn't want to hear about them. He sighed, and poured himself another whisky. A fine state they'd arrived at when his wife seemed to enjoy only the company of blacks!

Thunder rumbled in the distance, and a crack of lightning blasted the sky. They stopped to watch the deafening display, as bolts of fiery light split the darkness and thunder crashed all about them. Eventually, the thunder faded, but continuous sheet lightning turned night into day.

156

'Pretty good, eh?' Jimmy seemed disappointed the action was over.

'Useless damn storms!' Josie said. 'I'm frightened they'll start a bushfire. Never any rain in them.'

'Hey! Don't ask for rain,' Logan said. 'If we get too much, the mines flood.'

Jimmy stood looking out at the trees. 'Plenty rain up here,' he said.

'I'll believe it when I see it,' Josie told him. 'I haven't seen a speck of rain in months. You get to dream of rain.'

Maybe Jimmy misunderstood her. 'Big Dreaming country, this.'

'What do you mean?' Logan asked.

Jimmy replied in a whisper, 'Plenty magic. Strong magic country, this.' Then he changed the subject. 'When we go, boss?'

'Go where?' Josie was instantly alert.

'I have to go to Pine Creek tomorrow,' Logan said. 'There's no one else to take the gold in.'

'I see.' Her voice was terse. 'And when were you planning to tell me about it?'

'I'm telling you now,' he snapped, defensively because he had been postponing breaking the news to her. 'You'll be all right. The black girls will stay with you. I'll be away only a few days.'

'Only a few days? You're so damned offhand about everything, Logan. What am I supposed to do while you're away?'

'The same thing you do every day. Nothing!' He looked about him. 'That bloody Jimmy's done his disappearing trick again. I didn't even see him leave. He could have said thanks for his dinner.'

'Thanks isn't in their vocabulary,' she said tartly. 'If they allow you to do them a favour, it means they like you, and that in itself is a compliment. And they'd never ask a favour if they didn't like you.'

Logan was in no mood for her lectures on folklore: he was thinking he'd give Simon a few pounds to act as foreman at the mines while he was away.

The journey into Pine Creek wasn't so bad after all. They didn't have any problems on the way, and being able to ride freely, without the encumbrance of the buckboard, was a pleasure. His fear of bushrangers subsided to the extent that he was considering making this run more often. It was a good break from the daily operations of the mines, where he had to pitch in himself whenever they were shorthanded.

He handed over the gold at the police station, introduced Jimmy to the lawmen by his Aboriginal name, and strolled outside, pleased with himself.

Jimmy followed him, and stood fingering the old pouch around his neck.

'You'll wear it out,' Logan teased, but Jimmy was very quiet.

'Spirits talk,' he whispered. 'Chat-chat.'

'What's chat-chat? Are you talking like a Chinaman now?'

'No, woman comen. Woman close.'

'What woman?'

Jimmy looked puzzled. 'Dunno . . . singing strong but.'

Logan couldn't hear anyone singing, but then the blacks had several

157

meanings for singing in their mystic world, or so Josie said. All super-stition. A load of bulldust. He stepped down into the street and headed for the store, with Jimmy hurrying beside him. Then the blackfellow stopped in front of a hotel. 'That place,' he pointed. 'We wait now.'

'What for?'

Jimmy patted his precious pouch. 'This feller strong magic. He say wait here.'

Exasperated, Logan left him there. 'When you get sick of waiting, I'll be at the Chinaman's store.'

Moving back, Jimmy squatted on the ground beside a horse trough. He didn't know how long he'd have to wait, nor did it matter. With some-thing akin to a sixth sense, he was certain, beyond even the possibility of a doubt, that it was necessary for him to be there, and even before she emerged, his trance-like state had afforded him the knowledge of who to expect.

As Sibell walked out of the front door of the hotel, he felt no sense of surprise, simply acceptance. He ambled over and took off his hat in the polite manner of white men, and Sibell stared.

'Well! For heaven's sake. Jimmy! You pop up everywhere.' She ran down the steps to talk to him, and he answered all her questions with a grin.

'You got my horse yet?' he asked.

Sibell remembered. She had promised him a horse one day.

'No got the horse yet?' he asked sympathetically, sorry now that his request was causing her concern.

'No, not yet. But I did promise, and I will get one for you.'

'Ah, yes,' he replied. 'By 'm by.'

Sibell knew that 'by 'm by' meant 'later' to the blacks, but it was also an evasive term which could mean 'never'.

'No,' she said stoutly. 'Where I live, they have plenty of horses. I'll get you your horse, I really will.'

Jimmy let that pass. 'Mr Conal brung me up here,' he told her. 'I go get him.'

He darted away, and Sibell put her hands to her face to cover the blush. Jimmy had taken off before she could stop him. Logan! In Pine Creek? He was the last person she wanted to see. What if he'd heard that stupid story of hers? That he would be coming back to marry her. 'Oh, my God!' she said, wishing she could run away. Wishing she had gone to Katherine with Zack and Cliff. But what had Jimmy said? That he had come up from Katherine. 'Oh, my God!' she said again, and rushed back to the hotel veranda to sit down, before her legs gave out.

She would receive him here, pleasantly but coolly. And she would not encourage his company. What if Josie was with him? How awful! And what were they doing here? Her nervousness, always simmering close to the surface, threatened to overwhelm her, and she took quick, sharp breaths to force more air into her lungs, to fight off the choking sensation that, lately, seemed to have reappeared. Charlotte's collapse had shaken her, reviving old fears.

Sibell wished she were dead rather than having to face Logan, and that made her angry. By the time he came striding towards her, tall and handsome despite a dark beard, with those piercing eyes, so familiar, shining with anticipation, she had composed herself.

He sprang up and took her hand. 'My God! It is you! And don't you look marvellous?' He didn't notice her cold stare, or maybe he thought she was just as surprised as he was.

'Well, the country suits you, my girl. I've never seen you looking so tanned and healthy. But what are you doing here?'

'I'm with friends.'

'Marvellous!' he said again. 'It's such a pleasure to see you. Talk about the rose among the thorns,' he laughed. 'You certainly pretty up Pine Creek!'

Sibell's resistance crumbled. Flattered by his attentions, she found herself telling him that she was living at Black Wattle Station, boasting about Black Wattle Station to get the better of him, to upstage him in punishment for his behaviour.

'It's a huge property, and the homestead is so comfortable. Brand new, not like the pigsties on most stations. Counting the black housegirls, they employ about thirty people on the station, and I am the book-keeper.' It sounded better than secretary.

'That's great,' he said. 'I always knew you were the clever one.'

'The Hamiltons are absolutely charming,' she continued. 'I have my own room, my own horse – a gift from the family – and I can come and go as I please.' As she spoke, she remembered that it was Josie who had first mentioned Charlotte Hamilton, so she avoided mention of her by asking how Logan came to be up this way.

'I'm managing gold mines in Katherine,' he said. 'It's a dump of a place, but the salary is good and I can claim bonuses on the gold output. That gives me the incentive to make certain the mines pay.'

'How did you come by that job?' she asked, curiosity defeating her efforts to be distant.

'I work for the GGC. The Gilbert Gold-Mining Company. Your friends own it. The Gilberts.'

'Percy Gilbert?' Was there no end to these betrayals? 'You're working for him? That's the bottom of the barrel.'

'Beggars can't be choosers,' he shrugged. 'What the hell if I work for him or anyone else as long as they pay me well.'

'He owes me money, a lot of money. He misappropriated the compensation that should have been paid to me by the shipping company.'

Logan whistled. 'Did he now? I didn't know that.'

'I could present you with the bill and you could pay me through his offices here,' she suggested, but he shook his head.

'Come on, Sibell. You know I couldn't do that. Just keep after him for the money.'

'I am,' she said. 'But he never replies.'

'I'll see what I can do when I get back to Perth.'

'Would you do that for me?'

'Yes. It'd be a pleasure. But what are you doing now? Where are your friends?'

'Zack and Cliff,' she said, pleased that her friends were two men, 'have gone off into the countryside, exploring, I think, or selling cattle. I decided to stay here for a few days.'

'Couldn't be better. I did intend to ride back this afternoon, but I don't have to. I can go tomorrow. So that leaves us an afternoon to ourselves. Could you stand my company again?'

'I suppose so,' she said, trying not to appear too pleased.

'Why don't we go for a walk along the creek and do it in style this time? After that murderous trek we had to take along the western beach with starvation rations, I reckon we deserve a rerun.'

'How?'

'We'll take a picnic basket and some wine, nothing but the best. And we'll have afternoon tea in comfort and watch the sun go down.'

His enthusiasm was infectious. Why not? she thought. It would be fun. And even though there was still the question of Josie to be answered, she was comfortable, even happy, with Logan, as she had known for a long time she would be. A tinge of spite entered her mind, too. Serve Josie right: she had no real claim on him, he hadn't even mentioned her.

'Well!' Logan exclaimed. 'Your Mrs Stirling has done us proud. That was the best cake I've had in ages.' He sprawled out on the rug. 'Pour me another glass of that wine, Sibell. It's not bad, considering.'

She laughed. 'Considering she only stocks about half a dozen bottles of wine. They've got a better cellar at the station.'

'This station must really be some place. Are you going to invite me to visit?'

'You can come any time you like,' she smiled. She was feeling happy now, totally relaxed, better than she'd felt for a long time. Logan understood her.

'I could come back with the gold consignments,' he suggested. 'At the end of each month, the police guard goes from here to Idle Creek and then on to Palmerston. I figure Idle Creek Junction would be the closest landmark to your homestead. Do you know it?'

'Yes, it's a nowhere place.'

'I know. But I hear someone's building a store there now. Or probably a store-cum-grog-shop, but it's a start.'

Sibell had been paddling in the shallows. He reached over and stroked her bare ankle, and she shivered. 'We could meet at Idle Creek,' he said. 'Would you like that?'

She knew the real question was: did she like him stroking her ankle and running his hand gently along her leg? She nodded. 'Yes, I would.'

It seemed so natural, inevitable, that they should move closer together, that he should be looking down at her, lifting strands of her hair and twirling it around his fingers, lying beside her, propped on an elbow. 'Your hair is so beautiful,' he murmured, running his fingers across her lips. 'No, that's wrong, you're beautiful, Sibell.'

Then he was kissing her, and Sibell felt all her day-dreams had come true. He began to unbutton her blouse, but she took his hand, and held it. She was nervous of destroying this moment, but she had to know. 'What about Josie?'

'You know about her?' he murmured, caressing her again.

160

'She wrote to me from Perth. She said you were both going to Geraldton.'

'It didn't work out,' he said, kissing her again, his tongue searching for her response.

Sibell's heart surged. She turned aside, just a little, to whisper to him: 'I didn't think it would.'

What a perfect day! As Logan made love to her, so gently, so leisurely, knowing there was no hurry, hidden in this quiet grove, she gave way to the exquisite pleasure of his fondling, until, fully aroused, she was crying out for him with an urgency that both astonished and delighted her.

Later, his passion spent, he rested, holding her in his arms, but Sibell was reluctant to end their lovemaking. Finally, he fell back, laughing. 'You've worn me out. Look, there's the evening star.'

She looked up. 'Starlight, star bright . . . Do I get a wish?'

'That's the rules.'

'Then I wish . . . you'd make love to me again.'

'Sibell! You're insatiable.'

'Is that bad?'

'No, it's tremendous, but we'd better be getting back.'

She was wildly happy as they made their way back into the town, proud to be with Logan, making all sorts of plans in her head for their future together, hoping he would change his mind and stay in Pine Creek a few days longer.

As for Logan, the most important statement he'd made all day concerned Josie. He had said that it wasn't working out – though not mentioning the marriage – and now he felt it was true. The marriage was a failure, a mistake. Josie fretted too much, she whined, in fact. Sure, living at Katherine was no bed of roses, but fair go! He had to put up with the discomfort, too. And so did other women in the settlement. They worked, they laughed, they made their own fun. They were a cheerful lot, making the best of it.

But Sibell! She was something else! She was like a cat, in more ways than one: lithe, sensual, exciting. And, like a cat, Sibell always fell on her feet. A typical woman, she'd complained about having to live with the Gilberts after the shipwreck, but she'd lived well. And now she was ensconced on a station, being treated like a princess. That half-drowned brat he'd found on the beach had turned into a very classy lady, and a real stunner.

Logan knew now that Sibell was in love with him – he'd have no worries there – and he was mad for her. He had to have her.

But how to extricate himself from Josie? She was missing Ned. He should send her back to Perth. Why not? She couldn't argue with that. And then he'd be able to arrange a divorce. He took Sibell's arm, enjoying the open envy of the men who stared at this lovely woman.

Not only had Logan misjudged Sibell, he had underestimated his wife. Josie spoke her mind. If she did complain about Katherine, it was her way of coping. She cursed every damned thing that annoyed her, thus getting the anger out of her system. And she did talk to other women, who, while they might greet Logan in passing with a cheery wave, gathered together at the wells and washtubs to give the village of Katherine, and their men, a good going-over. They bitched to their own husbands just as much as she did: it kept them sane.

Josie didn't encourage visitors in their ugly hut at night, because she hadn't ever learned to entertain after the lonely years at Cambray Farm. Besides, entertaining here was only an excuse for the men to get drunk. What did sustain her was her genuine interest in the Aborigines. She loved to talk to Broula and Tirrabah, and she taught them more English so that they could relate their own stories to her. The Aborigine people fascinated her, and she was even learning words from their language. To Logan, this was a waste of time, but what was time out here?

She loved Logan, she loved him so much, and now that she had overcome the initial shock of Jack's suicide, she refused to countenance regrets, knowing she would have left him sooner or later. And Ned . . . She did miss him, but he was in good hands, better Perth than Katherine, where there wasn't even a school.

Logan didn't seem to realise that he irritated her at times, too, yet he saw himself as the hard-done-by husband, sulking or making for the grog shop if he was criticised.

Men! Josie smiled. She'd have to butter him up a bit more. It hadn't been so bad on her own after all. Quite peaceful, in fact. And now his homecoming was something to look forward to. She ordered a round of beef for roasting and paid an exorbitant price for some fresh vegetables so that she could cook a special dinner for him. They would survive the diggings, though Josie would never accept that this was normal living. Katherine was hell on earth, and she said so. Josie didn't believe in the stiff upper lip, she saw that attitude as a short cut to becoming a doormat instead of a wife. Again.

Zack was astonished to find Sibell in such high spirits when they returned to Pine Creek. She accepted Cliff's apology almost absent-mindedly, so lightly that Zack was suspicious. Of both of them. He wouldn't put it past Cliff to try again, except that next time he'd be more subtle. He was already turning on the charm.

And Sibell . . . He had watched her at home, where she was always eager to help, to do her best. That calm veneer, though, gave way occasionally, when, believing herself unobserved, she would sit with her hands clenched and her face set into a tight, grim frown. He'd mentioned this to his mother. 'She worries me. She looks so tense sometimes, sitting there pretending to read, all scrunched up as if she's waiting for the bookcase to fall on her.'

'That's understandable,' Charlotte had said. 'The girl has suffered a great shock. Losing your parents like that, it would be frightful, not to mention the shipwreck itself. These things take time, you should be nicer to her.'

But look at her now! The clash with Cliff had shown that the tense, nervy girl still had plenty of fight in her, and the few days with Kate Stirling had certainly cheered her up. Maybe, he admitted to himself, a break from the Hamiltons, even for such a short time, had been a tonic.

They were saddling the horses, preparing to leave Pine Creek, and Sibell was all a-bubble, chatting to Kate, making certain they didn't leave any of her purchases behind, the gun she'd bought safely stowed in a saddle-pack. She seemed to have forgotten that snide remark of Cliff's.

Zack still squirmed when he thought of it. And he couldn't even deny he had said she didn't belong. Explanations would have sounded pitiful and might have made things worse.

It was evident she didn't care, though, and strangely that made him feel worse than if she'd taken it to heart.

'You're in good form,' he said to her, and Kate laughed.

'Spring is in the air.'

'Since when?' Zack said, the sun already a ball of fire over the dry, faded bush.

'Didn't you tell them about your visitor?' Kate teased Sibell. 'A handsome gentleman came to see her.'

'Who?' Zack asked, surprised.

'A friend of mine from Perth,' Sibell replied, sweet as treacle. 'You wouldn't know him.'

'What's he doing here?'

'He's the manager of a gold-mining company,' she said grandly. 'I told him he could come to call at the station. You wouldn't mind, would you?'

Zack shrugged. 'Why should I?' He was irritated by Kate's crafty grin. 'Hurry up, Sibell, we have to be making tracks. And put your hat on.'

What little charm Katherine had was lost on Logan now, so he concentrated his energies on the mines. Josie seemed more amiable, or maybe he was in a better mood these days, still luxuriating in Sibell's loveliness. He couldn't put her out of his mind.

'I was thinking,' he said to Josie, 'that this place is too rough for you. I hadn't expected conditions to be so bad.'

'Don't blame yourself, Logan. I wanted to come,' she told him. 'And we won't be here forever.'

He nodded sagely. 'Yes, but they tell me this dry heat gets worse, and there's no respite until the rainy season. And when that happens we're cut off for months.'

'If you're trying to depress me,' she sighed, 'you're doing a good job. I don't want to know about "worse". I'm simply trying to take one day at a time.'

'That's fair enough,' he said. 'But this climate is very hard on women. I thought perhaps you might like to go down to Perth for a spell.'

'Perth?' she echoed. 'Are you serious? I'm the Jezebel, remember? The harlot. They were just about ready to burn me at the stake. They'd have a field day if I went back there alone.'

'You shouldn't let them worry you . . .'

'No, Logan, I'm not strong enough to face people like that on my own. I'll stick it out here.'

'But you hate it.'

Josie kissed him on the forehead. 'Stop fussing.'

Logan had forgotten about the scandal in Perth. But she was a married woman now, she should be able to ignore the gossips. 'What about Ned?' he asked.

'I'm dealing with that,' she said. 'All in good time. But why this sudden urge to send me off to Perth?'

'Because you could be on your own a bit more,' he told her. 'I'll have to do some field work. I'm closing one of the mines and another is near to played out. I want to do some prospecting on my own. There has to be more gold in The Territory: they only found these reefs by accident when they were putting down the cables.'

She looked at him curiously. 'Prospecting? For yourself or for the Gilbert company?'

'For myself.' That was an afterthought. Prospecting would give him an excuse to visit Sibell. And from now on he would take his own gold out of Katherine.

'That doesn't seem the right thing to do,' Josie was saying. 'Prospecting on their time.'

'I've tried a bit of fossicking on Sundays,' he said, warming to his subject, 'but this place has been turned over, so I'll have to search further afield.'

'That's not the point. It's in your contract that you are entitled to prospect, but on their behalf. If you freelance, you're breaking the agreement.'

'To hell with the agreement! If I find gold, I won't need their contract. Percy Gilbert can come up and run his own mines. See how he likes it.'

Logan had convinced himself that Josie would jump at the chance to depart from Katherine, and now he was disappointed. He'd have to think of another reason to make her leave, without forcing a confrontation.

Then Nature lent a hand. The gruelling heat and hot desert winds were all that was needed to cause a tall tree to explode into flames, and then the bush outside Katherine was burning fiercely. With no equipment to fight the raging fire, the locals could only watch helplessly as it roared towards the little town, a wall of crackling, spluttering orange.

On the outskirts of Katherine, men, women and children made their stand. They formed a bucket brigade to bring water from the wells, faces bound to protect them from the suffocating smoke. They chopped down trees to form firebreaks, and fought the creeping flames in the undergrowth with wet bags that dried in seconds. Others battled with mats, blankets, anything they could find, to beat out forward patches of fire.

Mercifully, the wind dropped, and the pitted mining areas, cleared of trees, broke the force of the fire before it engulfed the heart of the settlement. The ugly pub, the Pinwell store, the police station and the BAT office, and some shanties huddled close to them were all saved, but outlying camps and huts, including the Conal home, were reduced to blackened ruins.

Exhausted, her clothes filthy from smoke and ash, Josie sat listlessly on the pub steps, trying not to inhale any more of the smoke that hung like heavy fog over the town. The silence was ominous as all about her people wandered, dazed, too tired to talk.

Three men and a young lad had died in the fire, trapped by the furious leaping flames, but Logan, who had been out there with them, had survived.

A woman brought a dipper of warm water to the group resting at the post office, and Josie was grateful to be offered a drink. Her mouth was parched, her eyes stung and her nostrils still burned from the pungent smell of eucalypt.

What now? she thought. My clothes, every last thing I had in the world . . . gone. But the effort to think past the present was too much, so she sat and waited until Logan came to fetch her.

A child was playing with a tent peg, and Josie gave a wry grin. That's me, she thought, a little square peg that has been hammered and hammered until I'm just a tiny little mite, a speck in this monstrous country, where everything is on a huge scale, out of proportion to the rest of the world.

Maybe we ought to go back to England. Pack up, and go home to the lovely green, to the softer light, and the cold, cold, cold of winter. God, what she wouldn't give for a cold day! She studied the face of a woman sitting nearby, watching rivulets of perspiration form white streaks through the grime on her skin, and realised she must look just as bad – but who cared?

The men held a meeting and decided that women and children made homeless by the fire should be evacuated to Palmerston, since supplies of canvas for tents had run out and it wouldn't be practical to attempt to reoccupy the burned-out areas until the rains came and rejuvenated the land.

'We could build a log hut further south,' Logan said, without enthusiasm, as they raked among the charred ruins of their former home, finding nothing to salvage. 'If you really want to stay.'

'No,' Josie said. 'I'll go to Palmerston with them, just for a while. There's nothing left here. I'll need to restock completely. We haven't any clothes, nothing to cook with . . . not a damn thing.' She kicked aside a tin baking dish. 'Look at that,' she laughed. 'I burnt it plenty of times myself, but the fire finished it good and proper.'

He was surprised to hear her laugh. 'Are you all right?'

'Of course I am. Good God, Logan, we're still alive. And we're not the only ones in trouble. At least we're not short of money. A lot of the other women I've been talking to are flat broke. I'll go with them and see what I can do to help.'

'I don't know what you'll find in Palmerston,' he said. 'You'd better go on to Perth.'

'Don't start that again,' she snapped. 'I told you I am not going to Perth. If I'm in Palmerston you'll be able to visit until the job's finished here. I'll miss you,' she said sadly, 'but I really think it would be the best thing to do.'

'But where will you live in Palmerston?'

'Send a telegraph to your agent to tell him I'm coming into town. Instruct him to find me a house, let him make himself useful. You're the boss, tell him it's urgent.'

Finally Logan agreed. At least it was a start. He'd be free to move about as he wished now. Mrs Pinwell had offered to let him stay in their sleep-out for the time being, so he had a roof, and some of the other men were already planning to hire a Chinaman to set up a cookhouse for them. Logan decided to join their group and do away with domestic arrangements. It would be a relief.

'I'm looking forward to the sea breezes,' Josie said. 'Are you sure you can't come with me? Even for a week or so? You'd enjoy being back at the coast again.'

'I'd like nothing better,' he lied. 'But I couldn't possibly leave right now. I'm worried that some of my diggers might quit with their wives.'

Josie kissed him. Poor Logan, she felt mean about leaving him, but she had no choice. And she would find a house in Palmerston, make a proper home for them there, one that was fitting for a man in his position. She would encourage him to make the time to come to Palmerston and mix with other businessmen, and when the mine closed at Christmas, they could spend the holidays together, and enjoy themselves, for a change.

Sibell was in a state of euphoria as they cantered west. With a heightened awareness of her surroundings, she was taking more notice, as Cliff pointed out landmarks that would lead them back to the station.

Flat-fronted, almost fan-shaped ant-hills, eight feet tall, littered the bush like ochre tombstones, and Sibell listened carefully now as Cliff explained that they were bush compasses.

'They're all the same,' he told her. 'They're all built in the same direction – north–south – so you always know which direction you're travelling.'

Hearing that Sibell had entertained a male visitor seemed to spark Zack into paying her more attention, and that excited her, too.

'Country's getting dry as a bone now,' he commented, riding alongside her, 'but there's water around if you know where to look. Down there, for instance . . .' He pointed to scuff marks across the track, which was so dry that the ground had disintegrated into deep dust. 'They're emu tracks, they'll be heading for water.' He detoured to make his point, and hundreds of little finches twittered in the bushes as they passed by.

'They're another good sign. The little birds can't travel too far without water. Even if it's underground, they hang about for the emus or the kangaroos to dig out water holes. They can smell it.'

'Down there, I'd say,' Cliff offered patiently, and Zack jumped down from his horse to tramp down a dusty incline.

'You have to find the lowest level,' he called to Sibell, as he began to dig with his hands.

Sure enough, he came to water, like a child playing on the beach, and scooped the hole into a wide pool, encouraging his horse to drink. 'It's a bit too muddy for us, but then we're not desperate,' he commented.

Their sense of time was strange to her. They were all anxious to get back to the station, but these detours and leisurely stops didn't seem to be relevant: they counted travel in days, not hours, and overnight camps on the trail were part of life in the outback. Sibell remembered that Maudie had said she'd slept out so much that she found bedrooms a bit stifling. Sibell was not as enthusiastic as Maudie, but she had adjusted to the matter-of-fact way the brothers made camp, prepared a tasty meal, and nested her down in soft grasses with her blanket and net. She was beginning to find the simple pleasure of camping more like a holiday than a necessity, and the two men genial company. Later, as they rode on, her thoughts returned to Logan. She hoped he would take her to visit his mines in Katherine, for they'd have to travel in this same manner, together day and night – how romantic that would be!.

Her day-dreams were rudely interrupted when Zack suddenly wheeled his horse about, grabbed Merry's reins, and pulled back a few yards. She found herself halted on the track, with Zack and Cliff, rifles unslung, ranged up beside her.

'If you can use that revolver of yours,' Cliff said to her, 'now's the time to produce it.'

She scrabbled in her saddle pack, took out the gun and loaded it as Kate had taught her. 'What's wrong?'

'That clearing,' Zack said. 'It's not natural. It has just been cleared.'

'What's wrong with that?'

'It's too fresh, no one's used it. The blacks have set up a trap for ambush. Travellers come along and think it's a nice easy spot to pitch a tent, with water nearby.'

'Why don't we go around it, then?' Sibell asked.

'Because they know we're here, and we don't know where they've planted themselves, or how many of them there are.'

Sensing danger in the air, the horses were quiet, ears quivering as they waited for someone to make a move. The stillness of the bush was ominous, and as her eyes searched the lanky, white-barked trees that surrounded them like an army, Sibell felt a rising terror.

'Don't be frightened,' Zack said, his voice calm. 'We'll talk our way out of this.'

'I can't see anyone,' she whispered.

'They're here all right, but it's probably just a few of the local bad lads getting smart.'

'No, it's not,' Cliff said, raising his gun. 'Look what we've got over here.'

'Oh, no!' Zack said, as two muscular natives with huge feathered head-dresses stepped from the sharp shadows, spears levelled.

Without turning his head, Zack spoke to Sibell. 'When I say "go", you ride like hell. Straight ahead and keep going. Keep the sun square on your back and you'll be heading in the right direction.' He seemed to take an age before he spoke to the blacks. 'You're Daly River mob!' he called. 'What are you fellers doing down here?'

'Gibbit guns,' one of the men shouted.

'No bloody fear,' Zack replied. 'I'll give you tucker. Plenty tucker at my camp.'

'Plenty white feller, too,' Cliff shouted. 'Little bit close, so you be good fellers.'

The spokesman for the blacks grinned and waved his arm, and as he did so there was movement in the bush all around them. Although Sibell couldn't see anyone, she heard the crunch and rustle of feet in the undergrowth.

'What'll you give me for the guns?' Zack asked suddenly, and, surprised, the black leader hesitated, glancing at his partner as if to confer.

167

Zack pressed on. 'We talk,' he called. 'Men talk, make trade. Woman goes.'

'Hang on to that gun of yours,' Cliff told Sibell, 'and use it if you have to.'

'You heard me,' Zack demanded. 'Woman goes!'

The blackfellow shrugged and waved his spear, dismissing Sibell.

'Go!' Zack cried, and slapped Sibell's horse on the rump. Merry didn't need any more encouragement and took off as if she were at a starting gate, bolting down the track.

Sibell almost dropped the revolver in the sudden rush, but she clung on to the reins, trying to keep control of the horse and hold the gun at the same time, head down, racing forward.

The Aborigine laughed as he watched the horse bolt. Then he turned back to resume their confrontation.

'You feller gibbit guns,' he said resolutely.

'You boss man?' Zack asked, stalling for time.

'Big boss this feller.'

'Guns no good without ammo,' Zack informed him, lifting up a pack of cartridges. As he did so, he spoke to Cliff. 'What do you think? We pull off the track and ride him and his mate down?'

'Safest way to go,' Cliff replied. 'They mightn't be too keen on chucking spears towards the big boss.' He too was taking out cartridges. He threw them one by one into the clearing. 'Here's your ammo.'

To create a further diversion, Zack opened his pack, and as he scattered cartridges to the side, he nodded to Cliff.

They dug in their spurs and charged, rifles firing.

Zack shot the boss man, and Cliff's horse shouldered the other black aside as they plunged into the bush under a hail of spears. It was tricky riding through the thick undergrowth, crashing over barriers of rotting logs and swerving in and out of the trees, a shouting mob of blacks hard on their heels.

As if prearranged, Zack and Cliff took off in different directions, Zack riding headlong down a gully to turn about and fire at two Aborigines as they raced over the rise. There was a scream as a man fell, and no one else appeared, but spears flew over Zack's head. He knew he'd be at a disadvantage, below his pursuers, if he stuck to the gully, so he took a chance and pushed his horse up the steep incline on the other side, knowing he was exposing himself to attack.

Spears thudded around him, despite the distance, and he guessed the blacks were using woomeras to increase the deadly flight of the heavy weapons. Miraculously, though, he made it to the top, where he leapt from his horse.

He lay in the long grass overlooking the gully, and grinned. 'Now it's your turn,' he shouted. 'You try it!'

One brave black stepped forward to take aim, and Zack shot him. He continued firing right along the rise, with studied precision, and when he was sure his battle was over, he went in search of Cliff, at the same time praying that Sibell had had the sense to keep going, in order to put as much distance as possible between herself and their attackers.

His horse was trembling with fright as it picked its way along the ridge. Zack patted it, reassuring, but he still kept his rifle ready, alert for any sound.

It was rare, but not unknown, for Daly River blacks to make forays out of their own territory. They were among the most dangerous tribes in the north. Recently they had murdered the captain and crew of a Japanese pearler who had been foolish enough to take a couple of their women, but they were not averse to killing white men who rode into their country prospecting for land, gold or tin.

He guessed they'd woken up to the fact that spears weren't much of a defence against guns, hence this business of finding some for themselves. Zack decided that as soon as they got back to the station they'd round up a few of their own blacks to patrol the perimeters of Black Wattle and warn off the Daly River blacks. Some sort of communication was necessary to protect life and limb from these marauders, and charity began at home. His job was to keep his own station safe.

There was no sign now of any of the blacks, but he heard a horse whinny, and his own horse pricked up its ears. Zack let it lead the way and felt a shiver of apprehension when he found Cliff's horse standing nervously in the bush, its bridle hanging loose.

He gave a low whistle, waiting for Cliff to respond, and when there was no answer, he examined the horse. Its flanks were wet, indicating that Cliff must have ridden through the lagoon, which was shallow enough at this time of year. He headed in that direction, leading the other horse.

Still watchful, he tethered the horses and made his way down to the lagoon on foot, whistling again for Cliff, thinking that he could be hiding out around here somewhere. Then he found the tracks leading from the lagoon, heavy tracks, a horse . . . Only a horse; the blacks had not come this far. Cliff had escaped them.

Zack breathed a sigh of relief as he turned and looked back over this section of the mile-long lagoon. Suddenly, something caught his eye, and he stared, transfixed by shock. Stupidly, he called to Cliff. He whirled around as if seeking help, or someone to tell him this was not right, his eyes were deceiving him. Then he was running, wading frantically into the muddy water towards Cliff. At first he'd thought it was a large piece of driftwood out there, with a stark, bald branch set above the water level.

It wasn't a branch, it was a spear.

Zack found his brother's body, a spear in his back, half submerged in the lagoon. He sat beside him, letting the water wash around him as he nursed Cliff to him and wept.

She was too frightened to dismount. She had come to a wide river. What river? She had no idea. The very sameness of the country had rendered it strange to her eyes. The same trees – gums, acacias and the odd cabbage palm – the horizon almost a perfect circle, level at the treetops, the same anthills, mocking her now, ghastly old monuments large enough to hide lurking attackers.

What had Cliff said? They were compasses, they could show her north from south – but what good was that? What direction should she go?

Sibell was lost. In her panic she had given the horse its head, galloping furiously into nowhere, and when it slowed to a canter, knowing the danger was far behind, she'd been comforted by Merry's rhythmic gait, so steady, so sure.

And now this river. They hadn't told her, in the rush of it all, how far to go, and they probably expected her to wait for them down along the track. But she'd lost sight of it miles back. Sibell worried that they'd be angry with her for being so stupid: she should have kept her wits about her instead of riding away so blindly. By this time they'd have finished arguing with the two blackfellows. It seemed silly now that they'd made her leave.

When she'd ridden off she'd expected devilish blacks to leap at her from the bush, to grab at her and pull her from the horse, but the way was clear. She was confused now about what had actually happened in the space of just a few minutes, and she could only recall those two Aborigines demanding guns. Pathetic really. What chance did they have against men armed like Zack and Cliff? They even carried knives, large Bowie knives, and they were crack shots with their rifles.

No. The only one in trouble right now was Sibell Delahunty, who felt she ought to go back, but to where? Zack had told her to keep the sun on her back. Had she? Hysteria rising, she laughed nervously. He should have told the horse!

She decided, finally, that she'd better keep going, try to get home, and pray they weren't waiting for her back there somewhere. She could just see their stormy faces if they'd had to waste time hanging about in the bush while she was safely home. If she could get home!

Of course, this would never have happened to Maudie! Maudie could do no wrong in their eyes. She'd have stayed, they wouldn't have sent her away, and she'd have shot one of those blacks without a blink. Sibell recalled how she had ridden out with Maudie one day, invited along because Maudie had said she had a job to do. They'd ridden down to the cattle yards and dismounted near a tall timber contraption. With the help of two black stockmen, Maudie had bailed up a steer, roped it up, and, as Sibell watched, wondering what they were doing, had calmly cut its throat, blood gushing everywhere.

Sibell had screamed and run. And Maudie had teased her about it later. 'You don't mind eating beef. Do you think the cattle just hand it over?'

'You should have warned her,' Charlotte had said, but Maudie was unrepentant.

'She has to know what stations are all about.'

As she sat there staring at the river, Sibell wondered what Maudie would do in a situation like this.

The sun was sinking, but was still hot on her back. Her back? She could be wide of the mark, but the sun was directing her straight ahead, if she stuck to her instructions. Yes, and you'll probably end up back in Western Australia, she told herself grimly. Besides, there's the river, and it looks good and deep.

Would that have worried Maudie? Sibell doubted it.

'Oh well,' she said. 'Sink or swim,' and she nudged the horse down the bank.

170

'They say horses can swim,' she told Merry, to keep her courage up. 'I hope you can.'

She eased the horse gently into the shallows and on into deeper water, already beginning to think that this was a mistake – the current was much stronger than she'd expected – but Merry plunged forward and Sibell felt a surge of excitement as it began to swim, ploughing on across the wonderfully cool water. She clung on, exhilarated by this new experience, but fearful as they surged out into the middle of the stream, too late to turn back. Merry kept going, swimming strongly, snorting water, head high, and Sibell, amazed to find she was still afloat, was praising the good brave horse, talking to it. As they scrambled up the far bank, she shouted with sheer delight, 'We made it! We did it! They'll never believe me!'

To dry off, an easy process in the heat, Sibell dismounted and led the horse forward until she saw a mob of cattle in the distance. Still nervous of the beasts, always afraid they'd charge her, she climbed back on the horse to get a closer look at the brands, relieved to see the familiar 'NTH' – Northern Territory Hamilton.

'At least we're on home ground,' she told the horse, 'which doesn't mean much on a place as big as a county.' She stared around her at the wild, dry scrub, exactly the same as the country the other side of the river. Wallabies grazed peacefully, birds sat on the backs of the cattle busy with their duties, hundreds of white cockatoos lined the branches of nearby trees, cackling and screeching at one another as if they too were arguing about her dilemma. 'I give up,' she said to the horse. 'I've got no idea where the house is. Upriver or down.' The homestead was a couple of miles from the river, which wound all over the place. Even if she made a decision to go left or right, she could easily miss the house, and soon it would be dark. The sun went down like a stone out here, twilight was unknown.

Terrified of walking through scrub in the dark, with snakes and dingoes prowling, she stayed on the horse. 'Home, Merry,' she said. 'For God's sake, go home.'

It was easier to hand the responsibility over to the horse, and Sibell lost all sense of time and place as they plodded on. She was tired and suffering from thirst, her mouth like sandpaper from the dust. She tried to think of Logan, but her worries increased, worries that he'd never bother to try to find her again, that he'd go back to Josie, wherever she was. And she tried not to think of Zack and Cliff, who would be furious with her by now.

Zack was right: she didn't belong in this wilderness. Zack was always so damned right, and Maudie and the rest of them! She hated them all, because she didn't belong anywhere. Once again she wondered, dangerously close to giving up, why she bothered living. Disoriented, she considered slipping down from this hard saddle and just stretching out on the earth where no one would ever find her. But she was too weary even for that effort, and the horse kept on, slowing now, hardly moving. It was tired too after that wild, reckless gallop.

She realised that the horse had stopped – for how long, she didn't know. She rubbed grit from her eyes and peered into the darkness, and it was a while before she realised what was barring their way. A gate!

One of the station gates! Merry shook and stamped impatiently as Sibell leaned down, feeling for the latch, collecting splinters in her hand.

The long, low gate felt like a ton weight as she shoved it aside. Up ahead were the blessed dim lights of the homestead, and they headed up the track.

Dogs were barking as a horseman came cantering towards her. 'You left the gate open,' he shouted, and passed by to close it. When he returned, he was all apologies. 'I'm sorry, miss, I didn't realise it was you.'

He swung alongside. 'Are you all right, miss?' It was Casey, thank God, it was Casey! She was home.

He grabbed Merry's reins. 'Where are Zack and Cliff?'

Sibell's mind was a blank, but she managed to point to the house. 'Up there,' she mumbled. 'I'm sorry.' She clutched his arm. 'You'll tell them I'm sorry.'

'Jesus Christ,' he whispered. 'What's happened here?'

Casey carried her into the house, and they gave her some brandy, but no rest from their questions.

'Blacks? Where? How long ago? How far back? Are you sure they were blacks? How did you get away? Are you sure you didn't just get lost? Were they hurt?'

'She probably just got lost,' Maudie said, 'and the boys are out there, looking for her.'

'No!' Sibell insisted. 'I mean I did get lost. There were blacks, they wanted guns.' She searched her memory for some proof. 'Daly River blacks, I heard Cliff say, or maybe Zack did.'

And then she was alone. Aching all over, she struggled out to the veranda. They were shouting, raising the alarm. Men were rounding up horses from the home paddock, saddling up, lanterns swinging at the stables, and out of the mayhem, a posse of horsemen, led by Maudie, galloped past the house and away into the night.

As they cantered down the track, the moon rose high, glazing the bush with silver, and the thud of the horses' hooves in the soft dust lent an unreal atmosphere to this flight. To Maudie it was all unreal. Her husband was in trouble somewhere out here, and back there lay Charlotte. She was fearful of what lay ahead, and also aware that she was the bearer of bad news for the sons of Charlotte Hamilton. If she could find them. They were due back today, but no one knew what route they'd taken. Sibell hadn't been any help, except to say that they'd been bailed up by blacks mid-afternoon, and had come home via Pine Creek, not directly across country from Katherine.

Had she known that last night, Maudie would have sent riders towards Pine Creek to try to find them, but now all she could do was stick to wagon trails and hope to pick them up. Of necessity, wagon trails wound around the terrain, so horsemen only used them for easier rides on the straight runs, cutting away every so often to save time. She figured they'd have to be within three hours' ride of Black Wattle, and if she hadn't found them by then, the men would have to fan out and extend the search.

She fired her rifle into the air again and again, but with no response, so

172

she pushed on, reloading the rifle. 'Where the hell are they?' she muttered to Casey for the tenth time.

'We'll find them,' he said grimly, shouting to the men to keep close.

Maudie knew why. If Sibell was right and those bloody Daly River blacks were prowling this area, they all had to take care. She ground her teeth and held the rifle ready as the track wound in and out of the patchy light. Someone had put a hex on Black Wattle, she was sure or none of this would be happening.

Last night. It seemed years ago. Everything had been fine, everything under control. She'd spent the afternoon teaching Wesley to ride, on the little mare she'd been grooming for him, quite pleased that Cliff had been away the last few days so that he couldn't interfere. Men were too impatient, too rough, they expected too much of little kids. She remembered her own father teaching her to ride when she was only a little nipper, shouting at her, bullying her, whacking the horse into a gallop, laughing when she fell off. And when he taught her to swim, chucking her into a creek, where she floundered, terrified, caught her leg on a snag, her mother screaming on the bank. Her mother had had to dive in and rescue her. And what did her father do? Gave her a belting for being such a sook, for upsetting her mother. But, by God, she could ride now, and she could swim like a fish. The greatest day of her life had been the day she beat him in the bush point-to-point. Rode rings around her old man.

Maudie knew she was only concentrating on these memories to stave off panic. She wasn't one to panic, and she wouldn't lose control now.

Last night. Just as she was getting into bed, the screams had cut through her like a knife. She could still hear them, Charlotte's screams, even out here, so far away.

She had looked in on Charlotte before she went to bed. 'You shouldn't be up. You're supposed to rest.'

But Charlotte had laughed. 'People die in bed. I've just been to the lavvy. The nights are too long. When I sleep all day, I can't sleep at night.'

'I suppose so,' Maudie agreed. Maudie, who'd never been sick in her life. Charlotte looked fine to her.

'Where's my magnifying glass?'

'Here.' Maudie picked it up from the dressing table and handed it to her.

'Oh! Good. I want to try to read, I'm so bloody bored. The boys will be home tomorrow, won't they?'

'Yes.'

'You run along then, Maudie, I'll get back to bed in a minute.'

What else could she have done? Nothing.

And then through the darkness, the screams. Maudie running, tripping, fumbling with the door-knob of Charlotte's room, fighting the terror of that wall of agony beyond, Charlotte screaming. Charlotte standing there, on fire! A human torch!

Maudie knew instantly what had happened. She grabbed for something to smother the flames, the flaming nightdress, the flaming hair. No blankets, only sheets. Useless bloody sheets! She fell on the heavier cotton bedspread, rolling Charlotte in it, rolling with her, stamping out smouldering fire, smelling the burning flesh, seeing the scorched hair. Grateful that the screaming had stopped and that Charlotte was unconscious.

She sent two riders to find Brody, but she doubted he could do any more than Sam Lim, who smeared salve on strips of torn sheets and gently bound the poor woman, and, when she awoke to face the pain, dripped laudanum over the poor seared lips. 'Oh, Charlotte,' Maudie, lamented. 'What a bloody stupid thing to do. And with your gammy eyes!'

The horse had slowed, they had all slowed. Another rifle shot rent the air, and another, but still no response, no answering shot, no coo-ee for them to target. Only the creeping darkness of the brooding bush, a thousand trees challenging them, and another thousand thousand beyond.

If only Charlotte hadn't been so damned independent. Why couldn't she have asked someone to do it for her?

It was the kerosene lamp. At first Maudie had thought she'd knocked it over, setting fire to her nightdress, but once they had Charlotte settled, Maudie had found the real cause. The kerosene bottle was out of place, on the wash-stand. Charlotte must have decided to refill the lamp herself, spilling some on her clothes – that would account for the extra fury of the fire. Half blind, Maudie thought angrily, working by the dim light of the other lamp, she wouldn't have noticed the spill, and lit a match. Wax matches were notorious for spitting and spattering. It would only have taken one . . .

Maudie cursed. Lamps and bloody stoves! How many women, in their floppy dresses, have gone up that way? She had a right to be angry, Charlotte should have known better. Should have been more careful. 'Ah, but she couldn't see properly.'

'What did you say?' Casey asked.

'Nothing,' Maudie said. How long had they been on this track?

'It'll be light soon,' Casey told her, and Maudie nodded. The bush was stirring. Kookaburras, as was their right, broke the silence with a clatter, and Maudie resented their interference. She needed the quiet to listen for foreign sounds.

Left behind, in the sudden silence of the homestead, Sibell turned to Sam Lim. 'Where's Mrs Hamilton?'

He threw his hands up and answered her in Chinese, crying hysterically.

Sibell tried to clear her head. She was exhausted, unsteady on her feet, confused. She thought he was worried about Zack and Cliff, and realised that Charlotte would be too. She would go to her and tell her they'd be home soon. Lord, if she could get home, they could. She knocked gently on Charlotte's door, but Netta came out, finger to her lips. 'Doan wake missus.'

'I'm sorry.' Sibell retreated.

'Missus hurt bad,' Netta told her.

'What? What hurt? What's wrong? Did she have another attack?'

Netta lifted sorrowful eyes. 'Missus bad burnt. Catchem fire.'

She allowed Sibell to tiptoe into the room, to see Charlotte lying there, so still, under a large eiderdown, her head swathed in bandages.

She felt dizzy, the room was swaying, and Netta's strong arms held her, took her, knees sagging, down to her room. She was aware that Polly was helping. Polly took off her boots, and between them the two black girls put her to bed without bothering to remove her muddied clothes. She sank down on the pillow as they pulled the covers over her, too tired to think any more.

'You go bye-bye,' Polly whispered, in the same voice she used for Wesley.

Sam Lim, frightened and upset, went back to his kitchen. Shyly, Netta watched from the doorway as he took a joss stick and lit it, placing it in front of a display of bush orchids.

'What that fella?' she asked, and he lowered his head mournfully.

'Missus need good joss now, she go to heaven soon. Sam Lim pray for her safe journey.'

Netta padded across the room to pick up another joss stick. He allowed her to light it, pleased that she was showing respect, but he was startled when she made her tearful prayer. 'Two feller go to heaven,' she said. 'Poor missus got good joss allatime. No go lonely.'

'What two feller?' he asked, thinking she'd missed the point of the ceremony, but she backed away, eyes wide with fear.

'Bad joss to say name of dead feller.' And then she was gone.

He stared after her. From the distance he heard the lowing moan of a didgeridoo, and realised the station blacks had commenced their 'crying'. He had been in this country long enough to accept that the Aborigines had deep and mysterious sources of knowledge. Sam Lim considered them inferior to Chinese, but he was still wary of their magic, so, while he could rail and rant at the Europeans, he made sure he never crossed the blackfellows. He had seen men die after a bone-pointing ceremony. Right now, he knew they were not crying for missus: that would come later. So who had died?

All about him now, he felt a shuddering numbness, as if the ancient Aborigine spirits had entered the house and were waiting with him.

Zack wrapped his brother's body in a saddle blanket and sat cross-legged beside him, not ready yet to share his grief with anyone. 'Why now?' he groaned. 'Just when we were getting it right.' He reminded Cliff of that first cattle drive, when they'd brought their first herd of six hundred head all the way from Queensland. He'd been twenty-one and Cliff eighteen, only kids, but Charlotte'd had faith in them, so they'd made it. Six months on the worst stock route in the country.

And then the station. 'Jesus! Do you remember the bloody station then? Just a wilderness . . . the stockyard fences crumbling with termites, and we lost half the mob trying to do everything at once, with the blacks making bloody nuisances of themselves . . .'

He shook his head. 'A couple of years of heartbreak and I was ready to give it away. Give the bloody lot back to the blacks!

'But it was you who made me hang on. Everyone thought it was me,

175

big brother Zack, the bosso! What was it you said? "We're surviving, mate! Surviving is winning, isn't it?" '

Zack was crying again, unashamed, heaving tears. 'So why did you have to go and get killed now?'

After a while he patted his brother's shoulder. 'You can rest easy, mate. Maudie and the boy, I'll take care of them. Your work won't go to waste. All the way down the line,' he promised, 'they'll always own half share, they'll never want for anything. And I'll send the boy to boarding school in Adelaide, just like you always wanted . . .'

With the first orange streaks of dawn, he stood and lit a smoke, listening to the busy small birds twittering life into the day, despairing that Cliff would never hear them again. He was still there when the searchers came pounding across the lagoon. He hated the noise they made, horses trampling, men shouting, even Maudie's screams, their trespass on the thoughts he was sharing with his brother. His answers to their wild questions were short, abrupt, almost noncommittal.

They lifted Cliff's body on to his horse for the journey home, while Casey, encouraged by Maudie's agony, threatened revenge. 'Don't worry, Maudie, we'll get the bastards. We'll get a posse together as soon as we can.'

'Do it now!' she screamed. 'Don't let them get away! They've killed my husband.'

'She's right,' one of the men said. 'You blokes take Maudie home with Cliff, and we'll get after them.'

They turned to Zack. 'Which way did they go? Someone said they're Daly River blacks? We're with you, boss.'

They took it for granted that Zack would lead the posse, but he put an arm around Maudie. 'We're going home, Maudie, all of us.'

She shook him away. 'No! I'll take him home. You find the bastards, Zack. Find them and kill them.'

'We'll talk about it later,' he said quietly.

'No, we won't!' she screamed. 'How the hell did you let this happen? He's been speared in the back! Where were you? Why didn't you look after him?' She was shouting at him, blaming him, thumping at him.

He took hold of her flailing arms and handed her over to Casey. 'Take her home,' he said, 'and that goes for all of you. Every man back to the station.'

People came from far and wide for the funerals of Charlotte Hamilton and her son Cliff.

Zack was with her at the end, and Charlotte died mercifully unaware that Cliff had preceded her into eternity.

They came on horseback, in buggies and traps and high covered German wagons: diggers, cattlemen, friends from Palmerston, stockmen, women in newly dyed black dresses, with their shy children and baskets of home-made provisions, all travelling hundreds of miles. Some stayed in the house, others camped around the homestead.

A missionary, Pastor Kreig, conducted the service, and Doctor Brody led the singing in the new cemetery Zack himself had paced out on the east hill, looking into the morning sun. Then the mourners filed into the

176

courtyard for refreshments. Most of the women stayed, chatting quietly at the tables, or sneaking awed tours of Charlotte's famous homestead, the like of which few had ever seen before.

'A grand place,' they agreed, these hard-living country women, 'fit for a queen.' And some even shed more tears for Charlotte, 'Who never got the real use of it.'

Others went out to join the men gathered by the casks under the livid green of the black wattle trees, where anger was surfacing again.

Maudie was with them, hardly recognisable in her best dress, a black taffeta with balloon sleeves and a full double-draped skirt, from under which peeped a neat hem of fine pleating. It was a beautiful dress, much admired by the ladies, and Maudie's stiff bonnet, black also, lined with satin pleating, completed her ensemble. But Maudie had no time for fripperies. She had ripped the silk flowers from the hat and would have worn her boots with the dress if Sibell hadn't intervened. Now she stood with the men, downing a mug of home-made ginger beer well laced with rum.

Maudie's tears had been fraught with rage at the murder of her husband, and now, as the tears dried, her attitude hardened. She moved among the men agreeing that something should be done, encouraging them to speak up on her behalf, until the wake turned into a public meeting, with speakers demanding that Zack take action.

Finally, he stepped forward, both hands raised for quiet. 'No one here has the right,' he told them, his voice firm, 'to tell me what I should and should not do about my brother's death.'

'Except his wife,' Maudie shouted aggressively, sure of her strength in this company.

Zack glared at her, tempted to tell her to shut up, but guessed that would only swing public opinion her way, so he ignored her. 'Let me tell you again,' he said. 'There was a fight, we killed three blacks, possibly more, and they killed Cliff. Three for one is a lesson in itself . . . I don't want any more bloodshed.'

'You mean you'll let them get away with killing your own brother?' a voice yelled.

'I never saw any of the other blacks,' Zack replied. 'I don't know who they were. Even if we did track them over to the Daly River, we'd never know which ones were involved.'

'Who bloody cares?' someone shouted. 'We should take a posse and ride up there. Give the bastards a lesson they'll never forget.'

'Zack Hamilton,' a woman called. 'Are you trying to tell us you condone this attack? None of us will be safe here now if we don't retaliate.'

'Why won't you listen?' he shouted angrily. 'We did retaliate. Jesus, woman, do you want to start a real war? No one knows how many tribes are out there, or on past the Victoria River, or even on to the Kimberleys. If we want to make The Territory safe, we have to make peace with the blacks, give them room to move, not provoke them.'

There was a growl of resentment in the crowd, and a voice from the rear shouted: 'I suppose Cliff provoked them, did he? Did he bloody shoot the buggers who were trying to kill him?'

177

'You run your station, Joe Buckley,' Zack called, 'and I'll run mine. They came for guns, they didn't get any, and they lost at least three men. They'll think twice next time.'

'Yes,' Buckley replied. 'They'll be more bloody careful next time, that's all. And what about Maudie? I reckon she's more of a man than you are, Hamilton. She's not gonna let them get away with it.'

Judging by the mood of the crowd, Zack knew he was losing this argument, so he issued a directive. 'Any man from Black Wattle Station who joins a posse is fired,' he shouted. 'And that's the bloody end of it.'

'No, it's not.' A tall, grey-haired man in immaculate police uniform, with dress decorations, stepped forward. 'Ladies and gentlemen, I am Colonel Puckering, Police Superintendent. Some of you may know me. I must apologise to the Hamilton family for my late arrival, and deeply regret that I missed the funeral. Not possible to get here any sooner.' His accent and staccato delivery had their attention, so he turned to Zack. 'Condolences later, sir, sure you'll forgive me. Have to say, though, that you're all on the wrong track. Murder is murder. I will investigate this case, I will take any further action when and if I see fit.'

His powerful parade-ground voice stunned them to silence. 'The days of cold-blooded murder in The Territory are over as long as I hold the reins here. Any man who kills an Aborigine, man, woman or child, will be brought to justice, be he white or black.'

He heard the shuffling, muttering dissent, but stood his ground. 'I have seen reports of your men going out on blackfellow hunts, of wanton retaliation against innocent blacks for crimes committed by persons unknown. Murder, gentlemen, plain murder! Not to be tolerated. The police, the courts, are the law here, and you would do well to respect the law. Any man inciting murder by way of assembling a posse – for this is the matter under discussion – is liable to be arrested. Thank you, Mr Hamilton.' He turned to Zack. 'Damn sorry to intrude like this.'

The women, of course, had heard that there was a 'blue' on, a row between Zack's and Maudie's supporters, so they'd rushed out to the tail end of the debate, Sibell among them.

Not owning a black outfit, she had thought it would be acceptable to wear her best dress, that blue two-piece travelling suit, but the glares of the women, not one of whom was wearing anything but black, had sent her searching through Charlotte's wardrobe for a long black cloak and a plain black velour hat, which she felt looked horrible. They did, though, give her the protection of anonymity. She had never felt so out of place as she did now, among these strong, sharp-faced women who saw Maudie as Saint Joan, a fighter, the epitome of their ambitions. Maudie had succeeded in the long run: this peasant girl might have lost her husband, but she'd gained half of Black Wattle Station.

The women were in tune with Maudie. While they sympathised at her loss, they were more case-hardened than the men, for who hadn't lost a son, a brother, a husband or a lover in this bloody country? And they'd talked and watched and cast asides for the last couple of nights, as the mourners had gathered, as their men became maudlin in the drink. Men who drank, their legs buckling, to good ol' Cliff, 'One of the best.'

178

Never immune to the rare handsome man who crossed their paths, most of the women, in their hearts, spared Zack from criticism, but up front their loyalty had to be with Maudie. For the time being, anyway, until the furore died down, when they'd be looking to their sons and daughters, with not one, but two eligible spouses on the horizon. Maudie the widow, and Zack the bachelor. They'd remind each other that a man cannot marry his brother's widow, and that there was this lovely, lovely house . . .

But Sibell, with her toffy English voice, had no place among them. They listened to her, nudged, peered down their noses, 'took her off', for none could imagine what a flibbertigibbet such as her was doing on a station. And without Charlotte's staunch support, Sibell didn't know either.

Sibell was relieved to find the Colonel among the crowd as they made their way back to the house for their farewells. 'What a wonderful surprise,' she said, trying to overcome her misery.

'Heard you were here,' he said. 'Knew I'd have no trouble spotting you. Can't tell you how sorry I am, Sibell. Double tragedy. Damn bad luck.'

'It's the story of my life, I think I'm a jinx.'

'Poppycock. The Lord makes the rules, not you. And you're looking quite splendid, despite the troubles. I gather you found employment here. How did you get along with Mrs Hamilton?'

'She was lovely. She was always happy, always had a joke to tell, everyone will miss her. And Cliff, too, of course. I don't know what will happen now.'

'Will you be staying on?'

'No. I worked for Mrs Hamilton, they don't need me any more.'

He took her arm. 'Mr Hamilton has invited me to stop over for a few days. You might show me to my room. I have to investigate the circumstances of Cliff Hamilton's death. Believe you were there.'

'Only at first, they sent me on home.'

'Fortunate for you, my dear. I brought along two constables – I've sent them out to patrol the area to make certain none of those renegade blacks are still around. But after that we shall be pleased to offer you an escort back to Palmerston.'

'And then you'll send me back to Perth,' she said dully.

He smiled. 'We'll see. Had my work cut out smartening up that town – wouldn't win any popularity stakes, not too popular here either by the sound of things – but Palmerston's a relatively quieter place now, and by Jove, I'll see it stays that way.'

'Maudie and Zack are at odds,' Sibell told him. 'They've had terrible rows over Cliff's death. It would be a big help if you could talk to her.'

'See what I can do,' he replied mildly.

After he'd talked with Zack, the Colonel took Maudie into the sitting room and listened patiently to her side of the argument. 'Quite understand,' he nodded, as her mood fluctuated between bouts of tears and

179

harsh recriminations. 'A terrible tragedy for you, my dear, and for your little son.'

'Zack's weak,' she cried. 'The blacks understand pay-back. They understand bloody well. They never forget an insult or an injury. Any of them! Women, too. They'll be back, you mark my words.'

'It's possible,' he said. 'That's why I intend to open a police station at Idle Creek Junction. Law and order is a matter for the police, Mrs Hamilton. The men out here have work to do, you can't ask them to ride out on these risky forays.'

'Why not? I'd ride with them.'

'Mrs Hamilton,' he sighed. 'Have you ever heard of inciting to riot?'

'Yes, I think so . . .'

'Then you should be extremely careful. You are placing yourself at risk of arrest if you insist on these measures.'

'Me? You'd arrest me?' Maudie was stunned.

'One hopes it would not be necessary,' he murmured, and smiled grimly as Maudie slammed out of the room.

At dinner that night, they were all subdued. Sibell wondered what the Colonel had said to Maudie, who was now sulking. There was no more talk of posses.

Zack ate gloomily, and the Colonel made tactful small talk until Sibell decided she might as well speak up. 'If you don't need me here any more, Zack, I think I'll go on to Palmerston with Colonel Puckering.'

He clasped his hands under his chin, elbows on the table, and considered this for a few minutes. 'I'd rather you stayed, if you can,' he said finally.

'Why?' Maudie asked sharply.

'Because I'll be away for a good while . . .'

'Where are you going?' Maudie interrupted.

'We need cash, as you both know now, so I'm going to start mustering right away and take a herd down to Stuart.'

'That's more than a thousand miles from here!' Puckering said.

'It's worth it. I'll get a better price down there, meet up with the Adelaide buyers. Our cattle are as good as they'll ever see, and I can telegraph on ahead that I'm on my way.'

'Who'll run the station?' Sibell asked.

'Maudie can run it, and I'll leave Casey with her. You can do it, can't you, Maudie?'

'Course I can,' she said defiantly, but Sibell could see she was pleased, and flattered. 'Can't see that Sibell's going to be much help, though,' she added.

'You need her,' Zack said. 'She can read, she can write, she can do the books and pay the wages and run the homestead. What do you say, Sibell?'

'I won't stay unless Maudie wants me here.'

They all looked to Maudie who shrugged. 'I suppose she might as well stay.'

Sibell smiled, knowing that was the best Maudie could do. Secretly, she was relieved. Logan was at Katherine, and he'd promised to visit her.

180

If she were forced to return to Palmerston, that might place her too far away from him.

'That's settled, then,' the Colonel said. 'I can't think of a better combination than you young people: you ought to do very well. If you have any problems, you know you can call on me.'

7

The station was now all dust and energy as whips cracked and horsemen galloped away to muster cattle from all over the property. Sibell was amazed at the work involved in preparing for a drive of this size.

'Zack aims to take two thousand head,' Maudie said, 'so they'll need plenty of horses. You can give me a hand rounding them up.'

'Are they selling horses, too?'

'No, they're not bloody selling horses! The men need them! Four to a man: they won't get far if they tire their nags.'

Before she had time to think about it, Sibell found herself working, too: up at dawn every morning, back on her horse and out there with Maudie, cutting out the horses Maudie chose, riding hard to avoid angry stallions who snapped at their mares' rumps to chase them out of reach.

Maudie was everywhere, yelling at the men. 'Get rid of those bloody Mexican hooks,' she shouted at two of the stockmen. 'You injure our horses I'll skin you alive! Use our spurs or none at all.'

She ruled with the authority of experience and a tongue as biting as a whip. 'You can pick your mounts from the stockyards and not before,' she roared, when some of the drovers demanded to choose their own horses. 'I say which ones are ready and which aren't.'

Then, back in the sheds, she threw aside heavy leather saddle-packs. 'Put those bloody things back. Who brought them out? English rubbish! You're not going on a bloody picnic. Get our own canvas ones, give the poor bloody horses a break!'

On and on she went, with Sibell in tow, making certain all the horses were branded, then off to meet the mobs of cattle that were coming in to be assembled for the trail.

Day by day the huge herd of noisy, complaining cattle grew, until Zack came in with the last of them.

Sibell rode gingerly around the outskirts of the mobs, trying to be helpful, astonished and not a little nervous at Maudie's reckless riding. She could lasso and rope a steer to a skidding halt as well as any of the men, and she shot, swerving through the trees, after runaways as if she were out on open plains. But while Sibell admired Maudie's talents, her admiration was not reciprocated.

Sibell had made mistakes: she hadn't latched a gate properly, and cattle had pushed free; she was incapable, it seemed, of hobbling horses, having failed at three attempts, frightened that these half-wild beasts would trample her; and she'd fallen off Merry twice, fortunately without injury. Her efforts irritated Maudie.

They were chalk and cheese, she knew, and she worried about the strange partnership that Zack had delegated to run the station in his absence. But still trying to be pleasant, she remarked to Maudie that it was good to see Zack had employed Aborigine drovers.

'Why wouldn't he?' Maudie sniffed. 'They've got to learn to earn their keep just like the rest of us.' Somehow, Sibell felt, that jibe was aimed at her, since Maudie had already made it plain she considered bookwork a waste of time.

A young black lad, a stockman, rode by them with one of the station men, and Sibell smiled at him. Suddenly Maudie took off.

She rode after them and pulled the black lad from his horse with a thud, then turned on the white station hand. 'You bastard!' she screamed. 'You get the hell out of my sight! And you,' she yelled at Sibell, 'use your bloody eyes, if you've got any!'

'What's wrong now?' Sibell said angrily. 'What have I done?'

'Look at this!' Maudie pushed the lad ahead of her. She reached down from her horse, pulled off his hat, revealing frizzy hair, and then wrenched at his shirt. 'Don't you know tits when you see them?' she grated, and Sibell realised the 'lad' was a girl.

'Bastards,' Maudie said. 'They'll try anything, those pigs.' She gave the girl a shove. 'You get on back to the camp, you hear? And keep away from the whitefellers or you'll get a good hiding.'

'I'm sorry,' Sibell said.

'You were staring right at her,' Maudie snorted, and rode off.

But at last all was quiet. They were ready to leave. Zack had decided to take the station cook with him, and after much argument Sam Lim had agreed to fill that job as a temporary measure, since there were still eleven men at Black Wattle.

'There'll only be you and me and young Wes in the house now,' Maudie told Sibell. 'Can you cook?'

Rather than admit another failing, Sibell said she would try.

'Oh, shit!' was Maudie's caustic reply.

Dawn was just a glimmer when Sibell heard a knock at her door. She climbed wearily out of bed and put on a wrapper. This outdoor life was wearing her out, and obviously Maudie intended to keep her at it until the last bullock swished off down the track. 'I won't be long,' she called.

The knock was repeated, so she opened the door, to find Zack standing there, looming over her in a high-collared cow-hide jacket. 'Couldn't leave without saying goodbye.'

'Oh!' she said, surprised. 'I'll just get dressed and come out.'

'No, don't bother, Sibell. You've done a sterling job here. Don't give up on us. And don't let Maudie get to you, she's all bark and no bite.'

Sibell nodded, rather than disagree with him at this time.

'I've been wanting to say to you, Sibell,' he continued, 'that was some ride getting back here from the lagoon. From where Cliff was killed,' he added sadly.

'Not really,' she said. 'I was lost, Zack. Merry brought me home.'

'No horse would take on the river where you did, Sibell, without a lot of whip or a lot of faith. She must have had faith in you.'

'I don't know about that. I was scared stiff.'

'You shouldn't put yourself down so much,' he said quietly. 'God knows, in this world there are always plenty of people to do that for you. You took on the river with Merry, and it was a very brave thing to do. One helluva swim,' he grinned. 'You're famous.'

'Why?' she said bitterly. 'I didn't help. It took me so long to get home it was too late to get help.'

'Is that what you think?' he asked, surprised. He pushed the door open and put his arms around her. 'Don't do this to yourself, you're not to blame. A horse with wings couldn't have brought help in time.' She was folded in his arms, comforted by his strength.

'Are you listening to me?' he asked.

'Yes,' she whispered. 'Thank you, Zack.'

He released her and stood back, looking down at her with a smile. 'No need to thank me. I'm very fond of you. I'll keep in touch, the telegraph line will come in handy, since I'll be following that route.' He took her hands. 'I really appreciate your staying on, damn sure I do. And watch out for young Wesley, will you?'

'I'll be glad to.'

He seemed reluctant to let her go. 'I have to say this now, so that you can think about it while I'm away. I'm not just fond of you. I love you. And I hope you can see some merit in me. When I come back, I'll be wanting to ask you to do me the honour of becoming my wife.' He breathed a sigh of relief. 'There! It's said!'

'Me?' she asked, feeling foolish, at a loss to know how to reply.

'Miss Sibell Delahunty, to be correct,' he smiled. Then he kissed her, a warm, loving kiss. 'I'll be praying you're still here when I get back, or else I'll have to come looking for you.'

From the veranda she watched them ride away, embarrassed that Zack had kissed her like that, when she was so much in love with Logan, and sorry for him over that sudden proposal, knowing she would have to disappoint him. She should have refused him there and then, but he'd hardly given her a chance, and she'd been too confused to compose a sensible explanation. But now she felt bereft and realised she would miss Zack Hamilton. She really would.

Maudie was out there now, boss of the walk, shouting at the remainder of the station hands to report for work, rallying everyone by pounding on the cookhouse gong.

'Oh, go to hell!' Sibell said, and went back to bed.

Zack was wrong. Maudie didn't need her at all, she treated Sibell like a half-wit servant. Or rather she tried to, but Sibell fought back. 'As long as I am here, you will address me civilly,' she said.

'You don't have to stay,' Maudie retorted. 'We can get along fine without you.'

'I promised Zack I would do my work, and I will keep my promise.'

'Oh, yes, Zack. Still hoping to marry him, are you? Think you're going to be the lady of the house and push me out?'

'So that's it!' Sibell said. 'You don't care if the station isn't run properly, just so long as you're "the missus". Well, here's the journal!' Sibell flung the book at her. 'Write that up. And here's a letter from the bank, read that – it's rather nasty – and tell them how Mr Hamilton intends to continue repayments. There are a few more here, too, and bills to be paid. Answer them yourself!'

'I can get Casey to help me,' Maudie sulked.

'He can barely write his own name, and you know it.'

'That's right. Throw your education in my face! You're so bloody smart, you're only hanging about here because you've got nowhere else to go.'

'Oh, don't worry. The minute Zack gets back I'll be leaving. I can't get away from here fast enough. And in the mean time, you get your boots off that table, you'll scratch it. Charlotte paid a fortune for it.'

'This is my house, remember. I'll put my boots where I like.'

Later, though, Sibell noticed with a smile that the boots had been removed and were never again dumped on the dining-room table. She realised that in Maudie's mind, Charlotte still held sway, and so on occasion she invoked Charlotte in their arguments, with some small success.

It took a while for her to entice Netta to help her in the kitchen, since she still saw it as Sam Lim's domain. Sibell's initial problem was to keep the stove hot. The huge old range was forever going out on her, with the result that Maudie would come home to find their food only half cooked and would sit smirking on the veranda, refusing to help. But gradually Sibell had it under control, and with Sam Lim's guidance was managing to produce edible meals. Quite often, too, she cheated, bringing over stews and puddings from his 'chow-house', as he called his new premises.

She was appalled at Maudie's lack of interest in her son. Apart from teaching the little boy to ride, she left him with his black nannies, not even bothering to see him to bed.

'You ought to take more notice of him,' Sibell chided Maudie.

'What for? I never had nursemaids to look after me, and neither did my brothers. He's spoilt enough already.'

'He's talking pidgin all the time. He should eat with us now and spend more time away from the twins.'

'Easy to see you don't know nothing about kids. He's running around all day, good and healthy, so he eats at five o'clock and goes to bed. I don't get in till dark: I know what it's like to be bloody tired by the end of the day.'

That, Sibell felt, was the saving grace. Except for Sundays, Maudie was busy around the station most of the day. She usually came in for lunch – which she called dinner – but often she'd be away all day. Apart from, too often, burning the porridge in the early mornings, Sibell's routine was working. The homestead was a delight without Maudie's presence: she and Netta prepared the meals in the morning, then they did the housework together, and after lunch Sibell settled happily in the office, determined that Zack should have no complaints. In the evenings, when Maudie went to bed, she sat up reading, working her way through Charlotte's library. She kept Wesley with her as much as possible, correcting his English at every step. Unbeknownst to Maudie, she was also teaching him to hold a pencil and begin the rudiments of writing.

This meant she was teaching his nannies as well, so she set an hour aside each morning for the kindergarten class, where they were all progressing well, considering the lessons great fun.

By the time Logan rode in, she had almost forgotten him, so engrossed was she in her daily activities.

Thankful that Maudie wasn't about, she flew out and threw her arms around him. 'I'm so thrilled to see you. Why didn't you let me know you were coming?'

'It was quicker just to turn up,' he told her. 'I take the gold consignments to Idle Creek now, so it was too good an opportunity to miss. I heard there was trouble out this way with the blacks. And where is everyone? Are you here on your own?'

'Not quite,' she said. 'Oh, come on in, Logan. I've so much to tell you.'

She took him into the sitting room, pleased that he admired the house. 'Would you like tea? Or a drink?'

'Later,' he said, taking her in his arms. 'I'd rather have you. God, I've missed you, Sibell.'

She was so thrilled with the wonder of him. Her Logan, at last, and for him to make the effort to ride all the way out here just to see her . . . She pushed him gently away. 'Not here.'

She took his hand and led him along the polished passageway to her bedroom, where he could make love to her in the cool quiet of the afternoon. She prayed guiltily that there'd be no interruption.

And none came. This time, he undressed her slowly and completely; and she shivered at the sensuousness of his touch, his kisses and his strong caresses, fascinated by his casual nakedness as he turned back the sheets and took her into her bed. Her bed, where she would always remember him, where she would be able to think of him in his absence until they could be together forever.

Later, as she lay in his arms, she wondered what she would say if he asked her to leave with him. Right now. It would be hard to refuse him – terrible – but she had promised Zack. Oh, God, how much longer would Zack be away? Months. Long, slow, dreary months. Perhaps she and Logan could announce their engagement now, and marry when Zack came home. Poor Zack . . . But really, she told herself, he has probably changed his mind by now. It was just a spur of the moment idea on his part, just gratitude that she was helping out. He had probably forgotten all about it.

But Logan didn't mention marriage, he just asked if he might stay over for a few days.

'Of course you can,' she said. 'I'd love to have you stay.'

'What about the dragon lady, this Maudie you talk about?'

'She's no problem,' Sibell said, hoping Maudie didn't make a fuss.

Maudie didn't seem to mind at all. 'You didn't tell me you had a boyfriend,' she hissed when she managed to take Sibell aside.

'You didn't ask,' Sibell said loftily.

'He's bloody handsome,' the young widow said appreciatively. 'Are you going steady?'

'Not really,' Sibell said carefully, determined not to give Maudie room to criticise.

At dinner, Maudie was on her best behaviour, and she managed to entertain Logan with her deliberate jokes about Sibell's cooking. 'Tomorrow night, we'll have Sam Lim cook us a decent meal, Logan. We'll make a party of it, just like Charlotte used to do.'

Since Sibell's room was next door to Maudie's, she knew there was no chance of being alone with Logan that night, so she slept poorly, dreaming of him, so close . . . missing him. She consoled herself that they'd have the day together tomorrow.

'I thought I might have a look around the station today,' he said at breakfast. 'I've heard so much about Black Wattle.'

Sibell smiled. She had already decided to give herself the day off to go riding with Logan, and in the afternoon they could come home and be together again.

'Good idea,' Maudie said. 'I'll take you. Plenty to see if you know where to look. There are some great views from the escarpment way out towards Battle Creek. I'm going out that way today.'

Aghast, Sibell looked to Logan, who grinned and accepted the invitation.

Neither of them asked her to join them, and she refused to lower herself by offering to tag along, but when Maudie had disappeared she turned on Logan. 'What did you do that for? We don't need her around. I thought we could spend the day together.'

'I couldn't very well refuse,' he said. 'If I want to be allowed to come here, she's the last person I need to offend. But you can come too.'

'I'd rather not. I see enough of her as it is, without having to put up with her showing off all day.'

'It's just as well,' he whispered, kissing her. 'It'd be hell to be with you and not be able to touch you and make love to you.'

'I know, that's how I feel. I love you, Logan. Tell her you've changed your mind, and she'll have to go on her own.'

'I can't do that. Besides, I do want to have a good look around these districts, and she'd be the perfect guide.'

Sibell watched them go, Maudie trotting by with studied unconcern, and Logan looking down at her, smiling bravely, as if he were the victim of this ploy. She noticed he didn't look back.

Hurt and angry, Sibell marched over to see Sam Lim. 'I need your help. I want to put on a really nice lunch, maybe fish or a chicken.'

'Whaffor?'

'We have a guest, Mr Conal.'

'No, no . . .' He waved her away. 'Missus pack lunchie. Chop, chop, quick, sanliches.'

'Sandwiches? She took sandwiches? She took their lunch?'

'Velly good,' he replied, as if approving that she'd managed to work that out. He took a leg of beef from his meat safe, and she watched as he chopped off the shank and expertly boned the meat with his fine, sharp knives made out of a cross-cut saw. She felt leaden, unable to make herself move away. To where? To sit in the house all day and wait for them?

'You takee,' he said, wrapping the meat in a cheesecloth. 'Missus say you cook tea and not burn good meat.'

Furious, Sibell grabbed the meat and slammed back up to the house.

187

Obviously, Maudie was enjoying relegating her to the status of a servant – which of course she was! None of the other Hamiltons ever treated her like that. Wouldn't Maudie have a fit if she knew Zack really had asked her to marry him. It would pay them both back if she accepted! Who was Logan, anyway, compared to Zack? Just an employee, like herself. While Zack was a pastoralist, a highly respected cattleman.

Netta poked her head round the door of the office. 'What we do this day, missy?'

'Anything you like,' Sibell said, and Netta wandered off singing happily, leaving Sibell to her wild plan. She began composing telegrams to Zack, scrawling them over page after screwed-up page. 'Re your question the answer is yes.'

She could send one of the stockmen to Pine Creek to lodge the telegram: they were always pleased for an excuse to go into town. What about, 'I accept, signed Sibell'? That would be fun – he'd know. Or, 'Hurry home. All well, pleased to accept'?

But was she? This débâcle wasn't Logan's fault, he'd been manoeuvred into this situation by Maudie. Maudie, the widow, who maybe had designs on Logan herself. Sibell sat biting her knuckles in rage. But what a joke! Stupid Maudie! As Charlotte had once said: 'Maudie's like a heifer in the house.' And she was too, tramping around the place as if she was still out in the stockyards. As if Logan would look at her!

Another thought stole upon her. Maudie was no fashion plate, but she was Zack's partner in the station. Would that affect Logan's attitude? Surely not. Sibell began to tidy up the desk, deciding not to contact Zack after all, and then she came across the last letter from Percy Gilbert, which reminded her again of Logan. The letter had in fact been written by Gilbert's solicitor, warning Sibell not to harass Mr Gilbert further, as Mr Gilbert had demonstrated his goodwill by lavishing care and expense upon her in the most charitable manner. It was most ungrateful of her to be demanding money at this stage, after having run off without so much as a word of thanks.

Sibell knew the letter by heart, but now it served to fuel her rage. Well, she would not cook their dinner. Damn them!

When Maudie strode into the kitchen that evening she found the benches bare and the stove cold. A note on the kitchen table was held in place by the sugar pot. She stared at it for a while, and then grinned. Unable to read it, but certain it was some trick of Sibell's, she removed it to the bench by the woodbox, and called to Logan, 'I don't know where Sibell's got to. Would you mind lighting the fire, Logan, she's let the stove go out again.'

Right on cue, Logan made for the woodbox. 'There's a note here,' he said, 'from Sibell.'

'What does it say?' Maudie asked, busying herself in the pantry.

'She's indisposed,' he replied, disappointed. 'She has gone to bed and doesn't want to be disturbed.'

'That's bad luck. Poor Sibell, she's not very strong, you know. We'll let her rest. It's a bit late for me to start cooking. I'm starving. What say we join the men in the cookhouse?'

'Fine with me.'

Ears straining behind her locked door, Sibell heard them leave the house, and ran to the window to peer out from behind the curtains. Maudie was taking him down to the men's quarters. 'Damn and blast!' she said, realising she'd made another mistake. Maudie would probably enjoy eating with the station hands, she'd sit at the top table and lord it over them all. Neither Charlotte nor Sibell had ever intruded on the men, but that wouldn't mean a thing to Maudie.

The next morning, she left Netta in charge of breakfast, and went to work in her office, where Logan found her.

'Are you feeling better?'

'Yes, thank you.'

'That's good.' He ran his fingers along the nape of her neck. 'You're looking lovely this morning, as usual.'

'If you'll excuse me,' she said, 'I have to go and find Casey. The foreman reports every day, but I missed him last night.'

'Can't it wait?'

'This is my job, Logan. I have to keep tabs on all these things.'

'I know, but just spare me a few minutes.'

'I had all day yesterday,' she snapped, 'but you were too busy to bother with me.'

'Now don't get upset,' he said. 'I had a very interesting day . . .'

'I'm sure you did.'

He laughed. 'There's my snooty girl again. My God, Sibell, you really haven't changed. I want you to listen to me, because this is important.'

'What's important?' she asked, gentler now, softened by having him near her again, hoping that this important matter concerned them, just the two of them.

'Have you got maps of the station?' he asked.

'Yes, there are maps of the property in that leather case over in the corner. They're rather rough, though, I remember Charlotte saying that. I don't think they'd meet your standards, being a surveyor.'

'It doesn't matter. Can I have a look at them?'

'Yes, but why? Did she ask you to do the surveying?'

'It was mentioned,' he replied, taking out the maps and spreading them one by one on the desk. He scanned each map carefully, putting them aside until he came to the one he was looking for. 'Ha! This is it.'

'What is?'

Sibell stood beside him as he pored over the chart. 'Right here,' he said, placing his finger on a blank area. 'Do you know this spot?'

She peered down. 'I've been through there, but what's so special about it? And don't tell me you've found gold.'

Logan was excited. He took her face in his hands and kissed her on the lips. 'Promise me you won't tell a soul.'

'I promise,' she said, 'if you kiss me again and say you're sorry for leaving me yesterday.'

'I'm sorry, I'm sorry,' he laughed, arms around her, 'and my darling, I'm not sorry.'

His excitement was so infectious she shook him. 'Tell me! You did find gold?'

'No, darling, not gold, but something nearly as good. Write down these latitudes and longitudes as I call them.'

Sibell wrote them on a page and handed it to him. 'Logan, what is it? If you don't tell me, I'll start screaming.'

'Wolfram,' he whispered, 'tons of it.'

She was disappointed. 'What's that?'

'Tungsten's its other name, it's a pliant metal, very handy. And there's tin. A fortune in wolfram and tin! And I'm going to claim the mining rights.'

'Didn't Maudie see it?'

'Maudie wouldn't know tin from a tea-pot, so for God's sake don't tell her.'

'But it's their land. Wouldn't the Hamiltons own it?'

'They might own the land, but not what's under it. Anyone can claim the mining rights.'

Sibell was amazed. 'What happens now?'

'We keep very quiet. I'll have to stay where I am until I can get the cash and equipment together, and employ staff. I've learned my lesson at Katherine. I'll have all Chinese labour this time. They work harder and for less pay. I'm going to be rich, Sibell, very bloody rich.'

He danced her around the room, and Sibell was madly happy for him. She was happy for another reason, too. Maudie, the station owner, had just lost the attraction she might have had for Logan, and it was her own fault! If he had considered Maudie at all. Sibell felt foolish for having been so jealous.

'Not a word,' he reminded her, and she nodded, smiling, loving him. He was so smart, so intelligent, and God, so attractive!

Netta plodded into the room without knocking. 'What now, missy?'

'Did you make the beds?'

'No.'

'Then you can make the beds, please.'

As she departed, Logan packed away the maps. 'Let's go for a walk, Sibell. Just you and me. There must be somewhere we can get away on our own. Then I have to go.'

'Leave? I thought you'd be staying a few days.'

'My darling, I've so many things to do now, I have to be on my way.'

'When will you start the mining?'

'That will be months away, but it's safe there. I'll see you before then.'

They walked all the way to the pandanus lagoons, where he made urgent love to her. She was frantic at the thought of him leaving so soon, so much so that she discarded her Black Wattle responsibilities. 'Logan, darling, take me with you. I can't bear to be away from you again.'

'To Katherine? Never, it's a vile place. I'm living in a humpy. Don't you realise that when I start the mining, I'll have my camp right on this property. Nothing will keep us apart then.'

When Logan left, the animosity between the two women increased. Maudie seemed to go out of her way to snipe at her, and Sibell knew she should try to make the peace, to talk openly with Maudie about this problem. But every time she had almost persuaded herself to make the attempt, Maudie would upset her again.

'Why don't we ever have tripe?' Maudie asked.

'Tripe? I hate tripe. Anyway I don't know how to cook it.'

'That's nothing new. Tell Sam Lim to cook some and we'll have it tomorrow night.'

'You can have it.'

'I just said I would. And in future, when I come in at noon, I want something better than cold meat and chaff.'

'What chaff?'

'All that lettuce and stuff.'

'You mean salad.'

'I mean food for chooks. I want something solid, if you don't mind.'

'If you would let me know when you'll be home for lunch, I could prepare . . .'

'It doesn't take long to throw on some chops and potatoes.'

'But we have that for supper.'

'I don't care, I don't want to see that chook food again.'

'Maudie,' Sibell said quietly. 'If you don't stop picking on me, you can do your own cooking.'

'I could sack you, too.'

'Go ahead, then. Right! Sack me. I'll be glad to get out of this place.'

Checkmate. They finished their meal in silence.

They managed to agree that they would recommence inviting Casey and another stockman, Archie Sims, for dinner on Saturday nights. Those evenings were a strain for Sibell, though, because Maudie ignored her and talked with the men about station matters. Sibell supposed that was fair enough, since these men would have had little else to discuss, but she soon realised that they were aware of the clash between the two women and were very much amused. She was embarrassed that they had become the butt of station jokes.

On one such occasion, Maudie did direct the conversation at Sibell. 'And what has become of your boyfriend, Sibell? Have you heard from him?'

Sibell was furious. Maudie knew that she hadn't heard a word from Logan, and that was bad enough, but then she saw the two men exchange knowing glances. 'All in good time,' she replied, smiling. The men worried her, though, she had a vague feeling that she'd picked up something else, not just another of Maudie's barbs. Then she dismissed it: probably they were notching up another spicy bit about 'the ladies' to report to their mates.

She decided she would write to Logan, inviting him to visit the station since it would be difficult for her to get to Idle Creek Junction. That was certainly true. She had mentioned to Casey that she might like to visit the junction, one of these days, having Logan in mind, but he hadn't been helpful. 'I don't know, miss. We're short-handed as it is, and I couldn't let you go without a couple of men to see you got there safe. And in the light of what happened to Cliff, I wouldn't recommend it right now. The junction isn't much of a place for ladies, anyhow. Best you talk it over with Maudie.'

Like hell she would.

'Nothing much to do here in the wet,' he continued, 'so I guess you people will be going in to Palmerston for a few months. That'll give you a break.'

'Does everyone go?' she asked.

'No. I don't like towns. I stay put here with some of the hands, just to keep the show going. Maudie says I'll have to move into the homestead to keep it fresh, so that'll be a bit swish for me, eh?'

She learned that most of the cattlemen, the bosses and their families made for the coast in the wet, some even going by ship as far as Sydney. Some of the really rich ones, including mine owners, even went to England. She was intrigued. Logan would be rich once his mines were operating. How exciting to be able to travel, to be forced to travel by these great rains everyone talked about.

That night she searched among Charlotte's papers and found the title deeds to the house in Palmerston. Maudie never mentioned it and Zack seemed to have forgotten about it.

'If Zack needs money,' she suggested to Maudie, 'he could sell that house in Palmerston.'

Maudie looked at her as if she were simple-minded. 'He wouldn't sell that, it's our beach house. Talk about penny-wise! Palmerston is cut off from the world except by ship in the wet: where else would we stay? It's not just Zack and me: we'd have Wesley and the two gins and Netta to do the housework, it'd cost a packet to rent a house in Palmerston for three months.'

'I suppose so,' Sibell said, feeling desperately lonely. Maudie had made it plain that her services would not be required during that time, and no invitation was extended to join them in Palmerston. Where would she go? With a shock, she realised that unless Logan came for her she'd be forced to remain on the station or find another job. Unless, of course, she married Zack, and that was out of the question.

Despite her problems with Maudie, Sibell found the days were rushing past, hauled along by the routine of the station. She had become accustomed to the energy and clatter of early morning as the men turned out and saddled up, their shouts and laughter mingling with the jingle of harnesses and the excited barking of dogs anxious to get to work. She liked to watch them cantering past the house, intent on the day.

Every so often they'd bring mobs of cattle or horses down the homestead track and into the stockyards. When she'd first arrived, the noisy cavalcades had fascinated her, but now that she was housekeeper as well as book-keeper in this establishment, their progress simply meant clouds of dust and more flies. A daily trial was her battle with the dust and grit, that seemed to permeate every inch of the house, not to mention the hordes of sticky flies, and her especial enemies, huge cockroaches. All the food had to be kept in safes, which stood in tins of water to protect them from the armies of ants which constantly invaded the kitchen. Some of Charlotte's new furniture had already been attacked by termites.

Since insects were normal to her, Netta was not disturbed by them. 'Why you worry?' she asked when Sibell would stand in the kitchen in despair, food on the benches black with ants.

It was fortunate that Sam Lim was in charge of the fowl-house and the vegetable garden, because Sibell was too frightened of snakes to enter those precincts. She had almost come to accept lizards, from tiny to gigantic, but not snakes. She never saw them in the grass, but she knew they were there, and she had seen several hanging lethargically from trees.

When she finally had the house in order, and three hot meals prepared for Maudie, who ate enough for two men, she sent Netta over to Sam for their daily supply of cakes and scones, which she had discovered was another essential for station people. They made meals of morning and afternoon teas, 'smokoes', they called them, and Maudie could get very cranky if she found the cake tins bare.

Sibell moved her office time to the evenings so that she could enter station information into the records as soon as Maudie and Casey came in. With luck, that gave her free time in the afternoons to exercise her horse or to relax in the delicious quiet of the house, with Wesley asleep.

There was no word from Logan, but he could be forgiven: he'd be back soon. 'He has to come back,' she told herself with pleasing certainty. 'His wolfram stuff is on this property.' She was a little worried about Zack's reaction to mining on his land, but a few carefully posed questions to Casey reassured her that Logan would be within his rights to stake a claim. Not that she mentioned Logan by name, her questions had referred to miners in general.

'Miners?' Casey had said. 'They're a damn nuisance but a fact of life. We can't complain, because it's the miners who are opening up the towns, making markets for us. They move on eventually.'

On this particular day, Sibell was in the kitchen, ironing, since none of the black girls had any inclination to learn what was to them a pointless chore. They did like to watch, though. Suddenly a terrifying crack of thunder split the air, and Sibell reacted with such a start that the flat-iron went crashing to the floor. Netta shot under the table, and the twins came hurtling inside, clutching Wesley.

They cowered together in the kitchen as the thunder roared and high wind scorched across the land. There was no rain, though, and after a while the commotion faded into the distance. 'Debbil-debbils,' Netta said but Sibell picked Wesley up.

'No,' she told the frightened child. 'It's only clouds bumping together.'

'Whaffor?' Wesley asked, sounding like Sam Lim, and Sibell sighed realising that her reply was as silly as Netta's, and that this poor boy was growing up with two pidgin languages to complicate his English. She resolved to make more time for him: he was a delightful child, full of fun and curiosity. Sibell had become very fond of him.

That night, after Casey left the office, Sibell waited for Maudie. When there was still no sign of her, Sibell went down to the cookhouse, where Casey, Sam Lim and some other men were playing cards. 'Maudie isn't home yet. Have you seen her?'

'She won't be far away,' Casey said. 'Maudie can look after herself.'

'But it's after eight, and pitch black out there . . .'

With an effort, Casey dragged his attention away from the cards. 'Anyone see her today?'

The others shook their heads, so he climbed out of his chair. 'She might have decided to camp out, I'll check.'

He went off to the bunkhouse to ask the other stockmen, and came back shaking his head. 'Johnny saw her this morning,' he said. 'She was on her way out to check some water holes.'

'Which way?' Sibell asked.

'Well, that's a good question.'

'Checking water holes wouldn't keep her out all night,' Sibell said.

'Unless she got too far to make it back tonight,' Casey suggested.

'On her own?'

'No,' he admitted, 'she don't usually camp out on her own.'

'You mean never,' Sibell said. 'I'm worried about her, those black-fellows could have come back this way.' Cliff's death was uppermost in her mind, and that dark territory out there now seemed too quiet.

'Do you reckon we'd better go and look for her?' Casey asked, and Sibell realised why Zack had left Maudie in charge in preference to the foreman. He was a good worker and reliable, but obviously not anxious to make decisions.

'Yes,' she said, 'right away.' And she was surprised that they obeyed without further question.

The silence was eerie after the search parties left, and it was strange to see lamps lit over in the men's quarters well into the night. Horsemen rode in, dim shadows accompanied by the mournful cries of night birds. Sibell heard them call: 'Is she home yet?' and then the negative replies.

Unable to bear this waiting, she saddled her horse to join the search, just as the flames of sunrise lit the horizon. Netta came chasing after her. 'Miss Bell,' she called, 'you take these fellers. Them good lookers.'

Two Aborigine men in ragged dungarees and worn singlets moved shyly behind her.

'Do they want to help?' Sibell asked uncertainly.

'You take, mind you too,' Netta grinned, and Sibell thought she might as well. 'All right, you get them horses.'

'No horses,' Netta said disdainfully. 'Them fellers run.'

She was glad Casey wasn't around to witness her departure. Trotting after the two men who had already sprinted away down the track, she had a feeling he might not approve. She wouldn't go far, though, and with the daylight, the station men might find Maudie any minute.

By the time they reached the main track, a mile from the homestead, Sibell expected to meet some of the men, but the converging paths were deserted. 'Which way will we go?' she asked her trackers, but, ignoring her, they stood very still, listening. Sibell couldn't hear a thing, unless you counted the ever-present birds, and it seemed to her a futile exercise to be listening for Maudie. Suddenly they plunged into a narrow trail threading through the bush and she followed.

As they rounded a bend, Sibell heard their excited shouts, and catching up, she saw them racing towards a riderless horse which was making its despondent way home. 'Good Lord!' she called to them. 'It's Maudie's horse. Where is she?' But it was no use talking to the black men, they were studying the horse's hooves.

One man ran back with the horse to send it on its way, then the tracking began in earnest.

It was a slow business. They kept to the trail for a couple of miles, then broke away into the scrub, heads down, loping along, picking up the tracks of the horse. Sibell followed obediently. She was worried. There was no doubt now that Maudie was in trouble somewhere out here in this desolate country. Sibell tried not to think of the wild blacks and at the same time remembered that in her haste she'd left her gun behind.

She pushed on, watching the Aborigines pointing, conferring, trotting relentlessly on. She hoped something would come of this, because they'd been out for hours, and the slow rate of travel seemed to be more enervating than a good fast gallop.

Merry pricked up her ears, and was harder to hold back as they approached a water hole, and soon they were cooling off in the muddy waters. Sibell recalled that Maudie had been investigating water supplies. She told the trackers this, and they nodded enthusiastically, setting off again, running now.

Within half an hour they heard a faint call, and the men raced ahead.

They found Maudie propped against a tree, very much alive and on her usual form, shouting angrily at the delay. 'About bloody time!' she yelled. 'It took you long enough to get here. I'm just about out of water.' She pushed aside the rifle resting on her lap and drank greedily from her water bottle.

Sibell jumped down from her horse. 'Maudie! Thank God we found you. Are you all right?'

'Oh, for Christ's sake, of course I'm not bloody all right. I've broken my leg.'

'Good Lord, no. Let me see.'

'Don't you touch it,' Maudie snapped, pain evident in her face as she grimaced at her twisted leg. 'I tried to straighten it but I think I only made it worse.' She looked at the mournful faces of the Aborigines. 'My word, Jacky and Sol. You two bloody smart fellers, hey? Plenty present for you when I get home.' She handed over the water bag. 'Sol, you get me some water. And Jacky, you run home and tell Casey to bring the buckboard. You know buckboard?'

'Yes, missus,' Jacky said, and disappeared into the bush.

'I'll stay with you until Casey comes,' Sibell offered, and Maudie grudgingly accepted.

'If you like.'

Sol brought back the water, which Maudie sipped carefully. 'This is muddy but it's still good. I've been here since that storm yesterday.'

Sibell took her neckerchief, doused it in water, and mopped Maudie's face. 'You're dreadfully hot. I think you have a temperature.'

'I'm bloody lucky to be alive,' Maudie groaned.

'What on earth happened?'

'It's my own fault,' Maudie said. 'I can't believe I was that damned stupid.' She looked up. 'See this tree?'

Sibell peered up at the huge old tree. 'What about it?'

195

'They call them "widow-makers". Men have been killed sheltering under these trees. Boughs break off, heavy as lead, and crash down, and bang . . . broken necks.' She pointed at a huge branch lying nearby. 'That thing nearly finished me. You know about them, don't you, Sol?'

The Aborigine shoved at the branch with his foot. 'Debbil,' he said, spitting at it in disgust.

'Did the branch break your leg?'

'No. It clouted me on the shoulder, the horse took fright and bolted, and I got thrown. Broke my leg. The only thing to do was to crawl back here and wait. I figured if I stayed close to the trunk, it couldn't get me again.'

It was only then that Sibell realised Maudie's left arm was limp. 'Oh, dear God, you've hurt your shoulder, too.'

'Bloody busted it,' Maudie said, her teeth gritted.

'You must be in terrible pain. Can't I do anything at all to help?'

'I don't think so, I'm better to stay still. I'm not looking forward to being lifted into the buggy, but I have to get home somehow.'

'I'll tell them to be gentle,' Sibell said, but Maudie had closed her eyes. She looked exhausted, and Sibell let her rest.

After a while she asked Sibell, 'Did the horse go home?'

'Yes, it was nearly at the gate.'

'Good,' Maudie said wearily. 'I had to throw rocks at him to make him go. After his bolt he came back all sorry for himself.'

'The men have been looking for you all night,' Sibell told her, but she didn't seem interested, so Sibell bathed her face again, and very slowly, very carefully, began to remove Maudie's boots.

Maudie was not in the best of moods. She listened as Sibell read out stock figures. 'That's bunkum. There are plenty more calves out there yet. And they haven't mustered down near the south-west boundaries yet.'

'Casey said they have.'

'Casey! He's too soft. They could tell him anything, he'd believe it. Zack'll be back soon, or the rains, either way we're in trouble if we don't get this sorted out. All of those calves have to be branded or they're easy prey for rustlers. And it'll be a nice bloody picture if we've got cattle wandering around the scrub for three months and we can't even guess how many. Bloody lamebrains!'

She was propped up on the couch in the office, with her leg tightly bound in splints, and her left arm strapped to her side to protect her dislocated shoulder. Maudie had endured the journey back from the scene of her accident with a stoicism that amazed Sibell. And she had refused to take laudanum to ease the pain while Casey and Sam Lim straightened her leg.

Sibell had been terrified. 'Are you sure you can do this?' she asked Casey.

'We have to try,' he told her. 'It'll be days before Doctor Brody can get here, and if it starts to knit crooked then it'll have to be broke again.'

'Oh, my God! Have you done this before?'

'Yeah, but not on ladies. And not on someone like Maudie. She'll kill us if we bugger it up.'

196

'I think you should take the laudanum,' Sibell said, but Maudie was adamant.

'No bloody way. It's my leg, I want to see what they're doing. You can get me a whisky though, a large double.'

Uninhibited, she yelled in pain, and yelled at them, as, sweating nervously, they jerked her leg into shape. When it was over, the leg in splints, she instructed them to get leather belts and strap her arm to her body.

She lay back then, waiting for the pain to settle. 'I'll have another shot of whisky now,' she told Sibell, who rushed to bring it to her.

'I think you're incredibly brave,' she said. 'I'd have wanted a pint of laudanum.'

'Not brave,' Maudie sighed, her voice faint now from the exertion. 'The stuff makes me throw up.' She smiled drowsily. 'My ma was brave, though. She was the one. She got bit by a death adder, on the finger, and we were nowhere near a town, not that there's much anyone can do, so she chopped it off.'

'She did what?'

'Chopped it off! With a tomahawk. Her finger, above the knuckle.'

Sibell knew it didn't help to sit staring at her journals. If they were wrong, something had to be done. But she still had trouble keeping up with Maudie's complaints, because she really didn't understand the problem, or, for that matter, how Maudie knew there was a problem. 'Three months?' she asked. 'Why do you just leave the cattle for three months?'

'Because of the wet, we wouldn't be able to cross any of the rivers or creeks, even if we wanted to.'

'I'm sorry, I had no idea the rains went on that long.'

'Longer,' Maudie told her. 'October to just about April is the rainy season. We're bloody lucky they're late this year. That's what gets my goat, here it is, November already.'

'But how do you know there are more cattle out on the station than I've got here in the books?'

'Because we're down on last year. It's there in your flaming books, if you had the sense to look. And there's no reason for it. Last year we lost four hundred head in the floods, but this has been a good year. With natural increase the numbers have to be up. A bloody shame Cliff isn't here to see Black Wattle doing so well at last.' She rarely spoke of Cliff, and Sibell understood. She was still unable to talk about her parents.

'So!' Maudie shifted uncomfortably, frustrated by this forced inactivity. 'We have to get it right. I won't have Zack telling me I messed up. Get the buggy, Sibell. I'll make Casey take me out himself.'

'Definitely not. Doctor Brody said you're not to be moving around, you've got two bad breaks in that leg.' She could appreciate Maudie's concern, though, she, too, wanted Zack's approval.

'I'll go,' she announced.

'Go where?'

'I'll go out and finish the job for you.'

'The hell you will. You'll break your bloody neck!'

197

'No, I won't. What if we split the station into districts and I send the men out to recheck. I can bluff them. I can say that I know by the figures from last year that they're not mustering properly.'

'That they're cheating, the lazy bastards,' Maudie said.

'Righto, that they're cheating, and Zack will be cross.'

'Zack will fire every last one of the buggers,' Maudie corrected.

But then Sibell was worried. 'Who will look after you?'

'Netta, of course. God, I feel useless with one wing and one leg, but she can lump me around the place. I can sit in the kitchen and watch her burn everything.'

Wesley came barging in, and his mother grimaced as he shook her. 'Mumma tell allasame good stories?' he asked, and Sibell saw Maudie wince at his pidgin. Noticing at last.

'I don't know any stories,' she said gruffly.

'Of course you do,' Sibell said. 'You must have hundreds of lovely bush stories you can tell him, about your childhood.'

'What good are they?' Maudie grumbled.

'They're important,' Sibell said, and not wanting to upset her by making an issue of it, she changed the subject. 'I'll bring Casey in to see you, and you have to tell him I'm in charge or they won't listen to me. Will you do that, Maudie?'

'I suppose so. But if you get into strife out there, it's not my responsibility.'

'No one says it is!' Sibell took Wesley off to bed and read him the story of the Three Little Pigs, which he found hilarious. 'I won't be able to give you lessons for a few days,' she told the child, 'because I'll be out mustering, but you'll be a good boy for the girls, won't you?'

'Yes,' he said, and then he looked up at her. 'Has Zack gone to heaven, like my dad?'

'Oh, goodness me, no! Zack's just taking cattle down to another station, he'll be home soon.'

'That's good,' Wes said sleepily. 'I like Zack.' Sibell was surprised to feel tears prick at her eyes. She sat with him until he was fast asleep, pondering her own loss. At least she'd enjoyed the company of her father throughout her youth. Wesley probably wouldn't remember much about Cliff.

She nodded to the twins, who were settling down on the veranda outside the door, and tiptoed away, resolving to make more effort on behalf of the tousle-headed little chap, while there was still time.

There were days when Sibell regretted her foolhardy offer, days when her back and backside ached, burning like torches, from long hours in the saddle with the sun building to a fury. She soon lost her creamy complexion, first to sunburn and then to a shiny bronzed look, with a white flash across her forehead which was protected from the sun by her hat.

She rode with Casey and Archie Sims right to the far boundaries of the station, camping out overnight, as Maudie often did, in the company of a dozen men who came together at a prearranged location for safety from marauding blacks. She carried a notebook and pencil and took down numbers at makeshift stockyards, choking in the dust and smell of thousands of cattle, until she grew to hate them.

If Logan could see me now, she thought, as she was forced to assist with new-born calves, or watch, sickened, as the men struggled with moaning cows, trying to extricate calves hanging half out of the mother's body. But the men worked. Sibell shouted at Casey that time was running out, and Casey yelled at the men.

'Where do you come from, Casey?' she asked him one night.

'I grew up on the Dargo High Plains,' he told her, 'and I got the wanderlust. Worked as a stockman right up through Queensland, and joined a drive across to The Territory. Tried my hand at gold mining but couldn't make a go of that, so I drove cattle for a while, and then I wandered in here. Liked the place. Decided I was sick of living with a swag, so Black Wattle is my home. Staying here,' he told her, 'until my toes turn up.'

Sibell knew then that, at fifty-five, Casey dreaded being sacked from the station. So she kept on at him, and he responded, except that occasionally he was heard to remark caustically that she was a worse nagger than Maudie.

She gave no indication that she cared what he said, but his criticism actually pleased her. She was flattered.

At night she came home exhausted, which amused Maudie. 'You're worn out, missy, give it away.'

She'd love that, Sibell told herself as she stumbled into bed, she'd love to tell Zack I can't cope. But I'm not giving her the satisfaction.

The meals were terrible, mainly burned or half-cooked chops, with lumpy potatoes and tasteless soup. 'Why don't you get cooked food from Sam Lim?' she asked Maudie. 'The men are eating better than we are.'

'Because he's already whining about cooking for extra men, and I don't want him quitting.'

'What extra men?'

'I've hired some breakers. The mustering's about finished, and we've still got time. I've seen mobs of brumbies running wild out there, I want a hundred brought in. That's what you call a base figure. Double it if you can.'

Sibell was furious. 'You're just making work. You could have done that ages ago.'

'No, I couldn't,' Maudie said. 'Most of the men will be going in to Palmerston for Christmas. They might as well make themselves useful on the way and take a mob of horses into the sales yards for me. As many as I can supply. I want those brumbies.'

'I don't believe it's necessary.'

'You wouldn't. But I see money as necessary.'

Hoping there wouldn't be too many complaints, Sibell ordered the men to begin rounding up wild horses, and was surprised that they didn't mind at all. 'A change of pace,' Casey said. 'It's a ton more fun rounding up horses.'

'If they bring in two hundred,' Sibell offered, 'they can all have one each for themselves. Free.'

'And the station pays the breaker's fees?' Casey bargained.

'Yes,' Sibell agreed, not caring, so long as she made the quota and confounded Maudie.

She was now seeing the land in a different light. Prior to these weeks of work, she had ridden through as if she were in an empty park. Now she was seeing for the first time the most amazing wildlife, animals she hadn't known existed. Casey seemed to know them all. There were wallaroos, some of them black, tall monitor lizards, big, strange frill-necked lizards with their skittering run, wobbling echidnas, long-nosed bilbies, and hundreds of goannas. She found that this seemingly empty country abounded with night-life: owls, bats, quolls, Casey could spot them all. He knew every bird and its habits, from the pretty finches to the great wedge-tailed eagles, and took pleasure in pointing them out. He really loved the bush, and she often saw him with the station blacks, learning from them the intricacies of nature. It was easy to understand now why this man shunned towns.

On Sundays everyone rested – the precious day off – but Sibell was sure none of them enjoyed this break as much as she. To be able to sleep in was a joy, and now there was only a week to go before the work was finished. Unless, of course, Maudie thought of something else for them to do. Though Sibell doubted she would: there had already been a few afternoon showers, and sombre clouds were beginning to edge up from the direction of the coast.

She lay in bed, wondering what would happen then. She couldn't stay on the almost deserted station, so she decided she'd have to go into town with Maudie and her entourage, and, having drawn her pay, find somewhere to live. There was still no word from Logan, and she fretted about that, thankful that the last few weeks had kept her so busy and so damned tired that she'd forgotten about him temporarily. Where was he? With all that riding, that enforced exercise, Sibell had never felt better in her life, and mentally she felt stronger, more able to cope with disappointments. Logan! She loved him dearly, but if he let her down she'd never forgive him.

She stared at the ceiling and laughed, remembering how Maudie used to come tramping into the house, complaining about her hard day, making Sibell feel inferior, a parasite even, cocooned in the comfort of the homestead. Overseeing the stock workers *was* tiring work, but interesting. Come to think of it, Sibell mused, I've enjoyed myself. The men were kind and thoughtful, and a funny lot, always making jokes, playing tricks on one another, competing, betting . . . It wasn't half as bad as Maudie claimed.

Where was Zack? she wondered. They'd had a telegram from him, hoping they were well, advising that he'd sold his cattle and was on his way home. No one seemed to know when he would arrive, though. 'If they can't make it to the homestead before the wet, they'll go straight on to Palmerston,' Casey told Sibell. 'Once the rivers are up, we'll be stranded out here. Have to use boats for emergencies, and that can be a bit dicey.'

Netta came racing into her room – she'd never learnt to knock. 'Miss Bell. Strange blackfeller comen up house.'

Sibell leapt up. 'Is he dressed?' Tribal blacks who refused to wear clothes were forbidden on the station.

'Yes, him covered,' Netta replied, and Sibell laughed.

'Very well, I'll see what he wants.' She dressed quickly and went outside, to find Jimmy Moon waiting at the gate, holding out a bedraggled parcel.

'Present,' he called, 'for Missibel from Logan.'

Caught in his own web, Logan had mixed feelings about closing down a second Gilbert mine. He needed to earn as much as possible to build up the necessary capital for his own projects, but, on the other hand, he was eager to finish work in Katherine and move on.

He'd approached the manager of the Bank of South Australia in Katherine, for a loan, but that gentleman had to put the matter before his superior in Darwin, who in turn had to obtain approval from the head office in Adelaide. 'Money's tight,' the manager, Fred Crowley, told him. 'There've been some nasty spills in the share market, lad.'

'That's nothing new,' Logan said. 'I don't believe this talk of money being short.'

'You'd better believe it. Back there in London they don't want to see us going the way of America, with all this talk of making Australia a republic so the Mother Country has turned the screws.' He grinned. 'We can't run away from home with no cash, so they're making fair bloody certain we're kept short. Only the big British investors are getting easy credit . . . Take a look around you, the monster stations up here are mostly owned by them. Anyway, you didn't give me much to go on. What do you need the cash for?'

'It's a private matter,' Logan said, unwilling to give the slightest hint of his find.

'That usually means a man's on to something.' Crowley winked. 'But it's not much help on your application.'

'Never mind, just keep trying,' Logan told him.

He had troubles at the mines. Having brought in Chinese labour to boost the pace of work, he was very pleased with their progress, but the other men went on strike, and stayed out until Logan was forced to pay off the Chinese.

The coming wet season worried him, too. He couldn't seem to find a definite answer to his questions so that he could plan ahead. Some men told him the mines would be flooded, shut down for the season, others told him that only happened if the Wet was heavy, others claimed this country was so dry a wet season would only happen once in a blue moon. They all agreed, though, that the rivers could be up, and that Palmerston never missed a rainy season.

He realised then that few people had been in this territory long enough to sustain correct statistics, so he sent Jimmy Moon to talk to local blacks. He came back with the information that there were eight seasons, so Logan gave up and concentrated on pushing his miners as hard as he dared.

And then there was Josie. It was a relief not to have her in Katherine, not to have her around him at all. The marriage had been a mistake right from the start, he reflected, made worse by the shadow of Cambray's suicide, and the attitude of her son. He was weary of the Cambrays, and irritated that Josie had refused to go on to Perth. His nights were filled now with erotic dreams of Sibell, her youth and beauty, her spectacular body, her willing, exciting passion. Compared to Sibell, Josie had become, in his eyes, a dullard. Their love-making on the ugly old bed, he recalled, had hardly been worth the effort.

Not that their miserable surroundings had helped, living in the old cabin, but Logan still blamed Josie. She was more of a drag on him than a wife. It was her fault the marriage was over: he wished she had taken the initiative and left him, but since she had not, Logan decided it was time to call it a day.

He recalled his rash promise to Sibell before he left Black Wattle Station: that he'd arrange to meet her at Idle Creek Junction as soon as possible, sending Jimmy Moon for her next time he took a gold consignment north. That was too risky now. He was becoming too well known, down 'the track', as the locals called the route south from Palmerston. Someone would be sure to mention Josie, and Sibell would find out he was married. He smiled to himself, thinking of Sibell's temper – that in itself excited him. Josie was always so cloyingly kind!

Logan knew that if he wanted to hold on to Sibell he'd have to make a move right away. Disassociate himself from Josie once and for all.

Their agent had found her a house to rent in Palmerston, and from her letters she was happy enough there, though missing him. He could afford to support her for the time being. When his mines were operating and he was in the money, he'd make a settlement on her, once the divorce was final.

'Timing is all-important,' he told himself as he sat down to write to Josie, informing her that he wanted a divorce. She could be assured, he added, that he would take care of her financially. On condition that she returned to Perth. Once she did that, he smiled, he'd be clear to use her desertion as grounds for divorce. In this place, the heart of rough justice, he'd have a divorce over and done with before she even heard about it. There were several lawyers of questionable repute among the ranks of the miners on the goldfields, who could advise him in return for a few grains of Percy's gold.

Josie was happy in Palmerston, and planned to make their home there. Her house was on the edge of the Chinese quarter, a neat stone cottage set in lush grounds filled with tropical trees and bushes and myriads of beautiful chattering birds.

After Katherine, it was heaven. She had two bedrooms, an indoor kitchen, a real bath in the wash-house at the back. Best of all, she had a proper sitting room at the front of the house, and a pretty little porch where she could sit out of an evening and watch the brilliant sunsets.

The house was owned by an elderly Chinaman, Wang Lee, whom she found to be charming, and who had introduced her to her neighbours, all Chinese. Josie had been terrified of them at first, but now she found them happy, friendly people, whose main interest in life seemed to be food. They were forever plying her with prettily wrapped gifts of vegetables or eggs. Wang Lee himself had brought some Chinese women in to help Josie prepare a vegetable garden, telling her that vegetables grew here in a spectacular manner.

Contrary to all the tales she'd heard from the miners' wives when they'd straggled into Palmerston in the buggies that had been sent to collect them at a river port, she found the town a pleasant place, not a vile den of iniquity at all. There *was* a sleazy end of town, with brothels and sly-grog shops, a rough element around the wharves, and, nearby, the mysterious Chinese quarter, but a commercial centre was beginning to emerge, with two new hotels under construction.

Josie explored the town with interest. She was learning to cope with the heat by finishing her chores early in the morning and taking a siesta at midday. She took a sunshade with her on her walks and relied on the big leafy trees for shade in her travels, becoming quite well known about the town.

Accustomed to handling the family finances in her first marriage, Josie had continued to do so with Logan, who had no complaints, since she was a frugal housekeeper, and they both had access to his growing bank balance. Much daring, intending to explain later to Logan, she had sent a cheque for twenty pounds to Ned at his boarding school, and was delighted to hear from the bank teller that the cheque had been cashed. One small step, she told herself, a little smugly, not expecting thanks: at least the contact was made. She didn't care if she had to buy her way back into his good books, just so long as he acknowledged her existence. She was looking forward to the time when he would accept an invitation to take his holidays in Palmerston with her and Logan. What young boy could resist a sea voyage? Then he could meet and get to know Logan, who would make a fine father, a better father than Jack had ever been to the poor boy.

Wang Lee came to see her. 'You like my house?' he asked.

'I'm very pleased with it,' she told him. 'And the gardens are so lovely, with all these flowering trees. More like living in a park.'

'Ah, then you must buy,' he said. 'Velly nice house for sale now.'

'I can't do that. I only want to rent it.'

He shook his head. 'Velly sad. House for sale now. Best you buy or soon too late.'

Josie panicked. She knew how lucky she was to have found this place, and dreaded having to leave. There were better houses being built in a little area known as Doctors Gully, a pretty bayside spot, but they were for wealthier residents. Apart from that, decent houses were still difficult to find, especially to rent. 'How much do you want for it?' she asked him.

'Seventy pound,' he said. 'Velly cheap.'

Josie had spent enough time in the Chinese market to know that bargaining was expected, so she offered forty. They haggled over the price for a while, and finally agreed on fifty-five pounds, to their mutual satisfaction.

She rushed to the bank, drew out the cash, and by late afternoon was the proud owner of their home in Shepherd Street, Palmerston. She wrote a long letter to Logan, describing the house in more detail now, thrilled at their investment, explaining that if (God forbid) his business might take them away from Palmerston for a time, they could always let the house and so derive income from tenants. Josie even paid two shillings to a Chinese artist for an exquisite brush sketch of the house and surrounds, to send with the letter. She explained that since it was a rented house, she had not wished to spend any money on it, but now she would make new curtains and renovate the furnishings so that he would have a truly comfortable home to come to after the wretched conditions at Katherine.

The letter posted, she spent happy hours in the stores, choosing curtain materials for each room, and, on the way home, stopped at a cluttered Chinese shop, also owned by Mr Wang Lee, and bought a lovely Persian carpet for the sitting room. Wang Lee offered to deliver it himself in the morning. He intrigued her: she had discovered that he owned a great deal of property in Palmerston, and yet he walked everywhere, as humbly as his neighbours, notable only for his ankle-length tunics of heavy linen and his embroidered pill-box caps.

When he arrived, Josie was in tears. She had rushed out early to buy cottons and needles, and to pick up a newspaper, and had found a letter from Logan at the post office. Disappointed that their letters had crossed and he would not yet know of her great news, she had taken the letter home to read in comfort. Logan's letters were few and far between, so she treasured them.

Wang Lee saw her distress, bowed, and quietly laid out the mat, putting her chairs back in place. Then he stood miserably, feet together, hands hidden in his long, wide sleeves. 'Honourable lady not like the house now?' he enquired.

'No,' she said, in a fresh burst of tears. 'It's not that, Mr Wang.'

He bowed again. 'Bad news for dear lady?'

'Yes,' she wept. 'Terrible.'

'Someone die?'

'No. But it feels like it.'

'Ah so. I make you tea, feeling better.'

Not knowing what else to do, she followed him into the kitchen and slumped at the table, mopping her eyes with a tea-towel, embarrassed that he should find her in such a state but not wanting him to leave. She needed to talk to someone. Even old Mr Wang.

He clucked at the tea. 'This poor stuff. I bring you good tea next time.' Nevertheless, he made the tea and placed it in front of her. 'You drink, tea good in hot weather.'

'Thank you,' she sobbed. 'I'm so sorry, Mr Wang, I'll be all right in a minute.' Then she realised he had made only one cup of tea, and she invited him to join her.

He seemed so calm, sitting there with her, saying nothing, and his presence settled her a little. 'I've had very bad news,' she said eventually. 'And I don't know what to do.'

'Speak of bad news,' he said solemnly, 'give away half the sorrow.'

So she told Wang Lee what had happened, that Logan wanted a divorce. In her bewilderment, she was crying again. 'I don't know why. I don't know what I have done. Maybe the Lord is still punishing me for past sins. Oh, Lord, how could he want a divorce? I love him, he must know that . . .'

Wang Lee let her talk it all out without interruption, until she turned to him. 'What should I do? Should I go back to Katherine? Maybe he's just depressed. It's an awful place. If I go to see him, I'm sure he won't want to go on with this. But he's talking in his letter about going into the country, prospecting. I might miss him. I'll have to answer him. What can I say?' She was becoming angry with Logan. 'What on earth has got into him? How dare he ask for a divorce, after all we've been through? I think he must be touched by the sun out there.'

He allowed her to answer her own questions, until she asked him again, 'What will I do?'

'Miserable Chinaman not know hearts,' he said. 'But best suggestion, do nothing.'

'But I'll have to answer his letter.'

'No, write nothing.' He gave her a sly, toothy grin. 'Man hear nothing, man worry next. Maybe he think letter lost, you not hear about this divorce. Maybe he think again.'

He rose, bowed. 'Excuse please?'

Josie jumped up. 'Yes, of course. Thank you, Mr Wang. I'm sorry to burden you with my troubles.'

When he left, she did attempt to compose a reply to Logan, trying several approaches: her love for him, her shock. Maybe anger. Or refusal to countenance a divorce. Eventually she was so weary she gave up, and instead poured herself a brandy to steady her nerves. Since she couldn't make up her mind what to say to Logan, perhaps it would be better to wait. The next morning she decided to take Mr Wang's advice and do nothing. Let Logan work out what to do next. And damn him! Instead of replying, she went to the bank and drew out half of their savings, five hundred pounds, for a rainy day.

Jimmy Moon was restless. He hadn't come all this way just to sit around a boring white man's camp. They slogged at the diggings all day and knocked themselves senseless with grog at night. That grog stuff! Jimmy was terrified of it, certain from his observations that it contained poison, sent men mad. And women too, don't forget. In the mornings he took grim pleasure in listening to the miners groaning with grog headaches, struggling to work, their faces a sickly green. He wondered why they didn't drink his favourite, lemon cordial, which didn't hurt anyone and was as sweet as honey.

'Going on now, boss,' he told Logan, who jerked around in surprise.

'Going where?'

Jimmy pointed north. 'Maybe that way. Big walk nearly finished.'

'The Sergeant won't like that. You've done a good job here.'

And so he had, Jimmy knew that. He'd tracked down two men who'd escaped from the jail, and acted as a guide for strangers in the district, using his unerring sense of direction. But the Sergeant was still angry with him for refusing to go out and track the Daly River mob that had attacked two white men. 'Can't track blackfellers,' he'd said.

'Can't or won't?' the Sergeant had snapped at him, but Jimmy would not reply. He'd learned never to argue with white men: silence confused them and warded off the risk of a beating. Any blackfeller who gave them cheek got a hell of a hiding, and Jimmy took it on himself to haul the victims to safety, warning them to keep their mouths shut in future. Even though he'd learned to survive in their world, he still bore a smouldering hatred towards the race as a whole. They were cruel and greedy, chasing blacks off the land just as they did down around Perth. Up here, there was a bush war going on, because the dark people in this land were first-rate warriors. Jimmy had heard the talk around the police station, of hunting blacks as if they were animals, laughing about it. They were only upset when a couple of their whites walked into a spear.

But the Sergeant was right. He would not track a blackfellow, never, and anyway he couldn't hope to match any of the Daly River men in their own land. He'd much rather visit them in peace, because he found their exploits greatly daring. They weren't afraid of the whites, they were men after his own heart, coming out to fight, not pulling back all the time like his own people.

Logan seemed to have forgotten he was leaving. 'Go down to the store and see if there are any letters for me.'

Obligingly, Jimmy loped away. As he entered the shop, the storekeeper grinned at him. 'Your usual?'

'Yes.' He handed over threepence and collected his bottle of cordial. 'You got letters there for Logan?'

The storekeeper sorted through mail in a tea-chest. 'Yes, there's one here from his missus.'

Jimmy returned with the letter, which, when Logan read it, seemed to make him furious. Jimmy had never seen him in such a rage, stamping around and cursing like a crazy man.

'Going now,' Jimmy reminded him, not enjoying this scene.

'Wait a minute,' Logan said. 'Can you find your way to Black Wattle Station? That's where Miss Sibell lives.'

'Yeah, easy,' Jimmy said. 'Plenty blackfeller out there show the way.'

'Good, I've got a present for her.' He opened a small tin trunk and took out a soft pink crocheted shawl. 'One of the ladies here made this so I bought it for Sibell. I haven't had time to take it to her, so you take it for me.'

'Don't mind,' Jimmy said, which was his expression of pleasure. 'You like Missibel plenty, hey?'

'Yes,' Logan admitted.

'You make her wife number two?'

'Oh, Christ! You listen carefully, don't you mention Josie to her. She doesn't know I've already got a wife.'

'What matter? Man has two wives. You rich enough to have two wives.'

'It does matter. For God's sake, listen. I sent Josie away.'

'Then you're not married.'

Logan sighed and rolled a smoke. 'Do me a favour. Just don't say anything about Josie. Sibell will get angry. Jealous.'

'Ah.' That Jimmy understood. Jealous women could get very vicious, and bust skulls. 'Say nothing, boss.'

'Good.' Logan wrapped the shawl in brown paper. 'Put it in your swag, and whatever you do, don't get it wet.'

So Jimmy set off on his walkabout. There was no hurry and so much to see. It didn't occur to him that Logan expected him to go straight to Black Wattle Station, and instead he set off in the other direction – to the beautiful gorge along the Katherine River, with its abundance of wild life which would provide him with plenty of tucker. He knew, too, that families of the big man crocodiles lived in that territory, and they fascinated him. He then joined some members of the local Gagjadu tribe, who were pleased to show him their strange country further north. Eventually he would find Missibel, and then, after learning as much as possible from the dark tribes of this land, he would go into the exciting Daly River country. From there he was told he would meet the ocean again, his journeying across the continent complete.

A house! Josie had bought a blasted house! And with his money! Without even asking him. Fifty-five pounds down the drain! She'd sat down like a broody hen, right in Palmerston. Bloody woman, getting above herself! Talk about a weight around a man's neck! But now Josie wasn't just a weight, she'd blown his plans sky high. Set him back months.

And what about Sibell? In his anger, he lashed out at her, too. She'd just have to wait . . . stay there on the station until he had time to think this through. The wolfram mines were his first priority, he had to get his hands on some cash. In time, it could be easy enough from here, if he was careful. This month's gold supply was nearly ready for shipment, the books were in order, he couldn't touch them now. But next time . . . Logan decided to start skimming, to take a few ounces for himself here and there. And why not? Percy Gilbert was sitting pretty, raking in the cash, while he slogged away, living like a black. If he hadn't met Josie, he brooded, he would still have that easy surveying job, and the promotion that had been within reach.

The mail came, and there was no reply from Josie. What sort of a game was she playing? He would write again and instruct her to sell that house, inform her that he resented her high-handed attitude, that she had a damned cheek to think she could decide where he should live. Buying a house! He didn't know which was worse, her silence over the divorce or her news about the house, the trap to pin him down.

That was it! The realisation hit him like a hammer-blow.

She had received his letter and had gone straight off and bought the place, as a defence. To dig in. Or was it retaliation?

Either way, he promised himself, her tricks wouldn't work. Next time he was in Palmerston, he'd sell it under her, and damned fast too.

Clem Starkey, manager of the Arcadia Mines, joined Logan and young Constable Ralph Jackson in taking the two gold consignments through to Idle Creek. Logan found this a much more satisfactory arrangement than having to wait for everyone else, with all the delays that entailed. Rather than attract attention, they by-passed Pine Creek, looking forward to a rest there on the return journey.

They rode hard for a full day and camped well off the track at dusk. The constable stood guard while Logan and Starkey prepared their meal of bully beef and damper, washed down by bottles of beer.

'We should have lit a fire,' Logan said. 'The smoke would keep these bloody flies and mosquitoes at bay.'

'Yeah, and advertise where we are,' Starkey replied.

But someone already knew. Logan was unable to say where the two men came from, it all happened so quickly. The constable had patrolled the area and had come into the camp to pick up a bottle of beer to take back with him, when they heard the shout. 'Stand and deliver!'

Logan froze, and Starkey jumped to his feet. Logan saw Ralph lunge for his rifle and fire with one quick action, and he threw himself on the ground to avoid the cross-fire of two shots.

The constable gave a shout of pain and fell back, shot dead.

'You two bastards stand up!' the voice grated, and as Logan stood, he saw two men, with handkerchiefs over their faces, and battered hats pulled down, leaving only slits for eyes, hard, cruel eyes.

'Hand over those gold packs,' the outlaw said.

As Starkey stumbled forward, Logan, shaking, stammered: 'You killed him!' He stared at Ralph's body spreadeagled on the ground, his head thrown back, mouth gaping, a bloodied hole in his chest.

'Shut up, or you'll be next,' the outlaw said, his heavy shotgun at his shoulder.

The other man, holding a rifle, covered Starkey as he hurried over, and grabbed the leather bags from him. 'Now get back,' the outlaw ordered. 'Sit over there beside the copper.'

'You're not going to shoot us?' Starkey protested. Logan was glad the other man had made the plea, for his own mouth was too dry with fear to utter a sound. 'You've got the gold, mister,' Starkey pleaded. 'And you can have our guns.'

'Go on!' the outlaw said sarcastically as his mate collected their weapons and their food. 'Now we'll have your boots. Toss them over. You blokes look well fed, a good walk'll do you the world of good.' He laughed as Logan and Starkey frantically unlaced their boots. 'Get their water bags too,' he said to his friend. Later, Logan was able to report that he did not call his mate by name, nor did the other man speak at all, which was possibly because he had an accent that could be recognised. This fellow, the spokesman, had an Australian bush voice no different from thousands of his countrymen.

Logan didn't care about the gold, he was too stunned at the awful sudden death of the young constable. He watched their attackers carefully so that he could provide descriptions. They were both heavily bearded, both lean fellows aged thirty to forty, in moleskins and Blucher boots, both with check shirts. The silent one was wearing a cow-hide waistcoat, the sort that stockmen often wore, but with brass buttons, tarnished brass buttons, he had to remember that.

'Sorry about the copper,' the outlaw said, 'but it was self-defence. Silly bugger,' he said amiably. 'Bloody kids shouldn't be let loose in this country. I had the bead on him and he goes the hero.' He sighed. 'Too late to learn now.'

Logan heard the other man taking the hobbles off their horses, and he found his voice. 'For Christ's sake, leave our horses.'

208

'Can't do that, mate,' the outlaw said, giving a low whistle, calling up their own mounts.

As the horses came into view, Logan tried again. 'You can't leave us out here without water and without horses. We'll die in this heat.'

The other man, having packed up the boots, the food and water, and the gold, mounted up, leading the three spare horses.

'It'd probably be kinder to shoot you now,' the outlaw agreed, 'but that wouldn't be self-defence, so I can't do that. No hard feelings, mates.' He backed away, still covering them.

They disappeared into the bush and then Logan heard the pounding of hooves as the five horses galloped away. 'Which way did they go?' he asked Starkey.

'Who bloody cares?' Starkey said. 'Jesus, poor Ralph! He was a lovely fellow. It's a bloody shame.'

They buried Ralph and chopped a swathe through the bush to mark the spot. Then Starkey sat down, exhausted. 'I've got to get some sleep.'

'No, you don't,' Logan told him. 'Our only chance is to walk at night.'

'We'll cut our feet to pieces.'

'Better than marching in the heat,' he said grimly. 'I've done something like this before, but I was new at it. I didn't have the sense to walk at night.' And then he added, 'Bloody women!'

'What's women got to do with it?'

'I usually bring a blackfeller on these trips, you know, the tracker, Jaljurra. But I let him go, because I wanted him to take a present to a female of my acquaintance. If he was around now we could sit on our bums and send him for help.'

'Bugger your "ifs",' Starkey said. 'Let's get going. I reckon we're closer to Pine Creek.'

They were brothers. Joe and Joshua Phelps. And they were blow-ins. They'd come 'f-fair ac-cross the b-b-bloody c-country,' as Joshua would say, but they had to keep moving. Escapees from the Townsville jail, where they were serving time for bank robbery, they'd headed west, counting on the generosity of station folk and the rare travellers for sustenance. Joe preferred to call it generosity: his victims called it robbery-under-arms.

'God loveth the cheerful giver,' Joe liked to quote, as they replaced their tired horses with stolen mounts, held up isolated stations for provisions, grog and whatever cash might be to hand. They were always careful to trade with the blacks, though. They paid from threepence to a shilling for 'horizontal refreshment' with their lubras, depending on the attractions of the women. When cash was short, any thing would do: blankets, a bit of corned beef or even spare guns that they had acquired.

Joe considered himself a far-sighted man. 'We have to keep the Abos on our side,' he informed Joshua. 'They'll see that we shake off the coppers.'

'Where are we g-g-going ag-gain?' Joshua asked.

'West, I told you, you mug. We don't just cross one border, we cross two, and the coppers over there won't know nothin' about us, so we'll be safe as houses.'

It was Joe who did all the talking on their raids. 'I can just hear you,' he'd laugh, 'with your bloody stutter, trying to make them stand and deliver!' It was his favourite joke. Joshua didn't like it much, but Joe was his brother and his mate, so you couldn't complain.

'S-s-s-s-stand and d-d-d-d . . .' Joe would howl, doubled up laughing at the thought of frightened station women, their usual target, waiting for the bad news. 'By that time, the ladies would have grabbed for their guns,' he'd snigger.

They crossed into the Northern Territory, where the going was hard. 'Bloody shockin' bloody country, this is,' Joe complained, as they struggled across hundreds of miles of endless dried, cracked river beds, not realising that this was known as the Gulf Country, impassable in the wet. First Joe's horse collapsed, and then the other one, and the two men stumbled on, on foot, starving and dehydrated, ditching the last of their possessions in their fight against the grinding heat, until they were rescued by a mob of blacks.

'See, I told you,' Joe said, as they slowly recovered their strength. 'They're the only bastards worth a crumb in this whole bloody world.' And he meant it. Joe liked Abos, he sided with them. He reckoned they got pushed around just as much as poor bloody whites, and he liked their humour, the giggling women and the rumbling grins of the men. Not that he ever bothered to learn their names or their tribes, they all looked the same to him, and in this arse-end of the world, they were as numerous as kangaroos.

Fit again, he looked to his new friends for advice. 'Where's the nearest station homestead?'

'C-c-close?' Joshua whined, as they straggled along with the blacks for nearly a week. 'They said it was c-close!'

Eventually the blacks proudly pointed out the homestead. A deserted fenced shack.

The brothers poked about inside, and only managed to scrounge some tinned food and several bottles of rum. 'Jesus, what a dump!' Joe said. 'And they reckon a squatter lives here. He owns all this bloody land! I tell you it wouldn't do for Queensland.'

They spied some horses, though, and Joshua rounded up two decent mounts while Joe broke into a shed and took two saddles. 'Shit,' he said, scratching himself. 'They don't need bloody horses, they're jumping with fleas.'

But they were on their way again. Claiming to be gold prospectors fallen on hard times, they called at another station and were fêted in yet another miserable wattle-and-daub hut by the squatter and his missus, who were pleased to welcome visitors.

There were plenty of cattle on this station, and the brothers learned that this fellow owned land as far as the eye could see, and further. 'But why would you want to?' Joe asked his brother, as they rode away. 'Jesus, who'd want to live like that? With their dough.'

They'd been on their best behaviour with these people, since Joe had been flattered by their praise. They were impressed that the brothers had battled through to the Gulf on such a long and lonely trek, and sorry for them that they'd lost all their equipment on the way. 'Besides,' as Joe said, 'they could identify us if we pushed our luck.'

'He might have sh-shot us, too,' Joshua added. 'He n-never buckled h-his b-bloody holsters.'

Joshua was right about that. The squatter, who said they weren't called squatters up here, had swaggered around the whole time with twin guns hanging from his hips, the flaps of the holsters hanging ominously open. Joe appreciated that: their host had been a hard-looking bushie, not a bloke to tangle with.

'We gotta get guns,' Joe said, munching on fruit cake the woman had given them, as they rode on. At the next encounter, it was easy as pie.

They came across two real prospectors camped in a gully, but this time they copied the blacks and sat watching. They waited until the two men had finished eating, hoping they'd turn in and sleep. Even better, the pair were heavy drinkers. Within a couple of hours, both men were staggering drunk. It was only a matter of time, Joe knew, before they'd pass out, and sure enough, they did.

'You'll wake up with headaches that'll put you both off the booze for life,' he chortled, as he belted each one over the head with a home-made club for good measure. They stripped the camp – guns, ammo, tucker, water – and set the horses free.

'We going to P-Palmerston?' Joshua asked plaintively. He was getting heartily sick of this trek.

'No, I told you, we're going to the west, the golden west coast, I read about it in a book. This place is no good, it's too bloody hot and it's got everything that creeps and crawls. And you heard those miners, they reckon there's gold around here.'

'Are we going p-p-prospectin', then?'

'You could say that, mate. They dig, we lift. We'll hang about south of Palmerston and see what's offering.'

And that was how they came upon the best haul of their long, miserable journey: two bags of gold. Joe didn't have the faintest idea of its value, but he figured it would be enough to buy them a boat when they hit the coast, and they'd live free as birds.

He was sorry about having to shoot the copper, because that'd bring the law roaring after them. Even if they'd wanted to go to Palmerston, that was out now. Definitely out. So they rode fast, travelling west again, keeping clear of tracks, confident they'd be in Western Australia in a couple of weeks, according to Joe's sums and the information he'd picked up casually from the squatter.

'How will we know when we g-get there?' Joshua asked.

'We won't bloody know, there's no bloody line drawn, but if they send a posse after us, they'll know, and they'll have to give up the chase.'

'Why?'

Joe didn't rightly know, but he was certain they'd make it to the coast. He'd learned a lot from the Abos: how to live off the land, and best of all how to avoid the deserts, by sticking to the tropical north, and then following the coast south.

For several days, they pounded cross-country, congratulating themselves that they had a change of mounts with the three horses they had collected from the trio in the bush.

They camped deep in the sweltering forests, and Joe sent Joshua down to a muddy creek to pluck the two ducks he'd shot, while he lit a fire and boiled the billy.

'Jesus, it's hot,' Joshua said, as he stood sweating, out of range of the smoke. 'I never known a p-place as hot as this.'

'Take your shirt off for a while,' Joe replied. 'You're always whining.'

'Ah, yeah! And get eaten alive by bloody mossies. They're b-big as p-plates.'

'Well, take off that stupid waistcoat. I don't know why you wear it, you stew in it all the time.'

The waistcoat was Joshua's pride and joy – he'd won it fair and square in a card game. He took it off and placed it carefully on the branch of a tree, then squatted on his haunches beside Joe, licking his lips at the fat ducks roasting on a spit. 'When'll they be ready?' he asked.

'When they're bloody cooked,' his brother replied, lighting his pipe.

They seemed to come from nowhere, without warning, just melting out of the trees, a half-dozen big painted-up blacks, spears levelled at Joe and Joshua.

But Joe greeted them quietly. 'G'day, mates,' he called, without a trace of concern. 'You're just in time for tea.' He pointed to the ducks. 'You want one of these?'

'Gibbit guns,' one of them said, and Joe laughed. Both of their firearms were handy and fully loaded, but ten paces, he estimated, away from him, and too far for Joshua to reach them. Joe wasn't about to make the same mistake as the copper.

'You speak English?' he asked, and the man grinned.

'Mission fader learnem.'

Joe scratched his head. 'Is that right?' If they were mission blacks, what were they doing chasing guns? Renegades, by the sound of things, and he didn't like this situation one little bit.

'Can't give you guns, mate,' he said, 'but we've got a spare horse. You can have him.'

'Bugger horse,' the mission-taught Aborigine said, and strode forward to pick up the guns.

'Good-oh, you win,' Joe smiled. 'We got no quarrel with blackfellers. You fellers good mates. We're going west. What's in that direction?'

'Big river.'

'Can we get across?'

'Plenty big.'

'In the morning you show us how to cross?'

The spokesman nodded, and as far as Joe was concerned, that was that. He was disappointed at losing their guns and having to share their ducks with the blacks who hung about, but they could be replaced. He wondered where this mission was? Even holy men went armed here to hunt for game and protect themselves from snakes. They'd be easy to rob.

There was some joke going on among the blacks, and Joe grinned in

212

their direction. 'Gobble gobble,' he said to Joshua, because that's what their language sounded like to him. They talked a hundred to the dozen, words all strung together.

'Comen alonga this feller,' the spokesmen told them. 'See big river.'

'It's a bit late now, mate,' Joe said amiably. 'It'll be dark in an hour or so.'

But the blacks were on their feet. 'They're m-movin' on,' Joshua said. 'If we d-d-don't go with 'em, we could m-miss finding the b-best spot to c-cross.'

'By the looks of things,' Joe told him, 'we're not being invited, we're being took.' The Aborigines were ranging themselves around the two men, and their spears nudged. 'I shouldn't have asked in the first place.'

They set off in the company of their guides, travelling north-west, leading their horses, into heavy scrub which became worse at every step. 'This is a bloody jungle,' Joe complained, as he hacked a path for the horses, which were constantly becoming entangled in stiff, dry vines hanging greedily from ancient trees. In the end, he turned to the headman, who was right behind him in their single file. 'How much further?'

'Soon make river,' he replied. Their next hazard, though, was a mangrove swamp.

'We'd better sort this out first,' Joe told his brother. 'It could be quicksand in there. Leave the horses and we'll take a look at their bloody river, say "thanks, mates", and get rid of these characters. We were better off the way we were going.' He was still annoyed at losing their guns, and even more irritated to find they'd stumbled on the remains of wetlands that were still alive with game birds. Probably a big breeding area in the wet season. But how did you down birds without rifles?

Nevertheless, he maintained his veneer of good humour as they stepped from branches to caked mud in this twisted network of shaggy, uneven roots. 'How far this mission?' he asked his black companion, who trod easily nearby.

'Two day,' the fellow replied, more interested in a huge cloud of flying foxes that flapped chattering from their roosts.

'Through this country? Bloody hard work,' Joe commented, watching his step. The rope-like mangrove roots were brittle, waiting for water.

'Canoes,' he was informed, and that raised possibilities. If the blacks had canoes, more like dugouts, they could join forces and raid the mission. It was an idea he'd have to consider. Now, at last, as they pushed through the dense, porous trees, here was the river!

And the blacks were right: it was a wide river, still flowing strongly, and it smelled of the sea. To their left, the clutch of mangroves fell back, and Joe spied a small sandy river bank. 'Down there,' he instructed, feeling more in control now, and they all obeyed.

'This is a better spot,' he told Joshua as they surveyed the bush behind them. 'Easier to get to than the bloody march they brought us on. All we have to do now is find the horses.'

'Why d-don't you s-send them b-back for them?' Joshua said. 'It's g-getting dark.'

'I was gonna do that,' his brother said, although the idea had not occurred to him. He turned to make his request, but the atmosphere had changed. The Aborigines were done with smiling, and their coal-black faces were masks of iron dotted with white paint. They stood across the tiny beach, barring their return.

'You swim,' the headman said, swinging up the rifle. 'Good big river.'

The others had taken up warlike stances, spears poised.

'What's going on?' Joe cried. 'We ain't done you no damage. Jesus! I give you the guns, didn't I?'

'Him feller go first,' the headman ordered, and two of his men grabbed Joshua and manhandled him into the water.

Thinking they'd misunderstood, the stupid bastards, Joe screamed at them. 'No. Not yet. We can't swim that bloody river. We have to have the horses. Don't do that, he'll drown, you lunatics!'

But two more hard-muscled Aborigines held him as Joshua was forced, screaming to Joe for help, out into the deep. His captors raced back to the shore and watched grinning as their leader fired two shots, making certain that Joshua would swim.

Joe appealed to the headman but he was shoved aside and forced to watch, helplessly.

The Aborigines began to clap and leap around in excitement as Joe yelled at Joshua – poor Josh, he never was much of a swimmer – not to panic, to take it steady. Then he saw what it was that was really exciting them. Long snouts skimmed along the surface of the water like propelled logs. 'Look out!' he screamed at Joshua. 'Crocodiles! Go for your life! Keep going!' He struggled and kicked but was locked there with them on the sand, watching, as his brother screamed and the bloody attack began. At least four of the monsters reared and fought in the river over Joshua's body, tales lashing, wrenching their prey apart, the water washed pink.

Joe sank to his knees, weeping. 'Wotcha have to do that for?' he cried. 'He never done nothing to you bastards. He never done no harm to anyone in his life.'

'White feller kill my brudder,' the headman said coldly. 'So we make pay-back.'

'But, Jesus, it wasn't him! We just come to this country. We don't know nothin' about all this.'

The sun was setting, a lazy rose hue was resting over the land, and the headman was in no hurry. He stood over Joe with his rifle resting on his bare hip. 'No matter. Whitefeller hunt our people, we hunt whitefeller.' He grinned, mimicking Joe. 'Fair, mate?'

'No, it's not bloody fair,' Joe yelled at him. 'Not fucking fair at all. That was my brother you killed, I said I'd look after him and now look what you gone and done. Jesus,' he wept again, 'I think I'm gonna be sick.' He leaned forward to retch into the sand and at the same time saw another crocodile, at least twenty feet long, hurtling towards them, travelling at a pace Joe could hardly believe. Both captive and captors raced inland as the monster charged up the beach.

But Joe's freedom was short lived. They brought him back on to

214

the beach, all watching now for any sudden moves from the red-eyed armoured reptiles patrolling the river.

'We have to get out of here,' Joe told them. 'As soon as it's dark, they'll come for us, too.'

'You swim,' the headman said. Joe stared at the cruel, impassive face.

'Not on your bloody life,' he yelled. 'You won't get me in that river.' He whipped his knife from his boot and leapt away, his back to the water. 'Come on,' he shouted, wielding the double-bladed knife that had seen him through many a vicious brawl. 'Who's first?'

But the Aborigines didn't know the rules of this game.

Silently, almost dreamlike, a spear sailed towards him and thudded into his thigh.

Joe left it there, weighing him down like a chain, and screamed abuse at the headman. 'Come and get me, you bastard! You won't put me in your bloody river. You'll die for this! The troopers will get you.' Another spear struck his shoulder and he thought that was funny. 'You won't chuck me to the crocs, you'll chuck a bloody pincushion!' And even as he died, there on the sand, he wouldn't give up, calling on his old enemies. 'The coppers'll get you lot, they'll track you down. You're dead, you hear me? The whole fucking lot of you.'

They threw his body to the crocodiles, then went back and set the horses free, removing all trace of the white men's camp. They took the saddles and heavy packs, and threw everything belonging to the white men far into the river, amused that the hated crocodiles should also fight over those saddles. But far behind, unnoticed, they left a cow-hide waistcoast with dingy brass buttons hanging in the fork of a tree.

8

Netta stared in amazement as Missy ran out to greet the blackfeller, and brought him in the front door of the homestead and on through to the kitchen. She shook her head. Just as well Maudie was still in her bedroom, trussed up like a chicken. She'd really be angry with Missy this time.

But Sibell was unaware she was creating tension. 'Come through, Jimmy. What a lovely surprise! Sit down here. Would you like a cup of tea?'

Netta rolled her eyes in fear. No dark men were ever allowed in the house, let alone to sit down to tea, and she shivered at what Maudie would say. These ladies spat at each other like cats at the best of times! Nervously, at Missy's direction, she made tea and brought them some damper with jam, then watched as the new man talked to the white woman as if he had every right to be there.

Sibell opened the parcel to find an attractive crocheted shawl, rather grubby and watermarked, but retrievable. 'It's beautiful,' she said, 'and so kind of you.'

'Brung it long ways,' he told her, 'from Logan.'

Her eyes shone. 'Yes, thank you. I'm so pleased, I was beginning to think he'd forgotten all about me. How is he? Tell me all about him, Jimmy.'

Sibell didn't learn much except that Logan was working hard in his mines, living in a hut at Katherine on his own, taking his meals in a communal cookhouse, just like the station hands here. She felt sorry for him, having to rough it like that. She felt mean, too, that doubts had crept over her. 'Is he coming here?' she asked Jimmy, who nodded enthusiastically.

'Yes, he say he soon come to Black Wattle. I think he make you his wife, eh?'

Sibell nodded, thrilled. This truly was a heavenly day, and she was overwhelmed with gratitude for Jimmy's efforts, he had walked such a long way. She wanted to thank him somehow, and then she remembered the horse . . . 'I've a surprise for you, too, Jimmy. I can afford it now, so I'm going to buy you a horse. I haven't forgotten my promise, and there are hundreds of horses here.'

Netta managed to move Jimmy out to the courtyard before it was time to get Maudie up and help her out to the kitchen. Casey had made her a crutch from the fork of a strong tree, and she struggled around the house hoppity-kick like the strange little one in Missy's stories. She looked funny these days but no one dared laugh.

It only took a few minutes for her to spot Jimmy. 'Who's that bloke outside?'

Sibell explained the connection and Maudie was quite affable about him, so much so that Sibell had a sneaking feeling that it was more to do with Logan than with Jimmy himself. 'Is he staying on?' she asked.

'He'd like to, for a while,' Sibell said, and Maudie hitched herself to the back door.

'Do you want a job?' she called to him.

'Reckon,' Jimmy replied.

'You can work in the stables then. Go on down to the cookhouse and find Sam Lim. He'll give you a feed and point you in the right direction.'

'Good-oh missus,' Jimmy grinned, and padded away.

'I want to buy a horse, Maudie,' Sibell said. 'May I ask Casey to choose one for me?'

'What's wrong with Merry?'

'She's fine. It's not for me. I promised Jimmy a long time ago that I'd give him a horse, and I have to keep my promise.'

'You're bloody mad! Abos don't have their own horses!'

'I promised,' Sibell insisted. 'When we were shipwrecked, it was Jimmy who found us, he saved our lives.' Sibell had never given any details about the shipwreck, and now Maudie was curious.

'Was Logan there, too?'

'Yes, and a lot of other people.' That was true, she defended her lie, if I count the blacks at that camp.

'Oh, well, it's your money and another sale for me,' Maudie said. 'Talk to Casey.'

Sibell showed her the shawl. 'Logan sent it to me,' she said proudly. 'Isn't it lovely?'

'Might be when it's cleaned up,' Maudie sniffed.

That Sunday was the best day of Jimmy Moon's life. Netta had told the station blacks what was about to happen, and they'd come marching up from their camp in disbelief. They were Waray people, who spoke in a tongue much the same as the Jawoyn down around Katherine, and although they'd endured the whites for some years now, they'd never heard of a blackfellow owning his own horse. Some of the men, and women, too, were crack riders who had earned themselves jobs as station hands – mainly, Jimmy had noticed with grim satisfaction, because there weren't enough white men up here at what they called the Top End of the big country. Their horses belonged to the station, not to the black riders.

Jimmy liked Black Wattle Station, and since he was nearing the end of his travels, he decided he would make this his base, as he had done with the Cambray farm. Logan was always talking about leaving Katherine, and because Missibel lived here, Jimmy was under the impression that they would make their home on this station. That would be a fine arrangement, like family. Also, Jimmy had been making enquiries about Netta: she was a pretty nice gin, who would make him a good wife.

When Casey brought out the horse, a big speckled grey, the colour of clouds, Jimmy was over the fence in an instant.

'How about this one?' Casey called to Missibel, who laughed:

'Don't ask me, ask Jimmy.'

'Plenty good feller,' Jimmy yelled, and leapt on to his horse before they could change their minds. The black people cheered and clapped, and the cowboys, sitting on the high fence with their smokes, didn't mind: they were more interested in the breakers, who were getting ready to run in a high-kicking colt.

His heart singing with pride, Jimmy rode away from the house to be alone with this fine animal who would be his friend and his partner forever. He talked to it, patted it, and allowed it to go wherever it willed. Then, afraid of tiring his friend, he set it free in the home paddock and dutifully returned to work in the stables.

In the afternoon, he went bushwalking with Missibel and Netta. Missibel was wearing a little revolver strapped around her hips, and she was proud of it. 'There are so many snakes here,' she explained to Jimmy, 'I never move without it.'

Netta giggled and Jimmy smiled at her. Neither of them needed guns to catch snakes, but they humoured the lady. They tramped on past the big black wattles that were coming into bloom now. The long sprays of yellow flowers were different from the wattles he knew, the balls of yellow fluff that he'd always loved. He felt a little homesick, wondering about his mother. She'd know by now what had happened. Lawina's sister would have passed the word on through the people, and they'd never tell a soul. They'd know he got clean away and would be pleased.

'Come on up here,' Missibel called. 'I want to show you something, Jimmy.'

Startled, Netta drew back. 'No go up there,' she called. 'Bad medicine that feller place.'

'Don't be silly,' Missibel said. 'Missus Charlotte showed it to me. It's a bora ring, Jimmy.' She pushed through the trees, and he followed, not knowing that word, 'bora', until they came to a clearing.

'It's very old,' she said, pointing to a ring of stones.

Netta refused to go another step, but Jimmy kept going, wondering about this place overgrown with spiny grass. If it was so old, why hadn't the trees grown back? They seemed, like Netta, to have stopped at the perimeters, afraid to advance.

'Your people comen here?' he asked Netta, in English.

'No bloody fear,' she replied.

'Oh, go on!' Sibell said. 'I've been here before and nothing has happened to me.' She didn't add to Netta's terror by mentioning that she'd come with Charlotte, who had died in that terrible accident, though not, of course, because of this superstitious nonsense.

'Mebbe whitefeller doan catch magic sickness,' Jimmy murmured, and he was sorry he said that, because Netta challenged him.

'You plenty much whitefeller,' she whispered mischievously. 'You go.'

As he watched, the stones seemed to grow taller, like ghosts at a feast, and the air was heavy with the sweetness of the flowering wattles. Overhead, the trees rustled nervously, and suddenly, thousands of budgerigars shot up into the blue with a whirring of wings, and fled into the distance. Jimmy shuddered, but he couldn't lose face in front of Netta. He strode forward.

Jimmy Moon had known fear in his dealings with strange tribes, but never the creeping horror that overcame him now as he stepped into the ancient ground. There was a feel of death here. He understood that spirits were timeless, so he couldn't ascertain whether that powerful magic was centuries old or recent. Or worse, that he was stepping into the future, sensing his own death.

His interest in these mysterious northern tribes now seemed to him just rash fancy, but the women were watching so he would have to investigate. Every tingling nerve in his body was telling him to run, but if he did so he'd be a laughing stock among the Waray people. They had been mightily impressed with him, they'd made him welcome as a travelling man, a magic man afraid of no one. Hadn't he walked right into the homestead and sat at the kitchen table? Not even white stockmen could claim that respect.

He searched around mounds of crumbling sandstone, studying the grasses and seeds with care. 'Fellers bin here,' he called.

'What fellows?' Sibell asked.

Jimmy left the site and came back to them, still feeling nervy, unsettled. 'Her people,' he said, pointing at Netta.

She shook her head. 'Nebber, nebber. Devil place.'

'Blackfeller bin there,' he insisted. 'Which blackfeller?'

'Wadjiginy,' she whispered.

'Who are they?' Sibell asked, but Netta had said enough. She pursed her lips and dropped her head, staring at her toes.

'Are they dangerous?' Sibell asked Jimmy, who guessed they were because of Netta's response. He wouldn't be surprised if the visitors were the ones the white men called the Daly River mob, but he didn't want to upset Missibel. He looked at the trees standing stiff and mute before him, hiding a world of mystery, and he felt drawn towards them by a terrible power.

Without hesitation, without even wondering why, he spoke to Missibel. 'I go see.' He turned to Netta, who was watching him curiously. 'You take Missibel home.'

Alone in this mysterious place, he searched until he found the source of corroboree paints, white ochre. He mixed it with red berry dye, then stripped off his clothes and painted himself in his own signs, far removed from the patterns of the northern people which he was unable to interpret. He touched the magic pouch of his homeland for good luck, and set off to track the blackfellows as best he could.

There was very little to go on – hardly a trace except for some obvious old paths that could have been made by anyone, white or black, and the easy crunch of horse tracks – but he kept on, heading north, hoping to meet some tribal blacks who could explain to him the messages of that magic spot. It could have been an initiation place, hallowed ground in the old days, now too much tramped on by unbelievers for it to be useful. 'Still sacred, though,' he told himself. 'No need for spirits to run off.'

He found fresh horse tracks, two with riders, three riderless, and followed them out of curiosity, wondering why white men would have veered so far off their own trails, and with spare horses. He looked up and saw that thick, leafy vines had formed canopies over the trees, and decided that was a good idea. Jimmy slept that night wedged in high branches.

In the morning he came upon a campsite, where the horsemen had met up with blackfellows, leaving nothing but a shirt made of cow-hide, hanging from a tree. Jimmy examined it and found it very pretty. The hide was black and white and soft, so he tried it on. 'Bloody all right,' he said, feeling the comfort of the sleeveless article, which he now recalled that white men called vests. It sat well on him. If he met the white men he would have to give it back, but his plan was to find the Wadjiginy people: the white men were of no interest to him. He replaced the vest in the tree for the time being.

Having come this far, he decided he might as well keep going, and by midday he heard the voices.

'Talk to me,' he called in the Waray language. He stepped into a mottled patch of sunlight, unarmed, and waited until they came out of the bush. Six of the men wore tall coned head-dresses, but the other one, a gnarled old man with a stone-grey beard, was unadorned except for the mass of scars that ridged his dusty skin.

The strong, straight bodies of the younger men were white-painted, but the designs were patchy, entirely different from the various stripes and dots he had previously encountered, and they intrigued him. As the figures moved again, against the backdrop of trees, the mystery was solved. The paintwork was not tribal markings, but a reproduction of the dappled tree trunks and patchy sunlight of their surrounds, which, he realised would make them almost indistinguishable from the bush unless they chose to be seen. Jaljurra was impressed: warriors or hunters the disguise was efficient.

'Who are you?' the old man asked, his voice carrying the strength of authority.

Jimmy sat down, inviting them to join him, which they did, with caution. 'I am Jaljurra,' he told them proudly, 'of the Whadjuck people, and I come far to visit your land.'

They had never heard of the Whadjuck tribes, which was a good sign, since they couldn't be counted as enemies. 'I come to tell you of our nation,' he explained, 'travelling over six moons to meet Wadjiginy. Are you Wadjiginy?'

His visitors, unsure of this stranger, nodded, and allowed him to continue. 'Does your land meet the sea?' he asked.

'Why do you wish to know this?'

'Because I will have come to the end of my journey. Do you wish to hear my stories?'

Everyone loved stories and legends, they were passed down from father to son, from mother to daughter, and these fellows were no different. There was always plenty of time for listening.

They accepted him, believing from his tales that he was a magic man sent to cross the earth on a mission known only to the spirits, and Jimmy was inclined to believe that they might be right: that the spirits *were* with him on his travels.

Finally, they agreed to take him with them, to show him their sea. Before they left he indicated the vest. 'Where did this come from?' he asked, but they shrugged, not seeming to know. 'I will leave it here and take it back with me,' he informed them. 'It is a fine garment.'

He travelled in a dugout with the Wadjiginy men for two days, a marvellous, fast journey downriver, racing with them towards the sea. Eventually they came to the mouth of the river, spreading out into the great ocean, and Jaljurra was jubilant. He ran across a sandy spit and stood marvelling at the miles of pure white sand that lay in a lovely arc around a deserted bay. The sea was a magnificent blue, and the trees bordering the beach were solid green.

Jimmy's delight was infectious. Gurrumindji, the elder, sent the younger men to catch fish for a celebration, while he sat down with Jaljurra to accept his gracious pleasure in the wonders of their land, and to persuade Jaljurra to tell him important stories, which he as headman was entitled to hear. Sibell was worried. 'Where could Jimmy be?' she asked Maudie.

'Gone walkabout,' Maudie said. 'Nothing new about that. He'll turn up.'

'But he left his horse here.'

'That's why he'll turn up,' Maudie laughed.

'He thought there was something strange about that bora ring, though,' Sibell persisted. 'And Netta is scared stiff of the place.'

'Don't take any notice of them,' Maudie said. 'It's all a lot of rot. And better still, don't interfere with their superstitions. They can get bloody cranky about things like that.'

'I'm not interfering. I'm just worried about Jimmy. Do you think we should send someone to look for him?'

'For a blackfellow. That's a joke! If he could find his way right across the bloody country, he can figure out this lot. Anyway, if he's been tracking north he'll have come to the Timor Sea by now, so he'll have to turn back.'

'But what about those blacks? Even Netta is afraid of them.'

'Our blacks aren't scared of them, they're scared of strange spirits. It's a different thing. Just forget about it, he'll be back.'

There was an air of mystery about this sea-place, as if it were lost in time, inhabited by neither man nor spirit, the sweep of sands untouched, the greenness unmoved. These puny little humans, gathered on the beach, seemed to Jimmy to dwindle to mites by comparison.

The setting sun shimmered across the light waves, spreading a pink glow over the bay, and Jimmy breathed the fresh salt air, so alive after the turgid inland swamps.

In his turn Jimmy listened to Gurrumindji, to his Dreaming, and heard of the great warriors of the Wadjiginy. Because these were hard, forest men, secretive people, he had not seen another soul, not even a footprint, and yet he knew from their talk that their numbers were many, their clans strictly disciplined. Gurrumindji spoke of a whitefellow mission place that had been set down on another bay in their territory, and Jimmy didn't hold out much hope for the intruders lasting long there.

Gurrumindji asked him, in his wisdom, about the whitefellows who were beginning to encroach, breaking every rule known to nature, but

Jimmy could not offer advice, he would not presume to interfere in their lives.

Two men ferried him back along the rich velvety swell of the river, careful to beach at exactly the same spot where, they informed Jimmy, crocodiles did not dare nest. 'Wrong totem for crocodiles,' they said, and Jimmy laughed. 'He must be a mighty spirit to scare them off.'

On both river journeys he had observed the monsters baking on the muddy banks and drifting silently with the current, and although he hadn't shown it, he'd been terrified. It was one thing to watch them from above in the Katherine gorges, but to be at eye level in a flimsy dugout was tempting the fates. He was relieved to be ashore and on his way again.

The return journey was easier. He travelled fast, unerringly, collecting his prize, the cow-hide vest, on the way, brushing it free of the powdery mould that had already attacked its beauty. Closer to the homestead, he bathed in a lagoon, retrieved his trousers, and, wearing just the pants and vest, set out on the last few miles of the run home. Jimmy was no longer afraid of the bora ring, he was at peace now.

After Jimmy had left, the young men asked Gurrumindji why he had accepted the stranger, why he had given him the favour of their sea.

The old man's eyes glistened from his lined and weathered face. 'He has the blood of white men on his hands,' he said.

'But then why didn't you tell him to stay with us? He knows their ways, he can speak their language, he could have helped us.'

Gurrumindji shook his head. 'It is not possible. He has gone into his Dreaming.'

Rory Jackson led the posse, determined to track down his brother's killers. Conal, from the Gilbert mines, and Clem Starkey had been half dead themselves, dehydrated, incoherent, when a bullocky had come upon them as he was taking his team through to Pine Creek. Another few hours and it would have been lights out for them, too.

The bushwhackers, the murderers, had got a head start while Conal and Starkey stumbled around in the dark, losing the track and becoming increasingly disoriented by the sameness of the bush. It had been sheer luck that after three days they'd staggered back on course, only to be beaten down by the heat. Then it had taken time for the townsmen to make sense of their babblings. They'd been robbed and Constable Ralph Jackson was dead! Shot dead! With not too much regard for the health of the survivors, they were bundled into a trap and taken to the scene of the crime to locate Ralph's body.

Sergeant Bowles came up from Katherine with Rory Jackson, and Pine Creek was in an uproar of rage as posses were formed to scour the district for the killers.

'Find them and bring them into the nearest town,' Bowles ordered, as he plotted an orderly search.

'Bring 'em in? Like bloody hell!' Rory snarled to his mates. 'They'll bloody swing from the nearest tree. They never gave poor Ralph a chance!' And the four men in his posse agreed.

Cursing the absence of Jaljurra, and having no indication of what direction the outlaws might have taken in this vast wilderness, Bowles sent some men south, and others into Palmerston to raise the alarm. He took his men south-east, certain that these fellows would make for Queensland, across the wetlands, knowing they couldn't be followed once the rains set in.

Rory Jackson disagreed. He headed west, with his own mates.

'They've got nowhere to go in that direction,' Bowles argued. 'There are only a few isolated stations, and from then on they're into Western Australia. There's nothing out there.'

'That's just the point,' Rory said. 'I reckon they'll head west until the heat's off, then circle back to lose themselves in Palmerston. There are so many blow-ins in that bloody town, they wouldn't be noticed.'

Rory was a stockman, a drover, an odd-job man. It didn't matter now that he'd disagreed violently with his brother for his stupidity in joining the police force, or that Ralph had, at times, threatened to lock him up for being drunk and disorderly, and had abused hell out of him over that other business – when some do-gooders had claimed he had raped a gin. How could you rape a gin? They beg for it!

Anyway, now he was the man in charge, and he'd find the killers if it took him years.

The Jackson posse began at the ambush site and rode west, wide of the trail, fanning out over the countryside looking for cold camps. They found traces of fires left by white men and studied the refuse, having been given an inventory of the stolen goods, not to mention the gold. Rory had his own ideas about that – the price of his brother's life, he told his friend Buster Krohn, who smirked: 'Why not, mate? He died trying to protect their bloody gold, he earned it.'

They were only three days into the search when one of the riders brought in his collection of junk to be examined. A worn-out boot, a tattered saddlecloth, more tins, grog bottles, rusting pannikins – they could have been anyone's. But among the refuse, Rory pounced on a water bag. 'We've hit paydirt!' he shouted in triumph. 'This is Ralph's. Look here! Look! He painted his initials by the handles! See . . . they're worn now, but you can see the marks of the paint. This is his all right, damned if it isn't.' He rocked back on his haunches. 'Let all those other mugs go friggin' off on their wild goose chases, we've got them. We'll find the bastards now.'

He rallied his troops. 'You three go that way,' he yelled. 'Over to Black Wattle Station. Get to the homestead and find out if they've seen any strangers, then cut back and meet us up ahead. Buster and me, we'll keep going this way.'

'The chase is on good and proper now,' Buster grinned, as they saddled up. 'I reckon we'll get them.'

'Can't miss!' Rory told him. 'We can't miss now.'

The station appeared deserted when they rode in, but Maudie was prepared. She never took chances with strange men, she'd seen too many of them in her day.

'Netta,' she called, 'tell Bygolly to hang about. And get me out on to the veranda.

Bygolly was Netta's uncle, a black stockman who had been working with Zack and Cliff for years. Crippled as she was, Maudie liked to keep Bygolly within coo-ee, in case of trouble, and it was the black man who had galloped back to warn her that three men were headed her way.

By the time they reached the homestead gate, she was sitting in the big cane chair at the top of the steps, a rug over her knees to hide her gammy leg, and a loaded double-barrelled shotgun resting on her knees.

'What do you want?' she yelled.

'Police posse, missus, there's some bushwhackers at large.'

'Which one of you is police?'

They climbed down, hitched their horses and made for the gate. 'Not us, we're helping out Sergeant Bowles,' the first man replied.

'You can come in,' Maudie directed, the gun raised. 'You other two stay out. I'm not the only one watching you.'

He opened the wooden gate and stepped on to the path, his mates seeming content to wait. They leaned against the fence, taking the opportunity to light their pipes, but Maudie was still suspicious: she didn't like the look of any of them. 'Who are you?' she asked, 'and don't come any closer.'

'The name's Syd Walsh,' he replied, complaint in his voice, 'and there's no need for that there gun. My rifle's back on my saddle.'

Yeah, Maudie thought, and your knife's in your boot. She glared down at him. 'What bushwhackers?'

'Two blokes held up a gold consignment out of Pine Creek and they shot Constable Jackson. Shot him stone dead in cold blood. We're on their trails, so we've come to ask if you've seen any strange blokes riding through.'

'Only you,' Maudie said.

'No one?' he asked, disappointed.

'Not sight nor sound, and our men would know, same as we knew you were coming.' That was a lie – Black Wattle was so big they could miss an army passing through – but it sounded right enough.

'Whose gold?' she asked, relenting a little.

'Arcadia mines and Gilbert mines,' he replied.

'Then you'd know Logan Conal, would you?' Maudie asked, thinking she was being very shrewd.

'Can't say I do, missus. I'm not from Katherine. I met up with Rory Jackson in Pine Creek. He's the brother, like . . . of the bloke that got shot. He's leading the posse.'

'Where is he, then?'

'They're tracking the killers a bit north of here: we'll go on and meet them if you ain't seen no one.'

Maudie considered him. He didn't know Logan Conal, this tale could be a load of bulldust. But if they really were part of a posse, the Hamilton name would be mud if they didn't offer support.

'You can water your horses and get a bite at the cookhouse if you like,' she told him.

'Be obliged, missus,' he said, and she watched as they trailed around the homestead.

'Netta,' she called, 'slip out and warn Sam Lim to be careful.'

Maudie sat awhile, mulling over the conversation. She'd never heard of Constable Jackson, but there were quite a few new police down the track since Puckering took over. Could be true, poor bugger. Shot dead? By God, there'd be ructions now. And if those outlaws were anywhere near Black Wattle, the men would need to be warned to watch out for them. She decided that when Casey came in this evening he could take a few hands and check up on this posse, and find out more about the shooting. Maudie was hugely interested but didn't dare prolong contact with the strange riders.

And Logan's gold had been pinched! Wait till Sibell heard about that. She'd be all of a tizz. She was obviously mad about him, but he'd passed Sibell over to be with her, Maudie, that full day he spent at the station. Maudie sighed. Logan was what Cliff used to call a 'point-maker', always watching for the best bet for himself . . . Sibell would never keep him in line. She was too soft, and a cold fish. She always claimed she was so fond of Charlotte but she'd hardly shed a tear, not for Charlotte, not for Cliff, standing around like a piece of bone china . . .

But, by God, Logan was handsome, and men like that could be tamed if you owned the right carrots. Maudie had made certain he knew who owned what around here.

Syd Whatsisname and his posse mates were leaving, so Maudie whistled up Bygolly. 'Stick on your horse and follow them. Keep your distance, but see if they really are chasing bushrangers.'

'Righto, missus,' he grinned.

It was Rory who saw him, loping across open country blackened by a recent bushfire. 'Get on to this,' he said to Buster, reining in his horse. 'What's a white man doing out here without a mount?'

'Bit peculiar,' Buster agreed, so they began to close in.

'It's a blackfeller,' Buster announced as they came closer, but Rory was riding fast now, galloping across the burnt-out land.

'Do you see?' he shouted. 'Look what he's got on!'

Buster didn't register what was meant by that, but he came hard on Rory's heels as his mate swung his rope, standing in the saddle to make the loop wide enough to bring down his prey.

'By Jesus,' he yelled. 'Well done, Rory!' The lasso had caught the nigger in mid-stride like a calf, and felled him, squirming on the ground.

As the nigger tried to stand, Rory booted him in the face, and down he went again.

Both men sprang from their horses and trussed the black. 'Now do you see?' Rory asked.

'See what?'

'Don't you remember what Conal said? He said one of them was wearing a cow-hide vest . . . black and white? Now what have we got here?'

'Cripes, so he is.'

'So he's one of them, you dopey bastard.'

'They never said he was a nigger.'

'They never said he wasn't.' Rory contemplated the quiet form on the ground. 'You think about it, Buster. They said the second one never spoke, never said nothing. And Bowles thought it was because his voice would give him away. He thought the other bushwhacker was a foreigner. But we know better now, don't we? The partner was a nigger. This one.'

'By Jesus, you could be right.' Buster's voice quivered with admiration and excitement.

'I am right,' Rory told him.

'What you fellers want?' Jimmy Moon called, his mouth bloodied.

'See?' Rory almost danced with triumph. 'That's why he never spoke. Give the game away. Bowles is out there looking for a bushie and a foreigner, but we've solved it.' No detective, he believed, could have matched his brilliance.

'We want you, mister,' Rory growled. 'You and your mate shot my brother back there nigh to Pine Creek. But before you swing, Buster and me are going to have a little talk with you.'

Jimmy staggered to his feet. 'I am Jaljurra. Sergeant Bowles knows me. I work for him, tracker.'

'That's right,' Rory admitted. 'I heard of you. You know that country and you know about the gold. So where's your mate?'

'Doan got no mate,' Jimmy told them, remembering not to argue too much with white men. 'You fellers take me down Black Wattle Station.'

'Now listen to me,' Rory said, standing over him. 'Why don't we make a deal? We know you didn't shoot Ralph, the other bloke did. You lead us to him, and to the gold, and we'll see you get off easy.' He winked at Buster as he spoke. As he lied, Jimmy knew.

'Doan know nothin' about this stuff,' Jimmy said, and Buster kicked him in the groin.

'Try again, mister,' he snarled as Jimmy collapsed.

'We haven't got much time left,' Rory warned, 'before the other blokes turn up. We have to find the gold. Belt it out of him!'

Buster used his whip, he kicked and punched, but their prisoner wouldn't talk. 'I don't reckon he knows,' he said finally. 'Stands to reason the other bloke, the white man, took the lot. What would a nigger do with gold? We have to find the other one.'

'We'll find him all right,' Rory said complacently. 'He can't be far away now. We'll just get rid of this bit of baggage first.'

He fired a shot in the air, and then, after a patient wait, with the blackfellow in the cow-hide vest underfoot, he fired a couple more.

That brought the rest of the posse to heel, and Rory shoved Jimmy Moon at them, ripping the small pouch from around his neck and hurling it aside.

'No!' Jimmy screamed, lunging for it, but Buster was too quick.

'What you got in here, black boy? You got gold here, eh?' He tore it open, finding only a stone, and tossed it away in disgust.

'Who's this?' Syd asked.

'He's the accomplice,' Rory said, savouring the word. 'One of them murdering bastards.'

'A blackfeller?'

Once again, and with Buster's enthusiastic backing, Rory explained, pointing to the vest, and Jimmy listened to their angry mutterings which were rising over him like a swift-flowing tide.

He struggled to be heard – 'Not true, not true!' – but they kicked him aside and he sat with his hand to his throat, forlornly missing the cord and the reassurance of his precious tokens. He thought about his horse and wondered if it knew why he couldn't come back, why he might never come back.

The ugly white men were arguing, passing around a rum bottle.

'We can claim the reward for this one.'

'What reward? We won't get nothing for a nigger.'

'We have to go after his mate, we can't waste time taking in this bit of shit . . .'

'The gold's still out there . . .'

'I say we hang him now and get going!'

'Jesus! I don't know about that. There's that English bloke, the police inspector, he'd come down on us like a ton of bricks.'

'For Christ's sake! Whose side are you on? They killed Rory's brother . . .'

Bygolly's horse took the homestead fence in a headlong leap, crashing across the garden, Bygolly screaming, shouting for Maudie.

'Missus! Missus! They got Jimmy, them fellers!'

Maudie hobbled out on to the veranda. 'Cripes, you'll wake the dead. What's wrong?'

'They got Jimmy! They hurt him bad. Out past the debbil place.'

For a second, Maudie was unable to grasp what he was babbling about. 'Blaming Jimmy Moon? They can't do that. He wasn't anywhere near Pine Creek.'

'Oh, missus, you come quick!' Bygolly was crying, begging her.

'Get my rifle,' she shouted at Netta, who grabbed it from the hall.

'Bring your horse closer so I can get on him,' she told Bygolly, but Netta tried to stop her.

'No, missus. Nebber ride. You too much hurt.'

'Shut up and help me,' Maudie screamed at her, throwing away the crutch and hanging on to the veranda post. 'Steady now.' Gingerly she lifted the leg in its splints over the saddle and settled into place, digging the other foot into the stirrup. Her shoulder ached with the exertion and she took the bridle with her free hand, comfortable in the saddle now. But the rifle was difficult, and Bygolly had no saddle holster. 'Oh, damn, leave it!' she said. 'Open the gate.'

As she raced through the gate she shouted at Bygolly to find Casey. 'Find everyone you can!'

She was able to hold on as she sent the horse galloping down the track, but the pain in her leg was excruciating, so she concentrated on the men. Those bloody idiots. She'd give them hell. Jimmy must have run into them on his way home. Hadn't she told Sibell he'd be back? And that posse – if the others were bruisers like that Syd, poor Jimmy would be in for a bad time. That type liked beating blacks, it made them feel like big men. They had nothing else going for them.

The horse seemed to know exactly where they were going, as he pounded down the track, out past the black wattles and on towards the big scrub that had weathered a bushfire a few months back, only the hardier eucalypts withstanding the heat.

But where had the posse got to? They must be around here somewhere. She called out, slackening pace, but the bush was quiet and Maudie worried that she'd missed them: she'd been riding for a good half-hour now. They must have moved on and taken Jimmy with them. She couldn't go much further on her own . . .

Maudie walked the horse, listening for them, for voices, for horses, for a disturbance of birds in the area, but all was quiet. And then she saw him. It was Jimmy. Stripped to the waist, hanging like a rag doll from a tall tree. Deathly still. Dead.

'Oh, my God!' she wept. 'Oh, God. The bloody rotten bastards!'

Sibell was hysterical. She wouldn't believe what had happened until they brought his body in, and then she screamed and screamed, rushing wildly through the house to subside in a corner of her room, refusing to talk to anyone. A weeping Netta tried to console her, but she wouldn't listen, and the twins hid fearfully in Wesley's room with their young charge, certain that the debbil place had claimed a victim

'Let her be,' Maudie said. 'Do her good to yell it out of her. She's so damned ladylike, I reckon she's never made so much noise before in her whole life.'

'But what about you?' Casey asked. 'You've gone and buggered your leg again. I wouldn't be game to touch it this time.'

'It doesn't hurt as long as I keep it up and the splints stay tight. Have the last of the horses gone?'

'Yes, we're all done out there now. Do you want me to send for Doctor Brody?'

'No. It's time to pack up. I'll get myself to the hospital in Palmerston.'

'You're not going to ride again?'

'No fear, I've done my dash. I'll use the buckboard. Could you take us to Idle Creek? We can go by boat and borrow a couple of wagons for the rest of the way.'

Casey shook his head. 'I won't just take you to Idle Creek, I'll take you right into town and we'll lodge charges against that posse.'

'Oh, yes,' Maudie said grimly. 'We'll see to that, the bastards. Did you send someone to Pine Creek to report what happened?'

'I sure did. I told Fred, that new rouseabout, to report Jimmy's death as murder. We won't let them get away with it.'

'Poor Jimmy,' Maudie sighed. 'Netta said his real name was Jaljurra. Where did they bury him?'

'They wouldn't say. The blacks are all badly spooked, they didn't want any whitefellers around, none of us, not even Sam Lim. And you can't blame them. They said they wanted to put him away "secret", safe from white men now.'

It was time to pack up. Sam Lim dashed about, excited, delighted to be off on the holiday to Palmerston where he would be house cook again. Netta cleaned the house in double-quick time, and packed Maudie's clothes for her. The twins, anxious to help in case they were left behind, had Wesley ready in minutes, so Maudie had them bring her all the linen they'd need for the beach house, as well as town clothes and boots for Zack.

228

Where was Zack? The men should be home by now. She was worried. It could be dangerous on those long stock routes, even though they had disposed of the cattle. They'd sold a couple of thousand so he'd be carrying cash.

Maudie sat in state in the dining room, yelling instructions as the girls did the packing, trying to remember what would be needed. This was the first time Maudie had had to do this, as Charlotte had always made the house ready for them at Christmas, and she was overly concerned to do a good job, so that Zack would be pleased.

God knows, she thought shakily, we've been in enough strife lately. It seems like we just ran out of steam. What a tale of woe for Zack to come home to! A murder on the station, me with my crook leg and my arm tacked down, and her in there, half around the bend.

For days Sibell had been wandering around the house, ignoring all the activity, bursting into tears if anyone spoke to her, and Maudie was becoming impatient. She had decided they'd have to take Sibell to the beach house, since she didn't have anywhere else to go, but she wished she'd pull herself together.

Wesley was nagging her about the pony again. 'No,' his mother told him, 'once and for all. We can't take your pony with us. He'll be all right here. I'll find you another one in the big town.' She snapped at the twins, 'Take him and give him his tea. And tell missy I want to see her.'

Sibell came in, looking a mess, her face blotchy from tears, her hair untidy and the hem of her skirt undone. It dragged moodily behind her.

'We're leaving tomorrow,' Maudie said. 'Are you ready?'

Sibell stared sadly out of the window. 'I don't think I'll bother.'

'What do you mean, you won't bother? You can't stay here.'

'I won't be any trouble.'

'Yes, you will. Casey is taking us to Palmerston and then he'll be back. There'll only be a few white men around the place and they'll be completely thrown out of gear if you stay.'

'I can cook for them.'

'Oh, cripes, you're not staying, and that's that.' Maudie tried to be a little kinder. 'I want you to come with us to the beach house. We'll have a real good time in town.'

Her attempt at sympathy only brought on more tears.

'Come on now, buck up,' Maudie said. 'I know it's terrible, but what's done is done, crying won't fix it.'

Sibell glared at her. 'You don't seem to care about anyone, you don't know what it's like . . .'

'Don't I?' Maudie said sharply. 'My husband was murdered, or don't you count that?'

Sibell stopped, mopping at her eyes. 'I'm sorry,' she whispered. 'I don't know why I can't stop crying.' She looked vaguely about the room. 'It's strange. When my parents were drowned and the servants, too, everyone I knew, I didn't cry. I never have. And I've felt guilty about that . . .'

'It was probably shock,' Maudie said.

'No, I was angry. With them. With everyone, I think. It all seemed so horribly unfair. And then Cliff and Charlotte, I couldn't cry for them either. Wouldn't you think I'd have felt something, but I didn't. I mean,

I did, but I couldn't shed a tear for them. It was this terrible unfairness again. You probably thought I didn't care.'

'Of course not,' Maudie lied. She couldn't think of anything else to say as Sibell sat on the edge of a chair, looking small and vulnerable now, no longer the stylish, self-possessed lady. 'You've had a bad trot,' she said finally. 'You go and lie down. We've got a big day tomorrow.'

'But don't you think it's odd?' Sibell asked, her voice strained, 'that I can't stop crying for Jimmy, and yet I hardly knew him. I never took the time to find out anything about him.'

'I don't think it's strange,' Maudie told her. 'I reckon he's worth the tears.'

'Yes . . . he was, but so were the others. My parents, they'd be hurt to think . . .'

'Listen,' Maudie said sternly. 'You did care. In your own way you mourned for them, and you always will. It's just that with Jimmy the dam burst. You are right,' she said, tears brimming in her eyes now. 'It's all so bloody unfair.'

Both women were weeping, unable to reach out to each other, just two distressed people on either side of the room.

There was a cough at the door where Casey was standing, waiting, clutching his hat, embarrassed at having intruded. 'Excuse me, ladies, but you've got a visitor.'

'I don't want to see anyone.' Sibell jumped up and disappeared into the kitchen.

'It's Sergeant Bowles,' Casey continued. 'I told him what happened here, and he just wants to pay his respects before he leaves.'

'That's all right,' Maudie said, brushing at her eyes. 'Send him in.'

Sergeant Bowles was apologetic. 'I'm terrible sorry, Mrs Hamilton, I gave all those men orders to bring in the outlaws. Not take the law into their own hands.'

'But Jimmy wasn't an outlaw.'

'I know that, ma'am. God help us, this business has to stop. These louts have got to learn about the law. I know who they are, we've already arrested Rory Jackson and Buster Krohn, and we'll get the other three. They'll go on trial in Palmerston.'

'And they'll probably get off with all their mates on the juries.'

'That's possible,' Bowles admitted, 'but we'll do our best. It's a bloody shame, Jaljurra was a good bloke and a damned good tracker. Rory Jackson still swears he was one of the outlaws because he was wearing a cow-hide vest. It did belong to the partner of the bloke who shot Ralph – we identified that as fact – but Mr Conal and Mr Starkey swear the second fellow wasn't a black. He had a mask on, but they had a good look at him, they saw his hands. He wasn't a black. No, we're still looking for two white men for that crime.' He shook his head, puzzled. 'We can't figure out where they've got to.'

'Mr Conal?' Maudie asked. 'Logan Conal? It was his gold they took. Was he there when the constable was shot?'

'Oh, yes, he and Starkey were taking their own gold to Idle Creek.'

'Is that right?' Maudie said, wondering if Sibell was still in the kitchen. The door was open. She distinctly remembered Logan promising Sibell they'd arrange to meet next time he went to Idle Creek, but he obviously hadn't let her know he was going there.

'That's the bad part,' Bowles continued. 'If those mugs had done as they were told and brought Jaljurra in, Mr Conal could have cleared him right away. He was on the spot, he knew it wasn't Jaljurra. Not by a mile.' He planted his large hands on the table. 'He's terrible upset, I can tell you. Practically wanted to hang Jackson himself. Nice feller, Mr Conal, nice people, he and his missus. He said his wife has known Jaljurra for years.'

'His wife?' Maudie said evenly. 'I didn't know Mr Conal had a wife.'

'Oh, yes. I met her in Katherine. A fine lady.'

When Bowles left, Sibell returned to the dining room and slumped into a chair.

'You heard?' Maudie asked her.

'Yes.'

'Did you know he was married?'

'No.'

'You were keen on him, weren't you?'

'Yes.'

'I'm real sorry, Sibell, but you can't be blamed. He's a real charmer, I'll give him that. Bloody men! Does it hurt much?'

'Yes.'

'Well, if you want to bawl, you'd better get it over, get all your crying done in one hit.'

Sibell sat stony-faced. 'I'm not going to cry over him! He's not worth it.'

Maudie laughed. 'That's the spirit. Forget about him, there's nothing you can do.'

'Oh, isn't there?' Sibell said savagely. 'And Maudie, if it's still all right with you, I would like to come to Palmerston.'

'Good. Get packed.'

'I will,' Sibell said. 'I surely will.' And she headed for the office.

As they prepared to leave the station, Casey handed out mackintoshes which all seemed to be the same size. Even Wesley was enfolded, and lifted into the buggy, where he sat up front with Netta and Bygolly, their driver. The twins, bursting with excitement were in the back, legs dangling.

Maudie was placed on the tray of the buckboard, to protect her leg, among a motley collection of boxes, and Sibell was instructed to 'hop up' beside Casey, who had decided to drive the heavier buckboard himself.

The few remaining station hands, and most of the station blacks, turned out to bid them a boisterous farewell, and at last they were off, Sam Lim and two stockmen leading the way, their horses prancing impatiently.

No sooner had the strange little convoy set off for Idle Creek than the rain began to fall – steady, soaking rain.

'About bloody time,' Maudie said. 'I was starting to think we were in for a drought.'

Sibell didn't share Maudie's enthusiasm. She hadn't slept much since Jimmy's murder, still overcome with horror at the manner of his death,

231

and she was suffering from an inexplicable sense of anxiety. The soggy discomfort of this steaming rain didn't help, even though she and Maudie had been issued with large black umbrellas, since, unlike the buggy, their buckboard had no roof.

Casey was moving them along at quite a pace. 'I hope it isn't too bumpy for Maudie,' he said, 'but we have to keep moving. The deep dust on these tracks will turn into mud in no time and we can't afford to get bogged.'

'I hope the boat doesn't go without us,' Sibell said, not looking forward to being stranded in Idle Creek.

'They'll wait. Sergeant Bowles will have told them we're coming.'

No one else seemed to mind the rain. They were all in such high spirits that Sibell made a determined effort to be cheerful, reasoning that Maudie must be very uncomfortable. She felt a little more at ease with her after the conversation back there in the dining room. It still surprised her that she'd been able to unbend and admit her guilt over her parents to, of all people, Maudie. Somehow that seemed to have taken the edge off her depression, but she was sure that she and Maudie could never be friends. And that meant that a parting of the ways was necessary. Black Wattle was Maudie's home: she, Sibell, would have to go.

Oddly, that thought hurt, and Sibell realised she would miss the station, the people there, and all the everyday activities that she had come to enjoy. It had been like living in a small, vibrant village. She supposed they'd all forget her soon enough. She peered wistfully back down the road through the grey rain, wondering if she'd ever see the station again. And Merry, her lovely horse: one day she might be able to send for her, once she was settled. Somewhere.

They stopped for lunch in a glade of dripping trees, ignoring the rain as Sam Lim handed out sandwiches and tea. Sibell sat under the buckboard with Wesley and the twins, watching the men's muddy boots as they strung a tarpaulin from the seat of the buckboard to provide a better shelter for Maudie from the increasing rain. It was still hot, though! Sibell was amazed that the rain didn't cool them, it just caused her to steam inside her coat.

The horses slogged on, hauling them across gullies rushing with water, and the men came to assist as they forded creeks that were now springing to life in the teeming rain.

Sibell didn't feel well. She had cramps in her stomach, and she was so hot she wished she could discard her coat. She gave up on the umbrella and put it under the seat, her arms too weary to hold it any longer.

'You all right, miss?' Casey asked.

'Yes, thank you,' she said grimly, not wishing to hold them up.

'Only another couple of hours,' he said, and Sibell wished he hadn't told her that. She had thought they were much closer to the depot.

They came to a wider creek as the skies were darkening and the night threatening to close in on them, and the horsemen took the buggy across first.

'It looks deep,' Sibell said nervously.

'Early days yet,' Casey told her. 'It's not too bad.'

Having seen the buggy on its way, the men came riding back for the buckboard, and led it rattling and banging over the rocky creek bed, water sloshing around them as the strong current pushed past.

Just when Sibell thought they were over the worst, the buckboard lurched drunkenly to the left as a wheel collapsed, and, taken by surprise, she went over the side into the fast-flowing creek. She panicked, screaming, as she felt herself being swept away. Then her feet touched bottom, and she discovered the water wasn't so deep after all. She was wading in the waist-deep water, pushing against the current to get to the shore, when Sam Lim plunged in to pull her out and drag her, slipping and sliding in the mud, up the banks.

'Where's Maudie?' she asked him urgently.

'She still in wagon,' he told her. 'Wheel come off.' And he darted away to assist them.

Still shaking from the sudden fright of being dumped in the creek, and thoroughly soaked, boots and all, Sibell took a deep breath and tried to calm herself. She was utterly miserable, and had a splitting headache, too.

As she clutched her arms together, she felt something under her shirt, and she shrieked. A leech! And not just one, they were all over her, on her body, her legs . . .

Netta came running as Sibell tore at her clothes. 'Whatsup, missy?'

'Leeches!' Sibell screamed.

'Oh, dem tings. They doan hurt. You lie still.'

She was crying hysterically as Netta began searching for the horrible slimy things stuck to her body. Then she heard a familiar voice. 'What's going on here?'

'Leeches,' she screamed, not even trying to place the voice. 'Get them off me!'

Netta's hands moved efficiently, pulling away the parasites. 'All gone now,' she announced.

He bent down and picked her up as if she were as light as a feather, carrying her up to the buggy, and his voice had a smile in it. 'You girls have got yourselves into a real tangle.'

'Oh, it's you,' she said weakly. She put her hand to her forehead, which seemed to be burning in the heat. 'I don't feel very well, Zack.'

9

Children were playing outside the window, and their shrieks disturbed her. She turned on her side, wincing as her head ached, resenting the movement, but she couldn't see anyone – only the turbulent grey sky. The bed was so close to the window that she could reach out and touch the pane, which was strangely warm. It reminded her of a vague sense of overwhelming heat. Sibell felt as if she had walked through a fiery furnace some time recently, but now she was cool.

This room was cool, white. White walls, white bedsheets, white curtains. The black-painted iron bed-end stood out in stark relief. She had been very ill, she remembered now, glimpsing recollections of baths of perspiration, of people talking, of wild vicious dreams, of the pain – and that awful heat. It hurt too much to try to think any more, so she lay back, blinking to clear her eyes, relieved that the small movement no longer stabbed at her with those sharp knives.

She became aware that Zack was watching her. 'Is this a hospital?' she asked him.

'No,' he said, as if their conversation had been going on for days. Maybe it had . . . she couldn't recall. 'Maudie got the hospital, you got the beach house.'

'Palmerston?'

'Yes. The doctor says you're recovering now, so we have to start to feed you. You're a bit thin on it.'

'Why?' she asked, because it seemed the easiest thing to say.

'Feed a cold, starve a fever, that's the rule, and you've had the fever. Malaria.'

'Oh.' She thought about that. And then she went back to sleep.

The house sat forward on a low headland, looking over the bay.

Sibell liked to watch the rainstorms come bustling in from the sea. The humidity and the rain were trying, but they did not affect the holiday atmosphere that surrounded her. Visitors came, hearty, genial people, and the children played under the house while Zack entertained upstairs.

It was a small house with only two bedrooms and a sleepout, and another large room which served as a kitchen, dining room and sitting room. When it was wet, everyone sat at the long table as if at a family gathering, and in the intervals between the ever-hovering belts of rain, they placed themselves about the porch or on the steps.

Sam Lim was in his element as the caterer, but he preferred to do most of his cooking in a camp oven under the house, so that he could work without interruption and at the same time bully the two young Chinese gardeners who were employed to clear the wilderness around them that had once been Charlotte's garden.

Sibell was introduced to everyone – station people, townspeople, officials, men and women who were obviously the mainstay of this wild country – and they fussed over her, insisting that she rest, get her strength back. Even though Zack told them proudly that Sibell was the station book-keeper, they all seemed to take it for granted that she was Zack's 'girl', which embarrassed her. Apart from that, though, she began to enjoy herself.

The fever seemed to have taken all her old nightmares away with it, or maybe, she pondered, she had just worn them out, for she was sleeping soundly these days. Better than at any time since she'd landed in Perth.

She went for long walks with Wesley and the twins and Netta along the beach. The water looked so inviting that one day she became daring. 'There's no one around,' she told the girls. 'I'm going sea-bathing.'

They drew back in horror. 'No, missy! No!'

'Why not?' she laughed, unbuttoning her shirt. 'I'll wear my drawers and chemise, they'll dry in seconds when I come out. No one can see me. You come in too.'

Netta pulled her back. 'No swim in there, missy. All bad fellers there.'

'What bad fellers?'

They laughed at her, shouting: 'Sharks! Crocodiles! Stingems.'

'Oh, my God! In there?' She stared at the placid waters.

'Too bloody right.' They ran along the beach and found a large blue jellyfish with long threads floating lazily around it. 'Doan touch. Him kill you.'

'Poison!' Wesley told her, airing the knowledge obviously implanted in him by his careful nannies.

After that she was more vigilant when exploring the shores of Port Darwin.

Zack took them on daily visits to the hospital to see Maudie, whose leg had had to be reset and was now strung up to a wooden cage. She complained bitterly at her confinement: 'I hate this place, Zack. I want to come home.'

They had the same argument every day, and each time, Zack gave her the same answer. 'I'll take you home as soon as the doctor lets you out, and then we'll have a big party.'

'I'm getting sores on my bum lying here,' she complained one morning, uninhibited by male company. Sam Lim dashed away, to return with a salve which he said would cure her, and apparently it did, because they heard no more about it.

One day Sibell had a visitor. Lorelei Rourke. She came tripping up the front steps in a fussy dress of pink and lilac, and a huge straw hat decorated with masses of pink tulle.

Sibell wasn't too thrilled to see her, but Zack welcomed Lorelei with grave good manners, and Sibell was a little ashamed of her reservations. Nevertheless, she was glad Maudie was still imprisoned in her hospital room.

'I heard you were in town and that you were very ill,' Lorelei said, 'and I was so worried about you. I'm sorry, Mr Hamilton, to come barging in on you like this, I hope you don't mind. But I'm not one for sending cards.'

'Neither are we,' Zack said easily. 'Would you like a cup of tea, Miss Rourke?'

'Would I ever?' she replied, settling prettily into a chair and producing an ivory fan. 'I always say tea is a great thirst-quencher, don't you agree?'

'It sure is,' Zack said. 'I'll get Sam Lim on the job and leave you ladies to have a chat.'

She watched him disappear. 'My! Isn't he divine? I thought you'd be married to him by now.'

'I work for him,' Sibell said testily. 'That's all.'

'Well, I must say he treats his staff fine,' Lorelei giggled.

'And how are you keeping?' Sibell asked, to change the subject.

'Marvellously. I'm doing extremely well here. I have my own place – the Bijou Palace of Entertainment, I call it – and it's so popular, packed all the time.'

'You run it yourself?' Sibell asked. She knew it was a foolish question, because Lorelei had just said that, but the conversation was proving difficult.

'Oh, yes, I have six ladies working for me, and they're all very charming, very talented.'

The way she spoke, it sounded as though the Bijou was some sort of concert hall, but Sibell had been in this small town long enough to know that wasn't true: the Bijou Palace was spoken of in whispers. However, the explanation suited her.

She listened to Lorelei's talk about Palmerston – she seemed to know everyone and everything – and then Lorelei came back to Zack. 'Why haven't you married him? The way he looks at you . . . I picked it in seconds, he's keen.'

Sibell nodded. 'I know. Since we've been here, Zack has been so circumspect, keeping his distance, but I think he'll ask me again any day.'

'Again? Do you mean he's already asked you? Sibell, you must be quite mad. Do you love him?'

She smiled. 'I'm beginning to think I do. He's such a lovely person to be with, nothing's a bother . . . But Lorelei, I don't want to marry Zack because I have to.'

'Have to? What? Are you in the family way?'

'No, it's not that. But you see, the Hamiltons are sort of stuck with me, and me with them. If I don't marry him, I'll have to leave, and I haven't got anywhere else to go. And not much money.'

'That sounds like the best reason to marry him,' Lorelei said. 'You'd better grab him while you can.'

Sibell shook her head. 'No, it's not right. It just doesn't feel right.'

'Oh, go on with you! You've got another bloke up your sleeve, I bet you have.'

'There is another man. He's very attractive . . . you know . . . tall, dark and handsome – but I think he's a rotter.'

'What do you mean, you think? You listen to me, Sibell, if you suspect that he's a rotter, you'll be right. You stick by your intuition and get rid of him.'

They sat quietly while Sam Lim served tea and jam sponge, and then Lorelei spoke wistfully. 'I've got the opposite problem. I've got a man that I'm real fond of. He wants me to give up my business and be his mistress, to keep out of sight. But I'm making heaps of money. Why should I? If he'd marry me, that'd be different.'

It was Sibell's turn to give advice. 'Don't be his mistress, make him marry you.'

'It's not that easy,' Lorelei said.

Sibell looked at her carefully. 'Do you know anything about minerals?'

'Only that the men talk mining all the time. Mines, that's where you get the fast money.'

'I know where there's a big tin and wolfram supply. I mean, it's in the ground, and I don't think anyone has claimed it yet. I'd like to stake a claim but I don't know how, and besides, I think it takes money.'

Lorelei was interested. 'Well, now, aren't you the one? I could soon find out how you go about it, but you would need capital.'

'Would you have that sort of money?' Sibell enquired.

'I could very easily,' Lorelei said cautiously, 'but I don't lend money. If you have a viable mine and I have the capital, I reckon fifty-fifty would be a good idea. Like, I'd want half of all the works.'

'Not a bad idea,' Sibell agreed. 'I've got the map in my bag, it shows the exact location. What do we do now?'

'I'll meet you in town this afternoon and we'll go to the Mines Department and stake the claims, and then we'll see a lawyer. I like to have things all neat and legal.'

'Do you think we'll make money?' Sibell asked her.

'Can't say just yet,' Lorelei said. 'It won't cost much to find out, though. Once the mining leases are in order, we'll send out an official assessor, and if you're right, Sibell, we can make a fortune. There's a woman in town owns tin mines. She's a real old tartar, but she's got more money than the Queen. She goes for holidays in Monte Carlo.'

'Monte Carlo?' Sibell was amazed. 'From here?'

'Why not?' She primped her tight blonde curls. 'I'd go well in Monte Carlo. But hang on, where is this pot of gold?'

'On Black Wattle Station.'

Lorelei whistled. 'On the Hamilton station? Does your friend Zack know about it?'

'No.'

'You're pushing your luck, aren't you? Double-crossing him?'

'It's not Zack I'm double-crossing,' Sibell said, thinking of Logan. Now it would be his turn to be on the receiving end of bad news. 'If the mines look like making money, I won't be beholden to Zack any more. I'm practically a charity case at the moment.'

'So you're not going to tell him? I hope you know what you're doing.'

'Of course I do. I'll tell him eventually, but there's no point right now: this whole idea might come to nothing.'

'I hope not. You've got me half-way to Monte Carlo. Where is Monte Carlo anyway?'

*   *   *

Rain, mud, slush! Logan was convinced he'd never be dry again, and he cursed the sodding rain. It was like living in Turkish baths, except that every creeping, crawling thing invaded what little shelter he could find. Still in Katherine, closing down the mines, he wished, in fits of spite, that Josie were still with him: this would give her something to complain about.

At night he had to sleep with his mosquito net tucked in around his bunk, not just to ward off mosquitoes, but to keep the snakes out. And to make matters worse, his net was rotting and there weren't any more available.

A wave of malarial fever had swept through the settlement, and the shortage of manpower had given him the excuse he needed for a temporary shutdown. He was fed up with the place anyway. That trek with Starkey had just about killed him, thanks to those murdering outlaws.

He sat morosely on his bunk with a pint of rum, listening to the rain drumming down, remembering that march along the beach with Sibell, and he laughed grimly. He'd thought that was hot, coming from the old country, but when he looked back to those days, he realised it was a piece of cake, with ocean breezes and cool nights, marching with Starkey in bare feet had been like walking on an exposed hotplate. Everyone had told him since that they should have stayed where they were: there was not a lot of sympathy around for new chums mad enough to attempt a fifty-mile march on foot without water.

Logan had been suffering severely from sunstroke and dehydration, and one old-timer had told him to be careful of that sunstroke. 'It stays with you,' he warned. 'Like malaria. If you get too hot your body will overheat faster. You hafta drink gallons of water.'

Easier said than done in this place, where someone else told him not to drink the water unless it was boiled.

To be on the safe side, he added some extra water to his rum.

And then there was poor Jimmy. Those bastards had hanged him! Poor Jimmy, who'd never done anyone any harm. They'd hanged him on Black Wattle Station! What were Sibell and her high-and-mighty friends doing to allow that to happen? Sergeant Bowles had said that Maudie had tried to save him, but she'd been too late.

Logan appreciated that. Maudie had grit.

But Jimmy's death had caused Logan another problem. The whole situation was hell. None of them was as upset as he was over that terrible event, but all the talk and blame in the world wouldn't bring him back. That's why Logan wasn't enthusiastic about answering the summons from Colonel Puckering.

Rory Jackson and his mates had been rounded up and were now cooling their heels in the Palmerston jail, charged with murder, and Logan had been asked to give evidence for the prosecution. All very well for that police inspector, he didn't have to live here among the Jackson clan.

Now that he was adding to his finances by skimming gold from the take, Logan needed to stay on as manager of the Gilbert mines. He would go to Palmerston to register his wolfram claims and the tin, and to have it out with Josie, who was still ignoring him. But as for appearing in court, right out there in public, helping to condemn those men . . . why should he?

Local people had already hinted that if he gave evidence, his mines would be blackballed. No labour.

It would be bad enough to lose men on the Gilbert site, but if they ganged up on him, he'd never get his own mines going.

After discarding several plans, which included resigning from the Gilbert mines, Logan had decided to employ a foreman here in Katherine, which would allow him to proceed with his own projects at the same time. The bank was still holding out on him, but he'd heard Chinese businessmen in Palmerston were good for loans at higher interest rates.

What did the interest matter, though, when riches were waiting for him over at Black Wattle? That was another reason to remain as manager of the Gilbert mines. It gave him status in the community, important when seeking a loan.

But this damned court case had him worried.

He trudged down to find Sergeant Bowles. 'I can't see why the prosecution wants me in court. I won't be any help. I wasn't there when they hanged Jaljurra.'

Bowles looked at him shrewdly. 'They've been leaning on you, have they?'

'No. It just seems pointless having to go into Palmerston.'

'I heard you were going there anyway.'

'Possibly.' These bush policemen knew everything.

Bowles explained. 'The defence will claim that Jaljurra was one of the outlaws. Now it's still a crime to take the law into your own hands and hang a man, but if they can convince the jury that Jaljurra was one of the men who took the gold and shot Constable Jackson, then the jury will swing their way. Rory Jackson will pull in the sympathy vote.'

'Starkey can prove the other outlaw wasn't an Aborigine.'

'That he could,' Bowles said heavily. 'But Starkey's left town. He got the message, and jumped on a ship leaving Palmerston a few days ago, so you're it.'

'I don't know why they need all this rigmarole,' Logan argued. 'They hanged him, everyone knows they did, that should be the end of it.'

'I thought Jaljurra was a mate of yours,' Bowles said.

'Well, he was, but just the same, they can't expect me to get involved at this stage.'

Bowles stood, occupying the doorway of the tiny police station. He spat a chaw of tobacco at Logan's feet. 'You be there, mate,' he said, his leathery face grim, 'or I might have a word or two to say meself.'

'About what?'

'About why your gold output registered in customs at Palmerston doesn't tally with the returns at the battery.' He grinned meanly. 'But live and let live, I say. The last manager was up to the same tricks. Nothing's sacred here, is it, Conal?'

On his way to Palmerston, still trying to work out how to dodge the court case, Logan met some men from Black Wattle Station who informed him that the family had gone to town to wait out the Wet.

'Miss Delahunty? Has she gone too?'

'Sure she has. Casey took the women and young Wesley, the whole troop of them, himself, to make sure they got there safe and sound.'

And that was the only bright light in the present grey and miserable scene. Sibell and Maudie were both in Palmerston. He'd buy some decent clothes and call on them formally, they'd be easy to find. And then he'd see how the land lay. He yearned for Sibell, he got horny at the thought of her, but a man had to start thinking above his navel. Josie and her charms had taught him a hard lesson. Sex was one thing, ambition another. Josie had brought nothing but trouble to their union, she'd cost him a lucrative job, and more. With Sibell, he would end up supporting yet another woman, while Maudie was money, the door to easy living.

Finally, riding into town with groups of men who were also withdrawing for the season, Logan decided to forget Josie for the time being. He had earned a little enjoyment. He missed the crowd at Tommy's pub in Perth, in fact he missed civilisation and all its comforts.

This outpost, Logan thought derisively, as they plodded down Smith Street, will never amount to anything. He noticed that Palmerston couldn't even boast a two-storey building. It was squashed by the climate, and would remain so. It occurred to him then that the smartest move would be to make money here and get the hell out. Once his mines were operating, he could install a manager and live high like Percy Gilbert. He might even go to Sydney. Everyone said that was a fantastic town, the real jewel of the southern seas.

After inspecting the premises and finding them to his liking, the manager of the Gilbert gold mines took a front room at the Victoria Hotel. He bought himself some new clothes, returned to the hotel for a long, cool bath, and repaired to the barber.

'All-over trim, sir?' the barber enquired.

'No. Cut my hair and shave off the beard.'

'If I may say so, sir, you've got good healthy hair. What if I shave the beard but keep a nice thick moustache. All the fashion now, for them as got the face to wear them. And for them as not, too, many a time . . .'

'Let's see, then.'

'Certainly, sir. If you're not pleased we can whisk it off too.'

The job complete, Logan stared into the looking-glass. His black hair was trimmed neatly, not shorn as usually happened with scissor-happy barbers, and the thick, wide moustache gave him a superior air, rather rakish even. He liked it.

'Elegant, I'd say, sir,' the barber smiled, and Logan agreed.

'What's that place over the road?' he asked. 'The Bijou. Is it open?'

'Very popular,' the barber told him. 'Rather pricy, but good value,' he winked, 'if you get my meaning. Open all hours.'

'Good,' Logan said. 'Now, where's the Mines Department?'

'Next street across, on your left.'

Logan stood under the eaves in his cream tropical suit, feeling a new man, all sharp and shiny. He contemplated the steady grey rain and decided the Mines Department could wait. The Bijou Palace was a long, low stone building which, he guessed, had once been a storehouse but was now in use for a much more interesting purpose. He dashed across the road – amused to note the Bijou faced a charming church set back in serene gardens – turned the knob on the large solid door, and walked in.

Josie was shocked. She read about the arrest of five men charged with hanging an Aborigine called Jaljurra, and a few minutes later recalled that this was Jimmy Moon's tribal name. Surely not!

She hurried down to the police station and located the Inspector of Police, a very kind man, Colonel Puckering.

'I'm afraid so,' he told her. 'This fellow was indeed the black tracker from Katherine.'

'But he wouldn't have shot a man. He wasn't an outlaw.'

'Well aware of that, madam. Nasty business, this.' He looked at her curiously. 'Mrs Conal, did you say?'

'Yes. I live in Shepherd Street.'

'Would your husband be the manager of the Gilbert mines?'

'Yes.'

'A wonder he didn't tell you. He was one of the three in the ambush. He was there when Constable Jackson was shot.'

Josie went limp. Logan hadn't bothered to tell her anything about this: his letters, all three, had centred on his insistence that they divorce and his anger that she should dare to buy a house without his permission. 'He doesn't write much,' Josie muttered, to cover her embarrassment. 'He'll probably tell me all about it when he comes into town.'

'Of course he will,' Puckering said. 'Probably didn't wish to upset you. When do you expect him?'

'Oh!' Josie was startled. 'Any day now, I suppose,' she said feebly, needing to retreat from this interview.

'Be good enough to ask him to call as soon as possible, would you, Mrs Conal? Need his evidence. Most important.'

'Yes, I'll do that,' Josie said, gathering herself to escape. 'I'm terribly sorry about Jimmy. An awful thing to happen. We were very fond of him.'

'Jimmy?' Puckering asked.

'Oh, yes. Jimmy Moon, that was his English name. We knew him in Perth.'

Puckering stroked his chin. 'That fellow? Spoke English fairly well? Tall, well built, big smile.'

'Yes, that was Jimmy. How could they kill a gentle person like him? They must be monsters, those men.'

'Jimmy Moon,' Puckering repeated. 'What was he doing so far from home?'

Josie considered this. 'I don't really know. I think he just liked to travel, to explore. He crossed the Continent, you know, from Perth, right into the desert, and then north. He was really very clever. He relied on all the different tribes to help him on his way.'

'Jolly clever of him, I'd say,' Puckering agreed. He escorted her to the door, put up her umbrella for her and sent her on her way.

'Damn clever,' he said to himself. 'Rum business all around. She doesn't know her husband was robbed and nearly done for in the bush. And why did Jimmy Moon put so much distance between himself and his people?'

* * *

Josie was still distressed over Jimmy, but also mortified at having made such an ass of herself.

Since receiving Logan's bombshell, she had been trying to keep calm, to tell herself that maybe he'd gone a bit mental and that everything would be all right once he saw the house and settled, at least temporarily, into a sensible household. But all this about an ambush? What was going on?

It had taken time for her to adjust to normal living again, and, needing a friend, she had made enquiries about Charlotte Hamilton, only to find that Charlotte had died.

Devastated, she'd gone to the little church near the wharves to pray for her, finding consolation and a certain pleasure in the availability of a church. Except for that hectic time with Logan in Perth, Josie had lived so far from a town that she'd become adjusted to going without town amenities. It was only a few weeks ago that she'd realised she didn't have to keep supplies in the house, that shops were nearby, that she could buy fresh milk, fresh meat whenever she wanted. It was heaven.

And she'd occasionally purchase a newspaper, but they sold out in the mornings, and she missed them so often that she had finally put a paper on order. So, for the last few days, she had enjoyed the added luxury of collecting her own paper each evening.

She remembered that Jack had said newspapers kept back-copies and decided it was time to put this information to the test.

In the offices of the *Palmerston Gazette*, Josie was ushered to a corner table, where a clerk brought her a wad of papers bound together and held in place by a strip of varnished wood. And there she read in lurid detail, of the ambush, the death of Constable Jackson, and the gold robbery.

Logan hadn't said one word about it. He was deliberately cutting her out of his life. But why? Was there another woman? It was possible, but in Katherine? Unlikely.

She walked up the street, past the Bijou Palace and made for the church. Even though Jimmy hadn't been of the Christian faith, he deserved the respect of prayers.

'Who's Logan?' Zack asked Maudie, the first chance he got.

'A friend of Sibell's. Logan Conal. He manages the Gilbert mines at Katherine.'

'Boyfriend?'

'Past tense, I think.'

'Doesn't sound like past tense to me. She talked about him a lot when she was sick. Called him "Logan darling".'

Maudie grinned. 'With a fever people say anything. What do you care?'

'Because I want to marry her, dammit.'

'You what?' Maudie was stunned, and he took her surprise for granted, busy with his own thoughts. 'Trouble is, I never heard her mention me. I brought her all the way to Palmerston, minded her most of the time, but the only person she asked for in the fever was Logan. I didn't get a look-in.'

'Maybe I'm wrong then,' Maudie said, doubling back. 'Maybe he's not past tense.'

'Do you think I should ask her?'

'Ask her what?'

'About this Logan chap.'

'No, let me find out for you.'

'Would you do that for me? If I'm going to ask her again to marry me, I want to know that the coast is clear. It's my fault, of course. I didn't give her a chance to explain the first time, just popped the question and took off. I was scared she'd knock me back. Was Logan the fellow she saw in Pine Creek?'

'Yes, he's an old friend.'

'Is he now?' Zack said glumly. 'Still,' he picked up his hat, 'I might have known a girl like Sibell would already have a boyfriend.'

'I had no idea you were interested,' Maudie said, and that was the truth. She was shocked: Sibell, the two-faced witch, hadn't said a word. If Zack married Sibell, what was to become of her? She'd end up the maiden aunt, with Sibell mistress of the house. Her house. Black Wattle! Like bloody hell she would!

'Charlotte was keen,' Zack said. 'She kept hinting to me about Sibell, but that put me off, I felt I was being cornered. And then when Charlotte died, I was sorry, it would have made her happy. I was just too pigheaded to listen to her. I kept making up excuses why I shouldn't marry a town girl. Cliff and I talked about it.'

'What did Cliff say?'

'He agreed. I mean, compared to you, Sibell isn't exactly the right choice for a station wife.' He patted Maudie's hand. 'You'll always have that, girl. Cliff really appreciated you, he loved you.'

God spare me from maudlin men, Maudie thought. The lovesick bloody fool. She wished he would go away so she could think.

'It only hit me when I was leaving for the drive,' he continued. 'I looked at her and thought I mightn't be back for six months and she could be gone from here. She is beautiful, isn't she?'

In a pasty sort of way, Maudie thought. 'Yes,' she said. 'Not very strong, though, I don't think.' Obviously no one had thought to mention to Zack that Sibell had been station manager while she was laid up with her leg. Just as well, she chortled to herself, or Zack would be grovelling at Sibell's feet by now.

'Well, that's when I thought I'd better speak up, stake a claim at least,' he was saying.

'Leave it to me,' Maudie said in a firm voice. 'You can't ask her to marry you while you're in the house with her on your own.'

'We're not on our own,' he said. 'I'm tripping over people.'

'Only Wesley and the servants. People are talking, Zack.'

'Let them bloody talk.'

'I know. That doesn't matter, but if you ask her and she says no, the pair of you will be in a very peculiar situation. It will change everything. You'd better wait until I get home.'

'You're right. But in the mean time, you have a word with her, will you? Smooth the path. I'm a bit of a coward. It'd be a lot easier for me if you could find out if she'll have me. Then I could propose in style, with all the trimmings. Jesus, I really love that girl, the more I see of her. She's so sweet . . . but you know, she's got that English way about her, so standoffish . . .'

'Go home, Zack,' Maudie said, fed up with this conversation. 'I told you I'd fix it.'

After he left, Maudie fumed. Sibell sweet? Hell!

She felt sick.

The matron, Hilda Clarke, came by on her rounds. She was a hefty, no-nonsense woman with a voice like a foghorn, but Maudie liked her. They'd become quite good friends and Maudie had invited her to take her next holidays on Black Wattle Station.

'Hilda,' she called, 'can I have a word with you?'

'Yes, anything wrong?'

'Everything,' Maudie said. 'I have to get out of here.'

'You can go when you want,' Hilda told her.

'But the doctor said . . .'

'Bugger the doctor, he's a drunken old clod. You look after that leg, and no riding for a while, and I can cut you loose.'

She removed the winch, as Maudie called it, and gently lowered Maudie's leg to the floor. 'Have you been doing as I told you, wiggling those toes?'

'All the damn time,' Maudie said.

'Then you go easy and you'll be all right.'

Maudie tested the floor and allowed herself to be wheeled around on Hilda's strong arm, and then she was returned to her bed. 'It feels good,' she said, and the matron agreed.

'I'm in real trouble,' she told Hilda. 'I need help.'

'Say the word,' the matron offered, and Maudie poured out her tale of woe. That her brother-in-law was preparing to marry a woman who was no friend of Maudie's, not even a Territorian, an Englishwoman. And as soon as that happened, Maudie and her little son would be chucked off their own station.

Hilda was appalled. 'You poor girl! After all you've been through. I'd flatten that woman, stealing your home from under you. Don't you put up with it.' She turned to yell at a woman down the other end of the ward: 'Get back to bed, Mrs Flower. We don't need any martyrs here. Your baby's asleep, so leave him alone.' She nudged Maudie. 'Poor scrawny woman. It's her tenth kid. They ought to cut it off.'

'Can I get dressed?' Maudie asked.

'Yes. I'll give you a hand. You have to get moving, Maudie. Don't let the grass grow under your feet.'

'But I don't know what to do.'

The matron settled her bulk on to a rickety cane chair. 'Let's see, you have to take things one at a time. What was in your husband's will?'

'He didn't leave a will. He was so young . . .'

'I see. What about Charlotte's will? You could have knocked me down with a feather when I heard she'd died. She was a fine woman, I used to have dinner with her every so often.' Hilda laughed. 'What Charlotte didn't know about this town wasn't worth knowing. She should never have turned her back on her money, letting jumped-up lawyers mind it for her. If they had any brains they'd be as rich as her, not working for her.'

244

'She lost it all,' Maudie said gloomily.

'Not all of it or you'd have lost Black Wattle, too. She held the purse strings. So what did she say in her will?'

'I don't know. No one bothered to look. Zack's been away for a long time on a cattle drive, and I've been too busy. She always said she'd leave the lot to her two sons, so there's no point in chasing the will.'

Hilda sighed. 'You bushies, you're a lackadaisical lot. Letting things run on like that. The first thing you have to do is make certain the station is in your name and Zack's, or they could take your share.'

'Zack wouldn't do that,' Maudie said. 'It's just the house I'm worrying about.'

'No time like the present,' Hilda said, jumping up. 'I'll get your gear. You and me, we'll go and see for ourselves.'

'See what?'

'The will, girl! Charlotte's will. I'm always being asked to witness wills, I know all about them.'

Maudie was confused. 'Where will we look?'

'I reckon it'd still be lying around old Chester's office. Chester Pollard, her local lawyer. He never gets out of his own road, they have to jab him with a barge pole to make him move, he'd be waiting for one of you Hamiltons to turn up.'

'Are you sure it would be there?'

'Either there or out at the station. Did anyone find it in the house?'

'Not that I know of.'

'Righto!' Hilda was almost dancing on the bare boards. For a big woman, she was light on her feet. 'Let's you and I go and have a looksee. They won't miss me here for a while.'

Maudie was propped at the entrance to the bush hospital, the canvas awnings on the outer wards flapping gently in the warm breeze. Some children were playing on a see-saw across a half-drowned lawn, shrieking with joy as the downward sweep landed each one in a deep puddle worn by bare feet. She decided to build a see-saw for Wesley when they went home. Home? How long would she last there with Sibell running the show? And what good would it do, reading Charlotte's will? It was all plain as day. Zack and Cliff owned half of everything, and Zack had told her she was entitled to Cliff's share, fifty-fifty. What was he going to do? Cut the house in half?

But there was no denying Hilda, who was now determined to help Maudie. 'Charlotte would never forgive me if I didn't stick up for you,' she said as she bundled Maudie into her gig.

'Are you sure we're allowed to do this?' Maudie asked, also worrying that she might be expected to read. 'Maybe we ought to see Zack first.'

'Zack won't care,' Hilda shouted as she hurtled the gig into town. 'If the will hasn't been processed, you're doing him a favour. This is the first step towards getting that station in both of your names.'

Maudie hung on to the polished rails as the two horses shot around a corner, almost overturning the gig, but Hilda was in control, holding the reins with both hands and urging them on as if the hounds of hell were after them.

Not one to stand on ceremony, Hilda turned the gig into the back yard of a small, single-fronted shop. Once inside, half carried by Hilda, Maudie found herself in a musty room piled high with papers.

'Good God, Chester,' Hilda boomed. 'How do you find anything in this mess? And how's your gout?'

A clerk burrowed in a corner, chewing his pen and staring at them as Chester removed his glasses and stood up, pushing strands of white hair away from his ruddy face. 'Good afternoon, ladies.' He winced as he moved from his seat. 'Gout's bad, Hilda, it's this wet weather.'

'It's the port, more like it,' Hilda sniffed, pulling over a chair for Maudie. 'You know Mrs Hamilton? Charlotte's daughter-in-law.'

'Yes. My condolences, dear lady, on your double tragedy. I wasn't able to get out to the funeral – this infernal gout, hard for me to travel these days – but my thoughts were with you.'

Nervously, Maudie listened as they talked and Chester searched around for the will, pulling wads of papers out of pigeon holes, spilling them, replacing them, taking an eternity.

'Been expecting the Hamiltons, come the wet season,' he told Hilda. 'Been meaning to get the will out and ready, didn't want to post it, the mails being the way they are out here.'

Hilda winked at Maudie behind his back. 'Told you,' she mouthed. 'It's here.'

'Trouble is,' he muttered, still searching, 'she wrote that will some time back, that's why it's a bit difficult to put my hands on it right now.' His voice intimated that they might come back another time, but Hilda would not be deterred.

'We can wait,' she said stoutly.

'Not much left of her holdings now, poor Charlotte,' Chester said. 'Only the station and the little beach house. If I recall, when she made out that will she thought she was leaving the lads a fortune, what with her shares and so forth . . . But then, Black Wattle's a fine station, she still . . . Ah! Here it is.'

Maudie was spared the indignity of having to reveal her illiteracy as Chester read it out to them. 'By rights, Zack should be here,' he began.

'Zack will be in later,' Hilda said. 'You can read it to him then. Maudie here has to get her affairs in order. Cliff's share would pass on to her, wouldn't it? Since Cliff didn't leave a will.'

'Tsk, tsk. No will? Dear me . . . Yes, of course. Just more paperwork, that's all.'

'So she has to get on with it,' Hilda insisted, and Chester, bullied by Hilda, got on with it.

When they emerged from the solicitor's office, Maudie was stunned. 'What's happened? I don't understand.'

'Shut up and keep moving,' Hilda said.

She reined the gig in under a tree. 'Now listen. Obviously Charlotte was looking ahead. She knew two brothers and their wives running a station would be trouble in time, so she meant for the lads to each have a station of their own.'

'That's not news,' Maudie said. 'That was the idea all along.'

'Good. But Charlotte wanted to be fair to both of her sons, so she laid out options for Black Wattle Station. She's given her elder son, Zack, first

246

option, and if he doesn't take it up then Cliff can. Or could. It now means you can.'

'No, I can't. Zack will keep it.'

'An option, dear, means an option to buy.'

'That's worse,' Maudie said. 'Zack buys out my share and I'm really out on my ear. I only get the money.'

'You'll get enough to buy another station.'

'And let her push me out?'

Hilda smirked. 'Well, if you want Black Wattle, all you have to do is shut up for a few weeks. Until January the eighteenth, to be exact.'

'Why?'

'Because your brother-in-law's option is for six months. And the six months, from the time of Charlotte's death, will be up on that date. Then it's your turn. If Zack hasn't bought you out by then he's lost the toss. You can claim Black Wattle.'

'Hang on,' Maudie said miserably. 'No, I can't, I'd have to buy Zack out. Where would I get the money.'

'There's plenty of money in this town if you have the collateral, and you have that with your half share of Black Wattle. You could run the station, couldn't you?'

'Easy. But I'm not too good on the book side.'

'So you hire a book-keeper. All the big stations have 'em. That's not a problem.'

Maudie chewed her fingernails. 'I just have to wait until that day in January and I'm the boss?'

'That's about the size of it,' Hilda laughed, 'unless Zack finds out what's on. But he doesn't seem to be in any hurry.'

'No . . . he's too busy worrying about Sibell.'

'Well, then, Merry Christmas, Maudie! Come on now and I'll deliver you home.'

'What do I care if you've already checked it twice,' Logan roared. 'Check it again!'

'If you insist.' Clarrie Fogge sniffed and went back to the district maps. He'd been working in the Mines Department for years and already two years, practically a life sentence, in Palmerston. He prided himself on work well done and was looking forward to a promotion when he returned to Adelaide. He wasn't about to make any mistakes now.

He returned to the counter. 'It is as I have told you. Mining leases have already been registered in that area.'

'They can't have been. Who by?'

Clarrie peered at his records. 'A company by the name of Morning Glory Prop. Limited.'

'Who the hell are they?'

'I'm afraid I can't say, sir.'

'You mean you won't say!' the large natty man yelled at him, and Clarrie backed away, afraid the fellow would strike him.

'I can't divulge that information,' he replied.

'Not for ten quid?'

He looked down at the note slammed on the table and assumed an

247

air of offended dignity. Lorelei had slung him twenty. 'Not possible, sir.'

'Someone has jumped my claim,' Conal raged, but Clarrie shook his head.

'I beg your pardon, sir. Claim-jumping can only occur when a legally registered mine is appropriated by another person.'

'I know that, you bloody idiot!' He stormed out of the office. 'You haven't heard the end of this.'

'To be sure,' Clarrie smiled, rolling up the maps. Lorelei and the other young lady had warned him that someone might object, but there was no problem: first come, first served in the mining game. Mr Conal was just a bit slow off the mark, and he wasn't obliged to tell him any more.

Lorelei had been very generous. He'd had the time of his life at the Bijou, on the house, and had allowed himself to be persuaded to get the assessors out to the claim right away.

He giggled to himself. Lorelei was a trick! 'Without further ado, Clarrie,' she'd instructed, opening her best champagne. 'They can have ten quid each if they get out there and back before the rivers close the trails. And then, my beauty,' she'd kissed him on the cheek, 'if they bring back good news, they'll be guests of honour at the best party the Bijou has ever seen.'

The assessors had ridden out of town with a change of mounts, flying like express trains. Clarrie prayed the two ladies had struck it rich, he was looking forward to that party.

Clarrie hummed to himself as he shut down for lunch. Wolfram, eh? There was already one wolfram mine operating further south, and they were raking in the cash. There was plenty of room for another one.

He closed the door and strolled around the front to join the gentlemen of the BAT for lunch and a game of billiards.

Logan sank two whiskies at the nearest pub before he could get his breath. He saw himself in the mirror behind the bar, his face blotchy with rage, and tried to calm down. Who had done this? Had the Hamiltons stumbled on it? Or had someone else been prospecting. 'Jesus!' He thumped his fist on the bar. The Morning Glory company! He'd find out who was behind this. Had Sibell told someone? That was the most likely explanation. He should have known women couldn't keep their mouths shut.

'Oh, shit!' he exclaimed, and the barman grinned.

'Having a good day, are you, mate?'

'I'll have another whisky, without the lip,' Logan snarled.

He should have come to town sooner and registered his claim, but he couldn't be in two places at once, and it was more than a five-hundred-mile round trip from Katherine. He hadn't wanted to know the date the leases had been registered, it was easier to search around for blame. Logan didn't need to remind himself that he'd wasted two whole days – no, spent two whole days living it up in the Bijou with those luscious women and an endless supply of champagne. 'Ah, to hell with it,' he said to no one in particular. He felt like going back there again, right now, where he was appreciated.

But there was Josie, and this bloody court case. He was in no mood to talk to Josie now, she could wait. He had heard the Hamiltons were in town – everyone seemed to know them – and guessed Sibell would be with them.

Time to visit Sibell. To take her quietly and find out if she'd blabbed. He could bring her back to his hotel and make love to her. The whores were fine but they were only appetisers. Sibell was important. Nothing like a loving woman. And to be able to step out with a beauty like Sibell in Palmerston! She'd turn every head.

At least there was some social life in Palmerston. Logan was determined to be part of it, he missed the fun of Perth. There was to be a ball at the BAT headquarters on Christmas Eve, and he had scored an invitation from some of the lads during the fun and games at the Bijou. It would really be something to arrive with Sibell on his arm.

While he considered his next move, he decided to dig up his new friend John Trafford, who worked for the telegraph company. Not realising that he was following Clarrie, he made his way around to the Esplanade and studied the BAT headquarters. They were indeed very elegant: as Trafford had said, 'they do themselves proud'.

The single-storey sandstone buildings had a strange orange tint which gave them an opulent air, and the staff quarters, the dining room and smoke rooms, as well as the actual office building, were well cared for and set in neatly trimmed gardens. They looked so primly colonial it was hard to grasp that the élite of the town really kicked up their heels here, at the expense of the government.

He found Trafford in the garden lounge, drinking tall gins laced with a peppermint liqueur, and with him were three very pretty English ladies in fluffy summery dresses.

But they're still not a patch on Sibell, he told himself as he accepted their enthusiastic invitation to join them.

Across the road, the massive tide swallowed the beach and bumped restlessly against the land: foam flecked the sea grass, and pure white seagulls flapped impatiently as yet another squall growled grey on the horizon.

Zack jammed the long shovel into the ground and stamped it deep with his boot. Inactivity bored him, so he planned to fence the beach property, beginning with this section on the sea-front, to protect the garden from wind and sand. He dug a deep post-hole and lined up the next one, assessing the number of saplings he'd need in order to construct a strong closed windbreak. The house was built up on blocks, for coolness, so this fence would not obstruct the view.

While he worked, he thought of Sibell. He seemed to think of hardly anything else these days. Maudie had talked to her and reported that she was still keen on this Conal fellow.

'Best forget about her,' Maudie had advised, but Zack had no intentions of giving up that easily. People change their minds all the time. 'You're a prime example,' he told himself. 'Who was it resented being paired off with Sibell? You're paying for that now, my lad.' He should have listened to Charlotte. God, he missed her. And Cliff. They'd been close, the three of them, and then suddenly, they'd gone, and he remained. It was still hard to adjust, not to be able to talk things over with them. He smiled. If they were alive now, he'd be arguing with Cliff about the fence, what sort of a fence, how high, and so on, and Charlotte would be pacing around them in her old straw hat, giving orders, being the overseer.

He'd needed to get away on that cattle drive. He'd been so shattered by their deaths that Black Wattle Station had been unbearable. Every time he'd turned a corner, he'd expected to see them. So many times he'd thought he could hear Charlotte's voice, or Cliff's laughter. In a way he'd been like the blacks, gone walkabout, travelling all that distance with his grief until his 'crying' was done.

Someone was walking along the beach. Zack straightened up and watched, as a man in one of those sissy white panama hats trudged towards him.

'I'm looking for the Hamilton house,' he said.

'This is it,' Zack said, knowing instinctively that here was Conal himself. He'd known the fellow was in town, because the papers were full of the court case over the hanging of that black tracker at Black Wattle. Bastards, he thought, feeling guilty that he hadn't been there: perhaps he might have been able to prevent the outrage.

'You've got a good spot here,' Conal said, and Zack nodded. Sibell read the papers, too, she must have known Conal was in Palmerston. Zack had been crowing, secretly, that the boyfriend hadn't bothered to call, but that little win was short-lived.

'State your business,' he said, reasoning he wasn't expected to know the stranger.

'My name is Logan Conal. You must be Zack Hamilton.'

'Yes.' Zack made no attempt to be friendly, this was one visitor he could do without.

'Does Miss Delahunty live here?' Conal asked.

'She does.' He saw the flash of anger on Conal's face, and that pleased him.

'Could I see her?'

Zack picked up a towel and wiped the sweat from his face and neck. Maudie had said Conal was handsome, but he couldn't see it. Sure, he had a good build and even features, but he also had a loose, rubbery mouth that spelled weakness, and green eyes that glittered oddly. Like a snake, Zack thought, not caring that he could be biased. 'I'll see if she's in,' he said, and left Conal standing at the fence line which he'd marked out with string.

He went to the back steps and called to Sibell. 'You've got a visitor.'

She appeared at the door and looked down. 'Who?'

'Back there,' he said. 'Mr Conal.'

'Oh!' She was flustered. He watched her dither, hardening his attitude. This was his house, and if Sibell wanted to entertain her boyfriends, she could take them some place else. He was fully prepared to tell her this, but she finally made a decision. 'I'll come down.'

Sibell was agitated. Her first thought was to ask Zack to send Logan away, but she had to know the truth. From him. And if she asked Logan in, there was only the one big family room . . . Maudie was in there! Better to run down and head him off.

250

Zack seemed a large, disapproving presence as she hurried past, aware that he was watching.

'Hello, Logan,' she said, keeping her distance.

'Oh, my,' he grinned. 'You look better every time I see you.'

'What do you want, Logan?'

'I've come to invite you to attend a ball with me at the BAT on Christmas Eve.'

'Oh, have you? And is Josie coming too?'

'Josie? Why would I ask Josie? I told you that was all over.'

'You didn't tell me that she's up here with you.'

He sighed. 'Sibell, we're getting a divorce.'

'So you *are* married to her?'

'Oh, for Christ's sake, we can't talk here. I have to explain. Come for a walk.'

'Why should I?'

'Don't be so childish,' he snapped, knowing Sibell would respond to that accusation.

'I'm not childish,' she said, stepping over the line into the dunes. 'You've got a lot of explaining to do.'

When they had dropped down to the wide, flat sands, she turned on him: 'You are the most despicable person! And you're a damn liar. How dare you come around here making a fool of me again!' She stood firmly in the sand, out of sight of the house. 'And I'm not going for a walk with you, let alone to a ball.' He put his hand on her arm but she pulled away. 'Don't touch me!'

'Very well, I won't touch you, but you will hear me out, otherwise why are you here? You could have done your yelling back there.'

'Where's Josie?'

'I believe she's in Palmerston somewhere. I haven't seen her.'

'Where are you staying?'

'At the Victoria Hotel. I've had a lot of business to attend to this week, or I'd have called on you sooner.'

'Why didn't you tell me you were married?'

'Because I was so happy to find you again, and I didn't want to spoil everything.'

'Everything? Is that what you call it?' she said angrily. 'You mean you wouldn't have been able to seduce me?'

'Oh, come on, Sibell, who seduced you? You wanted me to make love to you, you could hardly wait, and you couldn't get enough. That's not the usual scene for seduced maidens. Be honest, I don't believe you'd have cared if I said I was married.'

'That's not true,' she flared, and ran away from him, but he stayed with her. 'Yes, it is, you can't run from the truth. I thought you loved me.'

He was wearing her down now, cornering her, so he pulled her to a halt, the battle almost won. 'Will it help if I tell you I still love you?'

'No, I don't think so,' she said. 'Tell me about Josie.'

'All right, I will, as long as you promise not to start yelling again. I think what happened at Cambray farm was that I felt sorry for Josie, you saw the life she had to live with Jack. And one thing led to another, and when I came back that way she left with me.'

251

'She wrote to me,' Sibell said. 'She said she was very happy with you.'

'She probably was. I took her into Perth.'

'You were living together!'

'I haven't denied it. But then when Jack Cambray died . . .'

'He died?'

'Yes. And there no longer being an impediment, Josie insisted we marry. She's older than me, I thought . . . Oh, God, Sibell, I don't know what I thought. I just got carried along by circumstances. To tell you the truth, I didn't want her to come north with me, but she insisted, and I'd never have got this job if I'd told Percy Gilbert, you know Percy, that I was taking a woman with me, not my wife. So we got married just before we sailed. And the whole thing has been a disaster.'

'Where's Ned? Josie's son?'

'She left him in a boarding school in Perth, with the result she's now pining after him. And she hates it up here. No pleasing her. I think she'll go back to Perth.'

Sibell took a twig and scratched absently in the sand. She was cross with Logan, but still angry with Josie, who had made a complete mess of a single man's life. And hers.

'I didn't realise you were so weak,' she said to Logan, and he took her comment without resentment.

'We're all weak,' he said blandly, congratulating himself that the worst was over.

For her part, Sibell was seeing him for the first time. Or maybe she was once again seeing the man she'd met on the beach, the man she had disliked. She flushed now, remembering what a silly fool she'd been, how ridiculously naïve to be concerned about appearances at a time like that, and her stupid remark about having to marry him. She still squirmed at that, but what had she known? Growing up in such a puritanical world, where the girls were kept ignorant, were always chaperoned . . . and for damned good reason, it suddenly occurred to her. She laughed. 'Do you know what I hate most in the world, Logan?'

'I have no idea,' he said. 'Tapioca custard, maybe. I always hated that.'

'I hate people who think they can bully me, ride roughshod over me.'

He laughed, sifting dry sand through his fingers. 'When has that happened?'

'Ever since I arrived in this country. I felt sorry for myself for a long while until I realised that other people . . .'

'Spare me the sermons,' he said. ' "I moaned because I had no socks until I met a man who had no feet." Is that your text for today? You can do better than that, Sibell.'

'Yes,' she said absently, 'you're probably right. What I was really talking about was self-pity, I suppose.'

She had led him into this reflective conversation for no particular reason, but she was startled by his reply. 'Yes, you're good at that.'

Was she? Indeed? Then it was time he had a go at it. 'Do you still want to take me to the ball?'

'Of course I do.'

'No matter what?'

'I don't know what that's supposed to mean, but it doesn't matter.'

'Promise.'

'Yes.'

'Then let's go back.' She would go to the ball, she would adore to go. Everyone was talking about it. She'd buy a new dress, or have one made . . . fast. She had hoped Zack would ask her, but he hadn't said a word, and Maudie had announced that Zack would have to escort her. Even with her bad leg.

'I'll still be there,' Maudie had said. 'I never could dance anyway.'

Sibell reasoned that if she went with Logan, that might spur Zack into action. He seemed to take her for granted, as if she were just part of the ménage at the beach house.

If they were both at the ball it would be a golden opportunity for her to break down Zack's steely reserve. She'd look her best, dance with him, flirt with him.

Logan interrupted her thoughts as they climbed the dunes. 'There's one other thing, Sibell. Someone has jumped my wolfram claims on Black Wattle Station. Did you tell anyone?'

'Why would I tell anyone?' she replied. Oh, yes, let's hear it for self-pity, Logan. She didn't want to let go of Logan until he found out from someone else – as she had about his marriage – that she had claimed the mines. He was so conceited. So sure of himself, and of her. This pleasure was worth waiting for!

Despite the rain – which seemed to have doubled in intensity, allowing fewer breaks for children to escape outside and ladies to walk abroad with some dignity – Palmerston was aglow with Christmas jollity. Shops were decorated with gum tips and streamers, silver tinsel and colourful paper lanterns, street vendors plied a busy trade in live chooks for Christmas dinners, and pianos plinked carols, becoming tinnier as Christmas Eve progressed, because this climate was cruel to the beloved instruments.

Dress for the ball was formal, and Logan was determined to keep up with the BAT gentlemen. He managed to buy an evening suit that was too short in the leg and smelled of mothballs, but there wasn't a stiff shirt left in town, so he went in search of John Trafford to borrow one, irritated by the necessity of these chores, which were wasting good drinking time. A party was already in full swing at the Victoria Hotel.

He walked moodily down Cavanagh Street, hanging on to his hat against a boisterous wind that was blowing in from the sea. It was a sodden wind, that brought no relief from the heat: only a warning that it had more rain in its tail. He would have to get after Trafford, too: he had promised Logan he would find out who were the directors of Morning Glory, but so far he hadn't got around to it, the lazy sod.

'Will do, chum, will do,' Trafford had said, and he had done nothing.

He can bloody well do it today, Logan thought – chase up the information before all the offices close down. They won't be open again for more than a week.

'Well, Logan!' a woman said, confronting him as he turned the corner. 'I heard you were in town.'

God! Not now! It was Josie!

253

'I was coming to see you,' he said curtly.

'And I should think you would,' she replied, standing firmly in his path. 'You're very good at putting things off. When were you coming to see me?'

'As soon as I can.'

'That's not good enough. You will come today. I am your wife, remember? This is a very small town, and I have known for days that you were at the Victoria Hotel, but I would not demean myself by chasing after you. I want an explanation about this divorce business.'

She wasn't bothering to keep her voice down, and people were peering at them, interested in this little drama.

'And I want to know what business you had to buy a house with my money?' he hissed.

'Our money,' she replied calmly. And then she was quieter. 'Logan don't be foolish. When you see the house you'll feel differently. Come home and we'll talk things over. Whatever has upset you, I'm sure we can sort it out.'

Standing on that windswept corner in a neat navy-blue dress, her skirts billowing around them, she looked a darn sight better than she had in Katherine, he noticed. She hadn't bothered with a hat, instead her hair was piled high and swathed in a long silk scarf which was knotted under her chin, the ends blowing wilfully in the breeze.

'Well?' she demanded. 'We can't stay here all day.'

'Later,' he said. 'I'll be down later.'

'Do you know where the house is?'

'Oh, sure. Down by that filthy Chinese quarter.'

'I like to say it's near the park,' she retorted. 'I'll be expecting you, Logan. Don't force me to come to the hotel.'

She stepped past him and went on her way.

'Shit!' he said, turning and bumping into a bandy-legged old stockman, who grinned, hitching his whip back on to his shoulder.

'We'll be in the shit if this keeps up,' he remarked, but Logan wasn't listening as he ducked for cover. A wall of rain came heaving over the town, almost blotting out the light and turning the streets into rushing rivers.

He waited in a doorway, worrying about Josie. He didn't want to see her at all, he wished she would just go away. Disappear. If he could find out who the directors of Morning Glory were, he would know where he stood. There was a time limit on these claims, and if they didn't act, he would still have a chance. And Josie could kiss the house goodbye: he wasn't having his money tied up in a house while there were prospecting opportunities all over the Territory.

By the time he reached the BAT headquarters, he was soaked to the skin, battling his way along the front as the wind slammed in from the sea. A servant handed him a towel when he squelched inside, and he dried his face and hands, slapping at his wet clothes. Others in the crowded lounge were equally bedraggled, but taking the weather in good part.

'Ho! Conal!' Trafford called to him from a group of revellers. 'Good weather for ducks, what?'

'Bloody awful!' Logan complained, but he was howled down.

'It's only rain, old chap. Not cold like back home. Have some champagne.'

Trafford's friend, Michael de Lange, was there, hovering over a table loaded with food. 'We're lunching buffet-style today, Conal. Have some of these oysters, they're tops.'

Logan took a glass of champagne. 'I wanted a word with you, Trafford.'

'Yes, of course. Have you heard the news?'

'What news?'

'The ball. We're changing venues. It's just too damn blowy on the front here, the ladies will be drenched and blown to bits before they make it to the door, so we're moving back a couple of streets to a more sheltered location, the Prince of Wales Hotel.'

'They've got a fine big room,' Michael said, cracking open a lobster claw. 'And he's decorating it grandly for us. Very sporting of Digger Jones to do this at the last minute.'

'He's not going to lose on it,' John Trafford laughed. 'We'll probably drink his pub dry.'

Logan drank some champagne, but it was too light for his mood, so he took a brandy from a tray and drank that to allay the confusion of the morning. Josie was trouble, he had seen it in her eyes, and it was only a matter of time before she met up with Sibell – it wasn't as if they didn't know each other. He downed another brandy, wondering if any woman was worth the complications she caused. He peered at the steaming grey windows. There were ships at anchor out there, sheltering in this great bay which they claimed was bigger than the famous Sydney Harbour. Everyone talked about Sydney, the hub of the down-under universe. He'd like to see Sydney. A man ought to just jump a ship and go. He'd done it before. Feeling mellow now in the company of these gents, who really knew how to enjoy life, he switched back to champagne, wondering if that dull-witted girl he had married was still in Liverpool. He had only married her because her hulking old man had practically frog-marched him to their Catholic altar.

Champagne! he laughed to himself. It was something you read about in books but never expected to taste, not the lads in Liverpool, anyway. But out here, next to beer, it was the national drink. 'Beer for the thirst,' they said, 'and champagne for the cheer.' And, by God, it was, too. It came to him, amid the glow and the chatter, that he'd had a damned good time in this country, even in Katherine after Josie left: always plenty of parties, plenty of pals. And food! He surveyed the table groaning with chilled oysters and lobsters, juicy cuts of beef, pork pies, kedgerees, cold collations, fat cheese wedges and fresh cobs of bread. They ate more in a day in Palmerston than a family back home could find in a week. And it had been the same in Perth. No wonder the locals were all such big, strong bastards. He laughed at the word, pouring his own champagne now. Everyone was a bastard – a good one or a bad one, it depended.

Logan was feeling no pain by now. Like these chaps, he decided, he had the measure of Australia and he was bloody well going to enjoy it. To hell with Josie and Sibell and Percy-bloody-Gilbert. No, not Sibell. They were stepping out this very night, he and Sibell, and afterwards he would make love to her . . .

'Hey, Trafford,' he called. 'I thought I asked you to check on something for me.'

'My dear Logan,' Trafford said, dodging around Michael, who was trying to balance a glass on a billiard cue, 'I expected you'd know by now.'

'How would I know?'

'Aren't you bringing the sublime Sibell this evening?'

'Yes.'

'Dear chap, Miss Delahunty is one of the directors!'

Logan was stunned. She'd sold him out after all, the bitch. He might have known she'd go after the lot, the station and the mines. 'Sibell's very secretive,' he said, forcing a grin. 'Who's the other director? Zack Hamilton?'

'No, not Zack, it's an absolute hoot! We've been in fits all morning. Sibell and Lorelei are partners.'

He gaped. 'Lorelei? From the Bijou?'

'The very one.'

'How does she know Lorelei?'

'We're old pals. Lorelei, Sibell, Michael and yours truly, we came to Palmerston on the same ship.'

'Drinks on the house,' Lorelei called, swishing into the main salon of the Bijou. 'This will be a Christmas we won't forget in a hurry.' She pulled on an over-large hooded raincoat that had been given to her by a sea captain and was ideal for this weather, and turned to Clarrie Fogge and the two road-weary assessors. 'I have to go out for a little while, so you gentlemen enjoy yourselves. I can't thank you enough, Clarrie, this is really wonderful news. Is the stuff really that good?'

'High-grade,' Max Klein, one of the assessors, told her. 'You'll do real good there, ma'am.'

As she was leaving, Clarrie followed her to the door. 'Max asked me to put in a word for him. He's German, very reliable, knows his business, would make a good mines manager. We'd be sorry to lose him, but properly managed mines put money in the government coffers, too, so we won't complain.'

Lorelei kissed him on the cheek. 'On your recommendation, Clarrie, he's hired.'

She blew into the police station on a torrent of rain, and the constable rushed to push the door closed after her.

'I'd like to see Colonel Puckering,' she said, and the constable grinned slyly.

'Yeah, I'll get him for you.'

Puckering loomed up in the doorway, scowling down at her. 'Come through,' he instructed, and led her out through the back door and along the covered walkway that he'd built to his bungalow. 'What are you doing here?' he said frostily, and when she was inside: 'I told you never to come here.'

Lorelei took off her coat and sat calmly by his desk. 'We have to talk.'

'What about?'

'Business.'

'The less I know about your business, the better.'

She fluffed her mass of crinkly blonde hair, taking no notice of his displeasure. 'I'm closing down the Bijou.'

He was relieved. 'That's good news.'

'I thought that would make you happy. Now what about us? You said you were fond of me, and if I gave up the Bijou then things would be different.' She watched his discomfort, and continued, 'Or was it just all talk? You and me, we get on well. Every Sunday night since we arrived has been our special time, and we do have a lovely time together.'

'I know that, Lorelei,' he said. 'Difficult for me, though, in my position.'

She smiled and folded her hands primly in her lap. 'You don't have to make excuses, Colonel. I wouldn't have held you to it. I just want you to listen to me for a bit,' she said. Her voice was calm, insistent, tapping into his conscience, for hadn't she been the joy of his lonely bachelor existence all this time?

On Sunday nights, the Bijou was closed in deference to the demands of vocal church-goers, closed to everyone except 'the Colonel' as she always called him. The other girls were given the night off so he and Lorelei could have their time together, undisturbed. He looked forward to those nights: they dined, they played cards, they made love, and, instead of diminishing, his desire for her increased so much it was a wrench for him to have to leave her at dawn. But now the orderly arrangement was under threat, and that upset him so much that his voice, when he spoke, sounded irritable. 'What do you want?'

'A favour,' she said. 'Are you going to the ball tonight?'

'I expect I shall have to put in an appearance,' he grunted.

'Take me.'

He stared at her. 'My dear girl, I couldn't do that.'

'Why not?'

'Not something I need to explain to you, surely? Complaints would fly, I get enough as it is, and I could very easily jeopardise my appointment here.'

'You mean you could get fired?'

'Quite likely.'

Lorelei considered this, and then she surprised him. 'What is to become of you, Colonel?'

'That's a strange question.'

'No, it's not. I'll tell your future for you. You'll stay on here, living on your salary – which you are always saying isn't much – living in this little cottage. And then you'll find, with luck, some nice lady, and you'll marry her and live poorly ever after.'

Puckering was amused. 'You make it sound pitiful.'

'I'm not finished. Your salary will then have to support two people, and after that they'll send you and the missus south to retire on a few lousy pounds, a couple of hundred a year. And you don't own a property, so you and the lady will end up stuck in a miserable boarding house.'

He laughed outright. 'Talking about the great days in India!'

Lorelei jumped up and took his arm. 'See! You know. All those retired

257

officers and civil servants end up in rented rooms somewhere.' She smiled artfully. 'Unless, of course, they marry rich ladies.'

'I shall have to look around then, shall I?'

'You don't have to look far,' she told him, standing back. She saw his jaw tighten, and hurried on. 'Steady on, don't freeze up on me. Give me credit for a bit of sense. I'm not suggesting you live on the earnings of a whorehouse.'

'One would hope not,' he said stiffly.

She took his hands. 'Come and sit down, I can't talk to you when you're playing the gent with a poker up your back.' She sat him on the couch and explained about the wolfram mines. 'That's why I'm shutting up shop. Sibell's entitled to fifty per cent, we agreed on that, but if you come in with me, on my half, you'll never look back financially, you won't have to be worried about what people say . . . you can quit this job . . .'

Puckering frowned. 'I will decide what I do about my "job", as you call it!'

'Of course you will, but you'll have the whip hand, you can please yourself. And, besides, we need you. If you are one of the directors, your name alone will clear the way for us, the company will be taken seriously.'

The small room, the cottage, seemed to be stifling now, and pathetic. Lorelei's predictions sounded cruelly real. Would he end up like that? But if he allied himself with Lorelei he'd have to walk the gauntlet of outrage from the respectable quarter of the town, a minority though they were. Would he have the courage to do it?

As if she'd read his mind, Lorelei kissed him on the cheek. 'After all, you're a cut above the lot here, why would you have to concern yourself with what they think? Look at the Administrator, he doesn't give a damn, he's always out prospecting. And the last one got run out of town for trying to close the pubs. You're a Colonel in the British Army, you've already set the pace.'

He shook his head. 'I'll have to think about it.' And Lorelei smiled. She knew the thinking had already been done.

'I've only got one condition,' she told him.

'What's that?'

'You have to take me to the ball tonight.'

'That's asking a bit much.'

'No, it's not. I see it as a sign of good faith. If you don't take me, the deal's off and we're finished.'

'You rascal,' he muttered. 'You drive a hard bargain.'

Lorelei didn't reply. She stood up, shook out her overcoat, and put it on.

'Very well, would you care to accompany me to the ball this evening?' he said.

'Charmed, I'm sure,' she giggled.

He lifted the hood for her, tucking her hair back, and then he kissed her. 'Damn the bloody mines,' he said. 'I couldn't bear to lose you, you're so soft and lovely.' He wrapped his arms around her, holding her to him. 'I'm really quite mad about you, Lorelei. I must be, even to be considering your wild plans.'

'Nothing wild about them. And you know how I've always felt about you.' She peered around him. 'Is that your bedroom in there?'

He nodded, releasing her. 'Yes.'

'We ought to try it out.'

'What, now? In broad daylight?'

She glanced out of the window at the teeming rain. 'You call that daylight? Only ducks and drakes are out in this weather. Come on,' she was unbuttoning his jacket, 'give Lorelei some loving. It'll be exciting here.'

'You are quite outrageous,' he complained mildly, as she began to undo his trousers. He picked her up and carried her into his bed.

Later, with Lorelei in his arms, he felt a huge sense of relief, even of happiness, that his life had taken a turn for the better.

A two-horse light carriage had been hired for the occasion, and even though he had clipped on extra waterproof covers for the protection of his passengers this stormy night, the driver was up front in all weather, so he gladly accepted Zack Hamilton's invitation to shelter his horses and vehicle under the high-set house while he waited for his 'parties' to emerge.

Upstairs, the would-be revellers were tense. A woman had come to the house during the afternoon to wash and dress the ladies' hair, and Sibell's blonde locks were now looking very elegant, waved back from the front in a fleur-de-lis style from the centre and tonged into a mass of curls from the crown. The clever woman, whose name was Lily, had wired pink frangipani into a band and pinned it like a small tiara across the centre of the curls, and it looked very attractive, matching the dusty-pink voile dress that Sibell had managed to buy.

Even though her dress wasn't as elaborate as Maudie's formal green taffeta, Sibell was pleased: it was light and cool, daringly low-cut, the neckline finished with handkerchief points of fine lace.

And Lily had transformed Maudie! The plaits had disappeared and her brown hair had been brushed wide and then replaced over an artificial roll of hair into the fashionable thick, face-framing style. Sibell was impressed. 'It looks beautiful,' she told Maudie, 'absolutely wonderful.' She brought another mirror so Maudie could see the back with the crown wound into soft coils.

'Why can't I have flowers like Sibell?' she complained.

'Mrs Hamilton, I think flowers would spoil the effect, hide the styling. But ear-rings would be perfect.'

'I hate ear-rings, I want flowers.'

In the end, more frangipani were collected, shaken dry and pinned at the back.

Zack was waiting in the family room when the two ladies were finally ready, and he complimented them both, pouring champagne. Sibell could see he was nervous. She was surprised to notice, too, how elegant he looked in his evening suit, the starched shirt and black tie not seeming to bother him at all.

He took his time with the champagne, refilling their glasses, drinking their health, and for the second time wishing them a Merry Christmas.

The twins and Wesley and Netta darted around, enjoying this special evening and gushing with pleasure at all the pretty clothes, but Maudie was impatient. 'We ought to get going, Zack.'

'I know,' he said. 'Are you sure your leg is all right, Maudie?'

'Don't worry, I'll get there, and I can prop it up on a chair.'

He walked through to the rear of the house, peering into the darkness. 'The seas are rough,' he told them when he returned. 'This storm is getting worse. I don't know that I should take you out on a night like this, Maudie.'

'What?' Her face was a picture of shock. 'Stay home because of a bloody bit of rain? What's got into you, Zack?'

'Even getting downstairs you could ruin your dress,' he said.

'Who cares about a dress?' she snapped angrily. 'I won't be dancing, no one'll see it anyway.'

'I don't know,' he worried. 'I don't like going out and leaving Wesley and the girls here. If anything goes wrong they'll panic.'

'What can go wrong?' Sibell asked, but he chose not to answer her.

'I can't speak for Sibell,' he told Maudie. 'She's going with Mr Conal, and he'll probably be here any minute. But I'm not sure we should go, Maudie. There'll be other nights.'

'Listen to you!' Maudie said, for once looking to Sibell for support. 'Choosing a time like this to get clucky. Wesley's got three people to look after him, does he need five? Well, you look here, Zack Hamilton, I only get to go to a ball once in a blue moon, and I'm going tonight come hell or high water. And if you won't take me, I'll go with Sibell and Logan.'

'Zack will come,' Sibell said hopefully, since Maudie's suggestion was taking the shine off the sodden night's programme. 'It is an awful night,' she agreed, and then she laughed. 'Talk about putting a damper on things, Palmerston's doing an excellent job. Once we're inside, though, it will be fun. Back home we have to go out in the snow at Christmas, and it's freezing: at least it isn't cold here. We're not likely to get pneumonia.'

Maudie was intrigued. 'Snow? Do you go out in the snow? I can't imagine what snow looks like. Did you hear that, Zack? They don't even let snow stop them, and you're carrying on like a tin of worms over a bit of rain.'

'It's not just rain,' he said angrily. 'This weather has been building for days, it feels like a cyclone to me.'

'Oh, my God!' Sibell felt a clutch of terror and the room seemed to spin. It was the first time she'd heard that word since those last hours on the *Cambridge Star*, and the horror of it came screaming back at her.

Maudie was standing over her with a cool cloth on the back of her neck. 'What happened?' she asked.

'You fainted,' Maudie explained with an edge of derision. 'See what you've done, Zack! You've frightened the daylights out of her.'

He was hovering around her, apologising, patting her hand, telling her not to worry, there was no danger. When she could breathe easily again, she joined in the apologies, for her foolishness. She saw Maudie grinning at her and realised that she must look stupid: she had never told them how the ship had come to founder, something else she'd been unable to talk about.

Zack was so upset at having caused her to faint that he was now doing

260

all he could to please, which included agreeing to take Maudie to the ball. 'We'll leave in a minute, Maudie,' he said, 'we'll just wait until Sibell's beau arrives and then we'll be off.'

'He's not my beau,' Sibell argued. 'He's my partner for the evening, Zack. There's a difference.'

'Who cares?' Maudie said, irritated by yet another delay. 'Just so long as he gets here.'

So they waited, the wind and rain whooshing around the house. They ate some Christmas cake and drank more champagne, with the conversation flagging and silences treading heavily upon them.

In the end Maudie had had enough. 'He's not coming,' she announced.

Zack looked at Sibell, who sat stiffly in her chair feeling her flowers and frock wilting about her.

'I'll stay,' she said at length. 'You go on.'

'Good,' Maudie said, gathering up her cloak.

'We can't leave you here,' Zack offered, but Maudie was on her way. 'If you don't get moving, Zack Hamilton, I swear I'll go on my bloody own. It's a Christmas Eve party, not New Year's Eve. If we don't go now, it'll all be over.'

'You'd better come with us, then,' Zack suggested to Sibell.

The fainting spell had passed as suddenly as it had come, and Sibell was feeling better, but she was thoroughly uncomfortable in this situation, especially since she'd brought it on herself. Allowing herself to be stood up was no way to make Zack jealous. 'You go on,' she said. 'I'll wait.'

'Don't be ridiculous,' Zack said. 'It's obvious he's not going to turn up now.'

'His wife's probably got him by the britches,' Maudie laughed.

Zack turned slowly about to face Maudie. 'His what?'

'You heard. His wife,' Maudie repeated sullenly.

'You never told me that,' he accused, and Maudie shrugged.

'It wasn't my business.'

'I asked you to do me a favour,' he said to her, a chill in his voice, as Sibell listened, bewildered, wondering why he was so angry with Maudie. 'It's my guess now you didn't bother,' he continued. 'You told me only what suited you. This will bear thinking about, Maudie.'

'Oh, cripes,' she retorted defensively. 'Some Christmas, with everyone in bad moods. If you wanted to know something, you should have asked her yourself, you just didn't have the guts to do it.'

'We'll see about that,' he said, and rounded on Sibell. 'So your friend Conal is married? And you're happy to be seen with a married man. That's hardly the behaviour I would have expected of you.'

'You don't understand, Zack . . .' Sibell tried. 'I had several reasons for agreeing to go with Logan.'

'I'm sure you did,' he said angrily. 'What a bright pair you are. Maudie playing tricks and you making a fool of yourself.'

'So now we're stupid, are we?' Maudie snapped.

He looked at them carefully. 'That's what I'm trying to figure out, but you'd better keep in mind that *I'm* not.'

'Oh, for heaven's sake,' Sibell exclaimed. 'Go to the jolly ball. I'm staying here.'

'Oh, no, you're not,' he said. 'You're coming with us. You're not going to sit here and sulk. As a matter of fact, I have been waiting for you ladies, if that's the right word, to tell me what you've been up to in Palmerston, and by God, you'd better make it soon.'

The two women looked at each other, mystified, neither of them knowing the other's plans.

Maudie was the first to speak. 'I don't know what you're talking about.'

'We'll see,' he replied. 'As for you, Sibell, if you so much as say one word to that Conal fellow tonight, you're sillier than I thought.' He jerked her chair back with such force that Sibell was almost tipped on to the floor.

The scene had made her so nervous, followed by this jolt to her feet like a naughty child, that she began to laugh.

'What's so funny?' he demanded.

'Everything, just everything.'

'You go on down,' he told Maudie, and called to Netta to assist her down the steps.

As the door banged shut, he handed Sibell her cloak. 'Come on, the sooner we get there, the sooner we can get home. I had hoped that once we were here in Palmerston and you were feeling better we might have been able to discuss my proposal, but you've been avoiding me, so we'll consider the matter closed.'

'By all means,' she said tartly. 'I don't have to explain myself to you.'

'That's what you think,' he warned. 'I didn't like the look of the Conal fellow in the first place, and I like him even less now. If he's at this dance and you want to join him, you go right ahead, Sibell, but keep him away from me. I won't associate with that type.'

'You don't even know him,' she retorted, not caring about Logan, but refusing to be dominated by Zack. It was bad enough that Logan had stood her up, without Zack reading her the riot act.

'I don't want to know him,' he said, 'but when we get home I believe there's something else you have to tell me.'

She guessed he must have heard about the mining claims, pre-empting her plans, since she had hoped to tell him herself. To surprise him. But would he believe her now? She deferred that subject and looked up at him. 'Zack, when people talk about marriage, they're usually in love.'

'That's true. But they're honest, they don't play games.'

'I didn't want you to think I had no alternative but to marry you,' she said.

He stopped and stared at her. 'And Conal's your alternative? Jesus!'

Netta interrupted them, charging back inside. 'Missus Maudie say "hurry up", boss.'

'Yes, let's go,' he said, and Sibell shrugged, annoyed that she hadn't been given a chance to explain.

'Father Chrismiss comen this feller night?' Netta asked hopefully, and Zack smiled.

'Sure, he'll be along.'

Not concerned with fashion, he pulled on the big, heavy mackintosh he wore when he was riding in wet weather. 'It's bloody marvellous,' he muttered to no one in particular. 'We've taken their world and given them Father Christmas.'

Outside, Sibell was relieved to find that the rain was steady but the wind had dropped. She was still shaky at the mention of a cyclone, and she grieved at the memory. There was so much Zack didn't know, didn't understand about her.

But a cyclone! She supposed that being on land was different. Safer. The danger lay at sea. She prayed no ships were out there, crews and passengers at the mercy of ocean storms.

He helped her down the slippery timber steps to the carriage. Sibell sat beside Zack, facing Maudie, who, despite her flattering hairstyle, and a touch of powder, had a face like thunder.

Logan stayed at the BAT bar all afternoon, dousing his rage with whisky and any other drink they cared to offer him. There was no way in the world he would take that double-crossing bitch to the ball now. Let her stay home and stew. It pleased him to think of her dressing, preparing for the grand event, primping and purring like the cat she was, in front of her fine friends, and then gradually realising that she had been stood up.

The numbers in the bar were thinning out as the gentlemen retired to dress for the ball. Logan took himself around to the Bijou Palace, intending to confront Lorelei Bourke, but she was nowhere to be found in the raucous packed salons.

Lorelei and Sibell? He wondered if Lorelei had told her that he was a customer? How was he to know the two women knew each other? That was a more likely reason for Sibell to turn on him, he decided, than just being married to Josie. After all, she knew he intended to divorce her. He mulled over that conversation with Sibell on the beach. He had told her that someone had jumped his claim, and he had asked her point-blank if she had told anyone about the wolfram. And Sibell had lied . . . No, wait. She had said, 'Why would I tell anyone?', with that blue-eyed, innocent smile of hers. And instead of pinning her then, he'd let that remark slip by, because he was so sure of her.

He was certain he could win Sibell back – women only needed a little flattery to come running again – and then, if he married her, everything she owned, under the law, would belong to him. It was a thought, a possibility . . . but God Almighty, a damn trap if ever there was one. But anyhow, two inexperienced women trying to set up a mine, they wouldn't get far!

Women hung around his neck, drunks spilled against him as he shoved his way out of the whorehouse and made for his hotel, passing the Prince of Wales, which was a blaze of lights in anticipation of the ball. The sight of it annoyed him.

Digger Jones had erected a canvas windbreak from the veranda awning, and it was flapping wildly as if urging the guests who were already arriving to hurry inside. They needed no encouragement. Gaudily dressed women and their escorts dived from swaying carriages into the hotel, screeching with laughter, while inside, the band was tuning up: single piano notes brought painful replies from violins, and a French horn pomped. Logan kept walking.

263

He passed by the Victoria Hotel, too, contrarily refusing to go in and dress in his newly acquired finery. The ball would last all night, he might attend later, he told himself loftily. And so he pushed on through streets deserted except for riders who dashed by, hell-bent on finding shelter, and whispering mounds of blacks who squatted in doorways. He travelled around the outskirts of the Chinese quarter, which wasn't safe for white men at night, stared in at the joss house that twinkled with ornate candles and lanterns, and at the granite-still Chinamen who sat or kneeled in their places. The sweet smell of incense stayed with him as he walked up the sodden path among dripping trees and banged on the door of Josie's house. His house.

Netta wondered why the big cupboard in the ladies' bedroom was locked, and she fingered it lightly as she wandered around their room, touching things. The two beds were scattered with clothes and the dressing table held all sorts of pretty things, which she picked up and studied. Combs, clips, ear-rings, hankies, were all examined in turn. She peered in the mirror, admiring her high frizz of hair that Missy had snipped into a neat ball enclosing her face, and bared her broad white teeth into a grimace, giggling at her reflection. There was a pretty pink powder-puff in a china bowl so she dusted her face liberally with powder and walked grandly into the kitchen.

She was in charge now, since Sam Lim had gone off to see his own friends, and it pleased her to be able to do what she liked in this strange whitefellow house built up on sticks – she shuddered – like burial posts. But she believed they knew what they were doing, white folks were damn clever.

The big meat safe had several plates of cold cuts, so she tore off a piece of corned beef with her strong fingers, ate it, and then went to the other coolgardie, where she eyed a jug of thick custard. Too good to resist. She poured some into a cup and drank it, delighting in the slow, sweet dollops.

Missy had left some champagne in her glass, so Netta took a mouthful. Then, spluttering, she spat the sour liquid into a bucket. Chastened by that experience, she resumed her idle patrol.

In the other room, which Zack shared with poor fatherless little Wesley, the child was sprawled across his bed, sleeping soundly, and the twins were curled up on their mats.

They stirred as she entered, their long, skinny legs creaking up defensively.

'What do you want?' Polly asked in their own language.

'Wesley's asleep,' Netta said. 'You two go to the sleepout now.'

'Missus Maudie said we can stay here until the boss comes home,' Polly told her, and Pet sat up. 'Father Christmas come yet?'

'No, not yet,' Netta said, losing interest in the sleeping arrangements. She studied the four pillow-cases hanging on the end-posts of the two single beds, and mentally counted them again. She had done this at least ten times since Maudie had told Sibell to put them there. One for Wesley, one for Polly, one for Pet and one for Netta.

The ladies had argued – they still argued all the time. Missy had said they should hang up stockings, but Maudie said no, put the pillow-cases. Netta was glad Maudie had won: stockings wouldn't hold much of a present.

'How does the Christmas father get in with the doors closed?' Polly asked.

'He opens them stupid,' her sister said.

Netta sighed. She knew from last year that the spirit man with the presents only came when everyone was asleep, and she wished the family would come home so they could all go to bed.

Last year . . . she thought about that. The old missus, Charlotte, had been here, and boss Cliff too, and there'd been plenty laughing, not all the scowls around this time. Even on this happy night they'd been arguing and shouting at each other. The old missus wouldn't have stood for it.

With a heavy heart she left the house and stood on the back steps overlooking the dark ocean, allowing the cooling rain to stream over her body, which was sweaty from the stuffy heat of the house.

She lifted her head and licked the fresh water from her lips, patting rainwater into her face to freshen the skin.

For a long time Netta stayed out there, listening to the night, and gradually she seemed to become one with the elements, her light cotton shift clinging to her body. She sniffed the air and stretched out her hands, palms up, as the winds, awake again, began blustering inland. They battered palm trees that bent and swished, hurling dried fronds into the air, and they hammered hardier trees that refused to budge, causing great boughs to switch around like cats' tails. As she watched, enjoying the spectacle, one great bough broke away and was hurled skywards, up and over the house.

Instantly, Netta raced inside, yelling at the twins, 'Get up! Get up quick! Devil wind coming.' She grabbed Wesley, rolling him in a sheet, and lifted him from the bed.

The child was crying, upset by the sudden disturbance, but she ignored him and kicked at the twins. 'Get up I tell you! We have to leave here.'

They blundered after her, down the steps, and fled into the street. Running beside her, Polly screamed at Netta, 'We should hide under the house. Come back.' But Netta would not stop, and since she had the boy, they ran on with her across vacant blocks of land, being shouldered into erratic paths by the strength of the wind. Searching for shelter, Netta made for a nearby dry gully, the boy clinging around her neck, stumbling over uneven ground and scraping through thick scrub that barred their way in the darkness. All around them, huge trees swished and shuddered, lashed by winds and driving rain, commencing their own fight for survival.

She found the gully and slid down the muddy slope, finding it deeper than she remembered but all the better to hide them from the storm. The twins, scrambling behind her, whimpered in fear, and Netta screamed at them to stay close, as she found flat ground and selected a refuge at the base of a tree. There they huddled together, listening to the storm building up overhead.

They were all so wet by this time, it was a while before Netta realised that water was beginning to swirl around them. She jumped up in fright, trying to think where else she might find safety. Looking up, she could discern a solid branch that might hold them. She handed Wesley to Polly and dug her toes into the ridged bark of the tree. 'Give him to me,' she shouted, after she had tested the branch, and the girls handed Wesley up to her. Netta wedged him with her into the crook of the tree, and as her eyes became accustomed to the darkness, she studied the branch and found that it thinned out. 'No room on this branch,' she called to the twins, 'and the next one is too high up. Go back!'

At first they argued, weeping, clinging to the tree below her, so she shouted at them, 'Do as you're told, or Missus Maudie will take the strap to you!'

Still crying, they melted away into the night. Netta clutched Wesley: 'Now we just sit still, and we'll get down in the morning. We'll be like little bears, sleeping in our tree.' He accepted her explantion mutely, allowing his head to droop against her, his small hands hugging the tree. As they hung on, the rains increased and the winds rose to a scream. Down in the gully, Netta could hear the swish of floodwaters, and she cursed herself for a fool for not thinking of this possibility. She could smell the sea again, a strong smell now, and she remembered that it was time for the big tides to come rushing in.

The gully itself became part of a new threat as the sea broke through to the old watercourse, thrusting sand-dunes aside, to hurl on unencumbered and join forces with the floodwaters that were still being reinforced by relentless rain. Rejuvenated, the ancient waterway snatched back its glory. Its waters, rushing to the sea, met the stronger tidal surge, creating a wave that ploughed wildly inland.

Netta heard it coming. With Wesley pressed against her belly, she clutched the tree, her legs entwined on the branch, and screamed in terror as the tree rocked, lurched and finally toppled, twisting about as the ferocious wind changed direction. She was still screaming when they ditched in the black waters.

High on the banks, Polly and Pet heard Netta's screams as they cringed among the roots of a fig tree, and they began to wail, their voices lost in the roar of the devil wind.

10

For days, out in the Timor Sea, the cyclone had gathered its skirts and prowled the ocean in a zig-zag course, at first threatening tiny Bathurst Island and then careering down into the wide bite of the Joseph Bonaparte Gulf, hurtling huge winds around at its core. Even a cyclone with its accompanying rain torrents, though, can't go on forever. It headed like a powerful live animal for the Arafura Sea, and then held steady off Port Darwin, a brilliantly clever manoeuvre, as its winds accelerated. No one can predict where or when a cyclone will make its final move. The Australian Aborigines define this stage as a conference of the mighty spirits of wind and rain – retreat or attack?

The cyclone was a powerful rain-maker, and for days, even allowing for the wet season, these torrents lashing at Port Darwin had been exceptional, the proud outflingings of massive winds yet to decide their fate.

At approximately 10.15 p.m. on this rain-lashed tropical night, the cyclone, with its arsenal of wind, made its suicidal dash at the coast, suicidal, because once across the shoreline it would eventually die. It would not, however die alone.

A mountain of rain and wind reared up on the horizon and pawed angrily at the surface of the ocean, and then it set off with screaming thunderous precision towards the land.

No horses of the apocalypse could match this speeding, all-powerful wall of destruction. It dragged at the ocean bed, sucking at coral reefs and becoming dark with debris as it charged forward. The inhabitants of the ocean, from the tiniest fish to the great sea monsters, battered by the pressure, recognised that their only chance of survival was to turn about, to fight their way back out to sea, beyond this terrifying field of motion. But for many, it was too difficult. They were carried, drowned, at this awesome, swirling pace, to be smashed on to a distant dry grave.

The massive winds with their miles-wide sweep, wound themselves into a fury and ran at the shoreline, challenging the landmass to defend itself.

Sam Lim dined with his family and friends that Christmas Eve, at the home of his uncle Wang Lee. From the outside, the house was a dull weatherboard, unpainted, no different from the many European houses springing up around the town, but inside, it glowed. Red and gold drapes hid ugly walls, and splendid painted screens were used instead of inner dividing walls. The furnishings were carved timber or lacquered pieces with plush upholstery, and long glistening shelves held the best of china.

For this occasion, to make room for everyone at the banquet, the screens had been set aside, and long tables, decorated with flowers, fans, intricate paper figures and colourful baskets, welcomed the guests.

With their abiding interest in fine food and its preparation, the Chinese community of Palmerston embraced Christmas as another opportunity to celebrate in the traditional manner, so this twelve-course meal was a jolly affair.

Sam Lim was enjoying himself immensely, because he hadn't been expected to cook. Since Mrs Hamilton had removed him to Black Wattle Station he had not seen his own people for a year, so he was a special guest – and making the most of it. He sat at his uncle's left hand, listening to all the news of here and home, telling them of his role as boss cook on the big station, and, as the meal progressed, looking forward to Fan Tan later in the evening. But as the tables were being cleared, Wang Lee requested that Sam Lim accompany him to the temple, to remind their ancestors of their presence and to speak of continuing good fortune in this strange land.

Sam gave no hint of his reluctance, instead reminding his uncle that it was not the best night for an old man to be out, but Wang Lee smiled, stroking his long stringy moustache. 'The fates decide the weather. The weather controls the seasons. The seasons put food on our tables. I must pay my respects, but if honourable nephew does not wish to attend me . . .'

'No, no,' Sam Lim replied. 'Sir, I am honoured.'

The two men set off through the wet and windy streets, carrying offerings to place with due reverence on the red carpeted steps before the main altar of the joss house.

As they went in, Sam Lim noticed the new stone lions guarding the entrance, and he was glad he had made the effort. Regardless of his uncle's fortitude, it was a wild night – a tree had crashed to the ground right in front of them, and he had been frightened. But the lions spoke of strength and safety, so he was reassured.

A large brass gong swayed on its hinges with a mournful humming sound as they passed, and all around them hundreds of candles flickered, blowing out one by one. Sam Lim wondered if that was a bad sign for the petitioners who had placed them there.

As soon as she opened the door, Josie's worries evaporated. Christmas! She might have known Logan wouldn't ignore her at Christmas, although, since their meeting in town, she'd been waiting, hoping he wouldn't let her down.

'You're soaked,' she cried. 'Come on in.' He also smelled of liquor, but after all it was the festive season, and a man couldn't be denied drinks with his friends. Her words tumbled from her as she hurried him into the bedroom. 'Take off those wet clothes. I've been a fool, Logan, I shouldn't have been such a bother to you when you've got problems of your own. Look around here, isn't it a lovely house? When you see it in the daylight – all the lovely gardens – after this rain lets up, you'll agree. I've been expecting you all day, and I've made us a slap-up Christmas dinner. It won't take long to heat up.'

He took off his clothes and grabbed the towel she handed him to dry himself. 'Have you got a drink?'

'I certainly have. I bought your favourite Scotch whisky, and some claret. Give me those wet clothes and I'll dry them out in front of the fire. We've got an inside kitchen here, just like back at Cambray Farm, better than the hut at Katherine, isn't it?'

'I'll have a whisky,' he muttered, and she hurried to get it for him, measuring it in the whisky glass she had bought at the market, and adding a few drops more to please him. After the foul and primitive conditions at Katherine, she wanted him to enjoy the house, to appreciate the home.

He was sitting naked on the edge of her double bed, lost in his own thoughts. She gave him the whisky, she brought him 'the makings'. 'Look at this, I've been keeping it for you. This tin of tobacco has a gadget that helps you to roll a cigarette, and the little rough part on the side is for striking matches. What will they think of next?'

He rolled the cigarette and she handed him a tiny cylinder of wax matches.

'Where did you get this?' he asked, looking at the Chinese writing on the side. 'From your Chink mates?'

'No.' She laughed nervously. 'They sell them everywhere here. I use them in the kitchen, too.' She gathered up his wet clothes and took them to the kitchen, hanging them on a rack by the stove. She had been fighting to keep the stove alight all day, what with dry wood scarce, but she had known he would come. People always came home at Christmas, where else would he go? She wanted to tell him that she'd had a letter from Ned, only a few lines to inform her that he would be spending his holidays with school friends in Perth, but he had sent Christmas greetings. The letter had been stilted, a child having difficulty communicating, but to Josie it was the best Christmas gift she could have received.

This, however, was not the time to discuss Ned, or Logan's foolish talk of divorce. Josie decided that that subject had to be avoided at all costs. It occurred to her – not for the first time – that Logan might have suffered a mental breakdown; the Rector at St John's Church had told her that this was not unusual, given the hazards of the outback, given that toil in this climate was not fit for white men.

At his request she brought him another whisky. 'I have a fat roast duck in the stove now,' she told him enthusiastically. 'It was nearly cooked when I took it out, so we won't have much time to wait. And I put in plenty of potatoes and pumpkin to bake with it.'

'So this is the house,' he said, peering around in the dim light of the bedside lamp. 'It doesn't look much to me.'

'You're not seeing it at its best,' she said tenderly, looking at his brown torso which turned white at his waist where the dungarees took over, remembering that the men out there often worked bare-chested in the heat. 'You're looking well,' she said, wanting to touch those strong shoulders and the muscular arms, but afraid to do so. Instead, with the experience of years, she stood in front of him. 'Is there anything else you need?'

She gave the impression of being timid, and tried not to look at the inviting darkness between his spread knees, at the naked show of him that she needed so much.

'Come here!' he said gruffly, and Josie silently exulted as he unbuttoned her skirt, dropped it to the floor and dragged down her drawers. 'Get them off,' he told her. She found his roughness exciting: in the marriage, they had made love, but not on demand like this. Sometimes Jack Cambray had done the same thing, ordering her on to the bed, and that had made up for a lot, had he only known.

She stood there in her blouse, and when his hand reached out and grabbed her, she obeyed, allowing herself to be pushed to the floor, to have him plunge into her, assuaging his anger. There, in their own house, with her co-operation, he pushed and plundered her body. He ripped the blouse from her, and she helped. He sat her up and throbbed within her, biting at her, and Josie rejoiced at his strength. She went after him, matching him in this powerful loving session, believing she had him back, while Logan gripped her, forcing her around the floor, taking her again and again.

At last, he was too tired to punish her any longer. And Josie, having reached sexual heights that she could never have imagined, stretched her weary body like a cat, rolled over luxuriously, and then remembered the roast dinner.

She was sore and bruised, but she didn't care, she had her husband back, better than ever. Here, in the warm heart of their first home, she delighted in their abandon. She brought in a pail of cool water and sponged her husband's strong, taut body, noting the scratch marks she'd made on his back. 'Get into bed, darling,' she told him. 'Have a rest, I'll call you when dinner's ready,'

She put him to bed and covered him with a sheet, thrilled to see him at last in their bed.

While he slept, she set the table in a festive style with a skein of tinsel and coloured bon-bons linking the wine glasses. She turned his clothes, lit the candles, changed into her best dress, turned his clothes again, brushed her damp hair into a pile atop her head and secured it with pins and a tortoiseshell comb. She carved the meat, made the gravy, tested the vegetables and ironed his clothes.

'Here you are,' she said, as she laid the clothes out for him, watching him stir to wakefulness on this Christmas Eve. 'Dinner's ready.'

He came up from the bed like a sulky schoolboy, and Josie left him to it. The fervour played out, she felt prim about watching him dress.

He stood in the doorway, buckling his belt. 'I have to go out,' he told her, but she was firm.

'Not before dinner, Logan.' She pulled out his chair. 'It's time you enjoyed the comforts of home. Happy Christmas, darling.'

It was far too late to make an entrance. The trio stumbled into the Prince of Wales Hotel, with Maudie hooked on to Zack's shoulder for support, and Sibell bringing up the rear, her soft skirts cloyingly damp. They pushed past streams of red, white and blue crepe paper which had done their duty as a flimsy welcoming canopy in the foyer while the pins held, but now hung limply like a discarded maypole. The lounge room was packed with gentlemen taking refreshments, smoking, and waiting for a chance to claim a lady for a dance. They moved aside to make way for the latecomers, exchanging greetings with Maudie and Zack, who pressed on to the dining room which had been turned into a ballroom, the floor scattered with sawdust.

Zack whistled to Digger Jones, who soon found them space in the crowded room by the simple process of shunting three young men away from the long official table set up near the band. At last they were seated, introductions made where possible in the crush. Their previous disagreements forgotten, Zack, Maudie and Sibell were soon caught up in the gaiety of the evening, which was certainly going with a swing.

Down the far end of the table, Sibell saw Colonel Puckering and Lorelei, who was dressed in a beautiful evening gown of lustrous pink satin, the bodice richly encrusted with beading.

'What's he doing with her?' Maudie hissed at Sibell, who realised that the Colonel was actually *with* Lorelei. She began to laugh. In this place anything could happen!

John Trafford came galloping over to ask Sibell to dance, and she was about to accept when Zack spoke up. 'Wait your turn, chief!' he ordered, and escorted her on to the floor himself, for a schottische.

'Is Mr Conal here?' he asked

'I wouldn't know,' she replied airily, as he swept her away.

After that there was a barn dance, at which practically every partner she greeted asked her for a dance. Since there was no sign of Logan, she was able to relax in this carefree atmosphere and enjoy herself. Even Maudie was smiling. The men far outnumbered the ladies, so, with a foot perched on a chair, she held court with several young men seated around her. As for Zack, the wines had had their effect, and he looked fondly on Sibell, proud of her popularity. 'I have to fight them off to get a dance,' he told her. 'You sure do look beautiful, Sibell.'

'Thank you,' she smiled. 'Listen to me, Zack. With Lorelei here, there's something I have to tell you . . .'

But he didn't allow her to finish. Instead he went off into fits of laughter. 'Your friend Lorelei! Did you know she's a madam? And a damned pretty one at that. She owns the Bijou.'

'Yes, I know,' Sibell tried, but he was off again.

'Apparently, when Puckering turned up with her . . .' he was almost choking with laughter at the telling, 'the Administrator and his missus quit this table. Put their noses right out of joint. Sorry we missed that.'

Sibell gave up, but she found time to go down and talk to Lorelei. 'I have to tell Zack,' she said. 'I think he knows.'

'Darlin',' Lorelei grinned, 'tell anyone you like now. The assessors came back with a brilliant report, we'll be laughing all the way to Monte Carlo.'

'That's marvellous!' Sibell said, but the intricacies of mining were still a mystery to her. 'Can we get it working, though?'

'Not a problem. I knew the first time I saw you I'd be moving up in the world, you're my good joss. And, let me say, you're the belle of the ball, my girl.' Then she winked. 'Even though I've got the best dress in the place. Do you like it?'

'It's the most beautiful dress, Lorelei, where did you get it?'

'Had it made, I've been keeping it for something special.'

Sibell looked around to make certain no one was listening. 'How did you get the Colonel to bring you? I mean . . . I don't want to be offensive, but I thought he disapproved of you.'

'He likes to think he does, but,' she giggled, 'I convinced him he ought to have some fun in his life before he gets too old.' Women stared goggle-eyed as she lit a slim cheroot in a long ivory holder, but she ignored them, and whispered to Sibell: 'The Colonel has not quite accepted it yet, but he's going to marry me.'

'That's wonderful!' Sibell said. 'I don't know how you managed it.' She looked over at Zack who was standing talking to some men. 'I'd like to marry *him*, but we're always at odds. There's always tension with him.'

'Because you haven't slept with him,' Lorelei said magnanimously. 'The poor bloke's probably busting his britches with you around all the time being untouchable.'

'No, it's not that,' Sibell said, but Lorelei waved her aside.

'The hell it isn't. You'd better go mind your territory, darlin', or one of these gals will grab handsome from under your nose.'

'It's not that easy,' she argued. 'He's a complex person. I have to take him carefully.'

'Complex, rot! Jump into bed with him.'

'In a house full of people?'

Their conversation was interrupted by the strains of a waltz. Sibell waited for Zack to come and get her, since this was his dance, but instead she saw him dragged on to the floor by a red-haired girl in swirling ivory taffeta.

'See what I mean?' Lorelei remarked.

It took just a few minutes for the cyclone slamming in from the sea to demolish the Hamilton beach house, to lift the roof and send it rocketing across the street, where it split apart, sheets of corrugated iron clanging dangerously in the wind. The walls of the cottage splintered, and the whole building collapsed into whirling wreckage.

Other houses along the front suffered the same fate, but the BAT buildings, carefully constructed by convict stonemasons, stood firm, only the windows shattered. The same strong hands had built the church, the warehouse – now the Bijou – and the Court-House, and they remained solidly clamped to the earth.

The driving winds crushed Wang Lee's house in one blow, leaving his family and guests screaming in the blackness. They roared into the tiny open joss house, which exploded on impact before Sam Lim could rush across to protect his uncle.

Josie had gone to bed, but Logan was still up, demolishing the last of the whisky, when the winds struck the side of the house. He dived for cover, hearing the roar as the building began to disintegrate.

By this time, the full force of the cyclone was concentrated on the town, blasting trees, wreaking havoc, the air alive with debris. Hilda Clarke, the matron, was talking to Maudie. 'By God, that wind out there would blow a dog off a chain.' As she spoke, the windows blew in, and torrential rain turned the room into chaos. Men fought to block the gale that extinguished all the candles and sent the lamps flying: women screamed, climbing under the tables for shelter as glasses and crockery smashed around them. They heard the awnings rip loose from their moorings, and panic set in as the building heaved and swayed.

From under a table, terrified by the noise, Sibell realised that people were escaping. They were fighting, scrambling over upturned furniture to get out of this maelstrom, and she tried to escape too, but a woman hung on to her. She recognised the booming voice of Hilda, Maudie's friend. 'Stay where you are. It'd be worse out there.'

'No!' Sibell screamed. 'Let me go!' She was in the dark caverns of the ship again: she had escaped before, this time, too, she could get to safety.

'Shut up or I'll belt you one,' Hilda said, her grip tightening. 'Are you all right, Maudie?' she yelled.

'I've got a bloody nose,' Maudie whimpered from somewhere nearby. At that moment a far wall collapsed. It seemed that the winds were taking the hotel apart piece by piece.

'Where's Zack?' Sibell called, but her voice was lost in the ferocity of the winds that were increasing by the minute. All they could do was wait and pray, as the roof splintered and subsided, the walls were whisked around them, voices screamed in agony, bodies were pinned under heavy rafters – but those still unhurt were unable to go to their aid.

Sibell was gasping for air as the world seem to crash and crack around her. She expected that the storm would pass any minute, that it would be played out, but it continued, on and on, rain deluging their fragile cave, as the elements raged over Palmerston. Boats were flung on to the beaches, the seas foamed and lapped over the Esplanade, more and more trees succumbed as the cyclone continued trampling the town.

Zack and the Colonel were among the men who worked with Digger Jones, trying to barricade the smashed windows, as their women took cover. It was too late for Lorelei, who huddled, whimpering, in a corner. Shattered glass had struck her full in the face, and she hid, frantically trying to remove the slivers, feeling for them in the warm wetness of blood, cutting her fingers in the process.

John Trafford stumbled over her. 'Lorelei! It's you! For God's sake, come away from this wall, it feels as if it'll give any minute.'

'No,' she cried. 'Leave me alone! Get away from me!' In her panic, her only priority was to protect her face. She thought if she could pull them all out, these searing, painful little knives plunged into her soft skin, her face would be saved. She screamed as a piece of glass wedged over her top lip came free.

John grabbed her hands and felt the blood. 'You're hurt,' he yelled over the nose. 'Where are you hurt?'

But Lorelei crouched lower, intent on her task, touching more sharp points of glass as she tenderly explored with her fingertips.

He knew Michael was nearby, so he called to him. 'De Lange! Where are you? Lorelei's hurt. Over here!' If need be they'd drag her away.

'My dress is ruined, too,' she wept, wincing as one piece of glass refused to budge.

'What's wrong?' he asked her urgently, frustrated that he was unable to see, trying to put an arm around her.

Like a terrified animal, she cringed away from him. 'For God's sake don't bump me.'

Michael struggled over to them through the rampaging winds.

273

'Help me get Lorelei away from here,' John said, feeling new gusts of wind from above as the roof began to bang loose, but at that moment the wall gave way. He threw himself across Lorelei as exploding timbers tore past, but he was too late. A heavy strut fell on him like the blade of a guillotine, breaking his neck.

'What was that?' Michael screamed, as a dark monster seemed to come rushing to fall upon him, crushing his chest, pinning him to the floor. He had used up his last breath.

Zack was thrown against a table with such force that pain jarred his chest and he had trouble breathing, but he crawled through the whirlwind to the Colonel, who was shouting for help. 'Are you hurt?' he asked.

'No, just stuck,' Puckering said grimly. 'But little Mai Lee is in here somewhere.'

Unable to stand against the force of the wind, Zack tore at the wreckage.

'Flatten out, man,' Puckering shouted, but Zack kept on, shoving aside soaked timbers and lumps of plaster that were a dead weight, until the Colonel was free and they were able to extricate Digger's wife, who was weeping hysterically.

'She'll be fine,' Puckering said. 'Just got a bump on the head.'

'Have you seen Sibell?' Zack asked. 'Or Maudie?'

'No. I thought I heard Lorelei screaming, but I can't find her.'

'Oh, Jesus.' Zack lay still, panting from exhaustion. They were in the open now, amid the wreckage of the hotel, in total darkness and disoriented by the teeming rain. Zack tried to get his bearings, inching forward on his stomach, but it was like trying to ferret through a rubbish dump, as nails and unidentifiable sharp objects tore his hands. Nearby, someone else was calling for help, so he began burrowing again, hopelessly, realising that every time he pulled planks or pieces of furniture away, they were whisked from his hands, creating more danger for someone else.

In the end, he, too, gave up, and dropped to the floor, his hands over his head, waiting for the cyclone to blow itself out.

God-fearing souls found shelter in the church, while the sinners across the road, behind the strong walls and barred windows of the Bijou, prayed that they'd be spared. Their prayers were answered. Paddy O'Shea, foreman of Corella Downs, who thought more of his horses than of his fellow men, indeed, of himself, broke away and raced for the stables, where he released the terrified horses, found his own mount, and rode madly for the bush. His miraculous ride through the worst of the storm became legend.

Max Klein, the German assessor, soon to be manager of the Morning Glory mines, hardly noticed the storm, he was too busy celebrating. Normally a sober man, Max felt he was entitled to a good and proper binge this Christmas. He sat behind the bar with a quart of schnapps singing 'Stille Nacht' in his deep baritone, like a rondo, over and over, round and round. For had he not done Lorelei a great favour by pegging out her claims with saplings, and marking them with cairns of dusty rocks? A necessity which the lady had overlooked, therefore he was sure she wouldn't mind when she heard that he'd also pegged a couple of claims

274

for himself. It was a good rich reef, and the thought of its glistening beauty brought tears to his eyes.

The houses at Doctors Gully fared no better than the shanties of the Chinese quarter, except for the brick stoves and the chimneys that were left standing amid the devastation. Only the two lions remained where the joss house had stood . . . where a weeping Sam Lim heaved aside heavy rafters to retrieve the body of Wang Lee.

Everyone who emerged from their shelters, like ghosts rising from a crumbled cemetery, drifted into the dismal dawn as though fascinated to find themselves among the living. The silence was almost a shock until a flight of sacred ibises, disciplined as ever, rode in soundless V formation over the flattened town, alerting other birds that the coast was clear. Hundreds of corellas began their loud mustering from the confines of the battered bushland, until they were ready to take off, wheeling in a white, shrieking stream against the dark skies. Zack moved among the stunned survivors to find Maudie and Sibell safe under an avalanche of panelling and plaster, protected by the sturdy cedar table.

'Wesley!' Maudie shouted at him. 'What about Wesley?'

'I know, I'll go now. You look after Maudie, Sibell.' He climbed over the wreckage and ran into the hardly discernible street, now a complete shambles.

Hilda lifted Maudie bodily from her refuge and dumped her in a cleared patch. 'At least the rain has stopped,' she said grimly. 'For the time being, anyway. And there's no need to panic, Maudie. Zack will find the boy. You . . .' she jerked her head at Sibell. 'Give me a hand here.'

All over the site, men and women, muddy and dishevelled, were working systematically to clear the debris from trapped guests. Many emerged unhurt and staggered away, but Sibell stayed with Hilda, removing planks and shingles, appalled at the disintegration of the walls, as thick dust rose around them.

'Stand back,' Hilda ordered her suddenly, and at the same time the Colonel joined them.

'Lorelei!' he called, and clutched at Sibell. 'Have you seen Lorelei?'

'We'll find her,' Hilda said. 'But we got a dead 'un here. Grab the other end of the piano, Colonel.'

Between them they heaved the toppled piano aside, and Sibell screamed! Michael de Lange had been crushed under its weight. Gently they lifted him out, his head flopping backwards, and men came to grasp his body and take it away.

'There are more here,' Hilda called. 'This is where the wall gave way.' As she spoke, Sibell recognised Lorelei's dress, crumpled pink satin unmistakable in the grey waste. The Colonel had seen it too. Frantically, he pushed past Hilda, using all his might to lift a heavy beam, causing other wreckage to scatter around it.

'Get them out!' he cried, his voice as strained as his muscles as he struggled to hold the massive log. Sibell realised John Trafford was there, his body sheltering Lorelei who was face down. She wept when she saw that John, too, was dead, and on her hands and knees she took his arms, pulling him away. Behind her, men scrambled to help as Hilda turned her attention to Lorelei.

'She's alive,' the matron called. 'Now take it carefully.' She had edged her way into the fragile tunnel and lifted Lorelei's head. 'Slide her out,' she called. 'Gently! gently!' and she inched out, lying on her side, with the girl. 'There now! She's free.'

The Colonel gave a sigh of relief and lowered the beam. 'Is she all right?' he asked, as the matron, kneeling, examined Lorelei.

'Yes, no broken bones, I don't think. She's got some nasty cuts. And she's awake, just in shock.' She nursed Lorelei on her wide lap. 'It's over, girlie. Do you hurt anywhere inside?'

'Get away!' Lorelei whispered. 'Leave me alone.'

Sibell, too, was in shock. Lorelei's face was a bloodied mess.

'We'd better get her to hospital,' Hilda said quietly, 'if the damn place is still standing.'

'My face!' Lorelei whispered, but Hilda held her hands down.

'Don't touch your face, dearie, we'll tidy it up for you.' But she looked up at Sibell, her eyebrows raised in an expression of doubt.

Zack ran and ran through the weird landscape, appalled at the devastation, skirting felled trees, skidding on swatches of wet foliage, past a small procession with the body of a woman in a wheelbarrow, past groups of citizens searching flattened blocks, and others who were just standing helplessly, staring at the ruins of their town.

A woman grabbed at him: 'My horse, over here. Will you help me get it on its feet.'

He glanced at the horse and its broken leg. 'Find a gun quickly, and shoot it!'

Some trees were still standing, but the sea was clearly visible where the view should have been blocked by houses, and then it dawned on him that he had passed his own house – or rather, he had passed the block where his house had stood. He rushed back, recognising the strewn palings of the front fence and the stocky bushes of the garden, to find the house had collapsed in a heap. He began shouting, the terror now real, fearful that Wesley and the girls were buried underneath. He began tossing aside wreckage, determined to remove it all piece by piece until he found them. Two men rode by, and he called on them for help, but they ignored him.

Rory Jackson and Buster Krohn were not about to stop for anyone. When the winds grew to cyclone strength, the jailhouse was unlocked and the prisoners set free to fend for themselves. Rory and Buster didn't run far. In these familiar surroundings, the cunning pair made straight for the one safe haven, the gallows pit. A shed had been constructed so that the hangings could be carried out in private, with just an invited audience. The gallows stood in the centre, a trapdoor underneath them. Once the execution order was given, the trapdoor gave way and the victim fell sharply through to his death, dangling over the pit.

Not superstitious, Rory and Buster knew instantly that this was as good a place as any to seek refuge, and they were right. The shed blew off its stumps, but the pit was safe.

At half-light they were out prowling the streets, looking for horses. They were disappointed to see that the Court House was intact, but that gave impetus to their flight. They were almost certain that they'd beat the charges, especially if Logan Conal could be induced to keep his mouth shut, but why wait to find out? They'd been given a reprieve by God himself, so the best thing to do was to get the hell out. They caught two horses, calmly looted the ruins of a general store for saddles and provisions – disregarding the cries and confusion around them – saddled up and made for the track, the only track that led out of Palmerston.

Logan Conal, too, staggered away unhurt. Furious, he surveyed the disaster. The house had been completely destroyed, the house that had been bought with his money was worthless, the money down the drain. He swore as he skirted the area where a tall ghost gum had crashed on to the house leaving a dark cavern where the deep roots had been wrenched free.

He heard her call, a feeble cry for help from deep within the tangle of branches and foliage. Interested, he saw that the tree had fallen right across the bedroom, squashing the back of the house, but simply busting open the section he'd been in, the sitting room. The outer branches had protected him, but the full weight of the trunk had caught Josie. He found his tobacco tin and rolled a smoke, searching in his pockets for the Chink wax matches. 'Well,' he said to himself, staring at the mass of foliage that imprisoned his wife. 'I can't shift that tree. She's brought this on herself. If she'd gone to Perth when I wanted her to, she'd be safe now. It's fate, really. This isn't my fault.'

The rain had ceased at last and the air was a cavern of steam as the sun began its climb behind the dense clouds. He had wanted Josie out of the way, hadn't he? Logan asked himself. And at this point he wondered, what if I just do nothing . . .?

He kicked angrily at a piece of wreckage. What did he have left now? Only the job. Josie had wasted his money on this ruin. Sibell had snatched his mines. Or had she? He might still have time, the storm would delay proceedings. He'd have his revenge on them in due time. He wondered who could have staked the claims for them. Not Sibell and her whore mate. Zack Hamilton, probably. Well, he puffed at the cigarette, two could play at that game. There was nothing to stop him getting out there, pegging his own claims and rearranging the Hamilton pegs – the Morning Glory mines. Then he would come back and register his sites. In the confirmation, when the ownerships clashed, he'd win something, he could appeal like the squatters down in Perth. He smiled to himself. Yes, he'd have a share, or he'd hold them up forever, give the lawyers a high time.

Josie's voice was fainter, and he stared coldly over the spot where the bed had been, well hidden under a mountain of foliage. To one side of the block, the parkland looked desolate, trees stripped of leaves, the ground swampy. On the other side, the blocks were deserted, winds had swept the Chinese humpies into oblivion and the area looked as if it had been cleared for building. 'Save a lot of time,' he remarked callously as he walked away.

Further into town he saw crowds of Chinese gathered together, crying over their misfortunes.

Animals were roaming aimlessly into the streets, so it was no trouble to acquire a horse. He led it to stables where he soon found equipment, then he had the same idea as the freed prisoners – to grab supplies while he could. As he dug out tins of food, a stranger challenged him. 'Hey! What are you doing there, mate? You could get shot for looting.'

'Who's looting?' Logan cried quickly. 'They need food at the hospital. Someone has to take it to them.'

'There's not much of the bloody hospital left.'

'The patients are still there, and plenty more besides,' Logan yelled at him. 'Why don't you quit complaining and help me.'

The bluff worked. 'Can't, mate, I've got my own family to look after.'

Logan took what he could carry, in sodden packs, and headed for the bush a few hours behind Rory and Buster.

Zack was toiling, sweat pouring from his aching chest, his heart beating in fear as he swung wreckage aside, working his way towards the centre of his ruined house, telling himself that he would find them, that they could still be alive in some hollow compartment under the debris. At first, the voice didn't register. He shouted a response, certain the sound had come from within the huge mound in front of him, then he halted and turned to see Sam Lim standing behind him, tears pouring down his face.

'Sam!' he called. 'Holy Christ! Help me! They're in here somewhere!'

'No boss,' Sam wept. 'They not there. All gone. Favourite uncle dead too!'

Zack stopped. 'Wang Lee? He was killed?'

Sam fell to his knees, but Zack pulled him up again, hoisting him to keep him on his feet. 'I'm sorry, I truly am, about Mr Wang, but you must listen to me. Did you say the girls are gone from here? With Wesley?'

'Ay-ee!' Sam screeched. 'Gone, I say to you, baby and Netta, they drownded!'

'What do you mean, drowned? How could they have drowned?' Zack glanced frantically towards the churning sea. His new fence had disintegrated but the tide hadn't come up this far. 'It's not possible!'

Sam began chattering hysterically in his own language, and divining a skerrick of truth in his previous remarks, Zack took him quietly. 'Steady on now, mate. Take it easy. Quiet down. Did you say Wesley had drowned?'

Sam gulped and nodded, unable to reply, and Zack's heart seemed to stop. He took several deep breaths, holding down his own panic. 'And how do you know this?' he asked softly.

'Twinnies tell me.'

'The twins? Where are they, for Christ's sake?'

'They run off,' Sam wept. 'Lose face. Frighten Missus Maudie kill them.'

'By Jesus, she will, too, and you as well if you don't take me to them.' He realised then that the Aborigine girls must have taken Wesley and run from the storm, and surely, if Polly and Pet were alive, Wesley would be too – they would never desert the child. 'Where did you see them?'

'Back there. 'Sam pointed. 'They running like mad, screaming baby drownded. I come to tell Missus Maudie.'

'Come on.' Zack pulled him forward. 'Show me where you saw them.'

As they raced towards the Chinese quarter, Zack tried to sort out this

278

confusing information. There was a blacks' camp on the outskirts of the town, but, more importantly, where were those girls running *from*? And why wasn't Wesley with them? Why? Why? He was short of breath, and he pressed his hand against a low rib to ease the pain, guessing that the rib had been injured when the bloody hotel fell on him. That seemed another age now. He couldn't waste precious time observing the destruction around them, needing all his concentration to find Wesley, Cliff's son: and by God, he would do that.

He found himself praying, talking to Cliff, calling on him for help. Tears flecked his eyes as he ran, and rain began to fall again, with a hiss like a sigh, over the tragic town.

'Tell me where he is! Show me!' he cried soundlessly to his brother. 'You can't let anything happen to him.' In his mind's eye, he saw the little kid face down in a creek, dead, like his father, red hair floating . . . and he cried out: 'No! Cliff! Where the bloody hell are you?'

In the hope of finding the twins, he was heading for the blacks' camp, with Sam puffing far behind him. He shouted to a group of Aborigines who were crossing his path up ahead, but intent on their own loping pace they seemed not to have heard him and travelled on by as if he were invisible. Zack was hit by a wave of nausea, fed by panic: he felt that none of this was real. Then a firm hand gripped his arm. 'Blackfellers bin lookin' for you, boss,' Bygolly said. 'We go find Netta and the boy.'

Netta! Yes, Netta. There was still Netta. How could he have forgotten her. 'Where are they?' he cried.

Bygolly hitched a coil of rope further up on to his shoulder. 'Dunno yet, but we findem.'

As they turned about and made for the gully, the stockman explained that the twins hadn't run away, they'd run to their own people for help. Zack began to piece their movements together. Netta had moved them to the shelter of the gully, but it had flooded, so she'd climbed a tree for safety, taking Wesley with her. But at the height of the storm the tree had collapsed. The girls had heard her scream but they could see nothing and do nothing. First light was a shock: the tree had gone and the landscape had changed. They had become so confused that even now they weren't certain where all this had taken place. So the people were searching.

Poor old Bygolly, known in the bush as Maudie's 'offsider', didn't need to enlarge. They had come out to search for Netta and Wesley. Dead or alive.

In all his years around Palmerston, Zack had never seen this dusty old watercourse in flood. Sometimes in the wet it had filled, forming a lagoon, but the water had soon evaporated when the sun returned. Now it had overflowed its banks, and, he guessed, broken through to the sea. His fears increased at his first glimpse of the wide and dangerous swirl, the ugly muddy waters filled with jagged branches like hacked limbs. Even a good swimmer would be at risk from submerged snags.

Aborigines, men and women, were prowling the new shoreline, so he pushed through thick scrub and rounded the bend to where he knew the gully must go directly out to sea.

He heard shouting in the distance, and Bygolly raced ahead, slashing at the tangled scrub with a tomahawk to create a path. 'They found somepin', boss,' he called. Zack, his mind on Cliff, beseeched him not to allow the 'something' to be bodies.

The Aborigines were shouting in excitement, but Zack had already seen them: Netta and Wesley, stranded out there in a half-submerged tree. Netta was waving, and Zack called to her, almost weeping with relief, and with gratitude that Netta had had the good sense not to try to swim out with Wesley. His first thought was for a dinghy, but he doubted that any small boats moored in the harbour would have survived, and he had no idea where else to look right now. Besides, time was against them: the stricken tree was swaying dangerously and could break free any minute to be at the mercy of the tide. Maybe it had already travelled a-ways downstream and was just snagged underneath.

Bygolly was tying the rope around his waist. 'I'll go, boss,' but a woman grabbed hold of him.

'No! You keep out. Stingems in dere.'

'Yeah, plenty stingems, you betcha,' another woman cried, looking to Zack.

He nodded. He had seen the frightful wounds those jellyfish could inflict with their yards of slimy tendrils. They bred in tidal creeks and rivers, and would have invaded the gully by now. He took the rope from Bygolly, regretting that he'd stripped to his trousers to search the wreckage of his house. Clothing was some protection.

The stranded tree lurched again, and Netta yelled to him to hurry.

'Hold on,' he called. 'We'll get you out.'

He borrowed an old checkered shirt from one of the men, fastening the only two buttons it possessed and rolling down the sleeves. Then he looked at his bare feet and the bare black feet surrounding him. No chance of any socks.

'We have to keep them out of the water,' he told Bygolly, knowing that a child could not survive the deadly lash of stingers. 'There's not enough length in this rope to tie it to a tree, so you fellers hang on. I want that tree pulled to shore like a raft. Give me the tomahawk, Bygolly, I might need it to cut the trunk free.'

Gingerly, he slipped into the warm murky waters, the rope tied to his waist, trying to ignore the gasp of fear from the women standing nearby. 'You're no hero, Hamilton,' he said to himself, flinching in fright every time he came in contact with submerged snags. He kept to the surface to avoid entanglements, and forced himself to glide gently through the water instead of making a fast dash to the tree. The last thing he wanted to do was to disturb any of the creatures, including snakes, that might be nearby. For such a short distance, it was the longest swim of his life, but he made it.

Netta, aware of the dangers, was now too terrified to speak, but Wesley had no such inhibitions. He thrust his small freckled face at Zack. 'She wouldn't let me go,' he complained. 'It's her fault. She's a bad girl. Me missum Fader Chrismiss.'

Zack laughed. 'His mother's son,' he said, and Netta smiled wanly.

He was anxious to get out of the water, but as he tried to pull himself up beside them, his weight caused the tree to shift in the current. He shoved the tomahawk at Netta and worked rapidly to secure the rope to the bedraggled tree. 'Start pulling!' he shouted to the shore, tugging on the rope in case they hadn't heard.

The tree creaked angrily as if indignant at this interference, and began its ponderous journey. Netta had managed, when the tree fell, to clamber with Wesley aboard the trunk – an easier perch than the branch – and now she reached down to Zack. 'Climb up quick, boss. It'll hold.'

He tested the makeshift raft and began to lift himself out of the sucking leafy surrounds, but not before a searing pain had scorched across the ball of his right foot. The pain sent a jolt through his whole being. It sped through his body like a hammer shot at a fair, clanging the bell in his head, causing the most excruciating headache he could ever have imagined.

Temporarily blinded, he grabbed for a hand-hold, but felt himself slipping back as his body doubled up in agony, every nerve screaming. Maybe he was screaming too, he didn't know. Netta had hold of his wrists, though, and was hauling him up, but the spasms of pain were making him a dead weight. His eyes began to focus again. Overhead, a dark shadow seemed to have shut out the light for an instant, and he understood that Netta was in the water with him. Not realising that every touch was agony for him, she pushed him up, lifting him, and he was amazed at her strength as she dragged him clear of the water, supporting him. Until darkness closed on him in blessed relief.

Zack thought he had drowned, but two Aborigine women were squatting beside him, cooling his face with a liquid that smelled strongly of eucalypt. Then he thought he had lost a leg, because there was no feeling there. He made a huge effort to reach down and touch the knee, and cried out when he felt nothing. They shushed him: 'Alri' boss, alri' now.'

'Wesley?' he croaked. 'And Netta?'

'They good. You get better now. Bloody crook, dem stingems.'

'Is my leg there?' he asked them, feeling stupid, and they laughed, so he lay back, not needing to hear their reply.

Netta was exhausted. She handed Wesley over to Polly, who whisked him away as if she were the rescuer, haughtily insisting that he needed his 'bye-byes'. Bygolly trotted away to find Missus Maudie and tell her that Wesley was safe. As for the boss, the two old women fussed over him, washing the vicious threads from his foot and ankle, and applying their own medicines to the wounds that looked like deep whip marks. While he was unconscious, they tore his good trousers and massaged life back into his leg, which was swollen red from the poison. But now he was awake, and quiet.

Sam Lim was kneeling there, sunk back on his haunches, a monument to misery. He told her that Mr Wang had been killed. And many many others. He told her that the town had been blown away. That trees were flattened like pancakes everywhere. That horses were running wild and dingoes were prowling, scavenging. All of these things, and more, he told her, about this great disaster, but she was too tired to care. She stretched out on the damp grass with no fears or feeling left. She wished she were back in her own country. She was not a sea-person, there was too much noise in this place. She missed the silence of the outback. And she remembered Jaljurra, without pain now, and thought she saw him

281

standing by, grinning at her. 'You can take your rest now, Tiranna,' he said to her in her own language. 'Good spirits will look after you.'

And Netta slept, a small smile dimpling her face, because he had known her proper name.

One wing of the bush hospital had survived, and it was now hopelessly overcrowded. Outside, the grounds were covered with makeshift wards in rows of tents like a military establishment, and the town's only two doctors, ably assisted by the matron, worked round the clock, performing operations and attending to the sick and wounded.

The Administrator and his wife, who had fortunately moved themselves away from the worst-hit side of that dining room, were not hurt, and returned to find that their residence had suffered only minor damage, so Zack, who moved quickly, was able to billet Maudie and Wesley and Sibell with them, along with a dozen other women and children, turning the reception room into a dormitory.

Wesley screamed when he found that he had to be separated from the twins, since black women were excluded from white households, but Zack built the girls a humpy near the gate from some of the numerous slabs of wood and iron flung around the town. The Chinese and the Aborigines soon salvaged wreckage to build their own go-downs; more families were accommodated in the BAT quarters, and the Bijou, in the absence of Lorelei, was thrown open to anyone who needed shelter. The monsoonal rains had begun again, nature back on course with a humid drizzle, as if nothing had happened.

All the men were working hard, roping off unsafe buildings for demolition and clearing the streets, while the women assembled clothing, blankets and provisions, and communal butcheries and food stores were set up. The fragile settlement was soon in danger of collapsing again, though. The Colonel noticed that most of the Aborigines were disappearing into the bush, where they knew they could find food, but the residents of Palmerston were feeling the pinch, and fights had already broken out over the distribution of the last of the town's supplies.

Everyone knew that the situation was shaky, and fear was abroad that history was repeating itself: three earlier attempts to colonise the north had already failed. Fort Dundas on Melville Island, Fort Wellington on Raffles Bay, and Port Essington had all been abandoned in their turn, leaving behind the lonely graves of men and women, brave pioneers, who had succumbed to the triple ravages of isolation, the difficult climate and tropical fevers.

Zack was worried, and he sought out Colonel Puckering for news. 'There's talk they might shut Palmerston down,' he said. 'Have you heard anything?'

'It's a possibility,' the Colonel said. 'I hear the South Australian government isn't too keen on sending good money after bad, and we'll need a solid injection of funds to pick up again after this cyclone. It's a tragedy.'

'But they can't shut down now,' Zack argued. 'They have to support Port Darwin, if only to maintain the telegraph overseas line.'

'They could do that with just a few men, as in a lighthouse situation.'

'I know,' Zack admitted, 'but that's a short-sighted approach. We need the port. God Almighty, given a chance, the Territory can export cattle and gold, and a wealth of minerals. We haven't scratched the surface of this country yet. And soon we'll have our own meat works: refrigeration is coming, we'll be able to export frozen beef. Haven't they thought of that?'

'I daresay they're nursing the pros and cons right now,' Puckering said. 'But in the meantime, the Administrator is about to issue orders that women and children are to be evacuated. Ships will be here in a few weeks to collect them.'

'That's dangerous,' Zack said. 'If they leave, they may never come back. It's the beginning of the end.'

'Not if we emphasise that it's temporary. They have to go, Zack, the town just can't support them right now. If we cut down on numbers it'll give us a chance to reconstruct.'

'Their men will go with them,' Zack grumbled.

'Let them go then. Fewer to feed.'

'But surely those ships will be bringing supplies?'

'And how long will they last? We can't rely on imported supplies, that's what brought down those other settlements. We're marooned here until the Wet lifts.'

'We're not going to give up on Palmerston that easily,' Zack said grimly. 'We'll go it alone if we have to.'

'Yes,' Puckering agreed. 'I think it is important that the powers in the south understand that Palmerston can survive, even after a cyclone of this magnitude. That the people of the Territory have the hearts of lions.' He looked at Zack. 'It seems to me that to get their backing, to set Palmerston apart from the previous unfortunate enterprises, you need prestige, not pity.'

'Who wants their pity?' Zack asked, surprised.

'I think that has been the attitude to date. There is no doubt the previous settlers men and women, in those other attempts at colonisation, suffered the most dreadful hardships in this same territory. In the end it was a kindness to give the order to abandon.'

'Oh, my God. We can't let that happen here.'

'No, we can't. So I suggest we barrage Adelaide with good news, not bad. Palmerston, you must insist, is here to stay.'

The police station had been blown apart but behind it, demonstrating the inconsistencies of nature, the chief's residence was still standing. Water had rushed in where the roof shingles had been torn off, but his resourceful Chinese servant had quickly repaired it by thatching it with palm fronds, so it was now the official station.

As he approached, the Colonel saw several men chained to trees. 'Who are they?' he asked Sergeant Coppedge.

'Looters, sir.'

'Good. We'll deal with them later. What's the count?'

'Another woman died this morning, that makes the death toll twenty-eight. Not bad, considering we've hardly got a town left.'

'Send a telegraph to Adelaide. Take this down: "Supplies still required but storm damage not as bad as previously stated. Death toll seven souls. Proud citizens of Palmerston rebuilding. God save the Queen".'

The sergeant grinned. 'You really want me to send this?'

'Forthwith. Any sign of Jackson and Krohn?'

'No, I reckon they've bolted.'

'Advise Pine Creek and Katherine to be on the lookout for them.'

'Yes, sir.'

'I'll be at the hospital if I'm needed.'

The Colonel rode through the town, pleased to see men hard at work clearing wreckage, burning the carcasses of dead animals, dragging logs behind straining horses to rebuild the streets, heaving back and forth with cross-cut saws, already making use of felled trees for new timber. At the cemetery, pathetic groups of mourners huddled around new graves. The cemetery itself told the grim history of this land. Puckering had made a point of reading the tombstones carefully, long before this disaster, and he'd been struck by the extraordinary number of Chinese buried there, as well as by the fate of so many young men who lay beneath the inscription, 'Accidentally killed'.

'Far too many,' he said to himself, looking up at the troubled sky, a sadness sweeping over him. He considered these young pioneers as much heroes as men who had been killed in action.

At the hospital he found the matron and enquired about Lorelei Rourke.

'A bloody mess, she is,' Hilda said. 'The poor girl. We've sewn her up the best we could, but when the swelling and bruising go down, she won't want to look in a mirror! She'll have some terrible scars. Bloody shame, pretty as a picture she was.'

'I'll go down to see her,' he said heavily.

'Yes, try to cheer her up. Lorelei's no dummy, she's got a pretty good idea of the end result. A girl like her, with her good looks gone, she'll bear watching.'

'Why?'

Never one to mince her words, Hilda turned to him scornfully. 'Because I'd say she's a prime candidate for suicide.'

The hospital looked as if a giant foot had stepped on one side of it, with some wall slabs pressed flat and others hanging unsteadily from the remaining wing. Puckering made a note to get another work party out here to clear this away. They'd done well to erect and man a field hospital so quickly, but the flattened part of the building would shelter rats attracted to the detritus of human suffering. The main section now housed only female patients, and he located Lorelei in a row of beds on the covered veranda. He had delivered her to the hospital himself, and had returned the next day, but they had been preparing her for surgery.

Her face was swathed in bandages and she was lying very still, covered only by a sheet. Puckering smiled, acknowledging other patients who watched him curiously. He approached Lorelei shyly, embarrassed to have an audience, and touched her on the small foot that peeped out from the sheet. 'Lorelei . . .'

She didn't reply.

He looked anxiously to the woman in the next bed. 'Is Miss Rourke asleep?'

'Don't reckon so,' the woman replied. 'She just won't talk to no one.'

Puckering moved up and took her hand. 'Lorelei. It's me, Puckering. How are you?' Her eyes moved and he saw the pain in them, but she still refused to respond, turning away from him.

'Come along now,' he said, with a confidence that he didn't feel. 'You've had a few bumps there, but Matron assures me you'll be better in no time. We've got a lot to talk about. Once the town is cleaned up, we can get back to normal, and you have your mining project to attend to.' He talked to her carefully, avoiding any mention of her friends Trafford and de Lange. He told her the Bijou was still standing, and checked himself as he was about to say, 'it hardly got a scratch'. Her eyes took on a flat, bored look, and her mouth, rose-pink against the bandages, was firmly closed. He began to feel he was intruding, until Sibell came squelching across the wet lawn, her long black skirt edged with mud.

'Colonel, I heard you were here, how nice to see you. How is Lorelei now?'

'I don't know,' he said helplessly. 'I rather think she'd prefer me to leave.'

'No, she wouldn't,' Sibell said as he helped her up on to the veranda. She moved beside Lorelei. 'The Colonel's here, he came specially to see you. All the other ladies are madly jealous.' When she didn't reply, Sibell bent over. 'Are you feeling all right?'

'Yes,' Lorelei whispered.

'Is there anything I can do for you?'

'No,' came the tiny whisper again.

'I'm a volunteer nurse,' Sibell told the Colonel. 'Matron has us all working like Trojans.' She smiled down at Lorelei, obviously trying to amuse her. 'We have to get everything just right, or Matron gives us hell. She'll turn me into a nurse yet. Lorelei's a model patient, she doesn't complain. Some people are so demanding, though, I don't know what to do first.' Gently, she fingered a lock of Lorelei's blonde hair protruding from the bandages. 'The Colonel can't stay here all day, surely you can say hello to him.'

Lorelei looked up at her. 'Tell him to go away.'

'I think she's just tired,' Sibell said apologetically. 'She'll be better tomorrow.'

'I see,' Puckering stammered. 'Should I come back tomorrow, then?'

'Yes, that's a good idea,' Sibell said. Lorelei's eyes were closed, shutting out the world.

'Then perhaps you could show me around your wards?' he asked, and Sibell took the hint, knowing that duty was Matron's domain.

They walked away together. 'Would you keep an eye on her?' he asked Sibell. 'I fear she's awfully depressed.'

'It's understandable. Don't take her reaction to heart. She really does care about you, but she's frightened about her looks. It'll be weeks, they say, before the bandages come off, so she might have settled down by then. It has been a bad shock for her. I won't be far away, I can pop in on her all the time.'

He left the hospital as the early darkness was gathering, feeling, possibly, as depressed as Lorelei. In spite of Sibell's expectations, the Colonel feared the day when the bandages were removed, and he wondered what he could do for Lorelei. He had been shocked to see her bloodied face, but more than that, he was heartbroken that she had sustained injuries of any sort. He also missed her terribly – her cheekiness, her gaiety. A logical man, he was not hurt by her rebuff, understanding the reason behind it. The matron was right: that cheerful, bubbling girl was already despairing, so he must not do so. He had to win her confidence back before those bandages came off, and maybe the best thing he could do was to suggest they marry as soon as possible.

As he rode towards the Chinese quarter, or what was left of it, a young Aborigine man hailed him. 'Mister Puckering! Sir! You come with me quick!'

'Where to?' The Colonel reined in his horse, but the fellow was already running into a side street near the park, stopping to beckon him on. Puckering decided he might as well investigate. He trotted after him, until the black fellow stopped in front of yet another devastated site. There was no one else around, the area seemed eerie, too quiet, and Puckering felt a tingle of apprehension. Involuntarily he touched his gun holster as he climbed down from his horse.

The blackfellow was standing near a dark cluster of bushes, and the Colonel shuddered, regretting that he had dismounted, for he could feel evil in this place: there was menace here somewhere. 'What do you want?' he asked as he stepped closer to the Aborigine. And then he stared at him, searching his memory. 'Don't I know you?'

The black man led him through the shrubbery to a lonely place where a huge tree had been uprooted and had fallen, crushing a small cottage. Scattered leaves, already turning brittle, crunched beneath his feet. 'Good God,' he said to himself. 'What a mess this is!' The old tree's massive weight had smashed and flattened its own underbelly of branches and was splayed out like a bonfire ready to be lit. No wonder the owners had given up on this one for a while. It would take a brigade of saws to clear this block.

He thought he saw the Aborigine standing near the felled trunk, and he strode over, but there was no sign of him. 'Bloody fool!' he called. 'Where have you got to?'

A voice answered, or maybe just a sound, certainly not the blackfellow. He felt that prickling sensation again, and the hairs stood up on the back of his hands. The blacks, he knew, had a strange and mysterious culture, and this place reeked of it. He called to the fellow again, but since there was no reply, he turned to leave, needing desperately to get away. At that moment, he heard a moan.

Startled, he stepped over a branch and hung on to another one, leaning forward, peering into the bowels of the tree. 'Is anyone there?'

'Oh, God, help me . . .' The woman's voice was faint.

'Jesus Christ! A woman's in there,' he yelled to the blackfellow, but he had disappeared. Frantically, he tried to penetrate the fallen tree, snapping twigs and spiky branches, calling all the while to her. But he could not reach her, and had to give up. 'Hang on,' he shouted. 'I'll go for help.'

Several hours later, working under lanterns, men with saws and axes extricated Josie Conal from the prison that had held her for days. A doctor was waiting as they lifted her gently on to a stretcher of canvas and saplings. He gave her water, told Puckering that she was suffering from dehydration and bruising, but that she had survived her ordeal quite well considering she was covered in hundreds of green-ant bites. 'Those little beasties,' he said, 'have bites like fire. There must have been a nest in the tree and they got all riled up.'

Puckering kneeled beside her. 'Mrs Conal. We're taking you to hospital. You've been very brave, and I am extremely sorry that we didn't find you before this.'

With her face distorted by the insect bites, her smile was a grimace. 'Jimmy stayed with me,' she told him wistfully. 'He minded me. He kept me company all the time, so I knew someone would find me.'

'Jimmy who?' he asked, bewildered.

'Jimmy Moon, of course,' she replied, drifting off to sleep now that she was safe.

Puckering looked about him. 'Has anyone seen a blackfellow here?'

They shook their heads. 'What blackfeller?'

But the Colonel didn't dare reply, in case they thought he had taken leave of his senses. Jaljurra, alias Jimmy Moon, had been a friend of the Conals! And now he realised that the man who had led him here was the same blackfellow he'd interviewed in Perth. Jimmy Moon! But Jimmy Moon was dead! That was not in doubt: both Sibell and Maudie, and many others, had identified him.

He turned and scanned the area, even as it dawned on him that the effort was futile. The fellow *had* spoken to him, had recognised him, and called on him for help. He wondered why he had felt an evil there when, logically, Jimmy Moon had been a benign presence.

Logically? he asked himself. There's no logic in any of this, you've let your imagination run wild.

But the woman, Mrs Conal, she had seen him too. Hadn't she said he was with her? How, under all that rubble? He watched as volunteers bent to pick up the stretcher, and gave a deep, audible sigh. For the sake of her sanity, the Colonel knew he would be duty-bound to confirm her story, but he didn't relish the idea.

As he tramped back to his horse, he felt a small glow of wonder that he had been privy to such an absorbing experience. But not one, of course, that he would care to discuss publicly.

Several times he visited Josie in hospital, but she never again mentioned the presence of Jimmy Moon after the cyclone. He seemed to have been buried in her subconscious.

Three days down 'the track', Logan was finding his journey heavy going. The landscape, at the best of times flat and uneventful, had taken on a completely new expression. Gullies full of rushing water had been gouged across the trail, dried-out creek beds had become swirling, murky rivers, and lagoons had overflowed into mile-wide floods with marooned trees sagging listlessly over new-born swamps. Insect life had increased a thousand-fold, and he had no protection. In his haste he had forgotten mosquito nets, so he slept on the soggy ground, his saddle for a pillow, wrapped, stewing, in a blanket. He was determined to get to Black Wattle Station where, he knew, he would be welcomed with typical country hospitality, and would be able to obtain better equipment for the return journey. No need to tell them why he was there, he could say he had become lost. Even though the Hamiltons were in town, which was convenient, those station owners always left some staff to supervise the properties.

The skies were thick with great flocks of birds taking advantage of the now abundant food. He looked crankily at elegant brolgas and herons as they dipped and stepped through the swamps, using them as a measure to urge his horse on, and he saw, too, a myriad of other birds that he couldn't identify. It seemed to be the meeting place for wildlife now, and he became nervous as more and more snakes slid by. When he reached a river, after fording countless creeks, he spotted well-camouflaged crocodiles nestling in the mangroves. He had changed direction so often, with no landmark to keep him on track, that his supplies had run out before he realised he was hopelessly lost.

Clouds lowered overhead, blotting out the sky and the stars, and not once had he seen the sun, which was hidden behind a thick blanket of grey. He thought of the mines at Katherine. Even with the cyclone, this was only the beginning of the wet season, which was expected to last until mid April. He shook his head, at last understanding the real meaning of the Wet. The whole region would be one huge swamp, and, as he had been warned, but never really believed, impassable. The residents of Katherine could only go south down the track from now on. Palmerston was well and truly isolated. He wished he could get back there, not giving a thought to Josie, merely accepting that if he couldn't make it to Black Wattle Station, neither could anyone else, unless they were hauling a boat. There was still time. All he had to do was find his way back to Palmerston, or even locate Idle Creek Junction. There had to be someone around in this godforsaken country, this trek was worse than that struggle back to Pine Creek after the ambush. Even though the blazing sun had disappeared, there was an insidious softness about the land, too green now, too damp and misty and rotting.

It never occurred to Logan that he could be in serious danger – except from attacks by slithering snakes or those watchful crocodiles – because he still hadn't adjusted to the emptiness of the land at this time of the year. Even the Aborigines had withdrawn to their home camps, no longer needing to travel far for food. So when he saw the smoke of a campfire, Logan simply turned his horse in that direction.

'Who have we here?' Rory Jackson asked, as he rode in.

'It's me, Conal,' he said. 'Jesus, am I glad to see you.' He saw the two men exchange suspicious glances, and remembered that this pair, whom he had met several times in Katherine, had been in jail in Palmerston. He decided to make a joke of it. 'Hey, Jackson! Weren't you in the lockup?'

'Who says so?' Jackson snarled.

'Don't get me wrong,' Logan purred. 'If you were released, it's fine with me.'

288

'Yeah,' Buster sneered, adding more damp, spitting logs to their fire. 'They let us go.'

'Good for you,' Logan said, encouraging them. 'It was a trumped-up charge anyway. Could you spare me a bite?'

'Depends on what you eat,' Rory said. 'Buster here's cooking wallaby stew.'

'Sounds good to me,' Logan said. The last people in the world he wanted to meet were these two, but he decided that beggars not being choosers was apt for this situation. He sat on his haunches with them by the fire. 'I'm sorry I can't offer you anything in return, I'm right out of tucker.'

'You ain't even got a firearm,' Buster noted. 'What're you doing in this country without a firearm?'

'I was just taking a look around and I got lost. I'd appreciate it if you could point me back to Palmerston, Rory.'

'So you can tell them where we are?' Rory asked, his voice rasping.

'No bloody way. What's it got to do with me?'

'The way I figure it,' Buster said, testing the meat on the spit with his knife, 'it's got a lot to do with you. Aren't you the bloke lined up to give evidence against us?'

'They asked me,' Logan said warily, 'but I wouldn't be in it. I don't need to be too close to coppers.'

'So you were just taking a look around out here?'

'Well, that's not quite true. I'm on the run myself.'

'Why would that be?'

Logan invented an interesting story. 'I got into strife in Perth. Killed a fellow. And when your case came up, the local coppers started checking on me too. It was only a matter of time before they found out, so I took advantage of the cyclone and left.'

'And you a mines manager,' Rory said sarcastically.

'Anything goes up here,' Logan said, relieved to see they weren't wearing their guns. 'The only reason I wanted to get back to Palmerston was because I'm bushed. But if you're going on, Rory, I'd appreciate the company.' He thanked his stars he hadn't mentioned Black Wattle Station. Talking to them was like trudging through quicksands. Black Wattle! Hell! That was where they'd hanged Jimmy Moon. He hated them, but was in no position to be anything but polite.

'Going on where?' Rory wanted to know.

Logan forced a laugh. 'Anywhere out of this bog.'

That seemed to placate them. They shared the scorched meat and a tin of beans with him, and a billy of tea, and Logan felt better. He decided that he'd cut loose from them in the morning.

'Get us some fish, Buster,' Rory said magnanimously, lighting his clay pipe. 'Show Mr Conal here how it's done.'

Buster produced a long, strong spear. 'You have to learn to save ammo in this country,' he announced. 'I can catch fish as good as any nigger.'

'Where did you get the spear?' Logan asked, trying to be sociable.

'He makes them,' Rory told him. 'Learned it from a nigger woman who used to live with him.'

289

They followed Buster down to the water's edge, yet another fast-flowing creek, and Buster waded in, standing immobile in the grey morning light, the spear poised. He seemed to stand there for ages and Logan was becoming bored, then suddenly his arm shot out, the spear flashed into the water and he brought up a large flapping fish. Logan was impressed. 'Good God, it must be all of ten pounds! he exclaimed, but even as he spoke, he watched the company carefully, sensing they were trying to distract him. All the while, with that murderous-looking spear poised, he had kept Rory in front of him.

'It's a barramundi,' Buster said, pleased with himself. Once again, Logan saw them exchange glances which he knew had nothing to do with the fish.

Buster removed the fish, took out his hunting knife, and handed the spear to Rory, but the big, lumbering man was too slow. As Rory lunged at him with the spear, Logan leapt aside and grabbed Buster's knife.

'Get him!' Rory yelled to his mate. Logan was fighting for his life now. He dived past the metal point of the spear and slashed at Rory's waist, vaguely surprised that the sharp blade had produced a wide gush of blood. Rory grunted, but kept on, not adept with the spear especially at such close quarters. He tried to change his grip, giving Logan precious time to strike again. This time he fell on Rory, wrestling with him, plunging the knife deep into his chest. Buster struck him across the back with a piece of timber, and Logan rolled away, realising the blow was meant for his head. He came up quickly, the big bloodied knife ready to take on Buster, but the fight was over. Buster fell on his knees beside Rory. 'Look what you done,' he screamed. 'He's dying! You killed him, you bastard!'

'Him or me,' Logan said, puffing from the exertion, his shoulders aching. 'Why did you mugs attack me in the first place?'

'We thought you was gonna jump us,' Buster replied, nursing Rory's head in his lap, knowing there was nothing he could do. A grey pallor washed over the dying man's face.

Not wanting to watch, and feeling sick to his stomach, Logan walked over to their tent and took out two rifles, just in case Buster turned on him again. He couldn't find their ammunition, but ownership of the guns made him master.

'He's gone,' Buster mourned. 'Rory's bloody dead!' He climbed to his feet, found a blanket and covered his mate.

'How could I have robbed you,' Logan insisted, 'when I didn't have any weapons?'

Buster turned teary eyes on him. 'You ain't got none? You ain't got none hid in the bush?'

'No.'

'You must be bloody mad then, out here with nothin'.' He stared forlornly at Rory's body. 'We didn't believe you.'

They buried Rory Jackson and stood contemplating the situation.

'What now, then?' Buster asked.

'Do you know this country?'

'Ought to.'

Logan still had the rifle. 'You get me over to Black Wattle Station and I'll let you go.'

'Black Wattle? Not on your bloody life. Anyway, you'd need wings to get there in the wet.'

'We can try,' Logan said, lifting the rifle to make his point.

'You can put that away,' Buster told him. 'It's not loaded and we're out of ammo.'

Logan stood dully, mesmerised by the crushing stillness of the swamps that now had him boxed in.

'Palmerston, then,' he said. 'You can take me back to Palmerston.'

Buster picked up Rory's pipe and lit it, taking his time. 'The way I see it,' he said eventually, 'is that if you kill me, you won't get out of here alive. So quit giving orders, Mister Manager. And I'm not as bloody stupid as you. A man don't get far out here without a partner, too many things can go wrong.' He began to pack their gear. 'I'm on my way now, and you're coming with me. I still don't believe your tales, but it don't matter now. And you can forget Palmerston, wild horses wouldn't get me back there with Rory gone.'

'I'd pay you well to get me there.'

'And I'd repay you in kind, mate. I'd tell Rory's mates you killed him while he slept. You wouldn't last a day.' He grinned, yellow teeth bared. 'So go get the horses.'

Logan tried to bluff. 'This country is impassable. Where could you possibly go?'

'We, mate, we . . . remember? We are not even going to try for the south, because the coppers'll be on the lookout. We're going east across the Alligator rivers into Arnhem land.'

'We'll never make it.'

'There are ways and means if we get a move on. And Abos can be helpful if we give them the rifles. We'll get up the plateau and sit out the Wet on the coast.'

'Impossible,' Logan said stubbornly.

'Yeah, it's risky,' Buster admitted. 'So you better hope I stay healthy, mate, or you're dead.'

As they mounted up, Logan, now the unwilling journeyman, knew he was entering the lost world, from which he would never return.

Zack found her at the hospital. 'Come with me, we have to talk.'

'Not that way,' she said, dodging the matron. 'Come through this tent. If Hilda sees me leave, she'll strangle me. I've never worked so hard in all my life.'

'Good training for you,' he remarked, as they dived through the flap at the back. 'A bit of nursing experience will come in handy on the station.'

'So I've still got my job, have I?'

'Yes, but I don't just need a book-keeper. I need a wife as well.'

Sibell took off her apron and looked at the heavy yellow-blooming trees. 'They're black wattles,' she said quietly.

'Black wattles are everywhere. Did you hear me?'

'Was it a question or a statement?'

'A question, dammit. Are you going to marry me or not?'

'How charming.'

'Oh, for Christ's sake, Sibell. Do you expect me to go down on my knee in this mud?'

'No,' she laughed. 'I suppose not. But Zack, there's something I have to tell you first.'

'Sibell, you'll hear me out for a change. I love you. I'm sorry if I misunderstood you in the early days. But I do love you and I think you care for me, now isn't that enough? Whatever else has to be said can wait, it isn't important to me. Will you marry me?'

'Of course I'll marry you, Zack,' she said impatiently, and he took her in his arms.

'Charming!' he teased. 'One of these days we'll have to learn to talk the same language, or we'll be in a permanent tangle.'

They walked further afield and he put his jacket on a felled log so that she could sit down. 'Now tell me this great secret of yours.'

Excitedly, she explained to him, as best she could, about the wolfram mine and the tin on Black Wattle Station. 'Isn't it marvellous? The assessors say it's as good as a gold mine. We're rich, Zack. Or we will be, once it gets going.'

'Is this what you meant when you said you didn't want me to think you had no alternative but to marry me?'

'Yes.'

'And Conal's not in the running?'

'No.'

'It doesn't make sense.'

'Zack, think about it. You people are so sure of yourselves. Even with the financial setbacks, you've got your feet firmly planted on the earth, you own all that land. And I had nothing. Maudie and I didn't get along. I needed to be sure, for both of our sakes, that I wasn't just marrying you for security.'

'Is money all that important to you?'

'Not just the money. Don't you see, I haven't got anyone.' Her voice shook but she continued. 'No family. Except for Lorelei and the Colonel, no friends. I'm sorry, I don't want to talk about it, I'm sounding pathetic.'

'We'd better talk about it,' he said softly, 'and right now. Tell me about your parents. We want them to live on with us like Charlotte and Cliff, so I have to welcome them into our family.'

He sat gravely, listening to her, encouraging her to let go, even wanting to hear about the vicious gossip that had dogged her in Perth concerning her relationship with Logan. 'You know so many people, Zack,' she explained, 'and I felt an interloper in your family. Imagine what a pleasure it was for me to come across someone I knew in Pine Creek. It was Logan. I got completely carried away.'

'We'd better not discuss him any more,' Zack said, 'or I might have to own up to my past.' He kissed her. 'No great love affairs,' he laughed, 'but I'd just as soon not tell.'

'That's fair,' she agreed. 'It's funny, though, I thought you must have found out about the mines.'

'I did,' he grinned. 'Clarrie Fogge told me right away. He was a great pal of Charlotte's. I wanted to see which way you'd jump, and then I thought, what the hell? Mine or no mine, it was time we got married.'

'You're a cheat, Zack Hamilton!' she cried. 'You let me go on with that story and you knew all along.'

'I liked hearing it, good news bears repeating. But something doesn't jell here. How did you know about the wolfram on the property?'

'Logan found it. He told me.'

Zack stared at her. 'Good God! you jumped the man's claims?'

'He deserved it,' Sibell crowed. 'He's a double-crossing rat. I had no idea he was married. Anyway, I didn't take his claim, he hadn't registered it. We simply got there first.' She was laughing, and all around, the world was singing with her. Fat birds twittered in low branches, currawongs, the happiest of birds gave out their la-la-lo, followed by their long brash whistle, little wallabies grazed nearby, everything was returning to normal, and her life was at last in order. In very special order. She was to marry this fine and lovely man, and they'd go back to Black Wattle . . .

'So this is a pay-out?' he asked, his blue eyes like steel, the fair stubble on his chin accentuating the set of his jaw.

'Not really,' she smiled, brushing damp hair from her face. 'It's a new beginning for us. You won't have to worry about keeping the station on its feet any more, Black Wattle will be the best in the north, all bought and paid for.' She reached out to him. 'Zack, dear, it will be wonderful.'

'For you, maybe,' he said, frowning.

'Oh, for God's sake, don't be like that. The mines are not just for me, they're yours, too.' She jumped up and put her arms up to him, joking with him. 'You know the old saying . . . what's yours is mine!' But he stood stiffly, refusing to look at her.

'I don't want any part of it.'

She saw the raw integrity in his face, and understood it well enough, but she would not accept his attitude. 'Zack! Don't be crazy! The company is being formed. Lorelei and the Colonel, you and I, we stand to make a fortune!'

'I know the arrangements, you own fifty-fifty of the Morning Glory mines when they get under way. But count me out. You go right ahead, and good luck to you, but I don't need money so bad that I'd trample on another man's rights.'

'What rights? Logan missed the post, that's all.'

'He trusted you, Sibell, and you've dishonoured that trust.'

'Don't talk rot,' she snapped at him. 'You said yourself you don't like him.'

He sighed and looked sadly at her. 'What you're doing might be smart, but it's still dishonest. You haven't left his team, you've joined it.'

Sibell felt trapped again, and she was furious with Zack for causing this problem. He was being ridiculous. 'Well, it's too late, the claims are registered and that's that.' She stroked his arm. 'Forget about it, Zack, he's just not worth worrying about. You've voiced your disapproval and I stand corrected. Maybe it wasn't the nicest thing I've ever done, but I was entitled.'

He was slow to reply, and she could feel a gulf widening between them.

'God knows I love you, Sibell, but I couldn't live with this, I'd choke on every penny. You've given away half of his entitlements, but you can give him back the rest. Do you know how many poor struggling bastards are out there all the time prospecting for minerals? Hundreds! You obviously don't have any idea how bloody clever you have to be to find the real thing. That tin and wolfram has been under my nose for years but I didn't twig. Now this poor bastard has hit a mother lode! He must have been over the moon! But he was stupid enough to tell you, and you've stolen it, the whole bloody lot. And to make matters worse,' his laugh was hollow, 'you handed half the fortune over, without seeking proper legal advice, to a woman as scatterbrained as you are. It's as if you were giving her a spare hat.'

'Would you have preferred I kept the lot?' she asked sarcastically, but Zack Hamilton would not be deflected from his point.

'I would prefer you gave Mr Conal at least your share of this miserable takeover.'

'I will not.'

'Fine!' he said. 'That's fair enough. You have your standards, I have mine.'

They lapsed into a terrible silence. A stand-off so familiar to lovers where neither is prepared to enter the cavern of consequence. Desperately, Sibell wanted to ask him if the engagement, their marriage, was still on, but she would not come begging.

Zack had never before felt so desolate. To see Sibell slipping away from him, and to know he was causing this rift, was almost too much for him to bear. He wanted to take hold of her, she looked so lovely and forlorn, and to tell her that this was foolishness, that it was a man's job to provide for his wife . . . But the stubborn set of her chin angered him. She had her hands on the reins of a dream, on the prospect of instant wealth, and she wasn't about to let go. So it was Zack who broke the silence. 'Your name is on the lists of evacuees from Palmerston, Sibell. You might as well go to Perth.'

She bristled. 'I don't wish to go to Perth!'

'You don't have any choice.'

'Where would I stay?'

'They are arranging to billet people who have no accommodation, but I'm sure, in your case, with the Morning Glory mines up your sleeve, that the banks will fall over themselves to extend credit. You won't have to travel alone. Maudie is going too, taking Wesley and a couple of other station women to help her. They're staying down until the end of the wet season.'

'I won't go!'

'Yes, you will. The Administrator wants the residence back, so all the women staying in his house are on the top of the list. There's nowhere else for you to stay in the town at present.'

He turned to leave. 'No hard feelings, Sibell. I wish you the best of luck.'

'Will I see you before I go?' she asked, but he shook his head.

'I don't think so.' For a few seconds then, it seemed he wanted to say something else, and Sibell waited, hoping they could find a way through the impasse, but then he was gone, striding quickly over to a row of horses that were tethered by the gate.

Sibell remembered that her horse, Merry, was still out at Black Wattle Station. You haven't seen the last of me, Zack Hamilton, she said to herself. Not by a long shot! Then she thought of Logan. Give him back the mines? Never! She had seen the casualty list, and his name was not on it, so he was still in Palmerston somewhere. Not that it mattered, she had no intention of looking for him. No matter what Zack said, Logan Conal wouldn't get a penny from the mines.

The Colonel was puzzled. They'd been unable to locate Logan Conal. He'd checked the town muster several times and sent the constables out to make enquiries, but the fellow was missing.

Piecing together Conal's movements on Christmas Eve, prior to the storm, he'd been surprised to find that Mr Conal had been staying at the Victoria Hotel, not at home with his wife. That could account for her being alone that night. But what was he doing at the hotel? And why didn't he go to the house to check on his wife after the storm? Unless he too had been injured or even killed. The Victoria had been wrecked, but everyone who had been in the hotel at the time was accounted for. So where was Logan Conal?

He organised a search party to scour the town, even the beaches in case he had drowned, but surely no one in his right mind would go near the seas in that weather? Later in the day, he could only place on report that Conal was missing, along with two prisoners from the jail. That pair he understood – Jackson and Krohn had obviously taken the opportunity to bolt – but Conal? He was no bushman, he'd never survive out there, and anyway, why would he want to leave?

Wearily, he decided he'd better have a chat with Mrs Conal. She had said she would tell her husband to call at the police station when he came home. So why didn't he go home? Must be some marital problem here, he told himself. He didn't want to upset the woman, he'd just ask her a few quiet questions. And it would be an opportunity to call on Lorelei.

Matron took him through the women's ward, which was so crowded that the new patient, Mrs Conal, had been relegated to a bunk by the back door. 'She's not too bad,' Hilda said. 'She still looks like a balloon, but the swelling will go down soon. Sharing a bed with a tribe of green ants must have been hell.'

Puckering nodded agreement. He'd sampled a few of those ant-bites and had yelped like a puppy. Poor Mrs Conal, stuck under the collapsed house and buried by a tree, unable to move, to defend herself against the angry insects . . . He shuddered! But though Matron had warned him, his first sight of Josie was a shock. The wretched woman looked plain comical. She was clothed in a huge white nightgown, so that all he could see were the swollen hands and face, and she had the countenance of a vaudeville minstrel, her skin covered in a vile-smelling black ointment, and her lips painted white.

'My own recipe,' Hilda announced proudly. 'Goanna fat, ti-tree oil and charcoal to set it. Does wonders! Takes the sting out. I can give you some if you like. The blacks put me on to it. And that's my zinc potash on her lips. Soothing, too, a great healer.' She was discussing Josie as if she were not present, as he'd noticed medical people were apt to do, so he turned his attention to the patient.

'Good afternoon, Mrs Conal. I hope you're feeling better.'

'Yes, thank you, Colonel,' she mumbled, having difficulty with the swollen white lips.

'She's still a bit weak on it,' Hilda informed him, 'but plenty of gravy beef will fix her up. She's dehydrated – all that time without water – and we can't hit that empty belly with too much food, so gravy beef does the trick. Plenty of body in gravy beef, Colonel.'

'Quite,' he said, wishing Hilda would push off, but no such luck. 'Mrs Conal,' he continued, 'as you know, the town is still in rather a tangle, so we haven't yet been able to notify your husband that you are here.'

'He must be looking for her,' Hilda said. 'Surely the first place he'd check would be the hospital.'

'Indeed,' the Colonel murmured. 'I don't want to alarm you, Mrs Conal, but I am concerned that we are unable to locate him.'

'Did you search her house?' Hilda asked. 'He's probably there too. He could be bad hurt.'

'We have searched the area thoroughly,' he said stiffly, watching Josie's eyes. He had the feeling she was following this conversation as an interested observer, not as the worried wife. 'When did you see him last, Mrs Conal?'

'Christmas Eve,' she replied, and there was real sadness in her voice. He felt guilty that he might have misjudged her. 'We had Christmas dinner together . . .' She wiped some cream from her lips with a rag. 'I'm sorry, it all seems so long ago, I'm having trouble putting everything in place. And yet it is only a few days, isn't it?'

'You had a bad fright,' Hilda explained. 'Shock does funny things to you.'

'Take your time,' the Colonel said gently.

'Yes. Christmas dinner, I made it specially for him. Just the two of us. We were having such a wonderful night, and we were so happy, and this had to happen. I remember we had a bottle of wine with dinner, and then we had a glass of port each, and the storm was getting worse. But there had been so many rain storms here, I wasn't really worried. I went to bed. Logan said he ought to take a look around outside and see how bad the storm really was. I think he was going to ask someone if there was any real danger.'

'So he left the house?' Puckering said.

'Yes.'

'How long before the cyclone hit was this?'

'Oh, a good while.'

'It wouldn't take long to check the surrounds. Where do you think he could have got to?'

'Earlier he was saying that since the hotels would be closed on Christmas Day, and we only had that little drop of port left in the house, he ought to go and get some liquor so that we could celebrate together.'

'So you thought he must have gone for some liquor. Where would he have bought it at that hour?'

There were tears in her eyes. 'I should have stopped him! But Colonel, you know there are Chinese sly-grog shops near my place – he would have gone to the nearest one.'

'He got caught in the storm and couldn't get back,' Hilda added.

'Yes, he must have,' Mrs Conal said. 'Something has happened to my husband, I'm sure of it, or he would be here now. I've been lying here too frightened to ask. When I saw you, Colonel, I thought you'd come to bring me bad news. Tell me the truth, is Logan still alive?

He pondered the question. 'By all accounts, yes. We just can't find him.'

'That's impossible,' Hilda said. 'If the man is still on his feet he'd be here right now.'

Mercifully she was called away, and the Colonel was able to touch on the more delicate aspects of this mystery. 'Mrs Conal, were you on good terms with your husband?'

'What a question,' she said tearfully. 'Logan and I were very much in love. Colonel, we'd only been married a year.'

She spoke in the past tense. Did she believe he was dead? And why?

'I understand Mr Conal was staying at the Victoria Hotel. Why was that, when you were at home?'

'Business reasons, that's all. He just kept the room there and came home to me.' She sobbed. 'We were hoping to have a child. I have a child from my first marriage, my first husband is dead. My son Ned is in boarding college in Perth.'

Puckering promised to continue the search for Logan Conal, made his excuses and left. He was certain she was lying, but why? He grimaced as he recalled how she had said that she was 'lying here', even then the thought had crossed his mind that lying she was indeed. Logan Conal was not in Palmerston, that was a certainty, the town was too small for him to hide. And why would he need to hide? So Mr Conal must have met with an accident. He was not a victim of the cyclone, the flimsy buildings had been cast asunder by the winds, there was no one else buried in the surface debris. A body, he thought grimly, would have been discovered by now . . . in this humid climate the smell would be enough.

For a fleeting moment he wondered if the wife had killed and buried him, since he didn't believe her excuse for his residence at the hotel. But no, not that woman with the soft brown eyes. Conal was a big man. She would have had to kill him on Christmas Eve, drag his body away from the house in torrential rain, dig a hole to bury him. Not possible, it would take a year of Sundays to dig a trench in that weather, with water washing away every spadeful. Of that exercise he'd had first-hand experience in India.

Outside the hospital he lit his pipe, feeling depressed by his problems and the heavy atmosphere. Mrs Conal's injuries were nothing compared to Lorelei's problems. At least Mrs Conal's face would clear up soon. Lorelei was slowly beginning to acknowledge people, to talk to him. She was not, he mused thankfully, the sort of girl who could shut up for long. He had spoken about her to the doctors, who had said they would have to wait for the wounds to heal. After that, if he could persuade her, she might be able to obtain further treatment. They'd told him there was a specialist in Sydney who could, possibly, do something about the inevitable scars.

Depression, he thought miserably. Lorelei had good reason to be depressed, as did so many other residents. Even apart from the cyclone, not for nothing did they call this time of the year the suicide season.

He stopped. Suicide! Had Logan Conal committed suicide that night? It would be easy enough to walk off into the sea. No one would last long. Apart from the waves pounding into the bay, stingers and sharks would make short work of swimmers. He sighed. So far, this was the only theory that made sense. Had Conal come back, found his house destroyed, believed his wife was dead and done away with himself? Who knows? he thought. Until Conal reappeared, it was as good an answer as any. However, rather than upset the woman any further, he would report Conal as missing. Just missing. Time might solve the mystery. In the mean time, he'd order another sweep of nearby beaches – probably a hopeless quest, since ninety per cent of the shoreline of this huge bay was unexplored. The Port Darwin peninsula was only one of several arms reaching out into the harbour.

When the Colonel left, Josie shivered. She was glad her face was covered in this awful paste. It felt like a disguise, a screen to help her hide the truth. She could never tell him what had really happened, it was too awful, too humiliating. Logan had made love to her, used her, and then when the opportunity came, he had coldly, callously left her there to die. She had heard him walking around outside after the storm had passed, long after the tree had fallen on the house, and he had ignored her cries for help. Oh, he knew she was there all right! She'd heard him scrunching about, and when she called, the movement stopped, he was listening and he was close. And when she called out to him again, he'd paused and then he'd gone away. Logan had wanted her to die. At first she thought, hoped, he might have gone for help, but his refusal to answer her was a clear message in itself.

The days and nights wedged down there had been frightening. She couldn't recall what she had thought about: maybe she just kept on passing out with the pain and the struggle for air. But now she was terrified, mortally afraid of Logan. He had tried to kill her once, if only by omission, by criminal neglect – of that she was sure. So what would happen next? She was just as mystified as the Colonel at Logan's disappearance but she prayed he would stay away. Thank God she'd had time in the hospital to invent a credible story as to why her husband did not, could not, come to her aid, but it still didn't account for the days he'd left her there, when he could have returned. The Colonel was a kindly man, at one stage she'd almost succumbed to her fears and asked him for protection from Logan. But that would have meant telling him the truth, and she could not do that.

No. She had made her decision. No one knew he'd wanted a divorce, except her only friend, dear old Mr Wang. And Hilda had said he'd been killed at the joss house. Poor Mr Wang, she wished she could talk to him now. He was such a wise man, she could have asked his advice. He'd already given her sound advice: do nothing. And she'd stick with it. She'd do nothing. As far as the world was concerned, she and Logan were happily married. If someone or something had struck him down, which, by his absence, seemed possible, then she could only assume that God was in his heaven. She remembered that Christmas Eve again, and their torrid wanton lovemaking, and she felt sick. She turned away and thought of Ned.

Meal times at the hospital were difficult in the primitive conditions. The cookhouse was a hessian structure with an iron roof, where two women laboured over a grid making soups and stews, at the same time keeping an eye on a succession of dampers cooking among the coals of a bush oven. There were no trays, so the volunteers carried the meals in billies, to be ladled out to two or three patients at a time. After that they returned with mugs of tea, slices of damper, or the cakes and scones donated by women in the town. It was a tiring, time-consuming business, and no sooner had they finished and washed up in tin basins than it seemed to be time to start all over again.

Sibell had been tramping up and down between the tents, delivering and collecting, when Hilda called to her. 'This one has gravy beef, no meat and spuds for her. Take this to Mrs Conal.'

'Who?' Sibell almost shouted.

'Mrs Conal. The new patient. She's down the far end of the ward.' She put a lid on the billy and handed it to Sibell. 'You'll have to feed her, her hands are like sausages.'

'Why?' Sibell asked stupidly.

'Because she's the one they found under the house, and she's all swelled up with insect bites. Get going, girl. Don't just stand there!'

Sibell had seen that woman, everyone was talking about her, but she hadn't recognised her. It had to be Josie! Nervously, she made her way to Josie's bedside, wishing she could push this job on to someone else, afraid that Josie might abuse her. What had Logan told her about them? And if Josie were here in the hospital, no doubt Logan would be about too.

Josie's surprise and pleasure were no pretence. 'Sibell! Of all people. What are you doing here? Oh, Lord, it's so nice to see a friendly face.'

As she fed her, Sibell explained how she had come to work for Charlotte Hamilton, on, of course, Josie's recommendation. Josie was delighted. 'My dear, I'm so glad. But I heard that Mrs Hamilton died.'

After further explanations, Josie asked her if she had seen Logan.

'No,' Sibell said, nervous again. 'Why? Was he hurt in the storm?'

'The Colonel says he wasn't, but I don't believe him. If Logan could, he'd be here with me. I'm so worried about him.'

To avoid discussing Logan with his wife, Sibell changed the subject. 'What happened to you?'

Josie's story was easier in the second telling. She spoke glowingly of the Christmas Eve dinner she and Logan had shared, and was even able to refer delicately to the earlier event of the evening. 'He was so loving, we are hoping to have a child. Or we were once we had our house. Now the house is a ruin. But I suppose we could rebuild. We were so proud of that house, our first real home.'

Sibell didn't want to hear any more, but when the soup was finished, Josie embarked on the story of her ordeal under the house. 'That's why I know something happened to Logan that night. He only left the house for a short while, he wouldn't have left me there. Are you sure you haven't seen him anywhere?'

'No. Of course not.'

'There you are. Logan was well known in Palmerston, someone would have seen him by now.'

'I have to go,' Sibell said, anxious to get away.

'You will come back?' Josie asked. 'When you're not so busy?'

'Yes,' Sibell said, backing away.

'I did write to you, Sibell, to tell you about Palmerston. We were only renting then, but I liked the town. I wrote to you care of Percy Gilbert. I thought if you were still unhappy in Perth you might like to come up here for a visit.'

'I never got it,' she replied, and fled.

She worked mechanically for the rest of the day, and walked home along the waterfront, feeling miserable and desolate, unable to put Josie out of her mind. In her anger and jealousy she had forgotten Josie's innate kindness, and as for her marrying Logan, well, now, it didn't seem such a terrible thing to do. Sibell pondered on how much she'd grown up in the last year, able to see things a lot more clearly. Not as clearly, as cut and dried, as Zack, though!

The incoming grey tide slapped endlessly at the sands, offering no solace. She dreaded having to go on to that house, packed with chattering women and screaming kids. She missed the cheerful little beach house. She realised, too, that she missed the marvellous night quiet of Black Wattle and the invigorating sense of space. Perth would be dreary after that, and so would Palmerston. She slowed as she passed the BAT buildings, knowing Zack was billeted there and hoping he would see her, but no one called to her. There were women inside, wives and friends, resuming their normal lives, and Sibell begrudged them their laughter, remembering her two friends John and Michael who were buried in the Palmerston cemetery.

Overcome with regret for her affair with Logan, something that would obviously hurt Josie terribly if she ever found out, Sibell decided to try to make up for it, to look after Josie at least until he surfaced, wherever he was.

Three days later, Hilda came to her with good news. 'Your friend, Mrs Conal, she's well enough to leave now. You'd better hunt around and find her some clothes, see what's left in that box the women brought in.'

'Where can she go?' Sibell asked.

'Damned if I know,' Hilda said. 'But she can't stay here, this isn't a boarding house. Put her up where you are.'

'They won't take anyone else, they've refused half a dozen people lately. Can't she stay here until we find out where Logan is? Her husband.'

'Listen to me.' Hilda took her aside. 'There's a rumour going around about him. Only a rumour, mind you, but I reckon there could be some truth in it. He's been missing a week now . . .'

'What rumour?'

'Some say Mr Conal has done himself in. Suicide.'

'I don't believe it.'

'Well, the only other story is that he's gone marching about too close to them back beaches or one of the creeks. There are croc tracks everywhere lately. They say a croc could have got him.'

'Oh, my God, no!'

Hilda shrugged. 'It's on the cards. One way or the other, I reckon her husband's a goner.'

'Have you told her this?'

'Oh, Christ, no. Just let it ride for the time being. She'll have to get on with her life like everyone else.'

Instead of passing on Hilda's message, Sibell kept away. She cringed at the thought of facing Josie, and yet another part of her put up a stout defence. Why do you invite guilt? You're not responsible for Logan Conal. He's a grown man. He makes his own decisions.

But what if he had committed suicide? Was losing the mines such a blow that he'd simply given up on the strain of living? In which case, I am directly responsible.

Some Aborigine women, babies on their hips, called to her from the perimeter of the tents. 'Hey, missus. You got sick fellers dere?'

She walked over to them. 'Yes.'

'Whaffor?' they asked, laughing and nudging one another. Apparently the idea of assembling the sick amused them. They were all young, a cheerful lot, from a nearby camp, and to them the hospital was an interesting phenomenon.

'They get better here. When you get sick you must come and ask for the doctor.'

They shook their heads. 'Whitefeller place.'

Sibell realised that they were right. No blacks were permitted in the hospital. 'You call out and the doctor will come to make your sick people better.'

The women smiled, doubt in their eyes, and went on their way. Sibell thought of Jimmy Moon. She remembered the way he'd laughed too, almost in a paternal way, as if his white friends were but children, to be indulged. Jimmy had been so clever. She mourned his terrible, cruel fate, and he seemed close again, at least in spirit. Jimmy would have found Logan, he would be able to tell them exactly what had happened to him or where he was. Jimmy was like that. She stared at the wall of ragged bush beyond the clearing, no longer still and brittle under the hard sun, but very much alive, the sweltering green home to all manner of wildlife, their croaks and calls filling the air.

Suddenly she knew! Logan wouldn't commit suicide. Not him! Nor would he have gone anywhere near crocodile haunts. And Josie would know that, too, no matter what she said. It seemed obvious to Sibell that somehow he had managed to get out of Palmerston after the storm without even bothering to see if his wife had survived. That was Logan. And, what's more, he wasn't coming back.

She raced up to the main building and through the ward, then stopped abruptly. There was no sign of Josie, and the bunk had been removed. 'Where's Mrs Conal?'

'She's gone home. Went this morning.'

* * *

The following afternoon, Sibell asked directions at the police station, and made her way to Shepherd Street. Josie's block wasn't hard to find. 'The one with the big tree down, dead centre.'

And there was Josie, picking among the ruins.

'What are you doing here?' Sibell called to her.

'This is where I live.'

'Where did you sleep last night?'

'Right here,' Josie shrugged. 'I made myself a burrow like a rabbit.'

'You can't stay here.'

'Yes, I can,' she said stubbornly. 'The Chinese will help me, I know they will.'

Sibell followed her, trailing around the smashed timbers. 'Josie, where is Logan?'

'The official report states that he is missing, presumed dead,' she replied dully. 'Look, here's my lovely mat, ruined.'

'But he isn't dead, is he?' Sibell insisted.

Josie looked at her thoughtfully. 'Let the report stand.'

'I will. This is just between you and me. He's not dead, is he?'

'Leave it be, Sibell.'

'No! Why do I keep thinking he got out of Palmerston? That he found a way to leave?' Sibell's question was urgent, but she was unprepared for Josie's calculated and forthright reply.

'Because that is precisely what he did do.'

'What? How do you know?'

Josie studied her. 'I might ask the same question of you.' She turned away and began lifting broken planks, but Sibell stopped her.

'Listen to me, Josie, this is important. He survived the cyclone, didn't he?'

'Yes,' she sighed. 'I believe he did.'

'So why didn't he help you?' She saw Josie's anguished face and regretted the question, appalled by the ramifications.

'I don't know,' Josie said, squaring her shoulders. 'But I think we have to say Logan will not be coming back.'

Sibell put her arms around Josie. 'Yes, missing presumed dead.'

'Thank you,' Josie whispered.

'I don't want your thanks, Josie. We have to talk.'

'Right now I'm not much in the mood for talking. I'm stranded and broke, but I've still got my block of land, and no one is going to move me off. I'm not getting on that ship.'

'I'm not trying to make you go. This isn't going to be too pleasant for either of us, but I have to talk to you about Logan.'

'Why don't you leave me alone?'

'Believe me, I wish I could. But there's a man called Zack Hamilton who's been prodding my conscience. His straight and narrow path is very clear, though I've been finding it a bit foggy.'

Josie shrugged. 'You do what you have to do, that's all.'

'True,' Sibell said to the older woman. 'That's why I have to talk with you.' She took a deep breath and faced Josie, who listened gravely and sympathetically to Sibell's words. She did not divulge, though, that Logan had demanded a divorce. Older and wiser, Josie deemed it better to remain silent on that subject and so retain a scrap of dignity. Initially, when they'd met in Pine Creek, Logan had not told Sibell that he was married, or that Josie was in the district . . . That was enough. And it seemed likely that if it hadn't been Sibell, it would have been someone else.

'We'll say no more about it then,' she told Sibell.

'But there's more!' She explained about the mines, glad that she was over the part where Logan had visited Black Wattle. 'The trouble is that Zack claims I have been dishonest, or less than honest. He says Logan, having discovered a rich source of tin and wolfram, should have first option.'

Josie stared at her. 'He wants you to give the rights back to Logan?'

'Yes.'

'Don't you dare!' She jumped to her feet. 'Do you hear me, Sibell? I don't care what Hamilton says. Don't even think about it.' She laughed. 'It's marvellous! Serves him damn well right! Sibell, I never imagined you were interested in Logan, you always seemed, if I might say, so superior, even when I first met you on that strange day, as if Logan was a pest you were stuck with. Beneath your notice.'

'Time mellowed me. I was lonely.'

'So was I,' Josie said, thinking back. 'I was desperately lonely on that farm. Jack was no company. But that's history. Our dear Logan set his sights on you and met his match! I couldn't think of a better result. Now you'd better be getting back.'

A familiar figure came trotting towards them, and Sibell looked up in surprise. 'Sam Lim, what are you doing here?'

'Come to get honourable lady. Esteemed friend of departed uncle Wang Lee.' He bowed to Josie. 'You come eat supper.'

'I told you,' Josie said to Sibell. 'They'll look after me. They're all living in humpies too. Only the élite of the town have proper shelter these days.'

Sam Lim was delighted to see Sibell. 'We all go home together, missy, when sun comes out again?'

'I don't know,' Sibell murmured. She turned back to Josie. 'There's still Zack. Couldn't you and I come to some arrangement about the mines. I'm damned if I'll give them up, but as Logan's next-of-kin I'd be willing to share my claims with you.'

'The letter of Zack's law?' Josie smiled.

'Something like that.'

'Sounds fair to me,' Josie said, thinking of her son. Had Logan solved the problem after all? If need be, she would buy her son back. She gathered her charity shawl about her and accepted Sam Lim's hand to step over a stricken palm. God was indeed in his heaven.

The ships tacked sluggishly into the bay and dropped anchor well off shore, like a trio of sea-birds resting warily on the grey-mottled expanse, cautiously considering their approach. When at last longboats were lowered, a great cheer went up from the watchers on the waterfront. Ships were always welcomed at the tiny outpost at the top end of the huge continent, for news of the outside world and precious mail, but this time they signalled a new beginning. Jeremiahs in the town had warned that in the first instance they should expect only one naval ship to make fast for Port Darwin, for it would be carrying orders to prepare to abandon the settlement, leaving only a handful of men to maintain the BAT, the all-important telegraphic communicator.

'It has happened before,' they said. 'It will happen again. This place is costing the South Australian government more than it's worth.'

A contingent of Royal Marines were the first to step ashore, looking curiously around them. They were bombarded with questions because many locals were still nervous of the evacuation orders. They believed that this could be a political manoeuvre to remove citizens permanently with a minimum of fuss. But the news soon spread that the Marines had arrived to help restore order, so they were allowed to form up and march proudly up the cliffside for their first glimpse of the flattened town and for their first groaning taste of the pounding heat and the hard work ahead of them.

When the crowds dispersed, Zack went in search of Maudie, who was resting impatiently on the veranda of the Administrator's residence. She had missed all the fun down on the shore.

'If it wasn't for this bloody leg,' she growled, 'I wouldn't have to go down to Perth. I hate bloody cities. And what am I going to do there?'

'Just get back on your feet. It'll only be for a few months. You won't know Palmerston when you return, they say that second ship is loaded to the gills with building materials.'

Maudie waved that aside. 'I'm not interested in Palmerston, I'm interested in Black Wattle. Are you going to marry Sibell?'

'Why?' he asked, not prepared to give her an answer at this point.

'Because Black Wattle's my home, not hers, and I don't want her there.'

'Don't I get any say in this?' he asked mildly.

'With Cliff gone, I have to look after myself now, and Wesley.' Her attitude was defensive, and he felt sorry for her. It must be hard for an active woman like her to be stuck in a chair for so long.

'Don't you think I'd do that?' he asked, but she shook her head. 'I haven't got any quarrel with you, Zack. People talk, though. You and I living in the same house – that would be bad enough. But then when you get married and have kids, where does that leave me? Stuck in the back room like a maiden aunt.' She was working herself up to the confrontation that he had been expecting. 'Wesley and me, we've got just as much right to that station as you have. As a matter of fact, more so.'

He leaned easily against the veranda posts. 'I'd sure like to hear you explain that, Maudie.'

So she plunged in. 'You had your chance. Charlotte gave you six months to take up the option for Black Wattle, and you never did. After that it was Cliff's turn, and it's mine now. I'm doing what Cliff would have done, I'm taking Black Wattle. You won't lose, I'll buy you out, you can get another station.' Having thrown down the gauntlet, she now looked pleased with herself. 'You were too slow off the mark, Zack.'

He sighed. 'I don't know why you people seem to think I walk around with my eyes closed. You're Cliff's widow: when he was killed I promised him I'd do the best I could for you – that's why I didn't take up the option. I didn't want you to think you were getting the bum's rush, and I wanted you to feel secure at Black Wattle. If you want that station, it's yours. You'll need help on the accounting side, so you'll have to make a real effort now to learn to read and write. You can do that while you're in Perth, you owe it to Wesley.'

'You'll move off the station?' She couldn't believe how easy this had been. She had been fully prepared for a fight.

'Yes, when we get things worked out. I've put in a bid for next door.'

'Which one? Corella Downs?' She was startled.

'Corella,' he repeated, watching her. 'There's no homestead to speak of, but I can build one. It's a few square miles smaller than Black Wattle, but good beef country and more water holes. It'll be easier to manage, I reckon.' He didn't state the obvious. Years back, Maudie's mother had died of the fever and her father had struggled hard to provide for the kids. A few weeks before Maudie, the youngest in the family, married Cliff, the old drover had been killed in a stampede and was buried on Corella Downs.

Zack let that sink in.

'By the way,' he added, 'don't think you're getting rid of Sibell. She'll be on your doorstep, not mine. She's taken out mining rights to wolfram and tin deposits on Black Wattle. She's going to be another wolfram queen along with her mate, Lorelei Rourke.'

'Who?' Maudie gaped.

'You know. The lady from the Bijou!'

'I don't believe you! I'll stop them.'

'Not possible,' he said, keeping a straight face. 'So you won't be lonely on Black Wattle. I daresay the mine owners will be around quite a bit, so you ladies will have plenty to talk about.'

'I thought you were going to marry Sibell,' she said, stupefied.

'I didn't say that,' he told her. 'Now you get yourself organised. The ships will be leaving in a couple of days, and I want to see you safely aboard.'

The wedding of Miss Lorelei Rourke and Colonel Puckering was scheduled to take place at the Chief Inspector's new residence on the Saturday afternoon, so on the preceding day he went to the hospital to visit his fiancée.

Matron came out to meet him, looking more like her old self now that clothing, overlooked in the first rush to send supplies, had arrived. She was back in her uniform – the black skirt and white blouse and large white wrap-around apron, topped with a crisp mobcap – and being very officious, insisting on showing him around the new building which was under construction.

'A private word with you, Colonel,' she said, dodging workmen.

'Yes?' He was irritated by the delay, any fool could see the building was going ahead according to plan.

'If you don't mind me saying, you've been very kind to Lorelei, but do you think it is wise for a man in your position to marry a girl like that?'

305

'Do you think she's too young for me?' he asked, deliberately sounding obtuse.

'Not at all,' she replied. 'A man like you, the same age as me, we're in the prime of life.'

'I'm glad you agree with me on that. But if you're referring to other matters, let me tell you, Lord Palmerston himself, after whom this town was named, was a notorious womaniser, with a squad of illegitimate off-spring, but the British public had the good sense to recognise his wisdom and goodness. Putting it plainly, Matron, my wife will be accorded the same respect.'

'Yes, of course,' she said, 'but . . .'

'No buts . . . you will recall that Palmerston, upon his marriage at the age of fifty-five, became a model husband. Lorelei is only twenty-four and her youthful follies are already behind her. And another thing – Palmerston went on to be Prime Minister. Nothing so grand in my life, but I am to be appointed Police Commissioner of the Northern Territory and I will make this very clear: woe betide anyone who upsets my lady.'

The big woman stood back and studied him and then she clapped him on the back with such force he almost stumbled. 'Good for you, Colonel,' she boomed. 'I thought you were just feeling sorry for her. And pity's what she don't need.'

Lorelei was dressed, sitting on the bed, but she was wearing a straw hat, her face covered in a mosquito net. 'Takes a wedding to get me out of here,' she said gloomily.

'The hell it does,' Hilda said. 'You're not sick. You're leaving here anyway. Let's have a look at you.'

Lorelei clutched at her hat. 'You turn around,' she told the Colonel but Hilda wrenched the hat and net away.

'Don't talk rot, he's going to be your husband. You can't live with your head in a sugar bag.'

The wounds in her young skin had healed but the scars were still raw and shocking, an eyebrow was split, one scar ran down her nose and across her cheek and another flared down to her mouth, giving the impression of a harelip, since her top lip had been sliced. 'See,' the matron said professionally. 'She's not too bad, only one side of her face was injured.'

'Thanks,' Lorelei said. 'So I walk everywhere sideways.'

'You're lucky you weren't killed,' Matron said. 'Am I invited to the wedding? I love weddings.'

'We're not inviting anyone,' Lorelei said.

'Yes we are.' The Colonel leaned over and kissed her. 'And Matron will be most welcome.'

Lorelei grabbed the hat and plonked it on again. 'At least brides get to wear veils,' she said, and then she whispered to the Colonel. 'Do I look that bad?'

'You'll always be beautiful,' he told her and she managed to smile. 'Sibell's coming. Why don't you ask that boyfriend of hers if we have to have people? She won't ask him.'

'He's gone fishing,' Puckering said, 'but I left a message for him.'

'I hope he turns up.' Then she found another worry. 'If you've asked people we ought to have food. What about food?'

306

'That's all fixed up. Sibell's friend Sam Lim is doing the catering.' And then he laughed. 'Where else but Palmerston would we have Chinese food at a wedding reception?'

Zack was late. They'd taken a boat upriver and come home with a good catch of barramundi, which he'd handed to the cook at the BAT. Eventually someone remembered to give him the message, so he dressed quickly and rode through the still, hot night to the Colonel's house. The ceremony was well over, but several people were still milling around on the front veranda, and, of course, the first person he encountered was Sibell. 'I'm glad you made it,' she said coolly. 'They'll be happy to see you.'

'I hoped you might be too.'

'Why not? We're still friends.'

'Maudie told me you were staying on. Where are you living?'

'At the hospital. Most of Matron's volunteers were evacuated, so she let me have free board in return for work with no pay.'

'Sounds fair enough,' he commented.

'It is not,' she argued. 'I work hard.'

'Ah, but it depends on the market,' he grinned. 'Right now the commodity in short supply is a roof that doesn't leak, so you have to pay a higher price.'

His reply annoyed Sibell, who had expected sympathy. 'I won't be there much longer anyway,' she said. 'I'm moving in with Mrs . . . with Josie, that lady over there, as soon as her house is finished.'

He glanced over at a good-looking woman in a neat brown dress that nevertheless accentuated a curvy figure, and realised that he should have complimented Sibell on her outfit. He supposed it was a bit late now, though. She did look lovely, in a full-skirted blue dress with a high, boned lace collar, her fair hair piled up under a pretty little hat.

The Colonel called to him, so he strode over to pay his respects. First he kissed the bride, who looked demure in a dress of cream silk and lace and a misty veil, which she didn't bother to remove. Knowing the circumstances, he gallantly kissed her through the veil and congratulated the Colonel, resplendent in full dress uniform.

'Care for a whisky?' Puckering asked him after the initial greetings. 'Had my fill of wines.'

'That'd go down well,' Zack agreed, and the two men withdrew to the kitchen, where Zack was surprised to find Sam Lim tidying up. 'What are you doing here?'

'He catered for the show,' Puckering said. 'Damn good job, too.'

But Sam Lim was horrified. 'Boss! You get no supper. Ay-ee! I find you food chop-chop!' He began yelling at the Colonel's young Chinese servant, who ran around in a panic until Zack stopped them.

'No! I don't want any. Not hungry! Whisky please.'

The bottle and two glasses were rushed to the kitchen table, and the Colonel picked them up. 'We'll take them outside, it's too hot in here.'

As they left, Sam Lim called to Zack, 'Hey, boss! Soon we go home, eh?'

'Next month,' Zack told him. 'You'd better put in the order for provisions now. And round up the girls. Missus Maudie and Wesley ought to be back by then.'

He clapped his hands excitedly. 'All go home.'

Outside by the lantern, the Colonel was slapping at mosquitoes. 'These bloody things,' he complained. 'They're huge.'

'Yeah,' Zack said, taking a whisky. 'Scots Greys, we call them.'

'Scots Greys?'

'They come in regiments, different types, so we call them Scots Greys, Black Watch, and so on . . .'

'Well I'll be damned!' Puckering said.

'To your good health and your lovely wife!' Zack raised his glass.

'And yours,' the Colonel said. 'Thought you'd be taking a bride back with you. Miss Delahunty, for instance.'

'Sibell?' Zack said moodily. 'She's got a mind of her own.'

'I would have thought that a very suitable trait for women in the bush. Important for them to be resourceful.'

Zack couldn't resist a grunt of amusement. 'Resourceful? That's her all right! Grabbing that bloody mine!'

'I wanted to speak with you about that. You realise that my wife and I have formed the Morning Glory company with Sibell?'

Unimpressed, Zack shrugged. 'It's nothing to do with me.'

'Quite. But it may interest you to know that Sibell has come to an arrangement with Mrs Conal.'

'Mrs Conal? His wife?'

'Yes. You must have heard that the man himself is missing.'

'I did, yes. What do you think happened to him?'

'Death by accident, I'd have to say. But getting back to the company, Sibell and Mrs Conal have agreed with us that they should own fifty-two per cent of the shares. I understand your view on the matter, and appreciate you have taken an honourable stance, but the situation has now changed considerably. Since Mrs Conal herself is a director, and an enthusiastic one at that, might I add, I hope you no longer have any reservations about this project.'

'I suppose not,' Zack said, still bemused by the turn of events. 'But Sibell and Mrs Conal? They're friends?'

'My dear chap, don't ask me how women manage to sort these things out. Not only are Sibell and Josie friends again . . .'

'Josie? Is she Mrs Conal?'

'The lady herself. She's here as our guest and they're all getting along like a house on fire. She and Sibell have been tremendous support for my wife, tremendous. Most grateful to them . . .'

But Zack was still wary. 'They might be mates now, Sibell and Mrs Conal, but what happens if the husband turns up again. Which one will he claim?'

'No need to worry about that.' The Colonel refilled their glasses. 'He won't be back. Logan Conal does not exist.'

'You can't be sure of that.'

'Oh, yes, I can. Found an interesting report among my papers yesterday. Haven't told the women yet. I want to break this to Josie myself. I like to keep records up to date, so I advised the registrar in Perth that Mr Logan Conal, a survivor of the ill-fated *Cambridge Star*, is missing, presumed dead. Their reply was most intriguing. No one by the name of

308

Logan Conal appears on the lists of passengers or crew of that ship. There is no such person.'

'No such person?' Zack echoed. 'Then who is he? I mean who was he?'

'No idea. Possibly someone with a criminal background who grasped the opportunity to change his identity. A simple matter under those circumstances.'

'Good God!' Zack said. Then he raised his glass. 'And good riddance. Here's to a long and happy marriage, Colonel.'

'And to yours, sir,' the Colonel smiled.

The bullock train rumbled through the streets of Palmerston on the first stage of a long and arduous journey, loaded with supplies for Black Wattle Station.

At the stables the large party of riders took the packhorses in hand and mounted up. The wet season was at last drawing to a close, and although small squalls were still scattering over the north, the Dry was fast approaching. A rejuvenated Palmerston rang with the noise of axes and anvils, and carpenters clambered busily through the skeletons of new buildings. The contingent of Marines, not sorry to leave, waved their farewells as they marched down to the reconstructed wharf. Everyone was going home.

Sam Lim, bursting with excitement, his young Chinese apprentice cook beside him, called 'Giddy-up' to the horses as his wagon pulled away. Sitting happily in the back among more supplies were the twins, Pet and Polly, with Wesley and Netta.

Maudie, with Bygolly mounted up beside her, sat her horse proudly, surrounded by the stockmen she had hired to run her own station, Corella Downs. She was looking forward to the next couple of months living at Black Wattle – it would give her time to sort out the extra stock she would need while her home was being built. Zack had been marvellous, and he had suggested that, for the time being, it would be best to run the two stations as a single entity, until she had her property under control. He had even promised to help her choose a home site near water but out of range of floods. She was determined that her son would grow up to inherit a fine cattle property. She had even agreed, as part of their deal, to send Wesley to boarding school when he was twelve to get an education. That had caused a few arguments, since Maudie still couldn't see what learning history and geography had to do with raising cattle. But Zack had insisted.

Milling around them were familiar faces. As their horses jostled, men with their tools of trade, rifles and stockwhips, adjusted swags on their saddles and traded jokes with their mates. After the long lay-off, they too were ready for a hard year ahead at Black Wattle Station.

Sibell, clad in her bush gear of trousers and shirt and a leather hat, rolled up an oil-cloth coat ready for the journey through damp forests, and strapped it on to the saddle next to her rifle. And Lorelei, her face still camouflaged by the mosquito net attached to her hat, remembered this time the previous year. 'Look at her,' she giggled, hanging on to her husband. 'She's looking like a cowboy again, have you ever seen the like?'

The Colonel kissed Sibell on the cheek. 'Good luck,' he said. 'Have a safe journey home.'

'You will come and visit?'

'And ride all that way!' Lorelei exclaimed. 'I'd rather you came to visit us. I'll never make a bushie.'

Another group of men rode down the street to join the cavalcade as they began to move out. Max Klein and his miners had decided it would be wise to travel with the Hamiltons to learn the best route out to Black Wattle. The German mines manager saluted the Colonel as he passed.

Josie was there to see them off, and Hilda too, and Sibell was still talking to them when Zack rode over. 'Come on, wife,' he called to her. 'On your horse. We haven't got all day.' He grinned as the Colonel legged Sibell up on to a big bright-eyed chestnut horse, then came closer to her, looking concerned. 'Are you sure you don't want to go downriver by boat?'

'No,' she replied, shades of Maudie. 'It takes twice as long and it's boring. We'll ride home together.'

After dinner on Saturday night, Zack took Casey out on to the veranda, where they sat, quietly content.

'It's good to be home,' Zack said, and Casey nodded, puffing on his pipe.

'I've been thinking,' Zack added, 'we ought to ask that fellow from the mines, Max Klein, to join us on Saturday nights whenever he can. If we keep in touch with him we should get through this mining stage without too much disruption.'

'Won't do any harm,' Casey replied. 'By the way, I've been meaning to ask you, what do we do about Jimmy Moon's horse?'

'Give it to Netta.'

'Netta?' Casey blinked.

'It belonged to a blackfellow, we can't take it away from them. And Netta deserves a reward for looking after Wesley and the girls in the cyclone. I had the fright of my life when I thought they were buried under that house.'

'Oh, yes, I forgot about that. She was sweet on him, you know, that Jimmy Moon. You never met him, did you?'

'No,' Zack growled. 'Bloody awful thing to happen here. I believe our blacks had a lot of time for him. How did they react?'

'Not good for a while, but they settled down. I found out where they buried his remains . . . Out there by the bora ring.'

'The bora ring? I thought they wouldn't go near the place.'

'Yes, but times have changed. The taboo seems to have been lifted. No more debbil-debbil. And I'll tell you something else strange, the emus are back.'

Zack jerked up in his seat. 'So they are! I saw a couple the other day but it didn't register. I wonder what it all means?'

'I don't think we'll ever find out. All Bygolly will say is that this is emu totem place.'

'So why have they stayed away?'

Casey laughed. 'You'll love this. Bygolly says they've been here all the time, we just couldn't see them.'

From inside, raised voices began to intrude on the peace of the evening. Maudie and Sibell were arguing again.

'When will Maudie's house be ready?' Zack asked.

'A couple of weeks, I'd say.'

'That soon?' Zack grinned. 'It'll be damn quiet around here then, won't it?'

'They sure go at it hammer and tongs, those girls,' Casey said, and Zack leaned back, stretching his long legs out in front of him.

'They have to,' he said lazily. 'If they quit sparring, they'd find out they're friends, and that wouldn't suit them at all.'

Postword

Palmerston did survive, as did Pine Creek and Katherine. The magnificent Katherine Gorge is now a National Park, and to the east of Darwin is the famous Kakadu National Park. The town of Stuart was renamed Alice Springs.

The great cattle stations of the north have prospered and some welcome visitors in the Dry season.

By 1897, Palmerston had weathered three serious cyclones, but the determined Territorians rebuilt their town again and again.

In 1911, the Commonwealth took over the administration of the Northern Territory, and the town of Palmerston was renamed Darwin.

Darwin flourished in the new century, only to be struck down by another cyclone in 1937, and then it was devastated by sustained Japanese bombing in 1942, forcing the evacuation of residents. They returned years later to a heartbreaking scene. But still this town would not lie down.

By 1974, Darwin was thriving again until that Christmas Eve when the worst cyclone of all, Cyclone Tracy, subjected the city to eight hours of terror. The people emerged to find that their city, once again, had been flattened, completely destroyed. Mass evacuations ensued, but the Territorians came back to rebuild, using methods and materials designed to combat the elements. Even after this, they still retained that easy-going northern nature.

Darwin, one of the world's last frontiers, is now a cheerful, cosmopolitan city, the gateway to the startling and unique scenery of the outback.